The Land of Cockayne
A Novel

by

Matilde Serao

Double 9
BOOKS

The Land of Cockayne
A Novel
by Matilde Serao

ISBN: 978-93-63057-60-9

Published by

DOUBLE 9 BOOKS

2/13-B, Ansari Road
Daryaganj, New Delhi – 110002
info@double9books.com
www.double9books.com
Tel. 011-40042856

ABOUT THE AUTHOR

Matilde Serao, an influential Italian journalist and novelist, left an indelible mark on Italian literature along with her insightful works. Born in 1856, Serao was a trailblazer for girls in journalism and literature at some stage in the past due 19th and early 20th centuries. Her masterpiece, "The Desire of Life" exemplifies her literary prowess and societal critique. "The Desire of Life" is a compelling exploration of the human situation, love, and the pursuit of achievement. Serao weaves a rich narrative that delves into the lives of her characters, depicting the struggles and aspirations of people in opposition to the backdrop of societal expectancies. The novel displays Serao keen observations of the complexities of human relationships and her capacity to dissect the cultural and social cloth of her time. Serao, acknowledged for her dedication to realism, brought a clean attitude to literature thru her engaging storytelling and bright characterizations. As a co-founder of the newspaper "Mattino," she additionally made huge contributions to Italian journalism. Matilde Serao legacy endures as a literary pioneer who challenged gender norms and societal conventions. Through works like "The Desire of Life," she is still celebrated for her profound insights into the human revel in and her have an impact on Italian literature.

CONTENTS

CHAPTER I
THE LOTTERY DRAWING

The afternoon sun crept into the Piazzetta dei Banchi Nuovi, broadening from Cardone's, the engraver, to Cappa's, the chemist, lengthening on from there up the whole Santa Chiara Road, spreading a light of unusual gaiety over the street, which always wears, even in its most frequented hours, a frigid, claustral aspect. But the great morning traffic, of people coming from the northern districts of the town—Avvocata, Stella, San Carlo all' Arena, San Lorenzo—to go down to the lower quarters of Porto, Pendino and Mercato, or *vice versâ*, had been slowly slackening since mid-day; the coming and going of carts, carriages and pedlars had ceased; everybody seemed to be taking short cuts by the Chiostro di Santa Chiara and the Vico 1o Foglia towards Mezzocannone Alley, the Gesù Nuovo, San Giovanni Maggiore. Presently the sun's brightness lit up a street by then quite deserted. The shopkeepers on the right side of Santa Chiara—as the left side is only the high, dark enclosure wall of the Poor Clares' Convent—dealers in old dusty or wretched mean new furniture, coloured engravings, shiny oleographs, wooden and stucco saints, were at the back of their dark shops, eating over a corner of wine-stained tablecloth, with a caraffe of Marano small wine, closed by a twisted vine-leaf, standing by a big dish of macaroni. The porters, seated on the ground at the shop entrance, were eating lazily at a small loaf of bread, cut in two to hold some tasty viand—fried gourd soaked in vinegar, parsnips in green sauce, pomegranates seasoned with vinegar, garlic and pepper. The sharp, greasy smell of the quantity of tomatoes all this macaroni was cooked in, from one end of the street to the other, mingled with the acute odour of sour vinegar and coarse spices. From some passing fruitseller, carrying a nearly empty basket of figs on his head, or pushing a barrow with purple plums, and tough spotted peaches at the bottom of the baskets, the shopkeepers, clerks and porters, lips still red from tomatoes or shining with grease, bargained for a penny-worth of fruit, to finish their meal; two workmen, in front of the Martello printing-shop, where the small visiting-card press had stopped, deeply coveted a yellow melon; and two seamstresses were waiting on a doorstep chattering, till the seller of *pizza* passed, which is the shredded rind of tomato, garlic, and wild marjoram, cooked in the oven, and sold at a farthing, a half-penny, a penny, the piece.

The *pizzaiuolo* did pass, in fact, but he was carrying his wooden tray, shining with oil, under his arm, without a bit of *pizza*; he had sold everything, and was going off to eat his own meal, down to the Porto quarter, where his shop was. The two disappointed seamstresses consulted each other; one of them, a blonde, with a golden aureole round her pale gentle face, moved off with that undulating step that gives an Oriental touch to a Neapolitan woman's charm. She went up Santa Chiara Road, bending her head so as not to get the sun in her face, and went into Impresa Lane, towards the wine-seller's dark shop—which was a drinking-shop, too—almost opposite the Impresa Palace; she was going to buy something to eat for her friend and herself. The Impresa Lane had got empty, too, after mid-day, when all go back to their houses and shops to eat, as the summer heat gets greater, and the *controra*—the time of the Neapolitan day that corresponds to the Spanish siesta—begins with food, rest and sleep for tired folk. The dressmaker, a little frightened by the darkness of the cellar, out of which came a sour smell of wine, had stopped on the threshold; blinking, she looked on the ground before going in, feeling that an open underground cave, with a black gaping mouth, was dangerous. But the shop-boy came towards her to serve her.

'Give me something to eat with my bread,' she said, swaying herself a little.

'Fried fish?'

'No.'

'A little dried cod with sauce?'

'No, no'—with disgust.

'A morsel of tripe?'

'No, no.'

'What do you want, then?' the boy asked, rather annoyed.

'I would like—I would like three-halfpence-worth of meat; we will eat it with our bread—Nannina and I,' said she, with a pretty greedy grimace.

'We don't cook meat to-day; it is Saturday. Only tripe for unbelievers on Saturday.'

'Well, give me the salt cod,' she murmured, withholding a sigh. Then she looked into the Impresa court with curiosity, while the youth disappeared into the black depths of the cellar to get the cod. A little ray of sunshine coming from the top turned the court golden; every now and then some man or woman's form crossed it. Antonietta, the seamstress, went on staring, humming a popular dirge, slightly swaying on her hips.

'Here is the cod,' said the youth, coming back. He had put it in a small plate; there were four big bits falling into flakes, in a reddish sauce strongly seasoned with pepper, the sauce, as it waved about, leaving yellow oily marks on the edges of the gray plate.

'Here is the money,' Antonietta murmured, pulling it out of her pocket. But she stood with the plate in her hand, looking at the cod falling to pieces in the juice.

'If I were to take a *terno*,' she said, as she went on her way, holding the plate carefully, 'I should like to gratify my wish of eating meat every day.'

'Meat and macaroni,' the boy called back, laughing.

'Just so—meat and macaroni,' the seamstress shouted triumphantly, her eyes still fixed on the plate, not to let the sauce fall. 'Morning and evening,' called out the boy from the doorway.

'Morning and evening,' Antonietta answered back.

'You should apply to that youth,' the boy shouted gaily from the cellar, indicating the Impresa court with his eyes.

'I'll come back later,' said the seamstress from the corner of the street; 'I'll bring you the plate.'

Again the Impresa Lane was deserted for a long time. In winter it is much frequented at mid-day by the young students coming out of the University, who take the shortcut to the Gesù and Toledo; but it was summer—the students had their holidays. Still, every now and then, as the hour went on, someone came round the corner from Santa Chiara or Mezzocannone, and stopped in the Impresa gateway—some with a cautious look, others feigning indifference. One of the first had been a shoeblack, with his block—a lame old dwarf, who carried it on his raised hips; he was bent in two, wrapped up in an old great-coat, green, stained and patched, a cap with no peak over his eyes.

He had put down his block under the Impresa portico, and stretched himself out on the ground, as if awaiting customers; but he forgot to beat those two dry claps with the brush on the wood to claim it. Deeply engrossed with a long list of ticket numbers in his hand, the old dwarf's yellow, distorted face was transformed by intense passion. As the hour got near, people went on passing before him, and a murmur of hoarse, strident Neapolitan voices rose in the court.

A man, a workman, stopped near the shoeblack; he might have been thirty-five, but he was wan, and his eyes were dull; his jacket was thrown over his shoulder, showing a coloured calico shirt.

'Do you want a shine?' the bootblack asked mechanically, laying down his list of numbers.

'Just so,' replied the other, grinning; '*I* want a shine. If I had another half-penny, I would have played a last ticket at Donna Caterina's to-day.'

'The *small* game?' asked the shoeblack in a whisper.

'Yes, a little for the Government and a little to Donna Caterina. They are all thieves—all thieves,' the workman afterwards added, chewing his black stump of a cigar, and shaking his head with a look of great distrust.

'You have taken a half-holiday to-day?'

'I never go there on Saturday,' said the other, giving a sickly smile. 'I go to look for Fortune; I must find her some Saturday morning!'

'When do you get your week's money?'

'Eh!' he said, shrugging his shoulders—'generally on Fridays: I have nothing to get.'

'How do you manage to gamble?'

'One can always get it for gambling. Donna Caterina's sister—she of the *small* game—lends money.'

'Does she take big interest?'

'A sou for each franc every week.'

'Not bad—not bad,' said the shoeblack, with a convinced look.

'I have seventy-five francs to give her,' said the glove-cutter. 'Every Monday there is a storm. She waits for me outside the factory door, shouting and swearing. She is really a witch, Michele. But what can I do? One day or other I will take a *terno*, and I will pay her.'

'What will you do with the rest of your winnings?' Michele asked, laughing.

'I know what I will do,' cried Gaetano, the cutter. 'In new clothes, a pheasant's feather in my cap, in a carriage with bells, we will all go to amuse ourselves at the Due Pulcinelli, at Campo di Marte.'

'Or at Figlio di Pietro, at Posellipo.'

'At Asso di coppe, at Portici.'

'Inn after inn.'

'Meat and macaroni.'

'And Monte di Procida wine.'

'Just so, one only lives once,' the glove-cutter philosophically concluded, pulling his jacket up on his shoulder.

'I don't get into debt,' the shoeblack added, after a minute's silence.

'Lucky you!'

'I would get no one to lend me a sou, anyhow. But I play everything. I have no family; I can do what I like.'

'Lucky you!' Gaetano repeated, with a troubled look.

'Three sous for a sleeping-place, five or six for food,' went on the shoeblack, 'and who says a word to me? I did not want to marry; I had a rage for gambling: it stands in place of everything.'

'May he that invented marriage be hanged!' blasphemed Gaetano, getting clay colour.

Four o'clock was approaching, and the Impresa court filled up with people. In that space of a hundred metres was a crowd of common people pressed together, chattering in a lively way or waiting in resigned silence, looking up to the first-floor at the covered balcony, where the lottery drawing was to come off. But all was shut up above, even the wooden shutters, behind the glass of the great balcony. As other people came up continually, the crowd reached to the wall of the court even. Women that were pushed back had squatted on the first steps of the stair; others, more bashful, hid under the balcony among the pillars that held it up, leaning against a shut stable door. Another woman, still young, but with a pallid, worn, fascinating face, rather strange, melancholy black eyes, hollow-rimmed, and thick black locks loose on her neck, had climbed on a stone left in the courtyard, perhaps from the time the palace was built or restored. She looked very thin in her dyed black gown, that went in folds over her lean breast; she was swinging one foot in a broken, out-at-heel shoe, pulling up on her shoulders now and then a wretched little shawl, dyed also. She overlooked the crowd, gazing at it with downcast, sad eyes. It was almost entirely composed of poor people—cobblers who had shut up their bench in the dens they lived in, had rolled their leather aprons round their waists: in shirt-sleeves, cap over the eyes, they pondered in their minds the numbers they had played, slightly moving their lips; servants out of place, who, instead of trying for a master, used up the last shilling from the pawned winter coat, dreaming of the *terno* that from servants would make them into masters, whilst an impatient frown crossed the gray faces, where the beard, no longer shaven, grew in patches. There were hackney coachmen, who had left their cab in the care of a friend, brother, or son, waiting patiently, hands in pocket, with the stolidity of a cabman used to waiting hours for a hire; there were letters of furnished rooms, hirers of servants, who in summer, with all the strangers and students gone, sat pining in their chairs under the board that forms their whole shop, at the corners of San Sepolcro Lane, Taverna Penta, Trinità degli Spagnuoli; having played a few sous taken from their daily bread, they came to hear the lottery drawn, being unemployed—and lazy. There were hands at humble Neapolitan trades, who, leaving the factory, warehouse, or shop, giving up their hard, badly-paid work, clutching in their worn-out waistcoat pocket the five sous ticket, or bundle of numbers at the *little game*, had come to pant over that dream that might become a reality. There were still more unlucky people—that is to say, all those who in Naples do not live by the day even, but by the hour, trying a hundred trades, good at all, but unable, unluckily, to find safe remunerative work; unfortunates without home or shelter, shamefully torn and dirty, they had given up their bread that day to play a throw. One read in their faces the double marks of fasting and extreme abasement.

Some women were noticeable among the crowd—slovenly women, of no particular age, nor beauty; servants out of place, desperate gamblers' wives, who gambled themselves, dismissed workwomen, and among them all Carmela's pale, fascinating face, the girl seated on the stone—a faded face with big, tired eyes. Later on, as the hour for the drawing got near, and the noise increased, among the few gray women's faces and torn calico dresses, discoloured from too frequent washings, quite a different woman's face showed. She was a tall, strong woman of the lower class, with a high-coloured dark face; her chestnut hair was drawn back, elaborately dressed— the fringe on her narrow forehead had even a touch of powder; and heavy earrings of uneven, round, greeny-white pearls pulled down her ears, so that she had had to secure them by a black silk string, fearing they would break the lobes; a gold necklace and a thick gold medallion hung over the white muslin vest, all embroidered and tucked with lace. She pulled up a transparent black silk crape shawl on her shoulders every now and then, to show her hands, which were covered with thick gold rings up to the second joint. Her eye was grave and quiet, with a slight look of quiet audacity, her mouth settled and severe; but on going through the crowd, on her way to sit on the third step of the stair, to see and hear better, she kept that bend of the head, rather coquettish and mysterious, peculiar to the Neapolitan lower class, and the swaying of her body under the shawl that a Naples woman dressed in the French fashion soon loses. Still, in spite of the natural sympathy that womanly figure inspired among the crowd, there was almost a hostile murmur and something like an indignant movement. She shrugged her shoulders disdainfully, and sat alone, upright, on the third step, keeping the shawl up on her shoulders, her ring-laden hands crossed in front. The murmur went on here and there. She looked at the crowd severely twice or thrice—rather proudly. The voices ceased; the woman's eyelids fluttered, as if from gratified pride.

But, finally, over all the others—over Carmela, with her faded face and great sad eyes; over Donna Concetta, with her ringed fingers and powdered fringe, the handsome, healthy, rich Concetta, the usurer, sister to Donna Caterina, the holder of the *small* game—above the crowd in the court, entrance, and street, a woman's form stood out, drawing at least one look from the people gathered together. It was the woman on the first-floor of the Impresa Palace, sitting sideways behind the balcony railings; one saw her profile bending over the bright steel fittings of a Singer sewing-machine, lifting her head now and then, whilst her foot, coming from under a modest blue-and-white striped petticoat, beat evenly on the iron pedal, regularly rising and falling. Among the stir of voices, the conversations from one end of the court to the other, and stamping of feet, the dull quaver of the sewing-machine was lost; but the seamstress's figure stood out in profile on the balcony's gloomy background, her hands pushing the bit of white linen under the machine needle, her foot untiringly beating the pedal, her head rising and bending over her work, with no ardour, but no weariness, evenly on. A thin, rather pink cheek was shown in profile, and a thick chestnut tress neatly arranged close to the nape of the neck, the corner of a fine mouth, and the shade of long eyelashes thrown on the cheeks, could also be seen. During the hour the crowd was pouring into the court, the young seamstress had not looked down twice, giving a short indifferent glance and lowering her head again, taking the piece of linen slowly along in her hands, so that the seam should be quite straight. Nothing distracted her from her work—neither angry voice or lively remarks, nor the noise or the increasing trampling of the crowd; she had never looked at the covered balcony, where in a short time the drawings would be called out. The people from below stared at the delicate, industrious white sewer, but she went on with her work as if not even an echo of that half-covered, half-open excitement came up to her; she seemed so far off, so reserved, so wrapped up in a quite detached, different world, that one could fancy her more a statue than a reality—more of an ideal figure than a living woman.

But all at once a long shout of satisfaction burst out from the crowd in all varieties of tone, rising to the most stridulent and going down to the deepest note: the big balcony on the terrace had opened. The people waiting in the road tried to get in at the entrance, those standing there crushed into the court; it was quite a squeeze, all faces were raised, seized by burning curiosity and anguish. A great silence followed. Looking keenly, one could see by the moving of some woman's lips that she was praying, whilst Carmela, the girl with the attractive, worn face and very sad black eyes, played with a black string tied round her neck that had a medallion of our Lady of Sorrows and a forked bit of coral. There was universal silence of expectation and stupor. On the terrace two Royal Lottery ushers had arranged a long narrow table covered with green cloth, and three armchairs behind it for the three authorities to sit in—a Councillor of the Prefecture, the Lottery Director at Naples, and a representative of the municipality. The urn for the ninety numbers was placed on another little table. It is a big urn, made of transparent metal, lemon-shaped, with brass bands going from one end to the other, surrounding it as the meridian line goes round the earth: these shining bands make it strong without spoiling its transparency. The urn is slung in the air between two brass pegs; a metal handle by one, when touched, makes the urn twist round on its axis. The two ushers who had brought out all these things to the terrace were old, rather bent, and sleepy-looking. The three authorities, in great-coats and tall hats, seemed bored and sleepy too, sitting behind the table; the Prefecture Councillor, with his deep, black dyed moustaches, was drowsy: he looked as if he had touched them in in brown on his sleepy dark face; it was the same with the secretary, a youth with a dark beard. These folk moved slowly, like automatons, so that a common man from the crowd called out, 'Move on! move on!' Silence again, but a great wave of emotion when the little boy who was to take the numbers out of the urn appeared on the balcony.

He was a boy dressed in the gray poor-house uniform, a poor little fellow from the *serraglio*, as the Naples folk call these deserted creatures' asylum, a poor *serragliuolo* with no father nor mother, a son of parents who from cruelty or want had deserted their offspring. Helped by one of the ushers, the little boy put on a white woollen tunic over his uniform and a white cap, because lottery superstition requires the little innocent to wear innocence's white dress. He climbed nimbly on to a stool, so as to stand as high as the urn. Below, the crowd tossed about: 'Pretty lad, pretty lad!' 'May you be blessed!' 'I commend myself to you and to St. Joseph!' 'The Virgin bless your hand!' 'Blessed, blessed!' 'Holy and old—live to be holy and old!' Everyone said something, good wishes, blessings, requests, pious invocations, prayers. The child was silent, looking from him, his little hand resting on the urn's metal net. At a little distance, leaning against the balcony rail, was another *serraglio* child, very serious, in spite of his pink cheeks and fair hair cut on the forehead. It was the little boy who was to take out the numbers next Saturday; he came to learn, to get used to the working of the urn and the people's shouts. No one cared about him—it was the one dressed in white for that day to whom all the numerous exclamations were addressed; it was the innocent little soul in white that made that crowd of distracted beings smile tenderly, that brought tears to the eyes of those who hoped in Fortune only. Some women had raised their own boys in their arms, and held them out to the *serragliuolo*. The tender, agitated, distressed voices went on: 'He looks like a little St. John, really!' 'May you always find grace, if you do me this favour!' 'Mother's darling, how sweet he is!' Suddenly there was a diversion. One of the ushers took a number to put into the urn; he showed it unfolded to the people, called it out in a clear voice, and passed it to the three authorities, who cast a distracted eye over it. One of the three, the Prefecture Councillor, shut up the number in a round box; the second usher passed it to the white-robed child, who threw it quickly into the urn, into its small open mouth. At every number that was called out there were remarks, shrieks, grins, and laughter. The people gave each number its meaning, taken from the 'Book of Dreams,' or from the 'Smorfia,' or that popular legend that grows without books or pictures. There were shouts of laughter, coarse jokes, frightened or hopeful ejaculations—all accompanied by a dull noise, as if it was the minor chord of the tempest.

'Two.'

'A baby girl.'

'The letter.'

'Bring me out this letter, sir.'

'Five.'

'The hand.'

'... in the face of him who ill-wished me.'

'Eight.'

'That is the Virgin—the Virgin.'

But as every tenth number, enclosed within its little round gray box, was thrown into the urn by the *serragliuolo*, the second usher shut its mouth and turned the handle, giving it a spin on its axis that made the numbers roll round, dance, and jump. From below there were cries of:

'Spin, turn it round, old man.'

'Another spin for me.'

'Give me full measure.'

The Cabalists did not speak, they did not even look at the urn spinning: the innocent babe was nothing to them, the meaning of the numbers, nor the slow lively twirl of the big urn; for them the Cabal is everything, the obscure but still transparent Cabal, great, powerful, imperious Fate that knows all, and does all, without any power, human or divine, being able to oppose it. They alone kept silence, thoughtful, absorbed, disdaining that loud popular rejoicing, wrapped up in a spiritual, mystical world, waiting with deep confidence.

'Thirteen.'

'... that means the candles.'

'... the thick candle, the torch. Let us put out the torch!'

'... put it out—put it out!' the chorus echoed.

'... twenty-two.'

'... the madman!'

'... the little silly!'

'... like you.'

'... like me.'

'... like him that plays the small game—*alla bonafficiata*.'

The people got excited. Long shivers went through the crowd; it swayed about as if it was moved by the sea. Women especially got nervous, convulsive; they clutched the babies in their arms so hard as to make them grow pale and cry. Carmela, seated on the high stone, crumpled the Virgin's medallion and the forked coral in her hand; the usurer, Donna Concetta, forgot to pull up the black crape shawl, which fell over her heavy hips, while her lips gave a slight convulsive flutter. No one cared any more about the sewing-machine's dull quaver nor the industrious white sewer. The Naples folks' feverishness got higher and higher as the dream that was to become a reality got nearer, getting a livelier, longer sensation when a popular, a lucky number was drawn.

Thirty-three!

These are Christ's years!

His years.

'... this comes out.'

'... it will not come out.'

'... you will see that it will.'

'Thirty-nine!'

'... the hanged rogue!'

'... take him by the throat—by the throat!'

'... so I ought to see what I said.'

'... squeeze him—squeeze him!'

Unmoved, the authorities, the ushers, the boy in white, went on with their work as if all this popular noise did not reach their ears; only the other infant, new to all that extraordinary sight, looked down from the railing, stupefied, pale, with swollen red lips, as if he wanted to cry—an unconscious, amazed little soul amid the storm of deep human passion. The business on the platform went on with the greatest calm; as every new tenth number was put into the urn, the usher made it twirl longer, making the little balls jump in a lively way inside the open network. Not a word nor a smile was exchanged up there: the fever stayed at the height of the people in the court, it did not rise to the first floor. Down there the gravest people now laughed convulsively, in a subdued way, shaking their heads as if the infection had seized them in its most violent form. The affair seemed to be hurrying to the end. Renewed shouts received seventy-five, which is Punch's number, and seventy-seven, the devil's; but loud, drawn-out applause saluted the ninetieth, the last number, partly because it was the last, also ninety is a very lucky number: it means fear, also the sea; it means the people too; it has five or six other meanings, all popular. All in the court cheered, men, women, and children, at the great ninety, which is the omega of the lottery. Then all at once, like enchantment, a great silence fell: these faces and forms all kept motionless, and the great excited crowd seemed petrified in feelings, words, gestures and expression.

The first usher, the one who called out the ninety numbers, brought a long, narrow wooden board with five empty squares to the railing, such as bookmakers use on a race-course, whilst the other gave the urn its last twirl with all ninety numbers in it. The board was turned towards the crowd. Then the Councillor rang a bell; the urn stopped; another usher put a bandage over the white-clad infant's eyes; he slowly put his little hand into the open urn and searched for a minute only, quickly drawing out a ball with a number. Whilst the ball passed from hand to hand, a deep, dull, anguished sigh came out of those petrified bosoms down there.

'Ten!' shouted the usher, putting it quickly in the first square. A murmur and agitation among the crowd; all those who had hopes of the first drawing were disappointed. Another ring of the bell; the child put in its slender hand the second time. 'Two!' shouted the usher, announcing the number taken out and putting it into the second square. Some muttered oaths mingled with the rising murmur; all those who had played the second drawing were disappointed, and those who had hoped to take four numbers, those who had played the great *terno* in one, greatly feared to come out badly, so much so that, when the lad's small hand went into the urn the third time, someone called out in anguish:

'Search well; make a good choice, child.'

'Eighty-four!' shouted the usher, calling out the number and placing it in the third space. Here an indignant yell burst out, made up of oaths, lamentations, angry cries. This third number, being bad, was decisive for the drawing and the gamblers. With eighty-four, the hopes of all those who had played the first, second, and third drawing were frustrated; all those who had played the five sequence, fourths, the two treys, or these doubled, which is the hope and joy of Naples folk, hope and desire of all desperate players, and those that only play once on chance, saw they had missed it. The *terno* is the essential word of all these longings, needs, necessities, and miseries. A chorus of curses arose against bad luck, evil fate, against the lottery and those who believe in it, against the Government, against that bad boy with such unlucky hands. *'Serragliuolo! Serragliuolo!'* was shouted from below, to insult him, and fists were shaken at him. The little one did not turn to look; he stood motionless, with his eyes down. Some minutes passed between the third and fourth numbers; it happened so every week. The third number brought the frightful expression of the infinite popular disappointment. 'Seventy-five,' the usher said in a feebler voice, putting the number drawn in the fourth space. Among the angry voices that would not be soothed, some hisses sounded revengefully. Abuse poured on the child's head, but the greatest curses were against the lottery, where one could never win, never, where everything is arranged so that no one ever wins, especially against poor people. 'Forty-three,' the usher called out for the last time, placing the fifth and last number. A last gust of rage among the people—nothing more. In a minute all the cold lottery machinery disappeared from the terrace: the children, the three authorities, the urn with the eighty-five numbers and its pedestal, tables, chairs, and ushers, all went out of sight, the glass and shutters of the great balcony were shut in a minute; only the cruel board remained, straight against the balustrade, with its five numbers—these, these, the great misfortune and delusion!

Very slowly and unwillingly the crowd cleared out of the court. On those most excited by gambling passions the wind of desolation had blown, and overthrown them all. They felt as if their arms and legs were broken; their mouth had a bitter taste from anger. Those who that morning had played all their money, feeling no need of eating, drinking, nor smoking, feeding themselves with vivid visions of Cockaigne, dreaming for that Saturday evening, Sunday, and all the days following, quite a bellyful of fat, rich dinners, tasting them in their imagination, held their hands feebly in their empty pockets. One could read in their desolate eyes the childish physical grief of the first pangs of hunger; and they had not, knew they could not get, bread to quiet their stomachs. Others, the maddest, fallen from the height of their hopes in a minute, experienced that long movement of mad anguish in which people will not, cannot, believe in bad luck. Their eyes had that wandering look that sees the shape of things no longer; their lips stammered incoherent words. It was these desperate fools who still kept their eyes on the board with the numbers, as if they could not yet convince themselves of the truth, and mechanically compared them with the long list of their tickets. The Cabalists, to conclude, did not go away yet; they held discussions among themselves, like so many philosophers or logicians, still wrapped up in lottery mathematics, where dwell the *figure*, the *cadenze*, the *triple*, the algebraic explanation of the *quadrato Maltese*, and Rutilio Benincasa's immortal lucubrations. But with those who went away, as with those who stayed, nailed to the spot by their excitement; those who discussed it violently, as with those who bent their heads, deadly white, courage all gone, without strength to move or think, the form of the desolation varied, but the substance of it was the same—deep, intense, making the inward fibres bleed, tending to destroy the very springs of life.

Michele, the lame shoeblack, still seated on the ground, with his black box between his crooked legs, had heard the drawing without getting up, hidden behind people who pressed around him. Now, while the crowd was slowly going off, he hung down his head, and the yellow shade of his rickety old face got green, as if all his bile had gone to his brain.

'Have you got nothing?' asked a dull voice beside him.

He raised his gray eyes with pink lids mechanically and saw Gaetano, the glove-cutter, who showed in his chalky face the depression of disappointed hopes.

'No, nothing,' said the shoeblack shortly, lowering his eyes.

'There is nothing for me, either. If you have a few sous for a combination, old fellow, I will give them back on Monday.'

'Where could I get them? If you get hold of ten, we could make up five each,' the shoeblack muttered desperately.

'Good-bye, old fellow! Good-bye!' said the glove-cutter in a rough voice.

While Gaetano was going off under the gateway, Donna Concetta came alongside of him, slow and grave, her eyes down, the gold chain waving on her breast and ringed fingers.

'Have you won nothing, Gaetano?' she asked with a slight smile.

'I have been hit by an arrow!' shouted he, provoked to be so near the usurer, who reminded him of all his wretchedness, annoyed by her question at such a moment.

'All right—all right,' she returned coldly. 'We see each other on Monday—don't forget.'

'I don't forget; I keep you in my heart like the Virgin,' he called out, alongside of her, in a hissing voice.

She shook her head as she went off. She did not come there for her own interests, because she never gambled; nor even to worry some of her debtors, like Gaetano. She came in her sister's interest, Donna Caterina, the holder of the *small game,* for she dared not show in public. Donna Caterina told her sister which numbers she dreaded most—that is to say, those she had played most on, for which she would have to pay the largest sums. Then Donna Concetta sent off a lad to her sister, who quickly made off, so as to pay no one. Three times already she had gone bankrupt so, with the gamblers' money in her pocket. She had fled once to Santa Maria, at Capua, once to Gragnano, once to Nocera dei Pagani, staying there two months. She had had the courage to come back and face the cheated gamblers, using audacity with some and giving a few sous to others, beginning the game again, while the robbed, cheated, and disappointed gamblers came back to her, incapable of denouncing her, seized by the fever again, or kept in awe by Donna Concetta, to whom they all owed money. So the concern went on. The money passed from one sister to another—from the one who held the bank and knew how to fail in time, to the money-lender who was daring enough to face the worst-intentioned of her debtors. Nor was her flight looked on as a crime, as cheating, by Donna Caterina and her customers; for did not the Government do the same thing, perhaps, on a larger scale? A gift of six million francs has been settled for each drawing for every *ruota* of eight: when, by a very rare combination, the winnings go above six millions, does not the Government fail too, making the entire profits smaller?

But that day there was no need for Donna Caterina to fail, to make off; the numbers drawn were so bad, perhaps not one of her clients had won; and Donna Concetta climbed up the Chiara way very easily, not hurrying at all, knowing it was a desolate Saturday for all gambling Naples, getting ready for her battle of usury on Monday. All these unhappy creatures with broken hopes passed near her; she shook her head wisely over human aberrations, and clutched the hem of her crape shawl in her ringed fingers. A woman who was coming quickly down the street, dragging a little boy and girl behind her, and carrying a baby, touched her in passing on her way into the Impresa court, where some people were still lingering. She was very poorly dressed; her calico skirt was so frayed and dirty it filled one with pity and disgust, and she had a ravelled woollen shawl round her neck; her face was so lean and worn, her teeth so black, and hair so sparse, that the children, who were neither ragged nor dirty, looked as if they did not belong to her.

The sucking child only was rather slight—it laid its head on her shoulder to sleep; but the poor thing was so agitated she did not notice it. Seeing Carmela, her sister, still seated on the high stone, her hands loose in her lap, and head sunk on the breast, all alone, as if petrified in speechless grief, she went up to her, and said:

'Carmela!'

'Good-day, Annarella,' said Carmela, starting, giving a sickly smile.

'Are you here too?' she asked in a sad, surprised tone.

'Yes, I came,' Carmela answered, with a resigned gesture.

'Have you seen my husband, Gaetano?' Annarella asked anxiously, letting the baby's head slide from her shoulder to her arm, so that it could sleep more comfortably.

Carmela raised her big eyes to her sister's face, but seeing her so dishevelled and ugly from privation and misery, so old already, so doomed to illness and death, asking the question so despairingly, she dared not tell her the truth. Yes, she had seen her brother-in-law Gaetano, the glove-cutter; she had first seen him trembling and anxious, thin, pale and downcast, but she felt too sorry for her sister, the delicate, sleeping baby, and the other two who were gazing around them, and she lied.

'I have not seen him at all.'

'He must have been here,' Annarella muttered in her rough drawl.

'I assure you he was not here, really.'

'You will not have seen him,' Annarella repeated, obstinate in her sad incredulity. 'How could he not come? He comes here every Saturday. He might not be at home with his little ones; he might not be at the glove factory, where he can earn bread; but he can't be anywhere else than here on Saturday to hear the numbers come out: here is his ruling passion and his death.'

'He plays a lot, doesn't he?' said Carmela, who had grown pale and had tears in her eyes.

'All that he can spare and more than he has got. We might live very well, without asking anything from anyone; but instead, with his *bonafficiata*, we are full of debts and mortifications; we only eat now and then, when I bring in something. These poor little things!'

Her voice was so broken with maternal agony that Carmela's tears fell, overcome by infinite pity. Now they were almost alone in the court.

'Why do you come to hear this lottery drawn?' Annarella asked, suddenly enraged against all those that play.

'What am I to do?' said the other in her sweet, broken voice. 'You know I would like to see you all happy, mother, and you, Gaetano, your babies, and my lover Raffaele—and somebody else. You know your cross is mine, that I have not an hour's peace thinking of what you suffer. So all that is over of my earnings I play: the Lord must bless me some day or other. I must get a *terno* then; then I'll give it all to you.'

'Poor sister!' said Annarella, with melancholy tenderness.

'That day must come—it must,' she whispered passionately, as if speaking to herself, as if she already saw that happy day.

'May an angel pass and say *amen*,' Annarella murmured, kissing her baby's forehead. 'Where can Gaetano be?' she went on, care coming back.

'Say truly,' begged Carmela, getting down from the stone on her way off, 'you have nothing to give the children to-day?'

'Nothing,' was the answer in that feeble voice.

'Take this half-franc, take it,' said the other, pulling it out of her pocket and giving it to her.

'God reward you.'

They looked at each other with such mutual pity that only shame of the passers-by kept them from bursting into sobs.

'Good-bye!'

'Good-bye, Carmela!'

The suffering girl kissed the baby softly. Annarella, with the languid step of a woman who has had too many children and worked too hard, went off by the Santa Chiara cloister, pulling her two other little ones behind her. Carmela, pulling her discoloured shawl round her, dragging her down-at-heel shoes, went down towards Banchi Nuovi. It was just there a cleanly-dressed youth, his trousers tight at the knees and wide as bells over the ankle, with a neat jacket, and hat over one ear, stopped her with the look of his clear, cold, light-blue eyes, biting lips, as red as a girl's, under his fair little moustache. Stopping before she spoke to him, Carmela looked with such intense passion on the young fellow she seemed to wish to enfold him in an atmosphere of love. He did not seem to notice it.

'Well, have you won anything?' he asked in a hissing little ironical voice.

'Nothing,' said she, opening her arms desolately. She held down her head so as not to weep, looking at the point of her shoes, which had lost their varnish and showed the dirty lining through a split.

'How do you account for that?' the young fellow cried out angrily. 'A woman is always a woman!'

'Is it my fault if the numbers won't come out?' the love-lorn girl said humbly and sadly.

'You should look out for the good ones. Go to Father Illuminato that knows them, and only tells women; go to Don Pasqualino, he that the good spirits help to find out the right numbers. Get it out of your head, my girl, that I can marry a ragged one like you.'

'I know—I know!' she muttered humbly. 'Say no more about it.'

'You seem to forget it. Masses are not sung without money. Let us say good-bye.'

'Won't you come this evening?' she dared to ask.

'I have something to do. I must go with a friend. Send me a couple of francs.'

'I have only one,' she exclaimed, quite red and mortified, taking it out of her pocket.

'May you die in want!' he cursed, chewing his stump of Naples cigar. 'Give it here! I will try to arrange my affairs better.'

'Won't you pass by the house?' she begged with her eyes.

'If I do pass, it will be very late.'

'It does not matter; I'll wait for you on the balcony,' she said, persisting in her humiliation.

'I can't stop.'

'Well, give a whistle. I'll hear you, and sleep quieter, Raffaele. What trouble will it be to whistle in passing?'

'All right,' he agreed indulgently. 'Good-bye, Carmela!'

'Good-bye, Raffaele!'

She stopped to look at him as he went away quickly in the direction of Madonna dell' Aiuto. The patent-leather shoes creaked as the youth walked in the proud way peculiar to the lower-class *guappi*.

'May the Virgin bless every step you take,' the girl said to herself tenderly as she went off. But as she went along she felt discouraged and weak. All the bitterness of that deceptive day, the sorrow she bore for others' grief—for her mother, a servant at sixty; for her sister, who had no bread for her children; her brother-in-law, who was going to ruin; her affianced, that she would have liked to make rich and happy as a lord, and who never had a franc in his pockets—all these sorrows, and still deeper ones, the greatest of all, the most afflicting grief, her own powerlessness, poured into her mind, her whole being. It was not enough for her to work at that nauseating trade at the tobacco factory for seven days a week; that she had not a decent dress to wear, nor a pair of whole shoes, so that she was coldly looked on at the factory. She fasted four times a week to give her mother a franc, Raffaele two, her sister Annarella half a franc; what was over went to the lottery. It was no use, she never could do anything for those she loved; her hard work, wretchedness, hunger, did no one any good.

She felt so miserable as she went down San Giovanni Maggiore steps at Mezzocannone, getting nearer as she was to her saddest charge, that she could have killed herself for being so helpless and useless. Still, she went on into an out-of-the-way court in the Mercanti, that looked like a servants' yard, then stopped and leant against the wall as if she could go no further. It was a dirty place, with greasy water, fruit-skins, and a woman's broken old hat thrown into a corner. Three windows of the first-floor had half-open green jalousies, just letting in a ray of light—mean little windows and faded jalousies, on which dust, rain, and the sun had left their mark; then a little doorway, with a damp step broken to bits, and a narrow black passage like a gutter. Carmela looked inside, her eyes wide open from curiosity and fear. Rather an old woman, a servant, came out, holding up her skirt not to dirty it in the gutter. Carmela knew her, evidently, for she turned to her frankly:

'Donna Rosa, will you call Filomena?'

The woman looked to see who it was; then, without going into the house again, she called from the courtyard towards the first-floor windows:

'Filomena! Filomena!'

'Who is it?' a hoarse voice answered from inside.

'Your sister wants you—come down.'

'I am coming,' said the voice more gently.

'Thanks, Donna Rosa,' said Carmela.

'Glad to serve you,' said the other briefly as she went off.

Filomena kept her waiting two or three minutes; then a regular beat of wooden heels came along the passage, and she appeared. She wore a white muslin skirt, with a high flounce of white embroidery, a cream woollen bodice, much trimmed with knots of velvet ribbon at the wrists and waist. She had a pink chenille shawl round her neck; patent-leather shoes with high heels, and red silk stockings showed under the skirt. In face she was like both her sisters, but her well-dressed hair, with light shell pins, and the rouge on her colourless cheeks, made one forget the likeness to Annarella, and made her much more attractive than Carmela. The two sisters did not kiss nor shake hands, but they gave each other so intense a look that it sufficed for everything.

'How are you?' asked Carmela in a trembling voice.

'I am well,' said Filomena, shaking her head, as if her health did not matter. 'How is mother?'

'Just as an old woman always is.... Poor mother!'

'How is Annarella?'

'She is full of trouble....'

'Wretched, eh?'

'Yes, she is wretched.'

They both sighed deeply as they looked at each other; a blush and a pallor altered their faces.

'I bring you bad news to-day, too, Filomena,' Carmela said at last.

'Have you won nothing?' Filomena asked.

'No, nothing!'

'My luck is bad,' Filomena said. 'I have made many vows to the Virgin—not, indeed, to the Immaculate one; I am not even worthy to name her—but to our Lady of Sorrows, who understands and pities my disgrace; but nothing has come.'

'Our Lady of Sorrows will grant us this grace,' Carmela said softly. 'Let us hope that next Saturday——'

'We will hope so,' the other answered humbly.

'Good-bye, Filomena!'

'Good-bye, Carmela!'

Filomena turned her back and disappeared into the passage, her wooden heels making her steps rhythmical; then Carmela was going to rush after her to call her, but she was already in the house. The girl went off, wrapping herself convulsively in her shawl, biting her lips not to sob. All the other bitternesses—all, even going without bread—were nothing in comparison to what she left behind: that came by itself, a constant poison, an eternal shame, to her heart.

At half-past five the Impresa court was quite empty and silent; no one came in, not even to look at that solitary board with the five numbers: they had already been put up at all the lottery-shops in Naples; there was a group of people before each, all through the town. No one went into the Impresa court; the crowd would only come back in seven days. Then there was a noise of footsteps. It was the lottery usher, leading the two poor-house children by the hand—the one who had drawn the numbers, and he who was to draw them next Saturday. The usher was taking them back to the asylum, where he would leave the twenty francs, the weekly payment the Royal Lottery gives to the child that draws the numbers. The two boys trod on each other's heels behind the usher, chattering gaily. The white sewer, working at her machine, raised her head and smiled at them. Then she began to beat her foot on the pedal and pull the bit of linen straight under the needle; she went on quietly, indefatigably, a pure humble image of labour.

CHAPTER II
AGNESINA FRAGALÀ'S CHRISTENING

'Agnesina Fragalà, papa's lovely daughter,' said the young father, leaning over the brass cradle that shone like gold, holding open the lace curtains with rose-coloured ribbons, and petting with words, glances, and smiles the pink new-born babe that was placidly sleeping. 'Agnesina, Agnesina,' he went on saying playfully, 'I think you are very pretty.'

'Be quiet, Cesare; you will wake the baby,' the mother said in a whisper, from the toilet-glass she was sitting at.

'She will have to be wakened later on, at any rate; ought we not to show her to our guests?'

'Yes; I just hope she won't begin screaming in the drawing-room!' the young mother replied, smiling, half from nervous fears, half from motherly pride.

'Bah!' said the young father, leaving the cradle and coming near to his wife. 'The guests will be taken up eating cakes, sweets, and ices. You will see a gourmandizing, Luisella!'

The light edifice of Luisa Fragalà's intensely black hair was skilfully and prettily arranged; some curls shaded her short brown forehead, with its black eyebrows in the youthful oval face; and the long Eastern eyes of sparkling gray, soft and piquant, the rather long, broad, though well-shaped nose, and baby mouth, pink as a carnation, had a charm of youth and freshness that made her still enamoured husband smile with pleasure.

Cesare Fragalà was young and handsome, too—rather effeminately handsome, perhaps; his skin was as white as a woman's; his chestnut hair curled all over up to the temples, showing in places the white skin underneath; his face was round, rather boyish still, in spite of his being twenty-eight; but his close-shaven cheeks had a warm Southern pallor that was quite manly, and a thick curly moustache corrected that effeminate, boyish look. Both of them of burgher rank, of no degenerate race, they had the characteristics of Neapolitan youth. The man was strong, but indolent; good-looking and rather inclined to care for his appearance; his softness was visibly mixed with roguishness, from the contrasts in his face, where a coarse look was tempered by good-nature. The woman, dark and elegant, with that blood that seems to have dull flashes, that resoluteness of will in the profile and chin that shows a secret latent force in a woman's heart, ready for passion and sacrifice.

The surroundings were like themselves, from the rather vulgar luxury of pink and cream brocade that covered the furniture and the bed, the French paper on the walls of much the same design, the toilet-glass draped in white lace—precious work done by the bride's own hands before the wedding—to the great wardrobe of dark wood, with gold lines and three looking-glass doors, the height of luxury at that time; from the numerous images of saints—Saint Louis in silver, the face in wax; a Saint Cesare of stucco in a monk's habit, with rosaries, reliquaries, and Easter candles, forming a trophy, on each side of the bed—up to the silver lamp, lighted, before the Infant Jesus, in a niche; and in the same conjugal apartment, from plebeian tenderness, and that strong patriarchal feeling of Neapolitans, was the cradle, gay with ribbons, where the little one of a month old was sleeping. Everything was striking, even their clothes. Cesare Fragalà, expecting his guests shortly, had on his coat already, a handkerchief stuck in his shirt, and his curly hair smooth by dint of hard brushing; but his watch-chain was too bright, his studs too large, and his necktie was white silk instead of white batiste. Luisa looked very pretty in her yellow silk, with a white muslin wrapper over it while her hair was done, but she sparkled too much from diamonds in her ears, on her neck, and on her arms. Just then the hair-dresser put a brilliant star in front as a finish.

'Is nothing more needed?' she asked, rather thinking she had too few ornaments.

'No,' said the hair-dresser decisively; 'the fewer things put in the hair, the better.'

'Do you think so?'

'Let yourself be guided by one who knows his trade,' the artist added, gathering up his combs and curling-irons.

'You look very nice,' the husband whispered, on an inquiring glance from his wife. He looked at her tenderly, carefully, to see if anything was wanting. 'If my combination comes off,' Cesare added, whilst the barber took leave silently, so as not to waken the baby, after getting five francs and one more as a tip—'if my combination comes off, Luisella, I will buy you a string of diamonds for your neck.'

'What combination are you speaking of?' she asked, as she put some powder on her bare arms. She frowned, with a woman's sudden suspicion of all affairs she does not know about.

'I will tell you afterwards,' he said, stammering.

'Tell me now,' she demanded, standing with her long gloves in her hand.

'There is nothing really yet to tell, Luisella,' he said, rather put out at having let out something.

'Promise me never to decide on anything without asking me first,' she said, raising one hand.

'I promise,' he said with deep sincerity.

She was appeased, and sat down reassured, putting on her gloves, while her husband stood before the looking-glass twirling the points of his moustache, smiling at his own image and at life. The Fragalà family counted up no less than eighty years of commercial prudence and rising fortunes. Cesare's grandfather had begun with a wretched shop in Purgatorio ad Arco Street in the Pendino quarter, rather worse, said the envious, for he was a wandering salesman of cakes at a half-penny each, heaped on a wooden board carried on his head, under the arm, or by a leather band round the neck. In fact, either on the board or in that shop, these sweets were made of middling flour, sugar of third quality, eggs of doubtful freshness, and very often cooked in rancid lard, filled oftener with apples or quinces roasted under ashes than peach or black-cherry preserve. But what did it matter? All Southerners, men and women, young and old, love sweets, spicy cakes and biscuits sprinkled with aniseed and sugar; the pastry at a half-penny appeared and disappeared in Fragalà's shop, also sticky coloured caramels and cakes called *ancinetti*. Grandfather Fragalà soon managed, by dint of heaping up halfpence, to produce pastry at three-halfpence, the so-called *sfogliatella*, of which there are two qualities—the *riccia*, broad, thin, and flat, that falls into fine flakes, crackling under the teeth, whilst the cream in it melts on the tongue; and the *frolla*, thick and fat, two fingers' width of pastry that powders as you eat it, a thick layer of cream inside that covers your lips and jaws. It is true Grandfather Fragalà was accused of mixing a lot of dirty noxious ingredients in his *sfogliatella*: starch, gum, raw sugar, beef-fat, strong glue, and even bran. But what did it matter? On Sundays and all the other appointed feasts the *sfogliatella* sold like bread, or, rather, more so, from nine to two o'clock in the afternoon; then Fragalà shut his shop, because he had no more to sell, however many he had made, also because he was a God-fearing man. He quietly opened another shop in San Pietro a Maiella, putting in one of his sons; then, later on, another shop at Costantinopoli

Street, towards the Bourbon Museum, with another son; and, finally, at his death, his eldest dared to aspire to Toledo Street, but in the upper part, opening a pastry-shop with *three doors*—that is to say, three shops—at the corner of Spirito Santo, a gorgeous place. The pastry-shops of Purgatoria ad Arco, San Pietro a Maiella, and Costantinopoli Streets still exist, owned by the younger brothers, all more or less black and dirty, full of buzzing flies, but giving out that intoxicating smell of burnt sugar, apples, fruit, and crumbling pastry that all Naples boys, women, and old men long for. Even at Purgatoria ad Arco the tarts were sold at a penny, halfway between grandfather's price and the three-halfpence of the modern shop. But the three shops in one in Toledo Street rejoiced in the inscription 'Founded in 1802,' in gold letters on black marble—it was all white marble, shining plate-glass windows full of coloured sweets, bright metal boxes, and clear glasses with biscuits, tall round vases of pastils, strong and sweet, for disordered stomachs or for coughs, and glass shelves with all kinds of pastry in rows. Via Toledo confectionery was superb, but among its innovations it had not neglected the safe old Neapolitan speciality, *sfogliatella*, always popular and long-lived, in spite of innovations in sweetmeats, in its two forms of *riccia* and *frolla*; on Sundays, all the patriarchal families that come out from Mass from so many churches round—Spirito Santo, Pellegrini, San Michele, San Domenico Soriano—bought in passing some six or eight *sfogliatella*, to give the final festive touch to the Sunday dinner. Cesare Fragalà's father had added to the *sfogliatella* all the other specialities in sweets eaten by Naples folk at all the feasts in the year: almond or royal paste at Christmas; *sanguinaccio* at Carnival; Lenten biscuits, the *mastacciolo* and *pastiera*, at Easter; *l'osso di morto* (dead men's bones), made of almonds and candied sugar, for All Souls' Day; the *torrone* for St. Martin's; and others—*croccante, struffoli, sosamiello*—all Parthenope's sweets, made of almonds, sugar, and chocolate, delightful to the palate and heavy to digest; but they are the joy of Naples crowds—they are sent into the provinces, every holiday, in all sizes of boxes by the waggon-load. Still among the Fragalàs' jealous rivals there were some whispers about the mysterious ingredients in these sweets; but it was harmless malignity, to which customers paid no heed; even if they believed it, they cared little about it. The Naples philosopher, Peppino, Fragalà's customer, said: 'If one knew what one was eating, no one would wish to eat anything.' The Fragalà house was solid: Cesare had inherited a good fortune and unbroken credit from his father.

It is true he had, as a rich citizen, an instinctive contempt for his uncles' and cousins' dark shops, where the flies buzzed annoyingly, as if cloyed and ill with indigestion from the bad sugar and honey; but he was prudent too—he did not scorn his origin, he willingly received his relations at family dinners, and when he had to make changes in his Toledo shop, he thought them over, and took advice—mostly from his wife. Luisa thought of all this as she put on her gloves slowly, whilst her husband went to the kitchen to see if the refreshments were ready, and that the extra servants, hired for the occasion, were properly dressed. She rose, and, picking up her yellow train, went to lift the lace curtain of the cradle, and passionately gazed on her daughter Agnesina. Never, never would her husband do anything without consulting her; he had married her for love, without a half-penny, against everyone's wishes, and he treated her like a lady, as if she had brought twenty thousand ducats as a dowry. Now that there was Agnesina too, father's lovely daughter, as he said playfully, it was impossible he would ever hide anything from her, his child's mother. Who knows? Perhaps it had to do with the pastry-shop in San Ferdinando Piazza, in the centre of the richest part of Naples, quite a modern shop, that Cesare had been dreaming about opening for some time past without daring to risk so much capital. Perhaps if was that, and the fresh, pleasant-faced mother blessed the little one, and prayed God would bless her father's plans and her mother's hopes.

On leaving the room she met her husband.

'Where is nurse?' she asked.

'In the room next the kitchen with Donna Candida.'

'Let us go and see them,' she said, going forward, followed by her husband. They crossed to the back part of the house, where were the servants' rooms, and came to the pantry. The wet-nurse from Fratta Maggiore, a fine, stout woman, with pink cheeks, great prominent eyes, and a calm, serene expression, wore her pale blue damask dress, trimmed with a broad yellow silk band, which went in such deep folds she seemed to swim at every step she took—it was stiff like a stuff building. She wore a white crape handkerchief, and a gold necklace of three rows of big hollow beads over it; the front of her dress was covered by a batiste apron, over which she spread her well-ringed hands. Her chestnut hair was tightly held back by a silver comb, from which fell a big bow of blue ribbon. Donna Candida, the midwife, was beside her, a guest who had to be asked; she had put on her red silk dress for big christenings, the portrait of her late husband, Don Nicodemo, in a brooch, and a red cotton camellia in her gray hair. Both she and the nurse, most important people, were waiting patiently, saying a few words to each other.

'I wish you all happiness,' called out the old nurse on seeing her patient.

'Thank you, Donna Candida. You have come early. Does waiting not bore you? Will you take something, nurse?' Luisella's voice showed tenderness for her little one's nurse.

'As your excellency pleases,' said the nurse, raising her soft, oil-coloured, rather stupid eyes.

Cesare went off, and brought a waiter with marsala and cakes for the women. The husband and wife stood looking at them quite touched, and when they stopped eating Luisella pushed the tray towards them. Donna Candida, who was a polite woman, held up her first glass of marsala, and called out:

'To Donna Agnesina's health!'

'To my little one's health!' said the other, laughing.

The husband and wife looked at each other with happy tears in their eyes, nodding their thanks. Suddenly the mother said:

'Nurse, the baby is crying.'

The nurse hurriedly dried her lips, put down the candy she was eating, and rushed off with a great rustle, opening her bodice as she went with an instinctive maternal movement.

But the guests were already coming into the reception-room, which was furnished with couches and easy-chairs in pomegranate brocade, their woodwork gilded; large *carcels*, placed on gray marble and gilt brackets, as well as big gilt-bronze lamps with crystal pendants cut in facets, lighted it up. Those who knew each other had joined in groups, and spoke to each other in a lively way under their voice, to look like people of spirit, society folk, and did not even look at the unknown guests; these had got into the corners by families, and brought easy-chairs and seats together to make a fortress for themselves, from whence they cast shy, inquisitive glances on the people and the furniture, suddenly dimmed by lowered eyelids if they felt themselves caught staring.

The family of Don Domenico Mayer (a clerk in the Finance Department) were like that. They lived in an apartment on the fifth floor in the Rossi Palace, a tall, deep building at Mercatello Square that looks on to four different streets, where the neighbours often do not know each other even by name, and can live for years without meeting, two large stairs besides two smaller ones make it such a puzzle. Don Domenico Mayer, with a misanthropic look and bureaucratic overcoat, led in a misanthropic family, composed of his wife, with flabby, colourless cheeks, always suffering from neuralgia; his daughter Amalia, a tall, stout girl, with prominent eyes, thick nose and lips, and heavy black tresses, who suffered from hysterical convulsions; and Alfonso, the son, called Fofò by everyone, who was troubled by a growing silliness and a huge appetite. The misanthropic family had formed into a square; the women pulled in their poor though tidy gowns round their chairs, and father and son sat at the edge of theirs stiff and silent. Like them, other families held themselves apart—clerks, little tradesmen, managers—with serious looks, keeping their elbows to their sides, passing their hands mechanically over their shiny, not to say glazed, beavers; whilst on the other side were all the Fragalàs, and with them the Naddeos, great ironware dealers at Rua Catalana; the Antonaccis, prosperous cloth merchants at the Mercanti; and the Durantes, great dealers in dry cod at Pietra del Pesce—the men in broad-cloth, the women in brocade or silk, with jewels, especially bracelets, like Luisella Fragalà. Her charming presence in the drawing-room was hailed by a general movement: all rose; the boldest or most intimate left their places and surrounded her, while the shy ones kept at a little distance, waiting composedly till they were seen and greeted.

All rejoiced with her on her restored health, calling her 'Mama, Mama,' wishing her in the Southern style this *and a hundred* others, all in good health—that is to say, a hundred more children, no less. She got pink with pleasure, bent her head in giving thanks, which made the diamond star in her hair sparkle: it was a subject for comment to the other Fragalàs, the Naddeos, the Antonaccis, and Durantes; it was the secret-sighing admiration of all the other humble guests, the so-called *mezze signore*. Then, while Cesare Fragalà chattered with the men, laughing, passing his gloved hand through his curly hair, there was a general return to the couches and easy-chairs: all sat down.

Luisella Fragalà, standing in the middle of the room, went to meet each lady that she saw coming in at the door, greeted her smilingly, and led her to an easy-chair, making a large feminine circle, where fans waved slowly over opulent bosoms encased in brocade. Only the middle couch remained empty—it was the post of honour; all were looking at it and towards the door, waiting the unknown guests who were to sit there: for they knew the party would not really begin without them, and no refreshments would be offered till the guests of high rank appeared; in fact, Luisella and Cesare as the time passed gave each other inquiring glances. Suddenly, as a couple came into the room, Luisella made a quick, joyful gesture, effusively embraced the lady, and pressed the gentleman's hand smilingly; a whisper went through the room, someone got up, a name was breathed. It was really him, Don Gennaro Parascandolo, the famous Don Gennaro, a tall, strong, agreeable man, with a countenance breathing honesty, good faith, good temper; his hand-shake was hearty, his smile cheered the most low-spirited people, his glance put life into one; a very rich man—in short, little Agnesina's godfather, a rich man with no children.

He had had children—he and his sickly wife with the grayish hair and sad eyes. She liked to stay shut up in her sumptuous silent house, and when she went about with him looked like a woman's shadow, a living image of grief. They had had three lovely children, two boys and a girl, healthy and strong, for whom Don Gennaro Parascandolo had worked at his cold terrible trade of aristocratic usurer to make them rich. He never lent less than five thousand francs or more than two hundred thousand at one time, always at 10 per cent. a month—cruel for his children's sake. But diphtheria had come into his house, furtively, irremediably; in twenty-five days the most distinguished doctors' science, father and mother's despair, money poured out, were found useless: nothing could save the three children. All died choking in such a painful way that Signora Parascandolo's reason seemed to give way for a time. Even the strong man seemed to reel for a moment; he only recovered very slowly. He travelled a great deal, he showed at all first nights, gave flowers and jewels to famous dancers—all with the greatest indifference, not as if he was bored, but with no brightness nor gaiety. Now and then, very seldom, his wife went out with him, a colourless taciturn creature, incapable of distracting her thoughts even for a moment from her three dead children; but at these times Don Gennaro got gay: he came out with a heavy commercial wit to which his wife responded with a slight distracted smile.

As Don Gennaro Parascandolo had persuaded his poor shadow to leave the shade that evening, he was quite lively; whilst Luisella led the signora to the divan of honour, he went about, followed by Cesare, joking and laughing; all made a chorus to him wherever he passed, with that tendency to worship riches that all, and Southerners in particular, are apt to have. The Naddeos, Antonaccis, Durantes, and Fragalàs were rich people; but things may change in this world from one day to another. And Don Gennaro was so rich he really did not know what to do with his money! As to the little people in the room—clerks, tradesmen, managers—they looked respectfully at him from afar, impressed by his broad shoulders, deep chest, and leonine head. His name was whispered here and there, with comments in a lower voice: 'Don Gennaro Parascandolo.'

But Cesare and Luisella seemed to get an electric shock when the third person they were waiting for arrived. She was an old lady, who came forward solemnly, in a very old maroon silk, stiff as a board, made in the fashion of thirty years before, with organ-pipe pleats and very wide sleeves. She wore a black lace shawl that was very old, too, fastened with a turquoise and ruby brooch, black lace mittens on her old, withered hands, that clutched a black velvet bag worked in point stitch—on one side a little dog on a cushion, a peasant woman with a broad straw hat on the other. Luisella, pulling up her train, ran to meet her, made a deep curtsy, and stooped to kiss the hand that the old woman held out; she had an old coquette's peevish expression, with round gray eyes and a drooping nose. Another whisper went through the room: 'The godmother, the Marchioness.' No one said she was the Marchioness of Castelforte; she was the godmother—that was all. There was only one Marchioness godmother in the Fragalà family; she was Luisella's godmother and patron, a lady respected and feared by the whole connection—in short, a Marchioness, a titled person, of superior race. Even Don Parascandolo, who had no need of anyone, as all knew, went to bow before her, while the old woman closely examined him.

Now there was no more room on the seat of honour. Luisella sat in the middle, the Marchioness on her right, and Signora Parascandolo on her left, in Parisian costume, covered with magnificent jewels, but bowing her head under the weight of remembrances, always and unfailingly. As all got seated, there was perfect silence for two minutes. All were waiting, still looking at the door furtively, pretending to think about something else. Ladies hid a little yawn behind their fans; girls had that sleep-walking look that makes them seem detached from all human interests; men twirled their moustaches; and the boys had that absolutely idiotic look of which Fofò Mayer was the highest exponent.

But Cesare Fragalà disappeared. Refreshments came in two minutes after that silence. Then all set to talking, loudly, noisily, to have an easy bearing, pretending not to care for refreshments. But they came in from all sides continuously, spreading through the room, to the delight of all who longed for sweets—men and women, boys and girls. To ices thick and round as a full moon, so hard the teaspoon had to be pressed down, followed Portuguese cream, fruit, strawberries, white and Levant coffee, chocolate; smaller ices of all shapes, prettily arranged in pink or blue glass shells with gold rims; sponges—half cream and half ice, of different flavours: chocolate, mandarin punch, pistachio, strawberries and cream, honey and milk. After sponge-cakes, the delight of women and boys, followed peach and almond tarts, and coffee and lemon ices, served in milky white porcelain glasses. For ten minutes nothing was heard but the rattling of plates, spoons, and glasses; but when the ladies saw the trifles coming, they cried out enthusiastically about their lovely colours, with the white foam in the middle, and held out their hands involuntarily, whilst others, quieter and more active, ate up one thing after the other to compare them.

Conversation got animated with such joy. Gentlemen ran here and there, fetching a plate or glass, serving the ladies and themselves too, speaking from a distance, asking questions, calling up the waiters with the trays, making them lose their heads in the confusion.

'A sponge-cake for Signora Naddeo.'

'Would you like an almond tart?'

'Take a glass of champagne punch. There is nothing better for digesting the rest.'

'Who will change a strawberry ice for a coffee ice?'

'I assure you it comes to nothing, after all; the ices are water really. What shall it be—strawberries?'

'I have one.'

'Mama, give me the cream.'

Quite pleased, Cesare ran from one side to the other, leading the waiters, as every tray came up, towards the Marchioness, who was always the first to take some. Signora Parascandolo was the next; but she hardly took a spoonful, when she put down her plate and cast down her eyes again distractedly, as if she neither saw nor heard what was going on around her. The Marchioness, on the other hand, without hurrying, ate slowly of everything with her fallen-in mouth and toothless gums, her jaw going continually and her hooked nose trembling over her upper lip.

'My lady, try this pistachio. Would you like mandarin better, my lady?'

She nodded 'Yes,' like an old Chinese idol. Her withered hands had let go the bag, after taking a big white handkerchief out of it to put under her plate.

Very happy, Luisella tossed her head, laughing at all that cheerful noise. Every now and then her husband stopped before her.

'Won't you take something?'

'No, no! Help the other ladies.'

'Take something, Luisella.'

'No; I like looking on better.'

The view all around was so interesting! The ladies, who were more affected in their greed, sipped the sherbet delicately, keeping the plate on the point of their gloved fingers, raising the little finger every time they put in the spoon, keeping a lace handkerchief on their knees, and biting their lips after each spoonful. Some men quietly followed the waiter's tray step by step, so as to make a good choice, after which they went into a corner to eat comfortably. Little children put their ices on a chair, covering themselves with cream up to their eyes, and stuck out their pink lips, their innocent eyes showing their delight as they slowly licked the spoon; whilst the sleepy-headed-looking girls refused this and that, and ended by taking a little of everything, leaving the half of it, not really fond of eating yet. Even the Mayer family had got over their misanthropy; the lady thought no more of her neuralgia, and Don Domenico hesitated between a sponge and an ice, whilst Amalia and Fofò exchanged ices, to get the taste of each.

In the other rooms, everywhere, in the passages, even in the cook's bedroom and the kitchen, the same jingling of glasses and spoons went on, and the joy was even greater. The servants from every floor in the Rossi Palace had run in. The porter came up; the hair-dresser returned; the nurse's husband, the Naddeos' and the Antonaccis' coachmen—for they kept carriages—came in; even the newspaper boy of the Tarsia corner and the postman, still in uniform from his last round, with letter-bag round his neck, stood beside Gelsomina and Donna Candida. All these humble common folk that love sweets and sherbet had a feast, by the master's orders, and he came out every now and then to the kitchen, delighted to see them enjoy themselves. He replied to the servants' congratulations, speaking to them familiarly in dialect.

Now there spread a feeling of gastronomic repose; people quieted down, got a composed look, and smiled happily after the first burst of gourmandizing. Conversation, languid at first, had taken the mild tone of quiet, easy people, full of good breeding. The ladies smiled slightly; the girls waved their fans; men set mild discussions agoing solemnly—about their affairs, about the small politics of the day, the stagnant state of trade, from which all suffered. They stood in groups, gesticulating and solemnly nodding.

The Marchioness had picked up her velvet bag and crossed her hands over it—a torpor came over her, and she looked like an old sleeping mummy; whilst Signora Parascandolo, with her head down, gazed abstractedly at her fan, a precious antique her husband must have got from some desperate debtor by forced sale. Luisella began to feel very much bored between these two silent women; her lively temperament made her feel inclined to get up and speak to her friends and relations, still more to go and see what Agnesina was doing, and what was going on in the kitchen and the dining-room to cause such a noise; but her post of honour was on the divan—it would have been a breach of etiquette to leave it; so she went on being bored, smiling to her friends at a distance, and waving her gold-spangled fan. All at once, she called her husband—she could stand it no longer—and whispered to him; he nodded assent and went off to arrange the procession. The guests, knowing the usual programme, understood, and began looking towards the door, occasionally, for another part of the show to begin. Some affectionate smiles began already; a slight whisper ran along. The procession appeared at the chief door. Little Agnesina, in a white cap with pale blue ribbons that made her face quite red, wore an embroidered batiste robe that covered the pink little hands. She was laid out on a *portabimbi* of pale blue silk and lace, her head raised on a cushion; this forms a bed, a cradle, a bag, and a garment, all in one; it lay on the strong arm of the Fratta Maggiore nurse, Gelsomina, who carried it with the deepest devotion, as a cleric carries the missal from one end of the altar to the other, not taking her eyes off Agnesina, who stared placidly at her with the clear crystal eyes of a new-born infant. Beside her was Donna Candida, all in the gravity of her office; to mark its continuity she laid her hand on the baby's pillow; then followed the father, Cesare Fragalà, and a little further back the waiters with trays of candy, sweets, and dried fruits, caramels, jujubes, then other trays with marsala, malaga, Lunel; and farther back still, venturing to peep in, some inquisitive servant gazing with open eyes.

The christening-party was not unexpected; the guests all knew the baby would be shown, so long, noisy applause greeted it, with a clapping of gloved hands, and a chorus burst out:

'Long live Agnesina!'

'May you grow up holy!'

'How lovely, how sweet she is!'

'Agnesina! Agnesina!'

'Cheers for Agnesina's papa and mamma!'

In the meanwhile the baby was carried straight to her godmother, the Marchioness, to be kissed; she had held her at the font that morning, and now kissed her lightly on the forehead, while she put a white paper into the nurse's hand, with a discontented movement of her long nose over her fallen-in mouth.

Applause followed the Marchioness's kiss. Then, bending down, Don Gennaro, the godfather, kissed her; his broad face was rather pale and contracted as by some evil thought: perhaps other christenings, his sons', passed through his mind. But he recovered quickly, and received the company's still noisier applause with a smile. After the mother had kissed the baby there was a long minute's silence among the joyous party; she kept her head down over the baby's face, as if inhaling its breath, blessing it, calling down on it blessings from heaven. A great noise followed; as baby was carried triumphantly round the room, the women gave little screams of motherly emotion, and kissed her enthusiastically, which made her whimper. Raising her head, Luisella suddenly noticed a queer figure leaning against a door-post; she did not know who he was; her curiosity was aroused. She tried to remember ever having seen him before, but vainly: it was someone new. Who could he be? Perhaps he had been brought by a friend or relation, without asking leave, with that calm familiarity that from the Naples populace rises to the highest classes. It was certainly someone unknown.

Whilst the overkissed baby went on whimpering, the nurse and the ladies trying to console it by loving little words in a singing tone, and the room was again filled with the joy of eating, Luisella, curiously interested, possessed by an inward feeling, could not keep her eyes off that queer, motionless figure. He was a man of between thirty-five and forty, with the pallid, cadaverous face of one who has made a long, disastrous voyage; a rather curly, ill-kept black beard on his sickly red-streaked cheeks hid all traces of linen or necktie; the forehead showed the same bloodless pallor, and two deep lines formed at every movement of the eyebrows; his chestnut hair was thrown back untidily, leaving the temples bare, it being rather sparse there, and a network of rather swollen blue veins showed to an observing eye. When he moved his head, the muscles of his lean neck stood out like a dead fowl's sinews; his loose-hanging hands were fleshless, too. The man was very poorly dressed: his pepper-and-salt trousers were too short, showing the ill-brushed shoes tied by a rusty ribbon; his waistcoat and jacket—yes, really a jacket—were of dark maroon. The man's whole appearance was sickly, mysterious, wretched, and mean; his dull eyes wandered here and there without settling a minute on the same spot; even his expression was mysterious and ignoble.

'Who can the ragged fellow be?' Luisella said to herself with an angry, frightened feeling.

All were rejoicing again round the sweet-trays, the choicest sweets in the Toledo Street shop. To a natural love of sweets was added curiosity to taste new kinds they had often admired in pretty boxes. Dates and pistachio cream, to which a glass of malaga gives such a good flavour; while comfits of roses, with a dash of lemon-peel to excite the palate, suits marsala best, they found; all that soft, attractive, enchanting odour of vanilla from the chocolates and creams, the sharp flavour of mint, cooling and exciting, for it burns the mouth and causes thirst—all these things, pleasant to the eye and palate, delicious in odour, gave a new excitement to the party, to which freely-poured-out wine added a slight intoxication.

'Who can that dirty fellow be?' Luisella was still saying to herself, feeling hurt in her pride as mistress of the house, in her love of tidiness, by that sickly, wretched, dirty man. She got up mechanically to find out from someone about that queer, ragged fellow who had got into her house, leaving the Marchioness, who again spread out her handkerchief and heaped all kinds of sweets on it, munching at them slowly; leaving the rich, unhappy

Signora Parascandolo, who was following little Agnesina about with her eyes full of tears. Just then Luisella Fragalà overtook the little retinue where her baby was now shrilly crying, having nearly made the round of the room. Gelsomina was going to stop before the queer individual as if she wanted to make him kiss the baby, but as he came forward to do so Luisella broke in instinctively and sharply, and scornfully eyeing the unknown, she said to the nurse, putting her hands on Agnesina's pillow to protect her:

'Go away, nurse; baby is crying too much.'

The nurse went out at once, followed by Donna Candida, whilst the mother looked at them through the door as they went off through the other rooms, as if still to protect her from some unknown evil. As she went back into the room the sight of the carpet amused her; paper cases of candied fruit, gold and silver paper, were scattered over it; the seats, tables, and brackets had little heaps of sweets from the pillaged trays; ladies had taken off their gloves to hold the bit of candy or caramel they were eating; men were leading from one tray to another children who whimpered, all covered with sugar and chocolate; others, having asked leave of Cesare Fragalà, who granted it laughingly, gathered up the sweets in a handkerchief, taking care not to crush them; whilst others, including Cesare himself, sent for paper to make into bags to hold what was left in the trays. All hands were sticky and mouths shiny. On the tables were red or yellow rings from glasses of wine put down, and a loud continuous clatter went on through the devastation.

'Cesare!' called out Luisella to her husband.

'What do you want, darling?' he answered, while tying a three-coloured string with the knack of a professional.

'Tell me one thing.'

'Two if you like.'

'Who is that man there, near the door?'

'That one?' he said, peering as if he did not see well; 'it is Giovanni Astuti, the money-changer.'

'No, no! I know him—that other one.'

'Oh, it is somebody or other,' he said, rather embarrassed.

'Who is it?' said she severely.

'A friend of mine.'

'A friend—that ragged fellow a friend?'

'One can't always have rich friends,' was the answer, with rather a forced laugh.

'I know; but that is no reason for bringing a dirty fellow among decent people, even if he is your friend.'

'How excitable you are, dear! Be charitable.'

'Charity is one thing, decency is another,' she replied obstinately. 'Don't you see how untidy he is?'

'Untidy!' he muttered, with his usual good-nature; 'he is a philosopher—he does not care about clothes.'

'Well, I want him to go away.'

'How can it be done?' he asked, confused and mortified by his wife's persistence.

'Tell him so!'

'I'll first give him a glass of wine; be patient, then I will make him go away.'

In fact, Cesare went up to the unknown to offer him sweets and wine, speaking in a whisper, and looking him in the eyes. He agreed, with a smile on his discoloured lips. He began to eat slowly, with a little grimace, as if he could not swallow well. The mysterious person looked at the sweets Cesare offered him with an undecided air, before putting them into his mouth; but he made up his mind to eat them at last, still with that nervous, pained look of having a narrow swallow. He was standing with that embarrassed shame of his own person that is some people's constant unhappiness; and he broke an almond noisily, gulped over big mouthfuls of Margherita paste, gazing vaguely around, as if he dared not lower his eyes on his legs and shoes. Then he slowly went on eating; for Cesare had had a tray put on a table beside him, and went on handing him chocolates, vanilla almonds, mandarins in syrup. A tray of wine-glasses was set down also; the queer fellow took three glasses, one after the other, without taking breath between, lifting his pale, streaked face and hospital convalescent's sickly beard. Cesare Fragalà, with a set, preoccupied smile, looked in the man's eyes, as if he wanted to read his soul, all the time this feeding went on.

In the meanwhile Luisella, to amuse herself, to calm the impatience that had burst out so suddenly, wandered about, chattering and laughing with her relations and friends. Now came a rumour that the diamond star in her hair was a gift from the baby's godfather, one worthy of so rich a man. In their hearts all the merchants' wives thought Luisella had been very sly, under cover of politeness, to choose so rich a godfather; they made up their minds, with their next babies, to do the same, to choose a godfather who knew his duty and would do it like that dear Don Gennaro. Malicious little aphorisms ran around: 'Those who think out a thing well are not sorry afterwards.' 'A gentleman is always a gentleman.' 'Live with someone richer than you, and get him to pay.' As Luisella Fragalà got near, this was all changed into a chorus of admiration of the magnificent jewel. She acknowledged it, and bent her head, blushing proudly, as the star sparkled in her black hair. The women gave that long, admiring murmur that flutters the giver and receiver—full of gratified pleasure, self-satisfied affection, whilst their eyes languished or flashed. Some, to be still more amiable, even if it was humbug, asked: 'Is it from the godfather?' 'Yes,' said Luisella, with a slight sigh. 'It could not be otherwise,' the other whispered, as if she had guessed well. Elsewhere Luisella had twice been obliged to take the pin out of her hair, because ladies wished to hold the precious star in their hands. A group formed, women's faces bent over, full of curiosity and that love of jewellery that is at the bottom of every woman's heart, however modest and obscure she is. There were shrieks of admiration; questions and interjections arose at the flash of the brilliants. Someone got to asking the price, even; but Luisella gave a shrug to show her ignorance, which increased the stone's value; this mystery, this unknown cipher, acquired a breadth in the feminine mind that imposed respect. So that at a certain point eight or ten ladies surrounding Luisella, with a growing burst of enthusiasm, called out, 'Hurrah for the godfather!'

Don Gennaro Parascandolo, pretending to hear nothing, ran up eagerly, with the easy good-nature of a travelled Neapolitan. He modestly disclaimed compliments: it was a nothing at all—two insignificant stones, bits of glass; the ladies, in lively contradiction, praised him, and overwhelmed him with civilities, from a deep womanly instinct that makes them profuse in words and smiles, knowing something may come of it. When he said Donna Luisa Fragalà was worthy of a starry crown, applause drowned his voice. In the meanwhile the mistress of the house had given side-glances now and then towards the shabby fellow who was so much on her nerves; but he went on evenly eating and drinking, with that slow movement of the muscles of his neck that was like a hen's claw. However, something more extraordinary was going on around, which Luisella had to give heed to, at the time the phenomenon burst out in the room. Whilst the horrid fellow pillaged the sweets, making a circle of cut-out paper round his feet, and prune-stones as well, he had drawn the attention of those who had finished eating ices. In these gourmands' vague hour of digestion, quite satisfied with a packet of sweets to carry home, having nothing to do, their eyes wandered round, and they noticed that queer beggar Cesare Fragalà was feeding so attentively; gradually one pointed him out to the other: by that glance, a poke with the elbow, raised eyebrows, or a smile, that makes the most expressive of languages, they showed each other that silent devourer, who began when they were finished, but looked as if he would never finish until he had demolished the last sweet and drunk the last glass of wine. Some looked at him rather admiringly, sorry they could not imitate that continual guzzling; some smiled indulgently; others had a compassionate look in their eyes for an unlucky fellow that seemed never to have eaten or drunken enough. Some phrases, here and there, jocular and good-natured, were repeated from one to another: 'What a digestion!' 'It is St. Peter's Church!' 'Health and protection to him!' 'I would make him a coat rather than feed him!' 'Santa Lucia keep him his sight, because he has no need of an appetite!'

But they were the usual rather coarse remarks about a great eater. Some man in search of amusement had come close to Cesare and the silent gobbler to watch them. Little by little, all now in the drawing-room had their eyes on the great eater. Luisella blushed with shame to think that everyone had now noticed the wretched ragged fellow her husband had brought into the house, that she had to submit to having in her room. Vainly she tried, by going about talking and laughing, joking and waving her fan, to distract attention: it was useless.

The people brought together in the drawing-room had eaten and drunken, praised the baby, the diamond star, and the giver of it; now, not knowing what else to do, they had fixed their attention on that queer ragged fellow, who was certainly out of place in Luisella Fragalà's drawing-room. She was a good woman, but very proud; though charitable, she would never have brought a pauper into her room. It was useless for her to fly in a passion, feeling tears come to her eyes. Now all had noticed the beggarly gobbler, all were looking at him, even the women and the sleepy-headed girls who looked as if they never saw anything. The same compassionate, laughing, tolerating smiles were on the women's faces as on the men's, except that their stronger curiosity could not constrain itself. Signora Carmela Naddeo leant forward behind her fan, and asked Luisella:

'Who is that starving fellow, my dear?'

'Who knows?' said the other impatiently.

'Cesarino certainly does; he is handing him glasses of wine.'

'Cesare gathers these wretched people up by the cart-load,' said she, shaking with rage.

But suddenly a subdued whispered word ran from man to man, woman to woman—a syllable breathed rather than pronounced. Who first said this hissing word? Who was it that recognised him, and softly breathed it in his neighbour's ear? Who had let it out, the unknown secret? No one knows!

But in a second, quick as a flash of gunpowder, all knew and repeated the mystic word throughout the crimson room. It came back on itself, its letters making a magic circle that went round, and everyone with it. When they all knew who the man was, they were seized with stupefaction; the lamps seemed to be suddenly lowered, their lively faces got pale, even the covers of the furniture lost colour; there was a deep silence, where the magic word still lingered feebly: 'The medium — the medium.'

Luisella herself, the intrepid, grew pale; her hands trembled as they grasped her fan. The medium had given up feeding; now he was resting quietly, casting his vague, uncertain glances about, not knowing what to do with his lean yellow hands. A little blood had risen in his pale cheeks, under the black beard; but it was in streaks, a sickly colour, the effect of fever. Still, ugly, dirty, miserable as he was, all attention was concentrated on him — inquisitive, wheedling, obsequious glances were directed on him, in which was combined fantastic fear, especially on the women's part. For even the women, in a nervous tremor, said to one another, 'It is the medium.' A circle gradually surrounded him, getting nearer, as if by a strong natural attraction — rather anxious faces, where one could notice the vivid working of Southern imaginations, in this land of dreams and fantasies. Shy folk were now joining the bolder ones who had come near at first, overcome, dreaming of the train of ministering spirits, good and bad, who are ever warring around the medium's soul. Don Gennaro Parascandolo, one of the first to come up, found himself so hemmed in that he turned to Cesare Fragalà, and said, smiling rather sceptically:

'Cesarino, introduce me to this gentleman.'

Cesare was much embarrassed, but, seeing no way out of it, he caught at this request, and said quickly:

'Don Gennaro Parascandolo, Pasqualino De Feo, a friend of mine.'

The medium smiled vaguely and held out his hand, which Don Gennaro found icy cold, though damp with perspiration, one of those repulsive hands that make one shudder. But not a word was said. The women standing outside the circle, not daring to come near, asked each other, troubled by a deep longing:

'What does he say?'

'He says nothing,' Donna Carmela Naddeo answered; she was nearest, and never took her eye off him.

The women bit their lips, the men's presence intimidated them; too bashful to go near, they shivered with impatience to hear the fateful words of the man living in constant communication with the world of spirits, who heard all the hidden truths of life from the good spirits, who was told by them every week five, or at least three, of the lottery numbers.

What was he saying? Nothing. For long hours these people stand concentrated, lost, perhaps, in a great interior conflict, listening to the high voices that speak to them. Now and then, torn from their visions, they pronounce some fateful phrase that contains the secret, wrapped up in mysterious words, often without form, that those of strong faith and hope can miraculously understand. All, men and women, overcome by a great dream, suddenly shaken out of daily realities into the ardent, burning region of visions, forgetting the present moment, listened to the medium as if to a superhuman voice.

Don Gennaro Parascandolo certainly kept up a well-informed traveller's smile; he had a large, secure fortune, but in the bottom of his heart the old Parthenope instinct, for big gains, illicit, if not guilty, costing no trouble, unforeseen, owed to chance, combination, or getting the better of Government, all came so naturally to a man who knew the secrets of hidden things. Certainly all these, Fragalàs, Antonaccis, Naddeos, Durantes, were accustomed to sell stale sweets, rough earthenware, moth-eaten cloth, and stinking cod, in dark shops, in cold storehouses in Via Tribunali, Mercanti, Petra del Pesce, Marina; they were used to all the dulness, vulgarity and meanness of commerce, where year after year, by putting one penny on another, after two or three generations, a fortune came; they all knew the value of money, of work, of economy, of industry: but what did that matter? To be able, by means of a mysterious phrase that only cost the trouble of picking up, of interpreting, to gain big sums with a small stake, get in one day the gains of twenty years' trade in dry cod, or forty years' trade in sugar and sandy coffee, was so delightful a gift, so dazzling a vision, to middle-class ideas!

Certainly all these clerks and tradesmen looked forward to a modest future. They had lived on nothing; they were living on very little; they wanted to have a little more, only that: humble in their wishes, even. But the sight of the medium, a shabby fellow, yet so powerful, who spoke every night with supernal and infernal spirits, suddenly threw them into a fantastic world, where poor folk get miraculously rich, where they, obscure working people, might become gentlemen. Ah! Don Domenico Mayer, the nephew, son, brother, and uncle of clerks, had faith only in sacred bureaucracy—a cold career of silent suffering. Still, buttoned up in his overcoat, he left his family in the corner and joined the group round Pasqualino De Feo, the medium, and his anxious, severe expression wavered as he, too, waited for the phrase that was to draw him away in a day from the sepulchral atmosphere of the Finance Department. But the women's imaginations were the most feverish. Certainly at least ten of them, by birth, marriage, by their own efforts, or by their relations or husbands, were rich; their fortunes were easy, their children's future secure. Ten at least enjoyed the middle-class luxury of brocaded sofas, jewels, any amount of linen. All the others, by their modesty, good sense, and economy, by their own virtues or their parents', had everything that was necessary; but a lively passion for dreams had awakened and burned in them. Their souls were filled with visions of comfort, riches, luxury; they flew through the regions of desire with womanly tremblings, with the force and intensity the quietest women put into these sudden follies. An overwhelming wish to know the great secret seized them; crumbling pyramids of gold and jewels lit flames in their eyes. Even the old Marchioness of Castelforte, so crooked, such a ruin of a woman, a solitary remnant, the only one of her family, with no relations or heirs, seventy years old, and nothing but the tomb in front of her, got up, carrying her velvet bag, and set her coquettish profile between two men's shoulders. Even Donna Carmela Naddeo strained her ears, trembling with curiosity, rich and lucky as she was, whispering to herself: 'If he tells me the numbers, I will buy a diamond star like Luisella's.'

The medium still kept silence, so that Don Gennaro Parascandolo, feeling the impatience of the whole room behind him, risked a question:

'Have you enjoyed the party, Don Pasqualino?'

He opened his mouth; at last a low, feverish voice came from the thin blue lips.

'Yes,' he said; 'it is a fine christening. The baptism of Christ on the Jordan was fine, too.'

At once there was an agitation in the room, commenting on the phrase, trying to explain it. They formed into circles and groups, the women discussing it among themselves, whilst the number thirty-three, the Redeemer's number, ran from mouth to mouth.

Placidly, as if he was taking a note of a bill of exchange, Don Gennaro Parascandolo put down the remark in his note-book. Don Domenico Mayer took it, too, hiding behind a curtain, without losing his bureaucratic and misanthropic gravity. The old Marchioness, who was deaf, went about asking wildly: 'What did he say? What did he say?' She ended by asking Luisa Fragalà, who sat motionless with staring eyes beside the melancholy Signora Parascandolo. Luisa could only say: 'I don't know, my lady; I did not hear.' However, Don Parascandolo was not satisfied; he went on:

'Did you enjoy the sweets, Don Pasqualino? I noticed you seemed to like them.'

'Yes,' he muttered; 'I eat, but I don't masticate.'

'Have you no teeth?'

'No, I have not.'

He cast his eyes around vaguely, without meeting anyone's glance, as if he saw things from *beyond*, and made a sign with his hand, leaning three fingers on his cheek.

Again the same murmur and agitation; there was uncertainty, too. The phrase was ambiguous, very. What did the motion with three fingers mean? Even Don Gennaro Parascandolo, whilst taking a note, stopped to think. The mystery of that second phrase, of the gesture, let loose all these already shuddering fancies of a supernatural world. Faith, faith, that was what was needed to understand the medium's words! Everyone, calling together all the powers of his soul, tried to have a sublime burst of faith, to know the truth, how to translate it into numbers, to exchange it into lottery money.

Late at night, when the house was emptied of people, Cesare Fragalà, with the sleepy servants, went putting out the lights, shutting the doors, as he prudently did every evening. When he came back to the bedroom, he found Luisella sitting half dressed in the shade.

Agnesina's cradle had been taken into the nurse's room; the couple were alone. Fatigue seemed to keep them silent. Still, on coming up to his young wife, he saw she was crying quietly, big tears rolling down her cheeks.

'What is the matter, Luisella? what is it?' kissing her, trembling with emotion himself.

'There is nothing the matter,' she said, still weeping silently in the shadow.

CHAPTER III
IN THE CAVALCANTIS' HOUSE

Prostrate on the dark old carved wood kneeling-desk, her elbows resting on velvet cushions, head slightly bent, her face hidden in her hands, Donna Bianca Maria Cavalcanti seemed to meditate after praying. As long as twilight lighted up the little private chapel the girl went on reading a chapter of the 'Imitation of Christ,' attentively, in her usual thoughtful attitude. But the shadows had grown deeper round her, first faintly purple, then gray, enfolding the little altar and a figure of Our Lady of Sorrows, with seven silver swords radiating from her heart, hiding a three-quarter figure of Jesus Christ bound to the column, the Ecce Homo, crowned with thorns, and bleeding in the face, hands, and side, blotting out Bianca Maria's slender, neat figure. Then she quietly closed the torn volume, put it on the cushion, and hid her face in her hands. Only the faint light before Our Lady of Sorrows shone on the white, clasped hands and the knot of dark brown hair on her neck. She kept so motionless for some time that the white figure in the shadow of the little chapel looked like one of those praying statues that medieval piety placed on tombs to kneel in constant prayer. She seemed not to feel the hours passing over her nor the faint, cold breath the autumn evening brought into the chapel. Gazing through her fingers at the Virgin's sad face, she seemed to go on praying and meditating as if nothing could wrest her from it.

Still, as evening came on the little chapel got very gloomy. In the daytime it was a poor, cold place, being only a narrow inside room, badly lighted by a window looking into a narrow court of the Rossi, formerly the Cavalcanti Palace. Once a wretched carpet covered the floor, but it was so old and dusty that Bianca Maria had it taken away. The floor was bare now, of shiny, icy bricks. The little altar was painted dull blue, an ecclesiastical shade, covered by a rather fine bit of linen, though yellow with age, as was also the lace round it. Everything was old and shabby—the candle-sticks, the printed prayers in metal cases, the red-leather-covered missal, the poor silver sprays of leaves placed as sacred ornaments, and the little gilt wooden door, behind which was the Pyx. By day Our Lady of Sorrows, in black silk, embroidered in gold, with a batiste nun's head-dress, and the seven swords in her heart, looked wretched and poor, carrying a lace and batiste handkerchief in her pink stucco hands. The great Ecce Homo, too, life size, of wood and stucco, looked as poor as its surroundings. In spite of the carved wood chairs, with the Cavalcanti crest on the velvet cushions, the chapel had a look of frozen wretchedness, showing by daylight faded colours, tarnished metals, stains in the velvet. Even the two lamps that burned night and day before the Virgin and the Saviour were only two yellow sputtering tongues of flame.

But at night—and that night, curiously enough, only one lamp was burning, that before the Virgin—the wretchedness disappeared; only great fluttering shadows filled the chapel. One could not see the colour of the wood and metal; only the white altar-cloth was visible. There were no sparks of brightness, only in the trembling light Mary's sad face seemed agonized; and as the flame, shaken by an invisible breath of wind, bent to the right or left, Jesus' hands and side seemed really to bleed.

Bianca Maria was deep in thought, and, accustomed to the chapel, she felt neither the cold nor the gloom. Suddenly she trembled, thinking she heard a great noise in the room. It was then she noticed the lamp before Christ was out. She shivered with cold and fear. The Virgin seemed to weep over her bleeding Son's agony. Bianca Maria went quickly out of the chapel, taking her book with her, crossing herself hurriedly as if followed by some evil spirit.

In the antechamber an old servant in the Cavalcanti livery—dull blue, piped with white—sat reading an old newspaper by the light of one of those old brass lamps with three spouts one still sees in the provinces and in very aristocratic houses. He rose as he heard Bianca Maria's light step, looking her in the eyes.

'Giovanni,' she said, in her pure harmonious voice, 'in the chapel the lamp before the Ecce Homo has gone out.'

The old servant looked at her, and hesitated a little before answering.

'I did not light it,' he then muttered, casting down his eyes, and crushing up the paper in his lean hands.

'Perhaps you had no oil?' she asked, with a little tremor in her voice, turning her anxious face towards him.

'No, my lady, no,' the servant eagerly answered at once. 'There is lots of oil in the pantry. It was by the Marquis's orders I did not light the lamp.'

'Did he give you such an order?' she asked, amazed, arching her eyebrows.

'Yes, my lady.'

'For what reason?'

But she regretted the question at once. It seemed to fail in the profound respect she owed her father. Still, the word had rushed out. She would have liked to go away and not hear the answer, whatever it was; but she feared to make matters worse, and listened with open eyes, ready to restrain her astonishment and fear.

'The Marquis is in a rage with Jesus Christ,' the servant said, in that humble but familiar tone in which the common folk in Naples often speak of the Deity. 'Last Saturday he asked a great favour of that miracle-working Ecce Homo, but he did not get it. Then the Marquis gave orders the lamp was not to be lighted again.'

'Did the Marquis tell you that?'

'Yes, my lady; but if you like, I will go and light it.'

'Obey the Marquis,' she murmured coldly, as she went on towards the drawing-room.

As she wandered about alone in the spacious room, ill-lighted by a petroleum-lamp, she searched for her work-basket and could not find it, though she passed it twenty times without seeing it. She still bitterly repented having asked the servant that question, since throughout the ever-increasing family decay what most embittered her was to be obliged to judge her father before servants or strangers. It was in vain she shut her eyes so as not to see, that she spent her days in her room, the chapel, and the Sacramentiste convent where her aunt was; in vain she kept silence, trying not to hear what others said: Margherita, who was the maid, and Giovanni's wife's remarks, her aunt the nun's uneasy questions, and the hints of some old relations who came to see her now and then; they spoke so pityingly, it brought tears to her eyes. She had to lower her eyes, for she could not help judging her father inwardly as they shook their heads, pitying her. What shook her most throughout the financial difficulties she vainly tried to hide in that decent poverty that could not be kept secret much longer were her father's unexpected, vexatious, often wild, eccentricities.

Now, quieted down a little, seated by a square baize card-table, where the single lamp was placed, she worked at her fine pillow-lace, moving the bobbins and thread quickly over the pinned-out pattern. Perhaps she would have liked better to call in Margherita to work with her at mending the house linen, which the old woman blinded herself at in her little room. But Don Carlo Cavalcanti, Marquis di Formosa, was very proud; he never would have allowed a servant in the drawing-room, nor permitted his daughter to stoop to such humble work. Bianca Maria would have liked to spend the evening in her own room reading or working, but her father liked to find her in the drawing-room when he came in every evening. He called it the *salone* pompously, not noticing its bareness; for the four narrow sofas of discoloured green brocade, the twelve slight hard chairs put along the wall, the couple of painted gray marble brackets, and two card-tables, with small bits of carpet before each sofa and chair, being lost in the immensity, increased the deserted look. The petroleum-lamp, too, just lit up the table Bianca Maria was sitting at, and her hands, whiter than the thread, as they moved over the dark pillow-lace. She stopped sometimes, as if an engrossing thought occupied her; the hands fell down as if tired; the young, thoughtful face gave a quiver.

'Good-evening,' said a strong voice at her elbow.

She got up at once, put down the pillow-lace, went up to her father, and bent down to kiss his hand. The Marquis di Formosa accepted the homage; then he lightly touched his daughter's forehead with his hand, half tenderly, half as a blessing. She stood a minute waiting for him to sit before she did; but seeing he had begun to walk up and down through the room, as he had a habit of doing, she looked at him for permission. He gave it with a nod, and went on with his walk. On sitting down, she took up her work, waiting to be addressed before speaking.

The Marquis di Formosa's still springy, firm step filled the empty room with echoes. He was a fine-looking man, in spite of his sixty years and his snow-white hair. Tall, graceful, dried up rather than thin, even at that advanced age there was much nobleness and strength in his head and his whole person, but sudden flushes over his face gave him a violent look. The gray eyes, strong nose, the thick white moustache and ample forehead inspired respect. It was said that when the Marquis di Formosa was young he had made more than one woman of Ferdinand II.'s Court to sin. He was said to have been a successful rival to the King himself with a Sicilian dame, and that in the bloodless strife of gallantry he had got the better of the greatest gallant in the Bourbon Ministry, the Don Juan of his day, the celebrated Minister of Police, Marquis del Carretto. His imperiousness certainly, which had increased with age, gave the Marquis a hard look, and rather a disagreeable expression sometimes.

But his family's antiquity, that boasted descent from the great Guido Cavalcanti, his high position and natural haughtiness authorized some imperiousness. Now the Marquis was growing old: his sparkling glance was often dulled, his tall majestic figure stooped in spite of his leanness. Still, he imposed great respect. His daughter Bianca Maria gave a respectful shiver when she saw him coming, and all her own and other people's unfavourable judgments on him went out of her mind.

'Were you at the convent to-day?' asked the Marquis on passing near his daughter.

'Yes, father.'

'Is Maria degli Angioli well?'

'She is quite well. She would like to see you.'

'I have no time now; I have important business—most important,' he said, with a wave of his hand.

She kept silence, working diligently to keep herself from asking questions.

'Did Maria degli Angioli complain much of me?' he asked, without stopping his excited walk.

'No,' she said timidly; 'she would like to see you, as I said.'

'To see me—see me? To recount her woes, and hear all about mine? A fine way of filling up the time. Well, if she liked, if she chose, our woes would soon be ended.'

Bianca Maria's trembling hand entangled the thread round the bobbins and pins of the pattern.

'These holy women,' the Marquis di Formosa went on slowly, as if he were speaking in a dream—'these holy women, who are always praying, have pure hearts; they are in God's favour and the saints'; they enjoy special protection; they see things we poor sinners cannot. Sister Maria degli Angioli might save us if she liked, but she won't. She is too saintly, she does not care for earthly things. Now, our sufferings don't signify to her; she knows nothing about them. She never will tell me anything; never—never.'

Bianca Maria looked up, let the work fall from her hands, and gazed at her father, her eyes full of wondering pain.

'You have never asked her for anything, have you, Bianca?' he said, stopping beside his daughter.

'For what?' she asked, wondering.

'Maria degli Angioli loves you. She knows you are unhappy; she would have told you everything, to help you. Why did you not ask her?' he went on in an excited voice, a storm of rage rising in it.

'What should I ask?' she repeated, still more frightened.

'You pretend not to understand!' he shouted, in a fury already. 'These women are all alike, a flock of sheep, silly and egotistical. What do you speak about by the hour together in the convent parlour? Whose death do you weep over? Think of the living! Don't you see the Cavalcanti family is going down to misery, dishonour, and death?'

'May God avert it!' she whispered, crossing herself devoutly.

'Women are selfish fools!' he shouted, enraged at her softness, at finding no resistance; 'and I who think of nothing else from morning till night, who kneel before the holy images morning and evening, for the preservation of the Cavalcanti! And you who, by asking your aunt the secrets of her dreams, could save me and the name by a word—you pretend not to understand! Ungrateful and treacherous, like all women!'

She put down her head and bit her lips, so as not to burst into sobs. Then, in a trembling voice, she replied:

'I'll ask her at some other time.'

'Ask her to-morrow,' her father retorted imperiously.

'I will do it to-morrow, then.'

Quickly his rage fell, suddenly calmed. He came up to her and touched her bent forehead, with his usual caress and blessing. Then, as if she could not help it, feeling her heart bursting, she began to cry silently.

'Don't cry, Bianca Maria,' he said quietly. 'I have great hopes. We have been so long unhappy, Providence must be getting ready a great joy for us. It is not given to us to know the time, naturally, but it can't be far off. If it is not one week, it will be another. What are hours, days, months, in comparison to the great fortune getting ready for us in secret? We will be so rich, all this long past of privation and obscurity will seem a short dream of agony, an hour of darkness faded in the light of the sun. Who knows what instrument Providence will use?—perhaps Maria degli Angioli, who is a good soul. You will ask her to-morrow, won't you? Perhaps some other good spirit among my friends who *see* ... perhaps myself, unworthy sinner as I am—but I feel Providence will save us. But by what means? If I could only know!' He had started walking up and down again, still speaking to himself, as if he was accustomed to think aloud. Only now and then, in the midst of his excitement, he noticed his daughter, and took up his obstinate harping on one idea with her again: 'Where else, Bianca, can rescue come from? Work? I am old; you are a girl. The Cavalcantis have never known how to work, either in youth or old age. Business? We are people whose only business was to spend our own money generously. Only a large fortune, gained in a single day.... You will see, we'll get it. I am sure of it; a thousand dreams and revelations have told me so. You will see. You will have horses and carriages again, Bianca Maria: a victoria for the promenade on the Chiai shore, where you will take your place again; an elegant shut carriage to go to San Carlo in the evening. You'll see. I want to buy you a pearl necklace— eight strings joined by a single sapphire—and a diamond coronet, as all the women of the Cavalcanti family have had, till your mother.' He stopped as he mentioned her, as if a sudden emotion seized him; but gazing on his dream of luxury and splendour quickly distracted him. 'Open house every day. We will think of the poor and starving—so many want help; we will pour out alms—so many suffer. I have made a vow, too, to give dowries to honest poor girls. I have made so many other vows so as to get this favour.'

He stopped speaking, as if gazing through the room's darkness on fortune's splendid mirage that excited fancy brought before his eyes. His daughter got calm and thoughtful again as she listened to him. Her father's voice in the usual rhapsodies of his overheated soul sounded in her heart with anguished echoes, like a slow torment.

It is true she did not believe in the visions, but her father's impetuous, angry, tender phrases frightened her every evening. She could not get accustomed to these bursts of passion that made her peace-loving soul start and shiver.

'Signor Marzano,' Giovanni announced.

A little bent old man came in with a rough, pepper-and-salt moustache, his eyes piercing and at the same time soft. He was very plainly dressed. On passing near Bianca Maria he greeted her gently, and silently asked permission to keep his hat on. He held his Indian cane, too. Falling into step with the Marquis, the two walked up and down together, speaking in a very low voice. When they passed near the light, one saw the advocate's eyes sparkling with satisfaction, and his rather military moustache moving as if he was making mental calculations. Sometimes Bianca Maria, who busied herself more and more in her work so as not to hear, caught involuntarily some cabalistic jargon of her father's or Marzano's.

'The *cadenza* of seven must win.'

'We might also get the two of *ritorno*.'

'Playing for *situazione* is too risky.'

'A *bigliettone* is needed.'

They went on speaking, quite absorbed, their eyes flashing, lost in these fancies that falsely take the precision and fascination of mathematics, when Giovanni again came in, to announce, 'Dr. Trifari.'

A man about thirty came in, strong-limbed and stout, with a big head, too short a neck, a red curly beard that made his face even redder than it was, swollen lips, and blue, staring, suspicious eyes that did not inspire confidence. He was roughly dressed: a tight collar rasped his neck, a big sham diamond pin shone in his black silk tie, and he still had a provincial air, in spite of his University degree. He hardly greeted Bianca Maria, put his hat on a side-table, and went to the Marquis di Formosa's other side. All three marched up and down more quietly. Sometimes Dr. Trifari said a word, or gesticulated violently, speaking in a whisper all the same, his squinting glance questioning his audience and the shades around as if he feared to be betrayed.

The learned Marquis di Formosa kept up his vivacious look like a headstrong old man; Marzano persisted in laughing good-naturedly with his cunning, gentle eyes; whilst Dr. Trifari went about cautiously, as if he always feared being cheated. When the two old men raised their voices a little, he quickly signed to them repressively, pointing at the doors and windows; he went so far as to point to Bianca Maria. The Marquis waved his hand tolerantly, as if to say she was an innocent creature, when again Giovanni came in, to announce, 'Professor Colaneri.'

At once on seeing him, one guessed he was an unfrocked priest. A thick black beard had grown on his shaven cheeks; but the hair cut short on the forehead, and growing thinly over the tonsure, kept the ecclesiastical cut. The shape of his hand, where the crooked thumb seemed joined to the first finger; the way he settled his spectacles on his nose; his trick of putting two fingers in his collar to widen it, as if it was the tight priest's collar; his way of making his glance fall from above—his features and movements altogether were so clerical, one quickly understood his character.

Formosa received him rather coldly, as usual; the apostate gave his religious mind a repulsive shudder. Colaneri, too, spoke very cautiously; four could not walk about without speaking aloud, so they stood in a dark window recess. It was there Ninetto Costa came to join them, a dark, handsome fellow, showing the whitest of teeth in a continuous smile; he was one of the luckiest stockbrokers on the Naples Exchange.

Last of all, Giovanni announced one man in a whisper, negligently, 'Don Crescenzio,' a type between a clerk and an agent, who slipped into the room rather timidly; still, he was treated as an equal. The discussion between the six men grew warm in the window recess, but they kept their voices low.

Bianca Maria went on working mechanically. She felt dreadfully embarrassed; she dared not go away without asking her father's permission, and she felt she was out of place in the room. This mysterious talk, in an incomprehensible, mad jargon, all so excited and eager, rolling their eyes about so sternly; a growing madness in their glances; their faces pale and then flushed from making such violent gestures, disturbed her at first, and ended by frightening her. Her father especially seemed lost in the midst of all these madmen, some of them coldly, others wildly, interested, and all extremely obstinate. She looked at him sometimes in despair, as if she saw him drowning, and could not take a step or give a cry to help him. Just then the six men came slowly filing out of the window recess, and sat down round another card-table, where there was no light. They drew in their chairs to get closer together, put their elbows on the table, leaning their heads on their hands, and all began talking at once in the half-light, whispering in each other's faces, breathing out the words, looking each other straight in the eyes, as if they were using magic and charms.

Bianca Maria could stand it no longer. Making as little noise as possible, she wrapped up her lace pillow in a strip of black linen, got up without moving her chair, so as not to make a sound, and went out of the big room quickly, as if she feared to be called back, with a frightened feeling as if someone were following her. She was slightly reassured only as she got into her own room. It was plain and clean, rather cold-looking, a good, pious girl's room, full of holy images, rosaries, and Easter candles. Margherita, the servant, came to join her, having heard her step. With humble affection she asked if she was going to bed.

'No, no; I am not sleepy. I will wait. I have not said good-night to my father.'

'The Marquis will sit up till all hours,' the maid muttered. 'You will get tired waiting here all alone.'

'I will read. I wish to wait.'

The old servant obediently disappeared.

Bianca Maria took from a little shelf a religious novel of Pauline Craven's, 'Le Mot de l'Énigme,' a pious, consolatory book. But her mind would not be soothed that evening by the French author's gentle words. Sometimes the girl listened intently to find out if her father's friends were going away or if others were coming. There was nothing—not a sound. The great weekly mysterious conspiracy was going on, breathed out from face to face as if it was a frightful piece of witchcraft. This impression grew so on Bianca Maria's mind, that now even the silence frightened her. She tried again two or three times to read the charming book, but her eyes rested on the printed lines without seeing them. The sense of the words she forced herself to read escaped her. Her whole mind was taken up listening to the noises in the drawing-room. Silence still, as if not a living soul was there. She shut the book and called the servant, not feeling able to bear that solitude full of ghosts.

Margherita hastened in, and silently awaited her young mistress's orders.

'Let us say the Rosary,' she whispered.

Sometimes, when the hours seemed longest to the lonely scion of the Cavalcanti, when sleeplessness kept her eyes open, when her fancies got too lugubrious, she loved to pray aloud with her maid to cheat time, hours of watching, nervousness. She dreaded speaking to servants—her natural pride made her avoid it; but praying together seemed to her only a simple act of Christian humility.

'Let us say the Rosary,' she repeated, seating herself by her white bed.

Margherita sat near the door, at a respectful distance. Bianca Maria said the first prayers, the Mystery, and half of the *Pater Noster*; Margherita said the other part. The same with the *Ave Marias*: the first part Bianca Maria said; Margherita took it up and finished it. They prayed in a low tone, but one could easily distinguish the voices, always taking up their part of the prayer in time. At every ten *Ave Marias*, or Stations of the Rosary, they piously crossed themselves, and bent their heads low in reverence to the Holy Ghost at every *Gloria Patri*.

Thus, between mystical absorption in prayer, the natural emotion these familiar, but poetical supplications aroused, and the sound of her own voice, the girl forgot for a little the great drama developing round her father. The whole Rosary was said thus, slowly, with the piety of real believers. Before beginning the Litany to the Virgin she knelt at her chair, with her elbows on the seat, and the maid knelt in her corner. The girl invoked the Virgin in Latin, with all the tender names her devotees use, and the servant answered 'Ora pro nobis.' But from the beginning of the Litany a rising sound of voices reached from the drawing-room. This noise disturbed Bianca Maria's prayers. She tried not to listen to it by raising her voice more; but it was impossible now to abstract herself from that clash of voices getting excited and angry.

'What can it be?' she said, stopping in her intercessions.

'It is nothing,' said Margherita. 'They are speaking about lottery numbers.'

'They seem to me to be quarrelling,' Bianca Maria timidly replied.

'They will make friends again on Saturday evening,' Margherita muttered, with her commonplace philosophy.

'How so?' the girl asked, letting herself be drawn into the discussion.

'Because none of them will win anything.'

'Let us pray,' said Bianca, raising her eyes to the ceiling, as if gazing on the starry firmament.

It was impossible now to finish the Litany. The discussion in the drawing-room had got so warm, they heard it all, the voices coming near and going off, as if the Cabalists had risen from the table and were walking up and down again, with the need excited people have of going backwards and forwards and round about.

'Shall I shut the door?' asked Margherita.

'Shut it; we are praying,' Bianca Maria said resignedly.

The voices did not come in so distinctly. They could follow the Litany to the end without interruption. But the girl's mind was no longer in the words she was saying. She was quite distracted, and hurried through the finishing *Salve Regina* as if time pressed.

'The Madonna bless your ladyship!' said Margherita, getting up after crossing herself.

'Thank you,' the young girl answered simply, sitting down again beside her bed, where she spent so many hours of the day thinking and reading.

Margherita had left the door open as she went away. Now the voices burst out angrily. The enraged Cabalists argued furiously with each other, each one boasting loudly of his own way of getting lottery numbers, his own researches, his own visions, each one trying to take the word from the other, interrupting, screaming louder, being interrupted in turn.

'You don't believe in Cifariello the cobbler's talent?' Marzano the lawyer shouted with the white fury of very gentle, good-natured people. 'Perhaps because he is a cobbler, and perhaps because he writes out his problems with charcoal on a dirty bit of white paper! Here it is, here it is! Twenty-seven has come out second instead of fourth, but it came out! Here is eighty-four, that turned round and became forty-eight, but it did come out! Here is the *ambo* made up of fourteen and seventy-nine I was so unlucky as to give up playing; it came out three weeks after I gave it up. These are facts, gentlemen—facts, not words!'

'They are the sixty francs a month you give him to leave off cobbling and work out numbers for you!' Dr. Trifari interrupted sharply.

'Cifariello is ignorant, but sincere; he gave me fourteen and seventy-nine, and I did not go on with it.'

'Father Illuminato gave me fourteen and seventy-nine, too,' Dr. Trifari retorted, 'but it was the right week.'

'And you won without letting your friends know?' the Marquis di Formosa asked excitedly.

'I won nothing. I divided it into two different tickets. I did not understand what a fortune Father Illuminato was giving me. He is the only one that knows numbers. He holds our fortunes, our future, in his hands. It is a queer thing. When I felt his pulse to see if he had fever, I went trembling all over.'

'Father Illuminato is an egotist!' Professor Colaneri hissed out in a sarcastic, biting voice.

'You say that because he turned you out of his house one day. You tried to get the numbers out of him by force. He won't give them to priests who have thrown off the habit. Father Illuminato is a believer.'

'I see the numbers myself!' Colaneri called out shrilly. 'It is enough for me to take no supper the night before, when I go to bed, and to meditate an hour or two before sleeping: then I see them, you know.'

'But they don't come out right!' shouted the Marquis di Formosa.

'They don't come out right because my mind is clouded by human interests; because I can't free myself from a longing to win; because one must have a pure soul, lay aside disturbing passion, raise one's self into the region of faith, to see clearly. I see them, but often, almost always, a malignant spirit darkens my sight.'

'Look here,' said Ninetto Costa, the smart, rich stock-broker, loudly. 'I have done more. I knew that a young woman, a milliner that lives in Baglivo Uries Lane, had the name of giving good numbers. She can't play them, as you know; they can't do so without losing the power. But she gives them. I made up to her, pretended to fall madly in love with her, gave her presents. I see her morning and evening. I have even got to promising her marriage.'

'Has she given you any?' the Marquis di Formosa asked anxiously.

'Nothing yet. She changes the subject, when I mention it, timidly; but she will give them—she will.'

How Bianca Maria wished that the Rosary she had recited so absent-mindedly was still going on, so as not to hear this mad talk, that she caught every word of! It made her brain reel, as if her soul was drawn into a whirlpool. How she would have liked not to hear the ravings of their disturbed brains so set on one idea! Now the Marquis di Formosa was speaking resoundingly.

'The cobbler's simple science, Father Illuminato's saintliness, our friend Colaneri's dazzling visions, are all very well; but what is the result? What comes of it? We who play our collar-bones every week, drawing money from stones, all of us, winning in a hundred years or so a wretched little *ambo*, or, worse still, one single number. Stronger hands are needed! a higher strength is needed! We need miracles, gentlemen. We must induce my sister, the nun, to give lottery numbers. My daughter must get her to do it. We need my daughter herself, an angel of virtue, kindness, and purity, to pray to the Supreme Being for numbers!'

A deep silence followed these last words. The entrance-door bell rang. Bianca Maria, shaking all over, dragged herself to her door-curtain and saw a wretchedly-dressed man pass, mean-looking, with pale, red-streaked cheeks, the beard like a hospital convalescent's. It was a painful, alarming vision. In spite of the extraordinary man going into the room, the silence was unbroken, as if the unknown had brought in a mysterious tranquillity.

Bianca Maria strained her ear anxiously, leaning on the door-post. Perhaps the Cabalists had gone back to their little table, taking the new arrival with them. The silence lasted a long time. Motionless, almost rigid, she clutched at the doorposts, not to fall; what she had heard was so sad and cruel it broke her heart. She was seized with humiliation and anguish, as if she could feel nothing but this sorrow. She suffered every way in her natural pride and outraged maidenly reserve, and from her father throwing her name about in a mad dispute. She felt ashamed for him and for herself, as if he had boxed her ears in public. Her anguish nearly suffocated her; it rose to her brain, and seemed to burn her in its hot embrace. How long she stood, how long the silence went on in the drawing-room, she could not tell; only, through her distress, she heard her father's friends pass behind her curtain and go out cautiously, like so many conspirators. Then, mechanically, she left her room to look for him. But the drawing-room was dark, so was the study, where the Marquis di Formosa sometimes consulted an old book of necromancy. Bianca Maria searched anxiously for her father. In the end a light guided her. The Marquis di Formosa had gone into the little chapel, filled up the lamp before the Virgin, and lighted the lamp before the Ecce Homo, put out by his orders, also the two wax candles in the candelabra, and set them before Jesus Christ. Not satisfied with that, he had carried the big lamp into the little chapel. In that illumination he had thrown himself down despairingly before Christ, trembling, shaking, sobbing. Praying aloud, he said to the Redeemer:

'O Lamb of God, forgive me! I am ungrateful and ignorant, a miserable sinner. Forgive me, forgive! Do not make me suffer for my sins. Do me this grace for the sake of my languishing, dying daughter. I am unworthy, but bless me for her sake. O sorrowful Virgin, who hast suffered so much, understand and help me! Send a vision to Sister Maria degli Angioli. O blessed spirit, Beatrice Cavalcanti, my saintly wife, if I caused you sorrow, forgive me! Forgive me if I shortened your life! Do it for your daughter's sake: save your family. Appear to your daughter—she is innocent and good; tell her the words to save us, blessed spirit! blessed spirit!'

The girl, who beard it all, was so frightened she fled with her eyes shut, holding her head. When she got to her room, she thought she heard a deep, sad sigh behind her, and felt a light hand on her shoulder. Mad with terror, she could not cry out; she fell her whole length on the ground, and lay as if she were dead.

CHAPTER IV
DR. AMATI

Not once for a month past had Dr. Antonio Amati seen that thoughtful, delicate girl's face between the yellowish old curtains in the balcony opposite his study window, which looked into the big court of Rossi Palace, formerly Cavalcanti. Two years had passed from the day that one of the youngest, though one of the most distinguished, Naples doctors had come to take up his abode there alone, with one man-servant and a housekeeper, but bringing a crowd of old and new patients after him, filling the spacious, but rather dark, stairs with a going and coming of busy, preoccupied people. From the very first day he had noticed opposite his study window in passing that pure oval, the faintly pink, delicate complexion, those proud, soft eyes, that touched the heart from their gentleness. He saw all that at once, in spite of the windows opposite being dull from old age and her appearing for a short time only. He was a quick observer; in fact, a great part of his medical skill was owing to his quick glance, his lively, true, deep intuition.

'A heart with no sun,' he said to himself, turning round to put his heavy scientific volumes into his carved oak shelves. Nor was he surprised when the Rossi Palace door-keeper, humbly consulting him under the portico, as he got into his carriage for his round of afternoon visits, about a feverish illness that had inflamed her spleen, told him, amongst a flood of other gossip, that that angel opposite his balcony was Lady Bianca Maria Cavalcanti, a lady of high birth, but reduced in circumstances, poor girl, not by her own fault.... 'But perhaps she will become a nun,' the woman ended up. 'A heart with no sun,' Dr. Antonio Amati thought again as he went away, after prescribing for the sickly, talkative door-keeper.

But he had no time to remark or think of aristocratic ladies come down by bad luck, or their parents' sins, to obscurity and wretchedness; he could not let his fancy linger long on that melancholy life alongside of his, but so different from it. He was a silent, energetic man of action; a Southerner not fond of words, who put into his daily work all the strength other Southerners put into dreams, talk, and long speeches, accustoming himself to this self-government, calling up every day the violence of his fiery temper to conquer it by strength of will, and make use of it for scientific practical work, keeping always in touch with life, books, and suffering humanity, which at thirty-five had made him famous. He was proud of his great reputation, but not conceited, though lucky fortune had not made him mean or lowered him. No, he could not dream about Bianca Maria's lily face; too many around him were ill of typhus, smallpox, consumption, and a hundred other severe, almost incurable, illnesses that required his daily help and energies. Too many people called to him, implored him, stretched out their hands for help, besieging his waiting-room and the hospital door, watching for him at the University and other sick people's doors patiently and submissively, as if waiting for a saviour. Too many were suffering, sick and dying, for him to dream about that slight apparition, and admire the pale, thoughtful face bending under the weight of black tresses.

Still, through that life of useful work for himself and others, through the seeming hardness, hurry, even scientific brutality of his constant activity, which was made up for by his noble daily sacrifices, that silently attractive figure pleased Dr. Antonio Amati's fancy. Gradually it took its place each morning among the things he admired and liked to find in their places every day: his books, old leather note-books, some mementos of childhood and youth, a wax model of his dead sister's little hand, an old photograph of his mother, who lived in Campobasso province, a local accent he had not lost, in spite of living eighteen years in Naples and his travels in France and Germany.

Bianca Maria came into this harmonious atmosphere, that gently satisfied this strong man's eyes and heart. Antonio Amati did not try to see her oftener, nor to know and speak to her; it was enough to see her in the early morning, behind her balcony windows, look down vaguely into the dull, damp court, then disappear as slowly as she came—a quiet, solitary figure, not sorrowful, but not smiling. Between one patient going and another coming, Dr. Amati got up from his desk, and went as far as the balcony; in one or other of these little walks, that seemed to serve him as a pause, a rest, a distraction between one bit of work finished and another begun, he caught sight of Bianca Maria's pale, thoughtful face; and for two years that satisfied him. It is true that sometimes in these two years he had met her on the stairs, or in the Rossi Palace dark entrance, with her father or Margherita; he took off his hat, and she acknowledged his bow unsmilingly. She, too, knew him well, seeing him every day; but she looked him in the face frankly, with none of that extreme reserve, half smile, half sham indifference, or any of the little coquetries of commonplace girls. Frankly and innocently she looked at him a minute, returned his bow, and then her proud, gentle eyes took their vague thoughtful expression again.

They did not make daily appointments to see each other—he was too serious, too engrossed in duty to do so, and she was a simple creature, living too solitary an inward life to think of it—only they saw each other every day, and got accustomed to it.

'But perhaps she is to be a nun,' the door-keeper repeated sometimes. She had got over her illness, and employed herself over other people's ailments, moral and physical.

But the doctor walked on without replying, thinking of the sad chorus of lamentations that went on around him, from rich and poor, for real, present, imminent sorrows, almost hopeless to cure, but worthy of his courage and talent to attempt. Still, in that damp, south-east wind this autumn morning, whilst bad coughs, heart complaints, fevers came by turns dolefully in his list of cases, this sickly atmosphere of bad weather in Naples making them worse, he had, as usual, filled up his leisure by going to the balcony; and not seeing Bianca Maria, he felt annoyance of a latent, indefinite kind, which every new country or suburban patient made him forget; but it came back when the patient left. The forenoon passed in the gloom of the great writing-table, covered with maroon; of these colourless, anxious faces held up to him; these weak, complaining voices; lean breasts, or flabby with unhealthy fat, that were bared for him to find traces of consumption or atrophy, with wheezing, funereal coughs. Never had he felt the disagreeables of his profession so much as that day. Bianca Maria did not appear.

'She is ill,' he thought momentarily. Having thought of this, he felt as sure as if someone had told him or if he had seen her ill himself. She was sick. He at once thought of helping her, with that instinct to save life all great doctors have. He thought it over a minute; but his mind came back to the realities of life at once. It was folly to be taken up about a person he did not know, and who probably did not care to have him. If they needed his skill, they would have called him. For all that, he was sure Bianca Maria was ill.

But another patient came into the room. There were two, rather—a youth and a girl of the lower class. He recognised the girl at once from her hollow, worn face and sad, black-encircled eyes, the lock of untidy hair. He had cured her of typhoid at San Raffaele hospital, when the epidemic was raging in Naples.

'Is it you, Carmela?'

'Good-day to you, sir,' said the girl, rushing forward to kiss the doctor's hand, which he quickly drew back.

'Are you ill?' he asked.

'As if I was ill,' she said, smiling, in a faint, melancholy way, while the doctor was trying to recognise the young fellow's face. 'I am going to have a misfortune that is worse than an illness, sir.' She turned to her companion as she spoke, and called out: 'Raffaé!' Then Amati saw the young fellow in all the *guappesca* style of bell-trousers, small folded cap, silver chain with a bit of coral, shiny squeaking shoes, and the half-scampish, impudent look of a lad of twenty who has given up the knife, the traditional *sfarziglia* of his ancestors in the Camorra, for the modern revolver. 'This is my lover, sir,' she said, humbly and proudly, whilst Raffaele looked straight before him, as if it was not his business. She gave the youth so intense a look, so full of tenderness and passion, that the doctor had to restrain an impatient shrug.

'Is he ill?' he asked.

'No, sir; he is very well, thank God! But he has—that is to say, we have—another misfortune coming on us; or, indeed, it is my misfortune, as I must lose him. They want to take him for the levy,' said she, in a trembling voice, her eyes filling with tears.

'That is natural enough,' answered the doctor, smiling.

'How can you say so, sir? It is infamous of the Government to take a fine lad that ought to marry. If you won't help me, sir, what will I do?'

'And what can *I* do?'

Raffaele, in the meanwhile, stood with one hand at his side, hanging his hat between two fingers; sometimes he looked Carmela up and down absent-mindedly and haughtily, as if it was out of mere good-nature he allowed her to look after his affairs; then he cast an oblique but dignified glance on the doctor.

'You are so kind, sir,' Carmela murmured. 'I want you to give Raffaele a medicine to make him ill, and get him scratched off the list.'

'It is impossible, my dear girl.'

'Why so, sir?'

'Because there are no such miraculous medicines.'

'Oh, sir, you mean you don't wish to do me this kindness. Think if they take him for three years!—three years! What could I do without him for three years? And, then, he won't go, sir! If you knew what he says——'

'I told her,' Raffaele interrupted emphatically, pulling down his waistcoat, a common *guappa* trick, 'that if they take me by force, we will hold a little shooting; someone will be wounded, they take me to prison, and what happens? A year's imprisonment at most. I must go to San Francesco some day, at any rate.'

'Don't speak that way—don't say that!' she called out in admiring terror. 'Beg the professor to give you the medicine.'

'Are you to be married soon?' asked the doctor, who no longer wondered at anything, from knowing the people so well.

'Very soon,' Carmela answered by herself, while Raffaele looked before him.

'When are you to be?'

'When we get the *terno*,' she retorted, quietly and with certainty.

'Then, not for some time yet,' the doctor replied, laughing.

'No, no, sir; Don Pasqualino De Feo, the medium, has promised me a safe number. We will be married very soon. But you must get Raffaele off.'

'There is no need of my services. Raffaele will be rejected, because he has a narrow chest,' concluded the doctor, after looking carefully at the dandy.

'Do you say so, really?'

'Really it is so.'

'God bless you, sir! if I had to have this sorrow too, I would die. So many sorrows—so many,' she said in a low tone, pulling up her shabby shawl on her shoulders; 'I am the mother of sorrows,' she added, with a sad smile.

'Good-day, sir,' said Raffaele. 'When you come to Mercato or Pendino district, ask for Raffaele—I am called Farfariello—and let me serve you in any way I can.'

'Thank you—thank you,' replied the doctor, sending them off.

The two again repeated their farewells on their way out—she with a smile on her suffering face, he with the look of a man that despises women. Other patients came in requiring his medical skill up to twelve o'clock, when the time for receiving visits was over. Bianca Maria had not appeared. She was ill, therefore.

He took breakfast very hurriedly, and ordered the coachman to bring round the carriage to go to the hospital at one o'clock. The day was getting more and more unpleasant, from the scirocco's damp, ill-smelling breath. He went out quickly, as he was rather late, and on the stairs, half in shadow, he met Bianca Maria going down also, with Margherita, her maid.

'Then, she is not ill,' thought the doctor.

But with the sharp eyes of an observing man, who finds out the truth from the slightest symptoms, he saw the girl was walking undecidedly; her face, as she looked up to bow, was intensely pale, so that again his medical instinct was to help her. He was just going to speak, to ask her brusquely where the pain was, but her proud, gentle eyes were cast down again absent-mindedly; her mouth had that severe silent look that imposes silence on others. She disappeared without his saying anything. Dr. Amati shrugged his shoulders as he got into the carriage, and buried himself in a medical journal, as he did every day, to fill up even the short drive usefully. The carriage rolled along silently over the thin layer of mud; the damp obscured the windows, and the doctor felt the scirocco in himself and in the air. Even the hospital could not soothe the doctor's discomfort, though to take his thoughts off it he went deeper into practical medical work and scientific explanations to the pupils than usual. He went backwards and forwards from one bed to another, followed by a crowd of youths, taller than any of them, with an obstinate man's short forehead, marked by two perpendicular lines, from a constant frown, showing a strong will and absorption in his work; his thick brush of black hair was roughly set on his forehead, with some white tufts showing already. So great was his activity of thought, words, and action, one expected to see the smoke of a volcano coming out. His orders to the assistants and his class, even to the nuns, were given harshly; they all obeyed quickly and silently, feeling respect for the iron will, in spite of his rough commands, mingled with admiration for the man who was looked on as a saviour. Even the room he had charge of looked more melancholy and wretched that day than ever; the dulness of the air saddened the invalids, the heavy, evil-smelling damp made them feel their pains more. A whispered lament, like a long, laboured breath, was heard from one end of the room to the other, and the sick folks' pale faces got yellow in that ghastly light; their emaciated hands on the coverlets looked like wax.

In spite of trying to stun himself with work and words, Dr. Amati felt the disagreeables of his profession more than ever. Through that long, narrow room, full of beds in a row, and yellow, suffering faces, and the constant smell of phenic acid; through the scirocco mist and damp, that made even the nuns' pink cheeks bloodless-looking, he had a dream, a passing vision of a sunny, green, warm, clear, sweet-smelling country place, and his heart ached for this idyll, come and gone in a moment.

'Good-bye, gentlemen,' Amati said brusquely to the students, dismissing them.

They knew that when he so greeted them he wished to be left alone; they knew, they understood, the Professor was in a bad humour; they let him go. One of the ambulance men brought him two or three letters that came while he was going his rounds; they were summonses, urgent letters from sick people longing for him, from a father who had lost his head over a son's illness, from despairing women. He shook his head as he read them, as if he had lost confidence—as if all humanity sorrowing discouraged him. He went—yes, he went; but he felt very tired, which must have come from his mind, for he had worked much less than usual. He was going along absent-mindedly, when a shadow rose before him on the hospital stairs. It was a poor woman, of no particular age, with sparse grayish hair, black teeth, prominent cheek-bones, her clothes torn and dirty, whilst the slumbering babe she carried was clean, though meanly clad.

'Sir—please, sir!' she called out in a crying voice, seeing the doctor was going on without troubling himself about her.

'What do you want? Who are you?' the doctor asked roughly, without looking at her.

'I am Annarella, Carmela's sister—you saved her life,' said Gaetano the glove-cutter's wretched wife.

'Your sister in the morning, and now you!' the doctor impatiently exclaimed.

'Not for me, sir—not for me,' the gambler's wife said in a low tone. 'I can die. I don't signify. I do so little in the world I can't even find bread for my children.'

'Get out of the way—get out of the way.'

'It is for this little creature, for my sick son, sir;' and she bent to kiss the little slumberer's forehead. 'I don't know what is the matter, but he falls off every day, and I don't know what to give him. Cure him for me, sir.'

The doctor leant over the little invalid, with its pretty, delicate, pallid face, purple eyelids, hardly perceptible breathing, and lips slightly apart; he touched its forehead and hands, then looked at the mother.

'You give it milk?' he asked shortly.

'Yes, sir,' said she, with a slight smile of motherly content.

'How many months old is he?'

'Eighteen months.'

'And you still suckle him? You are all the same, you Naples women. Wean him at once.'

'Oh, sir!' she exclaimed, quite alarmed.

'Wean him,' he repeated.

'What am I to give him?' she said, almost sobbing. 'I often want bread for myself and the other two, but never milk. Must this poor little soul die of hunger too?'

'Does your husband not work?' asked the doctor ponderingly.

'Yes, sir, he does work,' she said, shaking her head.

'Does he keep another woman?'

'No, sir.'

'What does he do, then?'

'He plays at the lottery.'

'I understand. Wean the child. He has fever. Your milk poisons him.'

After gazing at the doctor and her child, she just said 'Jesus' in a whisper, and a sob burst out from her motherly breast.

Amati wrote out a prescription in pencil on a leaf of his pocket-book. He went down the stairs, followed by Annarella, whose tears fell over the child's face, her dull sobs following him in lamentation.

'This is the prescription; here are five francs to get it with,' said the doctor, motioning to her not to thank him.

She looked at him with stupefied eyes while he crossed the big cold hospital court to his carriage; she began to cry again when she was alone; gazing on the baby, the prescription in her hand shook—it was so bitter for her to think of having poisoned her son with her milk.

'It must be cholera,' she kept saying to herself, for among Naples common folk stomach disorders are often called cholera.

Dr. Amati shook his head again energetically, as if he had lost confidence altogether in the saving of humanity. As he was opening the carriage door to get in, a woman who had been chattering with the hospital porter came up to speak to him. It was a woman in black, with a nun's shawl, and black silk kerchief on her head, tied under the chin. She had coal-black eyes in a pale face—eyes used to the shade and silence. She spoke very low.

'Sir, would you come with me to do an urgent kindness?'

'I am busy,' the doctor grumbled, getting into his carriage.

'The person is very, very ill.'

'All the people I have to see are ill.'

'She is near here, sir, in the Sacramentiste convent. I was sent to the hospital to find a doctor. I can't go back without one ... she is so very ill....'

'Dr. Caramanna is still up there—ask for him,' Amati retorted. 'Is it a nun that is ill?' he then added.

'The Sacramentistes are cloistered; they can't call men into the convent,' said the servant, pursing her lips. 'It is someone who got ill in the convent parlour, not belonging to the convent....'

'I will come,' Amati said quickly.

He pushed the servant into the carriage, got in and shut the door. The carriage rolled along the Anticaglia road, which is so dark, muddy, and wretched from old age; and they did not say a word to each other in the short drive. The carriage stopped before the convent gate; instead of ringing the bell, the servant opened the door with a key. The doctor and she first crossed an icy court overlooked by a number of windows with green jalousies, then a corridor with pillars along the court; complete solitude and silence was everywhere. They went into a vast room on the ground-floor. Along the white-washed walls were straw chairs, nothing else; at the end a big table, with a seat for the porter lay Sister. A crucifix was nailed on one wall. Along the other were two narrow gratings with a wheel in the middle, to speak through and pass things to the nuns. Near this wall, on three chairs, a woman's form was stretched out; another woman was kneeling and bending over her face. Before the doctor got as far as the woman lying down, the servant went up to the grating and spoke: 'Praise to the Holy Sacrament——'

'Now and for ever,' a very feeble voice answered from inside, as if it came out of a deep cave.

'Is the doctor here?'

'Yes, Sister Maria.'

'That is well;' and a long, feverish sigh was heard.

In the meantime Dr. Amati had gone up to the fainting girl. Margherita was bathing her forehead with a handkerchief steeped in vinegar, and whispering: 'My darling! my darling!'

The doctor put his hat on the ground, and knelt down too, to examine the fainting girl. He felt her pulse, and gently raised one eyelid; the eye was glassy.

'How long has she been like this?' he asked in a whisper, rubbing her icy hands.

'Half an hour,' the old woman replied.

'What have you done for her?'

'Nothing but use the vinegar. They gave it to me through the wheel; they have nothing else; it is a convent under strict rules.'

'Does she often faint?'

'Last night ... she had another swoon. I found her on the ground in her room. I called my master.'

'Did she recover of herself ... last night?'

'Yes.'

'Had she got a fright?'

'I don't know ... I don't think so,' she said in a hesitating way.

They were speaking in a whisper, whilst the servant stood right at the grating, as if mounting guard.

'Is she better?' the feeble voice inside asked.

'Just the same,' replied the servant in a monotonous voice.

'Oh God!' the voice called out in anguish.

Meanwhile the doctor bent down to hear the breathing better. He seemed thoughtful and preoccupied. Margherita looked at him with despairing eyes.

'Did she get a fright, half an hour ago, in here?' he began again to ask, whilst he carefully raised Bianca's head and placed it against his breast.

'No! ... certainly not!' Margherita whispered. 'I was in church. I did not hear what was said; they called to me.'

'Who is that nun?' he asked, pointing to the grating.

'It is Sister Maria degli Angioli—the aunt.'

Then he got up and went to the grating. The serving Sister pursed up her lips to remind him of the cloistral rule, almost as if she wanted to prevent any conversation between him and the nun.

'Sister Maria——' he said very gently.

'Now and for ever,' the feeble voice said hurriedly, hearing a man's voice.

'Has your niece had a fright?'

Silence on the other side.

'Did she tell you of anything disagreeable that had happened to her?'

'Yes, yes!' the voice breathed out, trembling.

'Can you tell me what it was about?'

'No, no!' she went on quickly, still trembling. 'Something very sad ... I can't tell you.'

'Very well—thank you,' he whispered, getting up again.

'How is she? Are you giving her anything?' the Sister's voice asked.

'We are going to take her to the house. Nothing can be done here.'

'We are poor nuns,' the Sister murmured. 'How will you carry her?'

'In the carriage,' he said shortly. Then, going up to Margherita, he went on in a low, forcible voice: 'I am coming with my coachman just now. She can't stay here; I can't do anything for her here. We will carry her out to the carriage and go home.'

'In this state?' she asked undecidedly.

'Do you want her to die here?' he interrupted brusquely.

'Please forgive me, sir.'

He had already gone out, without his hat and overcoat, across the passage and icy court. After a minute he came back with the coachman, who had evidently got his orders.

The doctor gently raised the fainting girl's body from under the arms, resting her head on his breast, while the coachman raised her feet. She was almost rigid and very heavy. The coachman had a frightened look; perhaps he thought he was carrying out a dead woman, all in black, through that bare parlour, deserted corridor, and chilly court; and although the sight of physical suffering was not new to him, being in a successful doctor's service, the idea of carrying a young woman's cold body, a corpse perhaps, gave him such a shudder he turned away his head. Old Margherita, coming behind, looked yellower, more like wrinkled parchment than ever, in the bright court. The procession of the anxious doctor, the frightened man, the rigid figure in black, and the old servant sadly bent by a strange new anguish, moved silently across the silent, tomb-like cloister, like a funeral. Gently, with the care needed not to waken a sleeping baby, the two men placed the poor lifeless creature in the carriage, her head against the cushions and her feet on the opposite seat. She had not given a sign of life whilst she was being carried; the two lines deepened between Dr. Amati's eyebrows, lines showing a strong will and deep thought, but which gave him an absent-minded look. Margherita still gently tried to rearrange the girl's loosened tresses that had fallen down, but she did not manage it, her lean hands trembled so; she, too, had got into the broad landau; she gathered up her mistress's hair caressingly, and the doctor heard her mutter, 'My darling! my darling!'

He had lowered the blue blinds against indiscreet eyes; the carriage went at a foot-pace; and in that bluish, misty shade the slow pace kept up the idea of a funeral still more. However, the carriage stopped at one point; after a little the coachman opened the door, and handed in to the doctor a hermetically sealed phial, which he held to the unconscious girl's nose. A sharp smell of ether at once spread through the carriage, which was still going very slowly. Bianca Maria never moved; after a little there was one sign of feeling: her closed eyelids got red, big tears burst out between the lashes and ran down her cheeks. The doctor did not take his eyes off her for a minute, keeping her hand in his. She went on weeping, still unconscious, without giving another sign of life: as if she still felt sorrow through her unconsciousness, as if through her loss of memory one bitter recollection still remained — only one. She did not recover consciousness.

When they got to the Rossi Palace courtyard, hardly was the door opened when a murmuring noise broke out, gradually growing stronger, impossible to restrain. Beside the carriage door the porter's wife called out and screamed as if the girl was dead. All the windows looking into the courtyard, all the landing-place doors, had opened to see the poor, fainting, pale creature in black, with hair hanging down, taken out of the carriage. The doctor vainly tried to insist on silence, but the cry of surprise and compassion grew louder, rising in the heavy air.

On the first-floor landing-place Gelsomina, Agnesina Fragalà's nurse, came out, holding the pretty, healthy infant in her arms; the happy mother, Luisella Fragalà, came behind her, dressed to go out, with her bonnet on. But she lingered, leaning on the iron railing, smiling vaguely at her baby, and looking pityingly on the strange escort. She had felt rather tired and preoccupied for some time past, for she had been going every day to the Santo Spirito shop, from an instinct, a presentiment, that was stronger than her pride, tying up the parcels of sweets and cakes with her ring-covered, white hands.

'Poor thing! poor thing!' Luisella Fragalà muttered; her compassion had a deeper, acuter feeling in it than the other people's had.

Raising the heavy yellow brocade curtains behind her double windows on the first-floor, Signora Parascandolo's bloodless face appeared — the rich usurer's wife who had lost all her children.

She seldom went out; she stayed shut up in her gorgeous apartment, full of rich furniture now quite useless and dreary, as she never received anyone since her sons died; only she looked out of the window now and then in a silly kind of way that had grown on her. On seeing Bianca Maria carried up in that way, the poor woman, who took an interest in nothing usually, opened the window, and her voice was added to the rising tumult, crying in prayer and supplication, 'Jesus, Jesus, help us!' All Domenico Mayer's misanthropic family came out on the third-floor landing, leaving their three-roomed little flat that looked on to the Rossi Theatre. First came the father's long, peevish face, and, having just left some copying work brought home from the Finance Office, he had sleeves on to save his coat; then Donna Christina, the mother, who had got rid of the tooth-ache but had a stiff neck instead; next Amalia, with her staring eyes, thick nose and lips, and sulky look of a girl who has not yet got a husband; and Fofò, still afflicted by the hunger which his relations said was a mysterious illness. The whole family nearly threw themselves over the railings out of curiosity, and shrieked out in a chorus: 'Poor girl! poor girl!' A woman in a muslin cap and a man in a blue sweeping-apron were at the window—even the doctor's housekeeper; nor did they stop gazing when their master came up, so overpowering was the excitement in all the Rossi Palace.

That carrying up the stair, amid the noisy compassion of all these different people, the frightened, pitying shrieks, that had a false ring about them, seemed endless to Dr. Amati; as for old Margherita, she shook with annoyance and shame, as if that noise and publicity were insulting to her mistress.

When the door was shut behind them, she asked Giovanni in a fright: 'Is milord not in? Milady is ill.'

'No,' he said, making way for the bearers.

Margherita shook her head despairingly. She went with the doctor and his man into Bianca Maria's room; the girl was laid on the bed. The manservant went away. The doctor again tried to bring her back with ether—no result. He bit his lip; he said twice or thrice, 'It is impossible!' Once again he raised the violet eyelids, looking at her eyes. She was alive, but she did not recover consciousness.

'Where is her father?' he asked, without turning round.

'I don't know,' the old woman muttered.

'There will be some place he goes every day; send for him.'

'I will send, as you order me to,' she said, still hesitating; and she went out.

He sat down by the bedside, and laid down the ether bottle, convinced now it was useless. That bare, cold little room, with a look of childish purity, had calmed somewhat the scientist's dull anger at not being able to cure nor find out the reason of the illness. He had seen, a hundred times, long, queer fainting fits; but they were from nervous illnesses, from abnormal temperaments, out of order from the beginning, and ordinary methods had overcome them. The colourless young girl seemed to be sleeping heavily, and she might remain so for many hours, wrapped up in the dark regions of unconsciousness. He armed himself with patience, turning over in his mind medical books that spoke of such fainting fits. Twice or thrice Margherita had come back into the room, questioning him with an agonized look; he shook his head, 'No.' Then he asked her for brandy. She stood hesitating; there was none in the house. Amati told her to go and ask for it in his flat next door. With a teaspoon, a wretched one that had lost its plating, he opened the girl's lips, and poured the strong liquor through her closed teeth, with no result. Again, he asked Margherita, who was fidgeting about, to heat flannel cloths; seeing her still embarrassed, he told her to go to his house, and ask the housekeeper for some.

Whilst she was away, Giovanni came back out of breath; he panted as he spoke.

'I have not found the Marquis anywhere, not at Don Crescenzio's lottery stand, nor at the Santo Spirito assembly, nor in Don Pasqualino the medium's house, where they meet every day.'

'Who meet?' asked the doctor distractedly, hardly listening to what he said.

'The Marquis's friends.... But I left word wherever he is to come back to the house, because her ladyship is ill.'

'Very good; send out this prescription,' said the doctor, who as usual wrote it with a pencil on a leaf from his pocket-book.

The old servant's pale face looked disturbed. The doctor, always taken up about his patient, did not notice him.

'Go, and get it,' he said, feeling Giovanni was still there.

'It is because ...' the poor man stammered out.

Then the doctor, just as he had done for Annarella, the glove-cutter's wretched wife, pulled ten francs out of his purse and gave them to him.

'... the master not being in and not being able to tell the mistress,' Giovanni muttered, wishing to account for the want of money.

'Very good—all right,' said the doctor, turning to his patient.

But a loud ring at the bell sounded all through the flat. A resounding step was heard, and the Marquis di Formosa came in. He seemed only to see his daughter stretched out on the bed. He began kissing her hand and forehead, speaking loudly in great anguish.

'My daughter, my daughter, what is the matter with you? Answer your father. Bianca, Bianca, answer! Where have you the pain? how did it come? My darling, my heart's blood, my crown, answer me! It is your father calling you. Listen, listen, tell me what it is! I will cure you, dear, dear daughter!'

And he went on exclaiming, crying out, sobbing, pale and red in the face, by turns, running his fingers through his white hair, his still graceful, strong figure bent, while the doctor looked at him keenly. In a silent interval the Marquis noticed Amati's presence, and recognised him as his celebrated neighbour.

'Oh, doctor,' he called out, 'give her something—this daughter is all I have!'

'I am trying what I can,' the doctor said slowly, in a low voice, as if he was chafing against the powerlessness of his science. 'But it is an obstinate faint.'

'Has she had it long?'

'About two hours. It came on in the Sacramentiste parlour.'

'Ah!' said the father, getting pale.

The doctor looked at him. They said no more. The secret rose up between them, wrapped in the thickest, deepest obscurity.

'Do something for her,' Formosa stammered, in a trembling voice.

But he was summoned; Giovanni whispered to him; the Marquis was undecided for a minute.

'I will come back at once,' he said as he went off.

The doctor had wrapped the invalid's little feet in warm clothes; now he wanted to wrap up her hands. All at once he felt a slight pressure on his hand: Bianca Maria with open eyes was quietly looking at him. The doctor's forehead wrinkled a little with surprise just for a moment.

'How do you feel?' he asked, leaning over the invalid.

She gave a tired little smile, and waved her hand as if to tell him to wait, that she could not speak yet.

'All right, very good,' the doctor said heartily. 'Don't speak;' and he made Margherita, who was coming in, keep silence, too.

The servant's poor tired eyes shone with joy when she saw Bianca Maria smiling.

'Are you better? Make a sign,' the doctor asked tenderly.

She made an effort, and very low, instead of a sign, she pronounced the word 'Better.' The voice was low, but quiet. With a medical man's familiarity, he took one of her hands in his to warm it.

'Thank you!' said she after a time.

'For what?' he said, rather put out.

'For everything,' she replied, smiling again.

Now, it seemed, she had quite got back the power of speaking. She spoke, but kept quite still, only living intensely in her eyes and smile.

'For everything—what do you mean?' he asked, piqued by a lively curiosity.

'I understood,' said she, with a profound look.

'You were conscious all the time?'

'All. I could neither move nor speak, but I understood.'

'Ah!' said he thoughtfully. He sent Margherita to let the Marquis know that his daughter had recovered consciousness.

'Were you in pain?'

'Yes, a great deal, from not being able to come out of my faint. I wept; I felt a pain at my heart.'

'Yes, yes,' he said. 'Don't speak any more—rest.'

The doctor made a sign to the Marquis, who was coming in, to keep silence. Formosa leant over his daughter's bed and touched her forehead with his hand, as if he was blessing her. Her eyelids fluttered and she smiled.

'Your daughter was conscious during her swoon—the rarest kind of fainting fit.'

'Was she conscious?' the Marquis asked in a strange voice.

'Yes; she saw and heard everything. It comes from sensitiveness carried to excess.'

Then he poured out more brandy in the teaspoon for Bianca Maria to take. Don Carlo Cavalcanti's face twitched. He leant over the bed, and asked:

'What did you see? Tell me—what did you see?'

The daughter did not answer. She looked at her father in such sad surprise that the doctor, turning round, noticed it and frowned. He had not heard what the father asked his daughter, and he again felt the great family secret coming up, seeing Bianca Maria's gentle, sad glance.

'Don't ask her anything,' the doctor said brusquely to the Marquis di Formosa.

The old patrician restrained a disdainful shrug. He brooded over his daughter's face, as if he wanted to get the secret out by magnetism. She lowered her eyelids, but suffering was in her face; then she looked at the doctor, as if she wanted help.

'Do you want anything?' he asked.

'There is a man at my door: make him go away,' she whispered in a frightened tone.

The doctor started; so did her father. In fact, outside the door, in his invariable wretched waiting attitude, was Pasqualino De Feo, dirty, ragged, with unkempt beard and pale, streaky red cheeks. The Marquis had left him in the drawing-room, but he slid along to Bianca Maria's room with the timid, quiet step of a beggar who fears to be chased from all doors.

'Who is that man?' said the doctor in that rough tone of his, going up to the door, as if to chase him away.

'He is a friend,' the Marquis answered, hurrying forward in a vague, embarrassed way.

'Send him away!' the doctor said sternly.

Outside the door the Marquis and Don Pasqualino chattered in a lively whisper. Bianca Maria looked as if she could hear what her father said outside; at one point she shook her head.

'Do you want that man sent away from the house?'

'Leave him,' she said feebly. 'It would annoy my father.'

Ah! the doctor knew nothing at all. Even now, on coming back to stern realities, he blamed himself for the sad, dark romance coming into his life; but an overmastering feeling entangled him, which he thought was scientific curiosity. Hours were passing, evening was coming on; he had made none of his visits, and he stayed on in that poor aristocratic sick lady's room, as if he could not tear himself away.

'I ought to go,' he said, as if to himself.

'But you will come back?' she asked in a whisper.

'Yes ...' he said, determined to conquer himself and not come back again.

'Do come back!' in a humble voice, beseechingly.

'I am here—just next door. If you are in pain, send for me.'

'Yes, yes,' she replied, quieted at the idea of being protected.

'Adieu, madame!'

'À Dieu!' she said, pointedly separating the two words.

Margherita went with him, thanking him softly for having saved her mistress; but he had again become an energetic, busy man, inimical to words.

'Where is the Marquis?' he insisted on knowing.

'In the drawing-room, Professor.'

And she took him there. It was just so. Don Carlo Cavalcanti, Marquis di Formosa, and Pasqualino De Feo were walking up and down silently. It was almost dark: still, the doctor examined the medium with a scrutinizing, suspicious eye.

'How is Bianca Maria?' asked Formosa, coming out of a dream.

'Better now,' the doctor replied in a short, cold tone; 'but she has been struck prematurely, owing to a growing want of balance, moral and physical. If you don't give her sun, movement, air, quiet, and cheerfulness, she may die—from one day to another.'

'Don't say so, doctor!' the father cried out, angry and grieved.

'I must tell you, because it is so. I don't know the reason of to-day's illness—I don't want to know it; but she is ill, you understand—ill! She needs sun and peace—peace and sun. If you want a doctor, I am always near; that is my profession. But I have made out a prescription. Send your daughter to the country. If she stays another year in this house, only seeing you and going to the nunnery, she will die, I assure you,' he persisted coldly, as if this truth ought to be announced decisively, as if he wanted to convince his own unwilling mind also.

'Doctor, doctor, do not say that!' Formosa moaned, asking for mercy.

'She is ill; she will die. To the country—the country! Good-evening, Marquis!'

He went off, as if trying to escape. The Marquis and the medium, who had not said a word, went on again with their silent walk. Now and then Formosa sighed deeply.

'The Spirit that helps me— —' the medium breathed out.

'Eh?' the other cried out, starting.

'Warns me that Donna Bianca Maria has had a heavenly vision ... and that she will tell you it in an allegory.'

'What do you say? Is it possible? Has the Supreme Being granted me this favour? Is it possible?'

'The Spirit does not deceive,' the medium said sententiously.

'That is true—it is true!' Formosa murmured, looking into the darkness with wild eyes.

CHAPTER V
CARNIVAL AT NAPLES

From the first days of January, Naples was taken with a mania for work that spread from one house and shop to another, from street to street, quarter to quarter, from fashionable parts to the poorest, with a continuous movement, rising and falling. A stronger noise of saws, planes and hammers came from the factories and workshops: in the shops, with doors left ajar, and in the houses they sat up late: the smallest as well as the big industries seemed to have got a mysterious impulse, a breath of new life, into their half-dying state.

The demand for gloves had increased beyond bounds, especially white and dove-coloured ones: the humblest general shops kept them. In the artificial-flower shops, that compete with the French trade with growing success, a great quantity of boughs, bunches, wreaths of flowers, and ferns were got ready; big and small bouquets of bright, warm-coloured flowers to take the eye—the finest intended for ladies' hair and bosoms, the coarser for decorating houses, shops, horses and carriages. Roses, camellias, pinks, were most in request. At all the tailors' and dressmakers', satin, velvet, gauze, crape, were draped in all styles, made into dresses, mantles, hoods, and scarves; whilst at the shoe-makers', binders spent ten hours a day making pink, blue, white, gray, and lilac shoes, fancy, gold-embroidered boots, and some bound in fur. The glove, flower, dress, and shoe makers' work began the first hours in the morning and ended at eleven at night; but the only others that came up to them were the cardboard shops. Here paper, in men and women's hands, was bent into a thousand shapes and sizes. It was painted, cut out, twisted, even curled up; it was made up with straw, metal, and rich brocade stuff, starting from the twisted paper that holds a sweet or cracker to the big expensive box. From the little chocolate-box, made of cardboard and a scrap of satin, to the handsome, neat satchel with a second cardboard lining; from the roll, made of two or three old gambling cards, a little Bristol board, and bright-coloured pictures, to straw cornucopias, covered with ribbons; from ugly, mean things to lovely and expensive ones, the work was never-ending. All this paper-work was arranged on large boards; the colours were dazzling and took the eye. Every day they were sent off to the sweet-shops, where they were filled with confetti, dainties, sweets, and sugar almonds.

Yes, the work was hardest, always, in the confectioners', from the humble Fragalà of San Lorenzo quarter and the gorgeous but middle-class Fragalà of Spirito Santo up to the exquisite fashionable confectioner in Piazza San Ferdinando. Above all, there was a grand making of caraways, white and coloured, of all sizes, with caraway-seeds and a powdery sugar covering; there were whole stores of them in tins, canisters of all sizes, overflowing baskets made like canisters, all kept carefully from damp, which ruins caraways. Such a stock!—if it had been gunpowder, there would have been enough to conquer an army. The other heavy work was getting sausages and black-puddings ready, all covered with yellow bits of Spanish bread—pig's blood, that is to say—made up with chocolate, pistachios, vanilla, lemon, and cinnamon, so presented as to hide the coarseness. In the back-shops they weighed cinnamon, sliced lemons, crushed pistachio nuts, boiled sweets of all colours and kinds; ovens roared, stoves were made red-hot, kettles boiled and gurgled, and workmen, in shirt-sleeves and caps, with bare arms and necks, stirring with big ladles, beating pestles in marble mortars, looked like odd figures in purgatory, lighted up by the furnace flames.

All trades were busy: advertisements were put up; whole sheets of them were spread on the city walls. Fashionable barbers took on new lads; the three celebrated Naples *pizzaiuoli* of Freddo and Chiaia Lanes, of Carità Square, of Port Alba, informed the public, which loves *pizza* with Marano and Procida wine, that they would be open till morning. The Café Napoli, the Grande, and the Europa covered their windows with thick cloths, and held a grand cleaning up all through the rooms; the theatres announced four times more illuminations, whilst at the door of fancy shops, the windows of miserable or fashionable bazaars, were shown black velvet masks, wax noses, and huge cardboard heads, three times the natural size, and much uglier than Nature; network masks, to protect the face from caraways, ladles for throwing them, long tongs for handing up sweets or flowers to the balconies, scarves and ribbons, fantastic ballroom decorations, and entire costumes of tissue-paper. Along the streets in Monte Calvario quarter, across and parallel to Toledo, in the darkest old-clothes shops and retail dealers', dominos hung on wooden pegs for the popular balls: Mephistopheles costumes in red and blue, Spanish grandees in cotton velvet, harlequins made up of old carpets, Sorrento peasant women's dresses in gay colours, Pulcinellos, and almost white dress; above all, shining helmets, with cuirass of cardboard to match, and wooden swords. Masquerading costumes were on hire everywhere for a few francs; they gave a jocular tone to these dull lanes, hanging even from the first-floor balconies, sticking out in a row from the damp, dark shops with grinning, devilish masks, or showing sickly faces of white or greeny-blue satin.

Wherever one went, in lower class neighbourhoods as well as in aristocratic parts, one could see a lively movement, cheerful labour, a noisy bustling about, a never-ending activity, a daily and nightly ferment of all forces, the constant, lively, energetic action of a whole peaceful, laborious town, intent upon one single piece of work, given up to it heart and mind, hand and foot, using up its nerves, blood, and muscles in this one tremendous work. Everywhere, everywhere, one guessed or knew it; it caught the eye; it was written up what this great work was—'For the coming carnival festivities.'

Nothing else but the carnival. The great city gave itself over to that impetuous, joyous exertion, not for love of work in itself—for work that is the cause and consequence of well-doing, which in itself is the ground-work of goodness and respectability. The great town had not given itself over to that lively activity for any immediate civic reason, for hygienic improvements, industrial art exhibitions, changing old quarters or making new ones: it was for the carnival only—a carnival by official decree of the Prefecture and of the Municipal Palace; a carnival warmed up by committees, associations, commissions, set agoing by thousands of people, arranged and carried out as a great institution, widely spread in the minds of the whole five hundred thousand inhabitants, made to resound as far as the southern provinces, echoing even to Rome and to Florence, putting in the place of any other project, initiative or work, this of the carnival; nothing but the carnival—enthusiastically, even deliriously.

But, as at the bottom of all joyous things in this land of Cockayne, there is an ever-flowing vein of bitterness. This carnival, that turned all the gravest persons and things in the town into fun and masquerade—this carnival was a merciful thing. From autumn to January the damp, grievous scirocco had blown in Naples' streets, overcoming the energies of healthy people, and making invalids' maladies worse. The winter crowd of foreigners was smaller than usual. Many works had been stopped for a time, and those just starting had been delayed, so that many poor people slept on the church steps under San Francesco di Paola portico and the Immacolata obelisk in Piazza Gesù. A great wind of fasting had blown with the scirocco, so that the official carnival, carried out by the desire of thousands, was intended, if it succeeded, to satisfy for ten days at least a lot of starving people, from shoe-binders to flower-makers, from tailors to shop-clerks, from wandering salesmen to the small shopkeepers. Twenty days' carnival!—that is to say, ten days' bread, and a relish with it. The idea had been taken up at once. All helped, even the least enterprising, knowing they were putting out their money at good interest. Carnival, carnival, in the streets and balconies, in the gateways and houses!

On that Shrovetide Thursday the damp winter scirocco had got a spring softness. Toledo Road, where the carnival spread from one end to the other, both in its popular and fashionable form, had put on an extraordinary appearance. All the big shops were shut. The tradesmen and their ladies wished to enjoy the day's outing, also they were nervous about their plate-glass windows. All the signs were covered with linen or tow, as were the gas-lamps. As to the common smaller shops, they had taken out the glass and put up wooden platforms, and the owners, with their friends and children, sat with a store of caraways, having to do battle almost face to face with the people on the pavement; but they bravely flourished their ladles all the same. The balconies on the first floor were all differently draped with bright, cheap muslins, put up with a few nails or pins, with a very Southern and rather barbarous love of gay colours, some in the style of church decorations, blue, red, white, and gold, some tucked back with big camellias, roses, and dahlias, to make the balcony look like an alcove, an actress's room, a saint's niche, or a wild beasts' show even. The finest and smartest hangings began near Santa Brigida. Some Swiss gentlemen had had a chalet put up in their balcony, and the ladies wore simple, rather silly costumes, with hair down, a big cap, and gold crosses at their necks. Just after that, at Santa Brigida, a great man's natural son had hung his balconies with dark-blue velvet, covered with a silver net, which might represent the firmament, the kingdom of the moon, or the sea, but, at any rate, it surprised the good Naples folk. A balcony near the Conte di Mola Lane was made into a kitchen, with a stove, kettle, frying and stew pans, and eight or ten youths of good family worked as cooks and scullions, with white caps and aprons. A famous beautiful woman, whose beauty brought her wealth and led her into deadly sin, had changed her balcony into a Japanese hut, all stuffs and tapestries. Now and then she appeared wrapped in flowing, soft robes, just gathered in at the waist, with her black hair caught up in a shiny knot held by pins, her eyebrows arched in an unvarying look of surprise.

The common people smiled admiringly as they passed. They said, with their vague one idea of the East, 'The Turk, the Turk!' All these balconies, draped from one end of the street to the other, and the shop decorations, began to make one dizzy with bright colours, firing the imagination, giving that quick feeling of voluptuous joy Southerners get from outside impressions. Towards eleven, wandering salesmen began to go about, shrieking out their wares. They sold little boxes of inferior sweets made in bright colours—red bags, green and white boxes, lilac and yellow horns, carried in big, flat baskets in one hand. They sold artificial flowers also, made into sprays, cockades, and bunches, tied on to long poles. Real flowers were sold, too—white camellias and perfumed violets, from big baskets; also masks, ladles, linen bags for caraways, red and yellow paper sunflowers, that twirled round at every breath of wind like wild things. They sold a bad quality of caraways, bought cheap, intended to be sold dear in the blind, furious time of the battle.

At mid-day the traffic in sweetmeat-boxes, flowers, musks, and windmills began. Already the crowd began to fill the balconies and pavements, running up hurriedly from all the side-streets. On the first-floor windows and balconies a living, many-coloured hedge of women swayed about. There was a shimmer of girlish forms brightly dressed; their faces gently moved up and down like big pink and white flower-heads, with a blood-red touch now and then from an open parasol or scarlet hat. The balconies and windows of the second story were filled with still more excited people, whilst on the fourth children and girls here and there had thought of letting down a basket tied to a long bit of ribbon to fish with, smiling from above on some courteous unknown, who put a flower, some sweets, or a chocolate-box into the baskets of these smiling beings so near the sky. The people increased everywhere. Traffic with the hawkers went on from the balconies to the streets, with loud discussions, offers, and rejections, making the noise twice as great.

Caraways were not to be thrown before two o'clock, by the committee's express order, but some stray fights were started already. At San Sepolcro corner a peasant nurse, slowly swinging her petticoats, was fired at by some school-boys at close quarters. A grave gentleman, in top-hat and long great-coat, was violently assaulted in Carità Square. He tried to go at them with his stick, but he was hissed. Then he called for the police, announcing pompously he was Cavaliere Domenico Mayer, a State functionary; but the police would not help, saying it was carnival, and that he should not tempt people with his top-hat. And then the misanthropic Secretary of the Finance Department, full of bitterness, had gone into the San Liborio Lane to escape. A lady in a broad-brimmed hat, not able to move from one spot in the pavement near San Giacomo, had a continuous shower of caraways poured on her by a child on the third story. She heard it fall on her felt and feathers without daring to move or raise her head, in case she got the caraways in her face.

At two o'clock exactly a cannon-shot was heard in the distance. Then there was a sigh of relief from one end of Toledo to the other, from the street to the upper stories, and the crowd swayed about.

The four Rossi Palace balconies, first floor on the right, looking into Toledo, were draped in blue and white linen, caught back by big red camellias. Luisella Fragalà and her guests had thought of white and blue dominoes, with high, ridiculous hats and red cockades, and all the Naddeos, all the Durantes, all the Antonaccis, fat or thin, young or old, wore dominoes made in the house themselves to save their clothes from white powder, and, according to them, give an elegant look to the balcony. Some looked like big bundles, others like long ghosts; but the carnival madness had overcome these middle-class women. Besides all, trade was flourishing in these days. So many goods were sold; the men came back to the house in high good-humour, whilst all winter had been one complaint, and economy had got narrower and harder to bear. How happy they were, all these placid, industrious little women! In this time of carnival excitement they could share, in their blue and white fancy dresses and red cockades. Luisella Fragalà had thought out the costume, and that monkey Carmela Naddeo took up the idea at once and made others follow suit. They were all there, ladles in hand, guessing what sort of carriages were to appear, exaggerating, contradicting, shrieking, laughing, hanging over the railings to see if any carriages were coming round by the Museum. Only sometimes a cloud came over Luisella Fragalà's face; some unhappy thought was behind her brown eyes. Perhaps she was troubled by the thought that the balcony hangings would be spoilt by the confetti. Perhaps she would have liked to keep the shop open even on that profitable Carnival Thursday, her love of selling having instinctively grown so great, as if by that alone she saw a chance of being saved from imminent peril. Perhaps she secretly regretted Cesare Fragalà's absence. He was often away lately, and had disappeared early that Thursday, too. But these clouds were fleeting. Luisella was going about from one balcony to another with her hood down, vainly looking for places for the Mayer family, who had come without being invited. All quietly snubbed them, so as not to give up their places, saying to each other that the mother and daughter had no dominoes, and they made a false note on the balcony. They set themselves in the third row, the mother, as usual, rheumatic, and wrapped in flannel to the finger-tips; the girl's big eyes still dully misanthropic, as were her swollen, discoloured lips; the brother, as usual, very hungry.

'We will not get even a chocolate-box,' they grumbled one after the other, muttering with their unending rage against humanity.

But the great carnival wave, with ever-increasing force, swallowed up their rage against mankind also. The noise among the carriages got tremendous. The confetti war had begun between them and the pony-carts, done up with myrtle as an attempt at decoration, all being well filled with masqueraders of both sexes dressed in bright-coloured calicoes. The Parascandolos, who lived on the other side of the Rossi Palace, kept their balcony shut, for the Signora considered herself in mourning; but Don Gennaro Parascandolo, in a Russian linen dust-cloak and cap, with a bag of sweets hung round his neck, after walking along Toledo, greeted from hundreds of balconies, where his past, present, and future clients were, had gone to his club at Santa Brigida, and from there, amid a group of young and old boon companions, made a life of it, as they said there. They joked about him, asked him how many cars he had lent money for, and if it was true his collection of bills was increased by many princely autographs. Ninetto Costa, the smart, lucky stock-broker, who had his own reasons for making a fuss with him, said, to flatter him, that not a handful of caraways was thrown that day he was not interested in either providing or scattering. Don Gennaro Parascandolo laughed paternally, not denying it. He answered those who asked him for coppers as a joke, 'I have had to get the loan of forty pounds from a friend to hold carnival with.' Others around shouted, whistled, but always flattered him. One never knew when one might fall into his hands. He stood out among them all by his great height and the little cap oddly set on his big head, throwing ladlefuls of caraways at the carriages and pony-carts.

Slovenly, in her black dress, grown greenish, and her torn shawl-fringe, Carmela the cigar-maker had set herself at the corner of D'Affitto Lane, looking at the passing carriages with her hollow eyes, her fine fresh mouth working impatiently, the only feature that was still young in her worn face. Handfuls, ladlefuls of caraways often new from the balconies and the street, frequently hitting her face or back; but she only moved a little to avoid it, smiling at the annoyance, and cleaned her face with a corner of her shawl.

She was waiting there to see her lover, Raffaele, called Farfariello, pass. He was in a carriage with four others, all dressed alike; and, indeed, to get this dress, she had had to sell some copper pans, a chest of drawers, and two long branches of artificial flowers under a glass case, all things she was keeping for her marriage. How it tore her heart to sell these things, bought bit by bit by dint of hard saving!

But Raffaele had insisted on having forty francs—blood from a snail— because he was in despair at making a poor appearance among his friends; and she, getting white when she heard him swear, had sold all these things, and, like a fool, was quite pleased at heart when she handed him the money, because he had smiled and promised to take her and her mother to an inn at Campo the last Carnival Sunday if she took as much as even an *ambo* on Saturday. She, quite proud of this fantastic promise, kept down her heart's bitterness, and went as slovenly as a beggar that carnival day, her hair falling on her neck, without a sou in her pocket, to see her handsome lover passing proudly in a carriage, smoking a Naples cigar, in new clothes and hat on one side, with that intensely indifferent look characteristic of the *guappo*, or aspirants to it. She waited patiently, thinking only of him, not caring about her day's work, as there was a holiday at the factory. She quietly bóre all the pushing about that noon-day carnival that she took no part in, for she was wrapped up like a Buddhist in contemplation of her lover.

On the people went, on foot and in carriages, through the clouds of caraways, flowers, chocolates, through the shower of coloured paper from the upper stories, where, as they were not able to take part in the caraway war, they amused themselves in that way. The noise got clamorous, swaying about sonorously, rising to the skies that gentle scirocco day.

Carmela, confused by the noise and wild sights that noon-day, when Naples' rejoicing became epic, screwed up her eyes, not to lose sight of the two-horse carriages going along at a foot-pace, white with powder. Now and then one of the large cars appeared. There was the Parthenope Siren, a huge, pink lady with blonde hair hanging down. She was made of cardboard, and the body ended up in blue waves. This Siren was dragged along on a car full of men dressed as fish—oysters, carp, bull-heads. One car represented a merchant-vessel, a Tartana. The ship had rigging and sailors dressed in pink and white stripes, also in blue and white with long red caps. There was a car with eight or ten Jacks-in-the-box, from which gentlemen dressed in satin burst out in the midst of flowers. On one car all the Neapolitan masks were shown: Pulcinella, Tartaglia, Don Nicolai, Columbrina, Barilotto the clown, the *guappo*, the old woman—even to the newest mask of a pretentious, fast youth, Don Felice Scioscimocca.

When these cars passed, very slowly, almost quivering on their wheels, showering down caraway, confetti, and presents, they were much applauded. The Siren excited rather risky jokes; the Tartana was thought picturesque; the Jacks-in-the-box luxurious and smart; and the Naples masks were hailed with shouts of recognition and quick-flying dialogues from all the balconies in dialect, which the masks replied to in a lively way. There was one swaying movement from the top to the bottom of Toledo, both in the balconies and the crowds round the carriages.

Carmela looked and looked. She saw the two sisters Concetta and Caterina, pass in a carriage, the horses covered with flowers stuck in the shiny brass harness. She owed Donna Concetta thirty-five francs since ever so long, and managed to give her a few francs now and then just for interest, and she had often staked on the *small game* with Donna Caterina when she had not enough money for the Government Lottery, or, perhaps, only one penny left. The sisters were in full dress, the hair done up like a trophy on the top of the head with gold chains, and they wore heavy necklaces, pearl earrings, thick rings, keeping up their usual discreet, severe expression, casting oblique glances, and pursing up their lips. Two men were with them in workmen's Sunday attire, with shiny long hair, hat over the ear, in black jackets, with a spent cigar in a corner of the mouth. The four, silent and solemn, looked at each other now and then with serious, pleased glances of gratified pride, shaking their heads to get rid of the caraways off their hat-brims, smiling at the people who threw them. They looked to right and left haughtily, just like rich, common people.

Carmela bit her lips on seeing the two calm, ferocious heapers-up of other people's money, but immediately after the usual words came from her heart to her lips:

'It doesn't matter, it doesn't matter.'

But a very original car was coming down from the top of Toledo, raising a colossal laugh, from right to left, up and down. It was a great bed, with a bright pink cotton quilt, such as are used in Naples. It had an open canopy, with images of the Virgin and patron saints on the hangings. In bed, tucked in with white sheets, were two people, with huge pasteboard heads, one an old man in a night-cap, the other an old woman in a mob-cap. Very caressing, affected old people; they nodded their great heads, pulled the coverlids from each other with that selfish, shivering habit old people have; offering snuff to each other, bowing, sneezing, and stretching themselves out; greeting people in the balconies, thanking them for the shower of caraways they got, and shaking off the bed-clothes. It was not found out who they were, but they displayed that familiar caricature—a corner of a bedroom—without anyone thinking it too risky; for Southerners are used to sleeping in the open air, they live so much in public in this warm, easy-going country.

What about it? Everyone laughed. Even the people in Don Crescenzio's shop at Nunzio Corner, just beyond Carità Passage, laughed. It was really the lottery bank, No. 117, a shop usually shut from Saturday at noon till Tuesday, the crush beginning on Thursday up to Saturday at twelve o'clock.

Don Crescenzio, the lottery banker, a handsome man, with a red beard, worked there with his two lads, who were anything but lads: one, an old man of seventy, bent, half-blind, his nose always on the gambling register, made people say their lottery numbers three times, to make no mistakes, and wrote them very, very slowly. The other was a colourless type of no particular age; his face had undecided lines, his beard was an indefinite colour, one of those queer beings that are employed as witnesses by ushers, as middlemen at the pawn-shop, as distributors of handbills, and agents for furnished rooms. Don Crescenzio lorded it over his two *young men*. That Thursday he had quite changed his shop, putting up a gallery in it draped in white and crimson, to which he invited his best customers. Yes, they were all there, those that came every week to put down the best of their income—money hardly earned, either snatched from domestic economies, or got by cunning expedient, bold at first, and then shameful.

All were there at the lottery shop, turned into a stand. The Marquis di Formosa, Don Carlo Cavalcanti, with his lordly air; Dr. Trifari, red of face, hair, and beard, bloated as if he were going to burst, a suspicious look in his false blue eyes; Professor Colaneri, more than ever that day, clearly showed the indelible marks of a priest who has given up the Church; then Ninetto Costa, come from his club in Don Gennaro Parascandolo's company, felt drawn by a powerful, irresistible desire to his haunt; and other eight or ten—a court judge, a steward of a princely house, a sickly painter of saints, and Cozzolino the barber, who was a great Cabalist, down to the shoeblack Michele, in a corner on the ground, a hunchback and lame, his wrinkled old face full of irrestrained passion; beside him was Gaetano, the glove-cutter, more worn and pale than before, his eyes burning with discontent, uneasiness in every line of his face. Don Crescenzio's clients held their carnival in the shop dear to their ruling passion, and as they were tormented to buy caraways, they, too, threw them at the carriages, but mostly at the passers-by, among whom they found acquaintances sometimes. No one was surprised to see such different sorts of people together—a Marquis, a stock-broker, a court judge, a doctor, a professor, down to a workman. Carnival, carnival! The gentle popular madness had seized all brains; the warmish day, the bright colours, the whims in the thousands of vehicles passing, the clamour of a hundred thousand people overpowered even those suffering from another fever, which was pushed back for a time into a corner of the mind.

When Cesare Fragalà passed on foot, laughing and shouting, in a Russia-linen dust-cloak and travelling-cap, two long bags of caraways at his sides, which he emptied against balconies of his acquaintance and went filling again at every corner of the street from wandering salesmen, joking with everyone, fat, strong, and jovial, needing an outlet to his spirits—when he passed before Don Crescenzio's shop there was a chorus of greetings. Under the Rossi Palace, before his own balconies, he had already had half an hour's fight from below with his wife and her friends. Luisella, Carmela Naddeo, the Durantes, and the Antonaccis had thought Cesare's idea so original and he so charming that they had knocked him down by dint of caraway showers; he had been obliged to run away, laughing, keeping down his head, pulling his cap over his ears. There were noisy greetings, therefore, from Don Crescenzio's shop, and calls for him to come in. Was he not a customer, too, always hopeful of getting eighty thousand francs hard cash to open a shop in San Ferdinando? But Cesare was too satisfied wandering about alone, laughing and shrieking with everyone, buffeted by the caraways, red, panting with health and fun.

He went among the carts and carriages, borne by the crowd, through a burst of excitement, which the time of day made keener. The quietest did silly things now. Those standing on the cars, at first only merry, looked like so many demons. Raffaele, nicknamed Farfariello, loving Carmela's betrothed, passed in a carriage; to be seen better, he and his friends had made up their minds to sit on the roof. From there they waved white silk handkerchiefs, tied to sticks like flags, at the crowd. Alas! he did not see her, the girl who waited so many hours for him at the corner of D'Affitto Lane. She, having cried out, waved her arms and a bit of white stuff, felt stunned at the neglect, but whispered to herself as a consolation, 'It does not matter.'

But she still stayed there, hemmed in by that growing carnival frenzy. A thicker crowd closed in under the balcony where the lovely lady dressed as a Japanese was. She, getting excited, began to send down a shower of confetti by handfuls and boxfuls, as if she had a store in the house, a servant handing them to her. A shout of rogues and enthusiastic common folk rose to the skies, whilst she from above, quite serious, but a pink flame in her cheeks, recklessly flung down confetti, sweets, and chocolate-boxes. On the balcony draped with blue and silver net, the exalted personage's son had thought of the joke of tying a bottle of champagne, a game pie or a big chocolate-box, to a long rod, and letting it down to the level of the crowd's outstretched hands, pulling it up, dancing it about, amidst the longing cries, uplifted hands, and open mouths of the people below, until a shout of triumph announced some lucky one had carried off the prize of the new Cockayne. The rod was pulled up, and the young fellows, who had taken a mad fancy to the game, tied on some other eatable or drinkable—a bottle of bourdeaux, a cheese wrapped in silver paper, or a bag of confetti, and the game started again, with an unutterable row and obstruction to traffic. The men in the cars now, having taken in new stores as the evening went on, danced, sang, and threw things, behaving like demons.

It was at this most exciting time of the day that a new cart came out from a side-street of Toledo, arriving late, the horses drawing it at a foot-pace. It was queer and fantastic, being a philosopher's chemical laboratory, where a wretched old Faust sat cursing all human things in a frozen, melancholy way. It formed a dark room, with two shelves of books, a furnace, and an alchemist's retort, and there was an open Koran on a carved wooden desk. A bent old man in a black velvet skull-cap, with a long yellowy-white beard, tottered about the car, throwing boxes of sweets shaped like books, retorts, alembics, furnaces, to the crowd in the streets and balconies, each having a figure of Mephistopheles. But they were good sweets. Then a chimerical touch got into the carnival fury. The sorcerer's car seemed quite supernatural. The old man, whom the laughing women in the balconies called the Devil, his bald head in the skull-cap quivering, threw out things, magically producing them from beneath the car. Now and then amid the clamour of the populace a shrill voice called out to the decrepit sorcerer, 'Give us lottery numbers! give us tips!'

Having got to San Ferdinando, Faust's car turned to go back the same way up Toledo, when a most curious, indescribable thing happened. The old man took out of a copper alembic, beside the boxes of sweets, long, narrow strips of yellow paper and threw them to the crowd, who rushed furiously on them. A shout went before, and followed Faust's car, 'These are *storni, storni!*'

To carry out a new, splendid, eccentric generosity pleasing to the people, the old man threw lottery-tickets of two or three numbers, ready paid for next Saturday, at two sous each. They are called *storni*. He nobly threw handfuls of them to the people, laughing in his thick, white beard, forgetting he was old, holding his head back with ferocious gaiety.

What a shout everywhere, from the streets and windows up to the sky paling at sunset! What a lengthened shout of desire and enthusiasm! The whole population raised their hands and arms as if to seize the promised land. They cast themselves on the ground and kicked each other, so as to snatch a lottery-ticket, with its conditional promise of ten or two hundred francs gain. What joyous excitement among men, women, boys, rich and poor, needy and comfortably off! What an irresistible rush, that from holy fear respected the sorcerer's car; they made a triumph for him of glorious shouts from one end of Toledo to the other! But when he had thrown ten thousand tickets to the crowd he disappeared, no one knew where or how.

Antonio Amati met Margherita the maid on the staircase as she was going in, too, rather tired. Brusquely, as if he would have preferred not to speak, perhaps, he asked her:

'How is your mistress?'

'She is better,' the old domestic said in a low voice. 'Why have you not been to see her, sir?'

'I have a lot to do,' the doctor muttered, without, however, knocking at his door.

'That is true; but you are so kind, sir.'

'And then there was no need of me,' he added in a hesitating tone.

'Who can tell?' Margherita retorted in a still lower and mysterious voice. 'Why don't you come in now, sir?'

'I will come,' he said, with his head down, as if he was giving in to a superior will.

She put a key in the lock and opened it, going before the doctor into the quiet house, right on to the drawing-room, and he, though accustomed to keep down his own impressions, felt at once the cold silence and emptiness of the big room. He found the girl in black before him, smiling vaguely, holding out her hand—a long, cold, tiny one, which he kept a minute in his, more as a doctor than a friend.

'Are you quite well again?'

He spoke in a low voice, feeling the oppressive surroundings.

'Not altogether,' she said in her clear, tired voice. 'I had another fainting-fit one night; but very short—at least, I think so.'

'Did no one come to your help?' he said regretfully.

'No; no one knew about it; it was at night, in my own room.... It doesn't matter,' she added, with a slight smile.

'Why did you not go to the country?'

'My father hates the country,' she said. 'I will not leave him here alone.'

'But why do you not go out? It is carnival to-day; why did you not go to see it? Do you want to die of melancholy?'

'Signora Fragalà did ask me, but I hardly know her. I think I would have had to wear a mask. My father does not like such things; he is right.'

She spoke in a gentle, pretty voice, with a tired sound in it. Amati, who had been working all that day by sick-beds while others enjoyed the carnival, felt rested by that harmonious voice and the tired, delicate calmness of the young girl. They were alone, facing each other—around them was a great silence; they hardly looked at each other, but they spoke as if their souls had long lived together, in joy and sorrow.

'Where were you a little ago?' Antonio Amati asked brusquely.

'I was in the chapel,' Bianca Maria answered, taking no offence at the question.

'Do you pray a great deal?'

'Not enough,' she replied, raising her eyes heavenwards.

'Why do you pray so much?'

'I must do it.'

'You don't sin,' the unbeliever muttered, trying to make a joke of it.

'One never knows,' she said gravely. 'One must pray for those that don't pray themselves.'

So saying, she gave him a passing glance. He bent his head.

'You spend too many hours in the cold church. It will do you harm.'

'I don't think so; and, then, what does it matter?'

'Don't say that,' interrupting her quickly.

'Few things can hurt me,' she replied in a tone he understood and did not want to inquire into.

'Let us go and see the carnival from Signora Fragalà's windows. She asked me, too;' and he got up promptly to carry her off.

'Let us stay here,' Bianca gently retorted. 'Here at least there is peace. Don't you think this calm and silence good for one, too?'

'You are right,' Amati owned, sitting down again quite subdued.

'My father has gone out with his friends to see the carnival,' she went on quietly. 'Everyone in the palace is out on the balconies that look on Toledo; no noise reaches here, you see.'

They looked at each other frankly. That strange hour of unconsciousness, when he saved her, and she knew he was saving her, had set up something like an inward life between them. What she felt was a humble need of protection, help, and counsel; his feeling was a very tender pity. He could not keep back a question that rose to his mind.

'Is it true you wish to be a nun?' he asked in rather a choked voice.

'I would like it,' she said simply.

'Why should you?'

'Just because,' she replied with a woman's favourite answer.

'Why should you be a nun? No one wants to be a nun nowadays. Why should you do it?'

'Because, if there is one single person in the world that should go into a convent, it is I; because I have neither desires, nor hopes, nor anything before me. As that is so, you see, I must at least have prayer across this void desert and the desolation that comes before death.'

'Don't say that—don't say it!' he implored, as if for the first time fatality had breathed on his energy and destroyed it.

CHAPTER VI
DONNA CATERINA AND DONNA CONCETTA

The two sisters, Donnas Caterina and Concetta, were sitting opposite each other at the dinner-table. They were eating silently, with their eyes down; and occasionally they bent down to wipe their lips on a corner of the tablecloth that was all marked with bluish wine. A large deep-rimmed dish stood on the table between the two, full of macaroni cooked in oil, salted anchovies, and garlic, all fried lightly in an earthen pan and thrown over the boiling pasta; the two women plunged their forks now and then into the shiny oily macaroni, put some in their plates, and began to eat again. There was a big loaf of white underbaked bread, too—the *tortano*: they broke off bits with their hands to eat the macaroni with. A greeny-blue glass bottle full of reddish wine, that made bluish reflections, stood on the tablecloth; big glasses, and a salt-cellar, also of glass—nothing else. The sisters used leaden forks, and coarse knives with black handles; they sometimes broke off a bit of bread and dipped it in the fried oil at the bottom of the dish. Caterina, who was the roughest and saw fewest people—she lived furtively almost—put her bread into the macaroni dressing with her fingers; Concetta, who was more refined, from always going about and seeing people, put the bread neatly on her fork to dip it in the garlic, and nibbled at it after examining it. At one point, indeed, Concetta, finding a burnt bit of garlic, put it aside with a frown. Otherwise the sisters were exactly alike in gestures, way of speaking, and style of dress, though not so much so in features. Both had their hair dressed by the same woman at two sous each: it was drawn up to the top of the head, the coil fastened by big sham tortoise-shell pins, and the fringe slightly powdered over the forehead. Both wore the dress of well-to-do Naples common folk—a petticoat with no jacket, merely a trimmed bodice, that keeps the Spanish name *baschina*; and they never went without a thick gold chain round the neck—it was the sign of their great power—and they wore high felt boots, with noisy wooden heels. It being dinner-hour, they had left their usual work—a great coverlet of calico, pink one side and green the other, stuffed with cotton-wool—stretched over a big loom, where they stitched at it in wheels, stars, and lozenges, working quickly, one on each side of it, their heads down and noses on the pattern, pulling the needle out and in monotonously. The loom was pushed into a corner; the displaced chairs were noticeable. Now a little servant of fourteen came in, red-haired, white-faced, and marked with freckles, carrying the second course—a bit of Basilicata cheese, like a dry cream cheese, called *provola*, and two big sticks of celery. She glanced at Donna Caterina to know what to do with the macaroni left in the dish.

'Keep two bits for Menichella,' said the holder of the *small game*, as she cut a big slice of cheese.

'Yes, ma'am,' the girl said as she went out.

Menichella was a poor old thing of sixty; her son, in the Municipal Guard, had been killed in a fight with Camorrists in Pignasecca Square by a revolver-shot in the stomach. She lived on alms, and every Friday arrived at the Esposito sisters' house, where she got a hot dish, half a loaf of bread, and some scraps. The Espositos did this out of devotion to our lovely Lady of Sorrows, whose day is Friday. On Wednesday they gave the same alms to a blind beggar called Guarattelle, because for many years he kept a puppet-show; this charity they dedicated to the Virgin of the Carmine, Wednesday being her day. On Monday, too, they fed a deserted boy of ten, that the whole Rosariello di Porta Medina Road were taken up about and fed, while the Esposito sisters helped him that one day for the sake of souls in Purgatory, their day being Monday. A beggar seldom knocked at their door any day without getting something. 'Do it for St. Joseph; his day has come round.' 'The Holy Trinity be praised! to-day is Sunday; give alms.' Something to eat, a glass of wine, some scraps, beggars always carried off—money never. The sisters had too great a respect for sous to give them away. It was better charity, they explained, to give food, than encourage vice by giving money.

The beggars stayed on the landing; the sisters never let them in, fearing always for the valuables in the house; they used to carry out the dish of macaroni, vegetables, or salad. Sometimes the beggar ate it on the stairs, muttering blessings. They had now eaten the smoked cheese and bread, slowly, moving their jaws rather voluptuously, tearing the celery off in strips, and munching it noisily, like fruit, to take the taste of oil out of their mouths. When they were done, they kept still for a little, gazing at the blue stains on the tablecloth, with their hands in their laps, silently digesting and making long mental calculations, as women of business. The servant-girl, Peppina, carried off everything in a trice; the clatter of her old shoes was heard in the kitchen next door, as she went backwards and forwards to wash a few plates, stopping now and then to turn her macaroni in the pan; she had set it to fry again, seeing it was cold.

Now the sisters got up, shook the crumbs out of their laps, and went to take their place at the loom again, bending over it, the right hand, covered with rings, rising methodically, the left held under the loom, to stitch through. There was a ring at the bell; the sisters glanced at each other, and quickly took up their work. Besides what they earned from it, it served as a screen, morally and physically.

Two girls, dressmakers, came in, pushing each other forward. The first, the bolder, was Antonietta, who worked with a dressmaker in Santa Chiara Street, the same that went to buy lunch for Nannina and herself at the wine-seller's opposite the lottery office. Both of them were, wretchedly dressed, in poor woollen skirts, a gaudy but shabby jacket of another colour, and a little black shawl, which they liked to let slip down on their arms, to show their bust; a bunch of red ribbon was tied at the neck. Nannina, the smallest, was a relation of the Espositos; she had a holy terror of her aunts, with their money and jewels, for they always received her with pensive and intentional coldness. Still, they let her kiss their hands.

The two girls were still standing near the loom, looking on at this alert industry as if they were put out.

'Have you not gone to work to-day?' Donna Caterina asked Nannina.

'I have been at it,' the girl at once volubly answered, being prodded by Antonietta's elbow. 'But our mistress sent us to buy some things near here, and, as this friend of mine wants to ask a favour from you, we came....'

'Who do you want this favour from?' said Donna Concetta, raising her head from her work.

'From you, aunt,' stammered the niece.

'You don't say so!' her aunt exclaimed, in an ironical tone, smiling and shaking her head.

The girls said nothing; they looked at each other: from the start the thing was going badly.

Caterina, as she took no interest in the subject now, cut the tacking with a pair of scissors, where it had been already stitched, which covered her maroon bodice with white threads.

'Have you lost your tongues? What is it about?' Donna Concetta asked, laughing.

'Well, now I will tell you, ma'am,' the blonde began, biting her lips to make them red. 'I would like a new dress for Easter, a pair of boots, and cotton to make three or four chemises. If I was frugal, and made them myself, after my day's work is done, forty francs would do. I have not got it;

it would take a year to save it. Knowing you are good and kind to poor folk, I had an idea you might lend me these forty francs.'

'It was not a good idea of yours,' said the money-lender freezingly.

'Why? I can pay off the debt at so much a week. I earn twenty-five sous a day; I don't owe a penny to anyone. Ask Nannina; she is my guarantee.'

'Nannina ought to find a security for herself,' Donna Concetta grumbled. 'But why do you need this dress? Is what you have on not enough? If one has no money, get no dresses. When my sister and I had no means, we got no clothes. You are all mad, you girls, nowadays!'

'Aunt, aunt, do her this favour; she has a lover, and she is ashamed to go ill-dressed,' the niece begged for her friend.

'I have had a lover too,' Donna Concetta answered; 'he was not ashamed when I was ill-dressed.'

'Men nowadays are quite different,' Antonietta murmured. 'So do me this favour.'

'I don't know you, my dear.'

'I work for Cristina Gagliardi, at No. 18, Santa Chiara, the first-floor. I live at No. 3, Strettola di Porto; you can make inquiries.'

Silence followed, and the girls again gave each other an alarmed look.

'At most—at most,' said Donna Concetta, looking up, 'I can give you stuff to make a dress on credit, and cotton for the chemises.... I will ask a merchant that knows me—a good man; but you will pay dearer for your clothes.'

'No matter, it doesn't matter,' Antonietta quickly interrupted; 'do so.'

'What colour is the stuff to be?' Donna Concetta asked maternally.

'Navy blue or bottle green; I like navy blue best.'

'It will suit you best—navy blue; you look well in it,' said Nannina, in an important way.

'It does not discolour so easily,' Donna Concetta settled it by saying. 'How many yards do you need?'

The girl counted to herself, moved her fingers as if she was measuring, looked at her figure, and counted over again.

'Ten metres—yes, that would be enough.'

'Ten metres; Jesus! so you want to be in the fashion.'

'Donna Concetta, be forbearing,' Antonietta answered smilingly.

'Very good—very good; for each chemise four metres is needed—sixteen in all.'

'And the shoes?' the girl asked hesitatingly.

'I know no shoemaker, my dear.'

'You will give me the rest of the forty francs in money?' the sewing girl risked saying.

'Listen, my dear,' said Donna Concetta: 'I am going to-morrow, or Saturday, to the dressmaker's to ask if you really get over a franc a day, and if you have taken any money in advance. Then I'll arrange with the dressmaker that, instead of giving you your whole pay for the week, she keeps back two francs for me as interest on the forty francs.'

'Two francs?' the girl cried out, alarmed at this long story.

'Of course. I should get four, a sou a week for each franc; but you are a poor girl, and I really wish to help you. The dressmaker gives me the two francs for interest. You pay off the rest of the debt as it suits you, five or three francs at a time. Do you understand?'

'Yes, ma'am, yes,' the terrified girl cried out.

'The quicker you pay the better for you, and it will suit me. However, I warn you, if you were to get the dressmaker to pay you in advance, go away, or play any trick of the kind, I'll come to you, my dear, and let you see who Concetta Esposito is. I would think nothing of going to the galleys for my heart's blood.... Have I made it plain?'

'Yes, ma'am, yes,' Antonietta stammered, with tears in her eyes.

'There is still time for you not to do it,' Donna Concetta ended up icily, bending down again to stitch the coverlet.

'No, no!' the girl screamed out—'whatever you like. Promise me to come to-morrow to Santa Chiara Road.'

'We see each other to-morrow,' said Donna Concetta, taking leave of her.

'You will bring the things and the money?'

'I must think over it.'

'Good-bye, aunt,' Nannina murmured, pale and more frightened than her friend.

'The Virgin go with you,' answered the Espositos in a chorus, beginning to work again.

The girls went off quite silently, with their heads down, not able to speak or smile. A woman coming up, hurriedly, knocked against them; and with a quick 'Excuse me!' she went to ring at the Espositos' door. It was Carmela, the cigar-girl, with her big, sorrowful eyes and worn face. Before going into the house she sighed deeply, and her face flushed.

'May I come in?' she said from the lobby, in a weak voice.

'Come in,' was the answer from inside. 'Is it you, good soul?' said Concetta, on recognising her; 'are you really come to give me back that money? your conscience pricked you at last? Give it over here.'

'You are joking, Donna Concetta,' said the poor thing, with a pale smile. 'If I had thirty-four francs, I would give as many leaps in the air.'

'It is thirty-seven and a half francs, with last week's interest,' the money-lender coldly corrected her.

'As you like: who is denying it? As you say, it is thirty-seven and a half, I am sure you are right.'

'You have brought the interest, at least?'

'Nothing, nothing,' the girl said desperately, holding down her head. 'I am eaten up by misery: I have got to earning a franc and a half a day; now I might live like a lady, but— —'

'Why do you waste your money?' asked Donna Concetta, giving in to her fad of preaching prudence to her debtors. 'You are a beast, that is what you are!'

'But why,' Carmela cried out desperately—'why should I not give a bit of bread to my old mother? When my sister is dying of hunger with her three children, and one of them wasting away piteously, can I refuse her half a franc? When my brother-in-law, Gaetano, has nothing to smoke, for all his vices, should I deny him a few sous? With what heart could I do it?'

'It is Raffaele that sucks you out—it is Raffaele!' the money-lender sang out, threading a needle with red cotton.

'What about that?' the girl cried out, throwing out her arms; 'he was born to be a gentleman. In the meanwhile, if I don't pay the landlord on Monday, he will turn me out. I owe him thirty francs: but I might at least give him ten! If you would just do me this charity!'

'You are mad, my dear.'

'Donna Concetta, what are ten francs to you? I'll give them back, you know: I have never taken a farthing from anyone. Don't have me thrown on the streets, ma'am. Do it for the sake of your dead in paradise!'

'No, no, no!' sang out the seamstress.

'Listen, look here,' the other went on sorrowfully: 'these earrings I am wearing my godmother paid seventeen francs for; I give them to you—I have nothing else. You will give me them back when I give you the ten francs.'

'I never take a pawn,' Donna Concetta replied, glancing at the earrings.

'But it is not a pawn; it is a favour you are doing me. If I were to pawn it, I would get five or six francs; they would take the interest beforehand, with the money for the ticket, the box, and the witness, and only three or four francs would be left. Do it only this once, ma'am—the Virgin from heaven preserve you!' She convulsively took out her rather worn earrings, rubbed them with a corner of her apron, and put them gently on the coverlet, still looking at them earnestly, taking leave of them. Donna Concetta took them with a scornful grimace, and glanced at her sister, who just raised her head and signed 'Yes,' with a wink. Donna Concetta got up stiffly; without saying anything, she carried the earrings into the next room, where the sisters slept; a noise of keys in locks was heard, an opening and shutting of strong boxes, with silent intervals. Then Donna Concetta came in again. She carried two rolls of yellow paper in her hand.

'They are sous: count them,' she said shortly, putting them down before Carmela.

'It does not matter-they are sure to be right,' said the poor little thing, trembling with emotion. 'The Eternal Father should give it back to you in health, the kindness you do me.'

'Very good,' Donna Concetta finished up with, sitting down again to work. 'But I warn you I'll sell the earrings if you don't pay.'

'Never fear,' Carmela murmured as she went off.

For a little the sisters were alone, stitching.

'The earrings are worth twelve francs in gold,' said Caterina. She had sharp ears.

'Yes,' said Concetta; 'but Carmela will pay; she is a good girl.'

Again they heard the bell tinkle.

'It sounds like the midwife's bell,' Caterina remarked.

A dragging noise was heard, the sound of a box put down in the corner of the stair, and Michele, the shoeblack, came in with his hip up, as if he was still carrying his block. He greeted them in the Spanish style, saying, 'La vostra buona grazia' (I am your humble servant), whilst the thousand wrinkles on his rickety boy's face, grown old, seemed to breathe out malice. The sisters looked patiently at him, waiting till he spoke.

'Gaetano Galiero, the glove-cutter, sends me— —'

'Fine honest fellow he is!' exclaimed Donna Concetta, putting a strip of paper in her thimble—it had got too large.

'If you don't make people speak, you can never get to understand each other,' the hunchback rejoined philosophically. 'Gaetano is under great obligations to you; but you are a fine woman, not wanting in judgment, and you will forgive his failings. What does not happen in a year comes the day you least expect it. Gaetano is here with the money.'

'Yes, yes,' the sisters said, grinning.

'You will see him afterwards. But I have come to speak of an affair of my own. I, thank God, work at a better trade than Gaetano does; I stand beside the Café de Angelis in Carità Square. I don't say it out of boasting, but I polish the shoes of the best nobility in Naples. I can earn what I like; I laugh at ill fortune. When it rains, I stand under the archway of the café door; the dirtier it is in the streets, the more shoes I polish. My good woman, if I had a clear head, I would be a gentleman now. But now, to carry out a big affair that may bring me my carriage, I need a little money; and as you oblige people that way, I have come to propose the business to you. Forty francs would do for me; I would pay it off by three francs a week until I have managed the *combination*; for then I will give you back capital, interest, and a handsome present.'

'Don't put yourself about,' said Donna Concetta ironically.

'If you won't lend me money, who do you lend to?' the hunchback asked audaciously. 'If I stand all day in front of the café, I earn two francs, do you know. Not even a barber's lad can say as much. So that stand is my fortune, my shop; if I go away from it, I don't earn a half-penny, so I can't run away. Do you see? Ask the coffee-house-keeper who Michele is. Your money is safe in my hands. You will hear all about me from the café-owner.'

'If he guarantees you, I'll give you the money,' Donna Concetta said at once.

'In that case, he would give it himself' the hunchback objected. 'No, no, Michele has no need of a guarantee. Come to-morrow, Saturday, at nine, to the café-owner; you will hear what he says; you will willingly give me sixty instead of forty francs. I am an honest man; I am subject to public scrutiny.'

'Good; we see each other to-morrow. You know what the interest is?' said Donna Concetta.

'Whatever you like,' the hunchback gallantly answered; 'you can have a cup of coffee, too, and a roll inside: I am master at the coffee-house! Can I do anything for you?'

'We wish for your prayers always,' the two women said in a low tone, as he was going away. After working a little, Caterina observed:

'You said yes to him too soon.'

'I will make the coffee-house-keeper guarantee him. He is a hunchback, too; that brings luck,' Donna Concetta replied.

'If it brings luck, it ought to bring an end to this hard life of ours,' Caterina began again. She liked to complain of her luck.

'Oh,' the other sighed, 'we have no man to give us a helping hand, ever; so we have to do justice for ourselves always. Ciccillo and Alfonso are simpletons. It is no use....'

'What can we do?' sighed the other.

The two sisters gave up working, let their hands fall idle on the red coverlet, and began to think of their secret sorrow—the tormenting pain they confessed to no one—of their betrothed lovers, two good workmen, brothers, at the arsenal, Jannacone by name, who loved them, but would not marry them, either of the two, because of their trade. The struggle between love and money had gone on for three years, but Ciccillo and Alfonso Jannacone would not hear of marrying a gambler or a money-lender; the whole arsenal would have taunted them. They were good workmen, rather simple, very silent, who did not spend their day's wages; they had some savings, and came to spend the evening with the two sisters. Obstinate on that idea, one of the few that got into their heads, neither love nor avarice could overcome it. Several times the sisters, being keen on gain and bitterly offended at that refusal, had quarrelled with their lovers and chased them out of the house; but only for a short time: peace was made, Concetta and Caterina naturally promising to give over their business. The women must have made a lot of money, but they never spoke of it, and, in spite of their love for Alfonso and Ciccillo Jannacone, they themselves put off the marriages so as to gain still more money, not knowing how to break through that round of money-lending business. They did not wish to give up old loans, and could not resist making new ones; they did not understand why their lovers were so ashamed, and complained of it as an injustice. The sisters thought themselves humane to lend money at usury; to give lottery tickets at a sou or two seemed an act of charity to them, because the Naples poor—skinned and flayed as they were when they took money from Concetta to give it to Caterina and the Government—thanked and blessed them with tears. When they were quite alone, in expansive moments, the two complained of their fate; anyone else but the Jannacone brothers would have been happy enough to have such industrious, hard-working wives with dowries. But the workmen would not given in; they persisted they would never marry unless that way of gaining money was given up. Ciccillo especially, Caterina's betrothed, was hard as a stone; indeed, he said to her sometimes: 'Caterina, one day or other you'll go to prison.'

'I'll pay for bail and get out. Then the lawyer will get me off.'

She knew the law and its intrigues.

'If you go to prison, you don't see my face again,' Ciccillo retorted, lighting his cigar.

Yes, when they were alone the sisters despaired. But love of money was so strong, it made them put off the time for the double marriage. The two workmen waited patiently, slowly buying furniture with their savings to set up house together, as they never left each other.

'Wait till Easter,' the sisters said, thinking of ending up all their affairs by then.

'Good; at Easter,' the brothers agreed.

'We will be ready by September,' said they in April, being more than ever involved in a network of sordid business.

'In September, then,' the workmen complied.

Always when they were alone the women complained of being badly treated by Fate, and of being misunderstood by the men they loved, ending up with: 'Ciccillo and Alfonso are fools.'

But they were not long alone that day, either. The wretched trade went on till evening. There came a painter of saints, so far an artist that he painted the face, hands, and feet of all the wooden and stucco saints in Naples and its neighbourhood's thousand churches: a sickly man, who asked for money, and only got it on condition he brought a statuette of the Immaculate Conception in blue, covered with stars, next day, that Madonna being Concetta the money-lender's patron. Annarella, Carmela's sister, came in to ask for a loan, being desperate: 'just two francs for the day, just as a charity.' She wanted to make a little broth for her sick child. A horrible scene followed: the women would not believe her; she just wanted to fool them again, for Gaetano and she had a big debt, and were not ashamed to take poor folk's blood and not give it back. Annarella screamed, wept, and cried out that she would go and get her baby, all burning with fever, to show to them. A stone would pity him. Then she sobbed out that they said what was quite true; but to pity the poor little thing, who was not to blame, and now that he was weaned, she could take another half-day service, which the Virgin would help her to find. At last, as Concetta felt bored, to get rid of the crying and weeping she gave her the two francs, cursing and taking her oath they were the last, as true as it was Friday in March—perhaps the day our Lord died, as it is not known what Friday in March Jesus died on. Other people, either embarrassed, furious, or sorrowful, came to pay up old interest, to offer goods in pledge, or ask for more money. The debtors went on from humility to bitterness, from threats to beseeching, from solemn promises to mean tricks. Concetta continued working opposite her sister through the disputes, quarrels, and threats till evening came. She never got tired, and always had an effective retort ready or some lucid remark, finding out a good or bad payer at once. Only for one neatly-dressed, discreet caller, shaved like a good class of servant, she got up and went into the next room, where they chattered in a low tone for some time. The usual noise of keys creaking in the locks, and opening and shutting of strong boxes, was heard; the servant went out, still looking reserved, followed by Concetta.

'Is that the Marquis di Formosa's steward?' Caterina asked when he had gone.

'Yes, it is,' said Concetta, without adding more.

That hard, fatiguing Friday came to an end. Now it was getting dark the sisters had given up stitching the coverlet. Caterina, for Saturday, her great day, got ready some thick registers, written in shapeless characters, all ciphers, which she understood very well. She leant over it under the oil-lamp, thinking whilst her lips moved; and Concetta, seeing her deep in her important weekly work, kept silence out of respect to that sagacious preparation, feeling sure that next day money would be flowing in to them.

CHAPTER VII
DON GENNARO PARASCANDOLO'S BUSINESS

With the odorous smoke of a Tocos cigarette filling the little room, Don Gennaro Parascandolo was deeply wrapped up in the study of his little pocket-book, turning over the pages of a ledger, and comparing the long rows of figures in it with the dark, enigmatic ciphers in the note-book; then he took the pen and wrote something occasionally—one word or a figure—on the full side of the ledger.

He was working very placidly in that little room of his flat in San Giacomo Street, opposite the door of the Exchange. He had rented it from time immemorial, and he called it the *study*; there he began, unravelled, and finished all his business, with a discretion and secrecy he kept up even with his wife. She was far off, isolated for whole days in that sad, solemn, splendid suite of rooms in the Rossi Palace. When it was said Don Gennaro Parascandolo was at his *study*, all was said. Those who said it and those who heard it felt respectful terror; a fearful vision of riches always increasing, a magical flow of money running to money by enchantment, rose before them. The study was the place where Don Gennaro Parascandolo, strong, wise, audacious, and cold in his audacity, made his fortune grow by leaps and bounds. It was composed of two rooms: one big one, with two balconies, was quite full of valuable things gathered in a queer way—pictures by good artists, foreign furniture, gilt-bronze candelabra, curious antique pendulums, rolls of carpet and of linen-cloth, terra-cotta statuettes, even a trophy of antique and modern arms.

It was quite a museum, that room. Salvatore, Don Gennaro's confidential servant, spent half the day trying to keep it clean, and it required the greatest care not to spoil or break anything. Occasionally, some rarity left the museum, either sold advantageously, exchanged for another, or given away in a fit of calculated generosity. But the empty place was soon filled by a new article, or by some of the things heaped on each other in the strange museum.

When Don Gennaro was alone, he sometimes opened his writing-room door and stood on the threshold, smoking his everlasting cigarette, to give a look over what he called his *omnibus*. But he did not venture to go in, the accumulation was so great. The other room was prettily enough furnished with the respectable pleasant luxury of easy-chairs, sofas, small tables with smoking accessories, and a writing-desk that seemed placed there purposely to make the name 'study' appropriate. The hangings were bright, but not gaudy; on the desk were dainty knickknacks that Don Gennaro Parascandolo often played with. Whoever came in there felt calmed; even if he had an incurable sorrow in his mind, he was reconciled to existence for a time. Don Gennaro Parascandolo's own genial face, clouded sometimes by melancholy, his lively, frank manner, managed to give a benignant look to the surroundings that overcame all fears, difficulties, and prejudices, and gave a weak, morally defenceless guest into the host's hands, vanquished beforehand. The whole round of Don Gennaro Parascandolo's business was regulated by the minute hieroglyphics in his pocket-book, and a ledger thickly written in also with names, ciphers, and remarks.

Whenever a caller was announced, Don Gennaro, without hurrying, shut up the ledger in the safe, and put the note-book back in his pocket; every trace of business disappeared. An inkstand of gilt bronze and rock crystal, shaped like a jockey's cap, with racing accessories, made a good show on the desk, as well as a silver paper-weight like a book, with five seals made of old guineas, an ash-tray shaped like a woman's shoe, and a long, carved ivory Japanese wand that Don Gennaro trifled with.

So that Friday in March, after breakfast, he went on smoking his Tocos cigarette, gazing at the smoke; but when the faithful Salvatore, clean-shaven and in black, like a high-class servant, a discreet, silent fellow, came to say Signor Cesare Fragalà wished to come in, Don Gennaro quickly shut up the ledger and put the note-book in his pocket.

'With your permission,' said Cesare Fragalà, coming in smiling.

'My honoured patron, how are the wife and child?'

'Very well indeed, Don Gennaro. They are Fragalàs, a strong house, with no bad luck. You keep well, do you not?'

'Quite well; but Naples bores me. Cesare, this is a beggarly country. In a week I go off to Nice and Monte Carlo; after that I go to Paris.'

'Do you play at Monte Carlo?' Fragalà asked, with a scrutinizing look.

'Yes, a little. I often win; I have luck; I am learning to play.'

'How will that serve you?'

'It is good to know everything,' Parascandolo answered modestly. 'Have you never been there?'

'No,' said Cesare thoughtfully, 'I have a wife and daughter; still, it is a fine thing to gain twenty-five or a hundred thousand francs in an evening!' One could read in his eyes, that filled at once with melancholy avarice, a great passion for heavy, immediate gains, depending on luck, and for the most part unlawful.

'What would you do with it?' asked Don Gennaro, taking another cigarette, and offering Cesare one from an elegant engraved-silver Russian cigar-case.

'What would I do with it? First of all I would let fifty thousand melt away to enjoy life a little with my friends. I am not selfish, and fifty thousand would do to open a shop with in San Ferdinando Square. I will never gain it in the San Spirito shop,' Cesare ended up low-spiritedly.

'Still, in the carnival you must have made great profits,' said Don Gennaro slowly, shaking off his cigar-ash.

'Yes, yes, enough! but Monte Carlo, or something else, is needed; if not, one must vegetate, and Agnesina's dowry won't be ready. Then I am always pushed to it—so many calls.... Why, yesterday I should have given you back those five hundred francs you lent me without security—you know I am always punctual—but I could not.'

'For one day it does not matter,' Don Gennaro said coldly, setting his face like a stone the moment Cesare spoke of the debt, gazing at his cigar-smoke as if not to look his friend in the face.

'But I can't even pay you to-day,' said Cesare quickly, as if he wanted to get rid of his worry all at once. 'I have had to take a lot of sugar out of bond, and then——'

Don Gennaro, quite indifferent to all this chatter, said not a word.

'Be neighbourly, and complete the favour. I have a little bill due to-morrow,' Fragalà said, passing through a sharp momentary agony; 'it is five hundred francs, and I have not got it. You might lend them to me, and I will give you a thousand francs next Saturday ... it is a great favour ... and you can be sure of my being punctual.'

'I can't,' Don Gennaro said icily.

'Why, you have the money,' Cesare cried out ingenuously.

'Of course; but I can't lend it.'

'Then, you think I am not solvent?'

'Not at all; it is to carry out a rule. With intimate friends and relations, people like you, I always lend five hundred francs; often, nearly always, I get it back again. Then I willingly lend it a second time; but once it has not been paid I never lend any more, so I can only lose five hundred francs.'

'But I am to give you back a thousand,' said the other in alarm.

'He who can't give back five hundred is very unlikely to give back a thousand. A man that fails to keep his word once may do it again,' said Don Gennaro ponderously.

'Still, I did not believe you would refuse such a favour to a friend,' Cesare muttered. 'You put me into great embarrassment.'

'I think I do well not to give you that money,' said Parascandolo, opening a gold matchbox like Dellachà's paper ones, with figure-painting on it. 'I think you are going a bad road; you frequent very queer company....'

'I have done some idiotic things, I allow,' said Cesare, with his big-boy's honesty; 'but I did it with good intentions. Besides,' he added, as if speaking to himself, 'that Pasqualino De Feo is always needing some hundred francs. He is a poor man, with no profession nor trade. The spirits torment him— beat him at night. I have to have Masses said and prayers to appease them; if not, they drag him to death. If I have thrown away some hundred francs, I had my reasons. This business with spirits is important! You are clever, and have travelled a lot; but if you knew all, you would see it is worth knowing about.'

'It may be,' nodded Don Gennaro assentingly; 'but you are going a bad road.'

'No, no!' cried out Cesare; 'something must be settled. Either in or out. Perhaps we will get it this week—that is to say, to-morrow; or it may be necessary to sacrifice some more, next week, and then win. Really, you should oblige me,' he added, going back to his trouble.

'I can't,' retorted Don Gennaro.

'As a fact, I am an honest trader: anyone would do business with me!' Cesare called out, beginning to get angry.

'If it is business, that is another thing,' said Don Gennaro, giving in suddenly.

'Well, let us treat it as business,' said Cesare, calming down at once.

Then Don Gennaro quietly opened the safe and drew out a blank bill, of a thousand francs' value. Taking a finely-carved wooden pen, with a gold nib, he wrote the sum in figures and words, and asked, without raising his head:

'To fall due in a month?'

'Yes, in a month,' agreed Fragalà. Don Gennaro handed the promissory note to him. It was headed 'Domenico Mazzocchi.' 'Domenico Mazzocchi— who is that?' asked Fragalà, astounded.

'He is the capitalist I work for,' Parascandolo answered icily. Seeing that after Fragalà signed he was going to put down his dwelling-house, he stopped him warningly. 'Put down the address of the shop.'

'Why so?'

'In business and commercial affairs it is better to take action at the firm's address.'

Fragalà felt a chill down his back.

'There will be no need,' he thought it necessary to say, to reassure himself. He gave back the promissory note to Don Gennaro Parascandolo, who read it over carefully, twice; then he opened another safe and took out bank-notes, and counted three hundred and eighty francs twice over: he handed them to Fragalà, saying:

'Three hundred and eighty francs. Count your money over again.'

'Three hundred and eighty only?' asked the other, again astounded.

'Twelve per cent. interest is taken off,' explained Don Gennaro.

'Is that by the year?' asked Fragalà stupidly.

'No; by the month.'

Then there was silence. While Fragalà was counting the money mechanically, he thought, but dared not say to Parascandolo, that the interest had been calculated on the first five hundred francs, too, that he, Don Gennaro, had lent him, and not the capitalist Mazzocchi. He said nothing about it, though; indeed, in the innocency of his soul, he remarked, as he got up to go away:

'Thank you!'

'Why thank me? It is business. Only, think of when it falls due. Mazzocchi stands no nonsense—he is an ugly sort.'

'Never fear,' said Fragalà, with a sickly smile. After taking leave, he went off, with a colourless face and bitter mouth, as if he had been chewing aloes. At once Don Gennaro set himself to his accounts. But it was only for a few minutes, as Salvatore came to say Ambrogio Marzano, the lawyer, was there, with another gentleman, wanting to come in. He expected them, evidently, as he frowned slightly and looked stiff. Marzano came in, with his usual gentle smile—he was a lively, excitable old fellow; the one that looked put out was his companion, a gentleman of about forty, fat but pale, with very clear eyes that rolled vaguely and sadly.

The greetings were short. For a fortnight Marzano and Baron Lamarra had kept coming to San Giacomo Street to see Don Gennaro, on money business. They talked it over, made suggestions, accepted and then refused, then started the arguments over again. Baron Lamarra, son of a sculptor, who had become a contractor by dint of chiselling in the open air, and rich by dint of laying one son on another, had left his son a lot of money, though he was now trying for a loan of three thousand francs. He kept up his beggar-on-horseback airs at first, but as the days went on, and difficulties came in the way, he dropped them, and did nothing but play with the charms on his watch-chain; his conceited blue eyes got to have a despairing expression, which Don Gennaro studied sagaciously—perhaps it was for his benefit that he looked so cold. Only Don Ambrogio Marzano went on smiling, obstinate in his good nature.

'The Baron is rather anxious to finish up the business now we have talked it over for days,' said the little old man, trying to encourage his client.

'Let us finish it, then,' Don Gennaro answered, without lifting his eyes.

'You have not thought out a better arrangement?' Baron Lamarra murmured.

'No, I have not,' said Don Gennaro.

The two looked at each other, hesitating; the Baron made the lawyer an energetic sign to go on.

'How would it be?' Marzano asked.

'Here it is. My capitalist, Ascanio Sogliano, has no funds; but he can dispose of about forty dozen Chiavari chairs at six francs each, seventy-two francs the dozen, over two thousand seven hundred francs in all. He would give these goods, which are easy to dispose of, on a three months' promissory note, with the Baron and the Baroness Lamarra's signatures, each bound for all, with the usual interest, in advance, of three per cent; three times three, nine—that is to say, ninety francs a month; three times ninety, two hundred and seventy francs for three months.'

'And you said there would be a buyer for these Chiavari chairs, did you not?' Marzano replied, keeping up his frank tone.

'Exactly so,' said Don Gennaro, still very cold.

'Buyer at how much?' asked Baron Lamarra rather anxiously, knowing the answer quite well, but almost hoping for a different one.

'I told you: at two thousand francs.'

The lawyer shook his head; the Baron fumed with rage.

'It is too great a loss, far too great!' he cried out; 'and, then, my wife's signature, too!'

'Excuse me, Baron,' Don Gennaro remarked, 'you seem to be under a wrong impression. I am doing you a favour, finding a tradesman and a buyer. I am not taken up about this business. I often have as good aristocratic names as yours on bills, I can tell you. This is to clear up the position. You come here shouting as if you were in brigands' hands and your ears were being cut off. Here we don't cut off ears. If the affair does not suit you, let it go. It is indifferent to me, I repeat.'

As a sign of the greatest indifference, he lighted a Tocos cigarette, and began smoking, looking up to the ceiling. Baron Lamarra, whose face got flabbier and more unhealthy-looking in that annoying struggle, was disturbed. Silence followed. Marzano shook his head gently, as if he was lamenting over human weakness; he gazed at the silver top of his cane, without saying a word. The Baron ran his fingers through his black locks flecked with white; then he made up his mind, and drew out a thick black pocket-book, took out a paper, and put it on the table opposite Don Gennaro.

'It is settled,' he said, in a choked voice. 'Here is the promissory note.'

Don Gennaro only fluttered his eyelids in assent. He opened the note and looked at it a long time, the figures, dates, and signatures, reading in a low voice, 'Maddalena Lamarra—Annibale Lamarra. All right,' he ended up aloud, casting a scrutinizing glance at the Baron, whose face got livid from suppressed rage or some other feeling. 'Do you want to see the goods?' he then remarked punctiliously.

'What does it matter to me?' the Baron said sulkily, shrugging his shoulders. 'Give me the money to use.'

Don Gennaro nodded assent. As usual, he opened the middle drawer, shut up the promissory note in it, opened the side drawer, took out bank-notes, and counted them methodically.

'Count your money over,' he said, handing the bundle to the Baron, who had watched the appearance of bank-notes with a flashing eye.

But he did not count; he put the notes into his pocket-book, and, without saying a word, rose to go away.

Marzano vaguely stammered some words of thanks and farewell, but the Baron was already on the stairs, and the old man ran after him, not to let him elude him. When he was alone, Don Gennaro Parascandolo opened the drawer again and took out the Lamarra promissory note; he studied the signatures a long time, saying over the syllables ironically: 'Maddalena Lamarra ... bound for whole amount ...; Annibale Lamarra for himself and the conjugal authorization.' He ended up with a smile, and pushed it into the drawer again.

Ninetto Costa had come in without being announced, and the dark, lively, elegant stock-broker, in a suit of English check, a flower in his buttonhole, ebony stick in hand, and big iron ring on his little finger as a seal, seemed the pattern of happy youth. He stretched himself in an arm-chair, threw his leg over, and lit a cigarette, humming.

'Good settling-day Monday was, eh?' Don Gennaro asked.

'It was bad—bad!' sang out Ninetto Costa.

'You don't seem much put out. It will be bad for your clients then, and not for you,' said Parascandolo.

'It is bad for me; I have thirty to forty thousand francs at stake,' said the stock-broker, beating his trouser-leg with his stick in an elegant way.

'And how are you to pay?'

'I will pay,' the other ended up by saying, in a vague way.

'You have had several bad settling-days, it seems to me.'

'So, so. It is Lillina that takes away everything,' he muttered, with a not perfectly sincere gesture of regret.

'Lillina? She says "No,"' remarked Don Gennaro.

'Did she tell you so? She is the greatest liar among women! You can't think what a liar she is, Gennaro!' and he cried out more against her, rather in a sham rage. 'Have you got these jewels?' he added anxiously, though he tried to seem indifferent.

'Yes. Are they for Lillina?'

'Yes—that is to say, I am not certain; she is too great a liar! Besides, I have someone else in my eye.'

'You are a devil, Ninetto!' Don Gennaro said laughingly.

From the same drawer from which he had previously taken the money, Parascandolo took out a leather case and opened it. The jewels twinkled on the white velvet: there were a pair of solitaire earrings, a row of diamonds, a bracelet, and an ornament for the hair. Ninetto Costa looked at them, beating his lips with the knob of his stick. He went further off, to judge them better. He did this very gracefully; but a twitching of the muscles now and then made his smile unpleasant.

'They are fine, eh?' he asked Parascandolo.

'I think so,' said the other modestly.

'You would give them? You are a man of taste.'

'I would give them—according to the woman. Not to Lillina.'

'I don't know if I will give them to her—I don't know,' Costa burst out again hurriedly. 'You think,' he added timidly—'you think they are worth twenty thousand francs?'

'It is not what I believe; Don Domenico Mazzocchi, who sold them to you, thinks they are. I don't know about them. Besides, you can get them valued. Remember, they will ask two per cent. for the valuation.'

He said all this in such a cold, disdainful way that Ninetto Costa tried to interrupt him more than once, without managing it.

'Are you mad? What valuation? I would not do such a thing, with you and your friend Mazzocchi. To take so much trouble! I would not dream of it. It would be offensive to a friend—two friends.'

'Have you noted the terms of payment?'

'Yes, yes! at three, four, five, and six months—five thousand francs at a time, with a consignment on my mother's revenues, and all the necessary papers. All is going right. Do you wish nothing on the Exchange? I'll buy for you.'

'I don't do business; I have retired,' said Parascandolo, smiling and bowing, as Costa went off, carrying the jewel-case.

When he had gone, the other, being now alone, looked at the clock. It was getting late. San Giacomo Street is dark naturally, and already, at four o'clock, it looked as if the day was failing. Don Gennaro was thinking whether he had given an appointment to anyone else, and if he could go away, having finished his day's work, one of those hard-working Fridays for all that provide money—bankers, money-lenders, pawnbrokers. No, he thought, he had not given an appointment to anyone, and he could go away. He felt sure his coachman had brought round his carriage to take him to Carracciolo Street. But once more the faithful Salvatore came in to say three gentlemen wished to come in.

'Are there three?' asked Don Gennaro, pondering.

'Yes, three....'

'Let them in,' his master said, recollecting.

Dr. Trifari came in, fat, thick, red of beard and face, embarrassed and suspicious, taking off the high hat he always wore, like all provincials settled in Naples. Professor Colaneri was with him; he had a false look behind his gold spectacles, and bowed in the ecclesiastical style. A student, a fellow-countryman of Trifari's, and Colaneri's pupil, was the third one—a youth of twenty-two, with sticking-out teeth, a tartan necktie, and a decidedly silly look. The two, while keeping an eye on each other, glanced now at Don Gennaro, then at the embarrassed provincial lad, who seemed not to know what to do with his teeth, quite unhappy at not being able to shut his mouth. There was a curbed ferocity in Trifari's suspiciousness—it was palpable in him morally and physically; while Colaneri's was oblique, sly, cold, and hypocritical. The student looked like a fly between them—a stupid little fly held between two spiders, one cruel, the other treacherous.

Don Gennaro looked at them with a smile, guessing all that. Only to look at the wicked intentness of Dr. Trifari's eyes on the shut desk, Professor Colaneri's humble but dishonest look, the student's silliness—for he seemed to see nothing, or saw and heard without understanding—explained Salvatore's hesitation. But Don Gennaro Parascandolo, who loved artistic things, had taken up a long Japanese carved-ivory scabbard, and half drew out, as if by accident, a knife's shining blade. It was a book-cutter, though there was not a shadow of a book on the desk. With a click he sheathed it and laid it on the desk, but his fingers trifled with it. He smiled, smoking his everlasting cigarette, without offering one, however, to his three visitors.

'So we have come on that business, Signor Parascandolo. What has been done?' Dr. Trifari questioned, with a sham politeness that ill-covered his roughness.

'Yes. What do you refer to?' Parascandolo said.

'The money—the bank bill,' the plethoric doctor burst out.

'It is an ordinary affair enough,' remarked Parascandolo with an easy air.

'What do you say? With three signatures—mine, Professor Colaneri's, and Signor Rocco Galasso's—you call it an ordinary affair? Whose signature do you want—Rothschild's?'

'Certainly I would prefer Rothschild's to all signatures,' was said, with a mocking little smile. 'Business is business,' he added in his solemn way.

'We are honest men, it seems to me,' Professor Colaneri yelped out.

'I have the highest respect for you,' said Parascandolo with exaggerated politeness. 'But signatories must be solvent; that is all. I have made inquiries on account of my principal, Ascanio Sogliano. You will understand, I must prevent him making any loss, as I make use of his money. Now, Dr. Trifari, here is an excellent young fellow—he will become a light in the scientific world—but his signature is not good for a thousand francs, nor is Professor Colaneri's....'

'This is infamous!' Dr. Trifari cried out. 'I did not come here to be insulted, by Jove!'

'These are slanderous statements!' shrieked Colaneri the hypocrite.

'Where did you make inquiries?' Trifari asked, yelling.

'In your own neighbourhood,' answered Parascandolo coldly.

'Of course, in my own neighbourhood.... It is political hatreds ... election struggles!' Colaneri and Trifari shouted in chorus.

'That may be,' said Parascandolo; 'I cannot know about that, and it does not matter to Sogliano. So there remains this worthy youth here, Rocco Galasso; he is solvent. So, instead of three thousand francs, Sogliano will give a thousand, with your three signatures as a precaution.'

'It is impossible for us to agree to that!' Trifari thundered, purple with rage.

'Impossible!' shrieked Colaneri, quite livid.

'As you like,' said Parascandolo, getting up to go out.

But the most dumfounded of the three was poor Rocco Galasso, the student. He turned his stupefied eyes from Colaneri to Trifari and gasped, as if his saliva choked him. The two left the office in confusion, without saying 'Good-bye,' talking to each other, and shoving the student before them like a silly sheep. Parascandolo quietly called Salvatore to brush his great-coat. It was done silently, while he filled his case with cigarettes.

All at once, without being announced, the three burst again into the room, looking queer: Colaneri and Trifari as if forcibly restraining their rage, and Rocco Galasso, pale and humiliated, behind them, like a beaten dog.

'We are to do the business,' Trifari muttered, as if he was swallowing the wrong way. 'One thousand francs, as you said.'

Professor Colaneri agreed. Then the usual scene was repeated: The money-lender pulled out a blank promissory note for a thousand francs from the drawer and put it before Rocco Galasso, who dared not take it, but went looking Colaneri and Trifari in the eyes one after the other. The two, as if they were putting him to the torture, made him sit at a corner of the desk, and bent over, one at each side, to give him directions, and they dictated the formula word by word. He put his nose down on the paper, being short-sighted and knowing nothing about the business, never having signed a promissory note before. Then, crushed down by the two leaning on his shoulders, he got confused and frightened, and held his pen up hesitatingly. The work took a long time. The poor fellow was just going to mis-state the time of its falling due, when Trifori was down on him with a shout: 'At two months!'

At last the work was ended, and the student's forehead dropped sweat as he raised it that cool March day. Don Gennaro in the meanwhile pulled money out of his drawer and counted it.

'Seven hundred and sixty francs,' he said, holding out the bundle of notes to Rocco Galasso. 'Count your money.'

But the latter dared not take it. He looked again at his tutors. Colaneri put out his fat, cold hand and pocketed the money quickly, while Trifori glared at him.

'You take the interest in advance?' asked Trifori with a sneer.

'Yes, in advance.'

'Could you not add it to the promissory note?' Colaneri retorted, putting his hand in his pocket over the money.

'No, I cannot,' said Parascandolo dryly, getting up again.

The three went out silently. Colaneri rushed on in front; Trifori followed precipitately, forgetting Rocco Galasso, who was now of no use, while his greatest torment was that Parascandolo had made him write his address at Tito di Basilicata; and the thought that his father would know about it one day or other brought tears to his eyes.

In spite of Don Gennaro's wish to go out, he had to wait five minutes more. A little old woman, neatly dressed in black, a lady's-maid, had arrived, bringing an introductory note from Signora Parascandolo. Looking around her, she spoke to Don Gennaro in a whisper, and he listened with a fatherly, amiable smile. Then she timidly showed him something in a case, wrapped first in black cloth and then paper, which he would not even look at. He pushed it away, but not contemptuously. Then, after a few words to the old woman, he signed to her to keep silence, as she wished to begin her speech again, and he went to the desk, took out money, counted it, and handed it in an envelope to her. She waited to thank him, but he, to cut her short, asked:

'How is Lady Bianca Maria?'

'Not very well,' the old woman said, with a sigh.

In a few minutes the victoria bore easy, contented Don Gennaro Parascandolo to the Carracciolo promenade, where all his debtors, past, present, and future, greeted him with smiles and raised hats; and he smiled and bowed in return.

CHAPTER VIII
IN DON CRESCENZIO'S LOTTERY-SHOP

Donna Bianca Maria Cavalcanti read that letter over eight or ten times before putting it in her pocket. She was working at her lace alone in the bare large room, thinking over what was in it, for she knew the words by heart already. She saw it before her eyes, going over its meaning in her mind. So the slender bobbins slipped from her hands while she dreamt.

The letter was honest and frank. It said that, as a doctor and friend, he once more advised her to leave that lonely old house where she just vegetated. He begged she would deign to accept a humble, plain offer of hospitality in the country, in the village and home he was born in, where his mother lived alone piously. Donna Bianca Maria Cavalcanti should not despise this offer so frankly made. She could go down there with Margherita. The air was good, the country around fresh and green; it was an agreeable solitude. Dr. Amati could not go because of his work; but his mother would be sure to be very fond of her. She would be quite cured down there in that lifegiving, bright air. He implored her tenderly not to say 'No,' to believe in his devotion. He could not hide the real state of her health from her. Travel and country air were necessaries of life to her.

So the great doctor wrote in that short, precise style of his, honest, like his face and voice; a deep, sincere vein of feeling ran through each phrase. Feeling this, Bianca Maria shut her eyes to keep down her emotion. When Margherita brought her the letter, she guessed at once who it came from on seeing the clear, straight, precise writing. She opened it quickly, without hesitation or false modesty. After reading it, a country landscape, poor and humble, but bright and perfumed with green, rose before her eyes with the sweetness of an idyll; a flow of heat enlivened the slow blood in her veins; a desire for life and happiness gnawed at her heart; a first rush of youthful eagerness came. Antonio Amati's letter, read so often, was fixed in her mind. As she thought it over that fresh Friday evening in March, the blood rushed to her heart and her eyes filled with tears.

The Marquis di Formosa came in that evening, about eight o'clock. He also was more excited than usual, with a quiver in his limbs and features, which he got every week on Friday evening, as if he shortly expected a great sorrow or a great joy. But his daughter took no heed at first. She was distrait; though she went on working mechanically, the good, decided words of the letter that begged her to save herself buzzed in her mind, delightfully disturbing.

'Well, is there nothing yet?' asked the Marquis.

'What are you asking about? I do not understand,' she said, coming back to herself.

'What am I asking about? Why, the revelation the spirit is to make to you. Perhaps you don't wish to tell it? Why not? You must tell me; I expect to hear it from you.'

'Dear father, I know nothing about it,' she answered, growing pale, but trying to keep her voice steady. 'I will never know anything of what you imagine.'

'I don't imagine!' he cried out. 'They are truths and religious mysteries. Don Pasqualino is a pious soul. He *sees*. You could see, too, if you liked, but you don't want to. Tell the truth: you sup before going to bed?'

'No, I do not,' she said, keeping down her head, resigned to the torture of the inquiry, touching Amati's letter in her pocket.

'A full body is impure; it cannot have heavenly inspirations,' he said in a mystical way. 'What do you do before sleeping?'

'I pray.'

'Do you not ask for this favour with all your strength? Do you ask for it?'

She looked at her father, and opened her mouth to say 'No.' She did not utter it; but he understood her.

'It is natural the vision does not come—quite natural. Faith is needed,' said he, with deep disdain. 'But what do you pray for? What do you ask for, unloving heart?'

'I ask for peace,' she said gravely, waving her hand.

He shrugged his shoulders disdainfully.

'I will make Don Pasqualino pray,' he added. 'You will get the vision, whether you like or not; the spirits will insist on it. They command, you understand. They are masters in this world and the next. You will have the spirit by you when you least expect it; you will see it....'

'God help me!' said she, crossing herself with an uncontrollable shiver.

'Are you afraid?' he asked sneeringly, no longer, in his mad excitement, seeing how she suffered.

'Oh yes, I am,' she said feebly, as if she were fainting.

She clutched Antonio Amati's honest, affectionate letter convulsively, as if to get strength from it. But the Marquis paid no more heed to his daughter. He had rung the bell, and Giovanni came in in his old livery. He looked undecidedly at his master as he handed him his hat and stick, as if he were alarmed to see him go out earlier on that than on other Fridays. But what he dreaded was unavoidable, because the Marquis said to him, 'Come with me,' going towards his bedroom, a poor, bare room like the rest of the house. Giovanni lighted a wretched candle to hold their conversation by. The servant respectfully stood right before his master, who kept up his aristocratic bearing and natural haughtiness, which even vice could not subdue.

'Giovanni, have you any money?' he asked in a lordly way.

The servant bowed; he did not dare to answer 'No' exactly, so he said nothing.

'You must have some,' the Marquis went on rather sternly. 'I gave it to you two weeks ago. Have you spent it all? You waste the little I have left.'

'My lord, last Friday you took it almost all. We must live. You would not like her ladyship to die of hunger,' said Giovanni in a complaining voice.

'Very good, very good; I understand,' the Marquis interrupted, irritated, but concealing his rage. 'I need at least fifty francs. I have a debt of honour to pay this evening. Then to-morrow evening'—emphasizing the words—'I will give it to you back. I will give you other money, too, a lot of money, so that you will not accuse me of letting my daughter die of hunger.'

'You are master, my lord; but if you knew what money it is——' And he took a torn note-book from his pocket.

'What is it you refer to?' said the Marquis, casting devouring eyes on the pocket-book.

'Nothing, my lord;' and he respectfully handed his master a fifty-franc note.

He did it in such a way as to try and prevent the Marquis seeing a second one he had; but the old gentleman dared not ask for it just then.

'You can go,' he said to the servant, who went off.

He walked up and down the room impatiently; then he rang the bell twice. Margherita came forward in the same trembling, almost hesitating way as her husband. The old nobleman, descended from Guido Cavalcanti and ten generations of gentlemen, now stooped to cheat like a rogue.

'Margherita, do you know if Bianca Maria has money?' he asked absently.

'Who would give it to her? The few francs she gets from Sister Maria degli Angioli and her godfather at Christmas she gives to the poor.'

'I thought she had some,' he said, putting on his great coat. 'I am much embarrassed; I have to pay a debt this evening, and I supposed Bianca Maria would help her father. I am very much annoyed. Perhaps you have some money, Margherita?'

'I have money,' said she, not daring to deny it, out of respect and fear of her master.

'Can you give me some? I'll give it you back to-morrow evening.'

'Really,' she replied, 'I have some money, but I wished to buy a dress for her ladyship. Your lordship does not notice it; but at twenty, and as lovely as a queen, my mistress has only had two dresses in two years—one for summer, the other for winter. She does not even notice it herself, poor soul!... I had thought of buying one for her. Your lordship could have given me back the money at your leisure.'

'Sister Margherita, give me that money now, and *to-morrow evening*, I promise you before God, Bianca Maria will have money for ten dresses.'

'Amen,' said Margherita sadly and resignedly.

She could not resist the emotion in her master's voice. Pulling out a silk purse from her bodice, she detached a hundred-franc note from a roll of notes. He took it and hid it at once in his purse, and went out, saying with wild joy, in a queer tone of certainty, 'Till to-morrow evening.' And he said 'Till to-morrow evening' again as he passed through the drawing-room, standing by his daughter at a window which she had opened to get fresh air to try and recover from her moral and physical weakness.

The Marquis di Formosa went down the steps quickly, lively as a lad going to a love-tryst. Someone, in fact, was waiting for him, walking up and down before the door. It was Don Pasqualino De Feo, the medium. His sickly, mean look was not changed at all; he still wore his torn, dirty clothes, but that evening his eyes were sparkling in his thin face. He put his hand on the Marquis di Formosa's arm. Formosa, who had not noticed him, greeted him with a smile.

'Have you the money?' asked Don Pasqualino, lowering his eyelids as if to hide the flame alight in his eyes.

'Yes; how much is needed?'

'Four Masses must be paid for in four parishes to-morrow morning. We will make it five francs each Mass. I must spend the night in prayer. The *spirit* told me to shut myself up in San Pasquale at midnight. I have promised a gift of ten francs to the sacristan; otherwise it would not be allowed. We agreed to light four candles before San Benedetto's altar; it is his day to-morrow. Ten francs—forty; yes, forty francs would be enough.'

He made his calculation coldly, keeping his eyes cast down, but his queer, mysterious talk was unusually clear. The Marquis di Formosa agreed with a nod to every new expense that the medium enumerated, thinking it reasonable.

'And how much for yourself?' he asked, after counting forty francs into Don Pasqualino's hands.

'You know I need nothing,' said the other, waving it off.

'When do we meet?'

'To-morrow morning after my vigil, if the spirit leaves me alive. Friday last I was so beaten I thought I was dying,' the medium said emphatically, but in a whisper.

'I trust in you,' Formosa murmured.

'Let us trust in *him*,' retorted the other fervently, showing the whites of his eyes.

'Pray to him—pray to him!' the Marquis implored.

They separated after the Marquis had pressed two soft, wet fingers that Don Pasqualino held out to him. De Feo went up again towards Tarsia; Formosa went down towards Toledo. He was going to the lottery bank, No. 117, at the corner of Nunzio Lane, where the handsome, chestnut-bearded Don Crescenzio was the banker, and where Formosa and his friends were in the habit of staking. The shop, lately white-washed, glittered with light. Three gas-jets were burning at full cock above the broad wooden counter and high wire grating that cut off the bottom of the shop from one wall to the other. Behind this counter, seated on three high stools in front of openings in the grating, Don Crescenzio and his two clerks were working, his lads, so called, though one of them—Don Baldassare—was seventy, and might have been a hundred, he looked so decrepit; though the other had one of those colourless faces, with indefinite lines and colouring, that might be any age.

They kept a big register open before them, called '*To mother and daughter*'—that is to say, with double yellow slips of paper. They wrote the numbers on them with heavy, sharp-pointed pens, so as to have a clear, strong hand-writing, putting down each number twice; one could see their lips move as they repeated it. Then they cut the ticket with a dry click of the great scissors held in the right hand, passed it quickly through a wooden saucer of black sand to dry it, and, after taking the money, handed it to the gambler. Don Crescenzio had the fine contented look of a good macaroni-eater, smiling in his dark beard; whilst Don Baldassare, so bent he seemed hunchbacked, his crooked nose drooping into his toothless mouth, worked very phlegmatically. Don Checchino, the pale clerk, wrote hurriedly, so as to finish and go away.

When the Marquis di Formosa came in about half-past nine, the shop was full of people putting down their stakes. The game began feebly on Friday morning, increasing at mid-day, and in the evening it got to the flood. The Marquis di Formosa beckoned, and Don Crescenzio opened his little door and attentively handed him a chair. The Marquis always spent Friday evenings there, seated in a corner, watching all the people gambling. He tried to get up an excitement by the sight, and succeeded to a great extent. He had the lottery numbers and the money in his pocket; but he never played when he first came in. He tasted the joy a long time, from seeing others do it.

The shop was full of people. They came in by two wide-open doors, one in Toledo Street, the other in Nunzio Lane. The flood rolled in and out, beating against the wooden counter, which was shiny from human contact. The crowd was of all ranks and ages, with every variety of the human face: good-looking and ugly, healthy and sickly, gay, sorrowing, stupefied, and dull. The crowd came from all the streets around, from Chianche della Carità and Corsea, San Tommaso di Aquino cloister and Consiglio ward, Toledo and San Liborio Lane. Certainly there was another lottery bank a short distance off, one in Magnocavallo Street, and another in Pignasecca Road. In a few hundred steps' radius there were several, all flaming with gas and overflowing with people. But if a lottery bank was opened for every three other shops in Naples, from Friday to Saturday, each would have its crowd. Besides, lottery banks go by favour, like other things; some are popular, others are not. The one in Nunzio Lane, like the Plebiscito Square and the Monte Oliveto Road ones, had a great name for luck. Large sums had been gained there. Many people, therefore, came from a distance to stake a franc, five francs, or a hundred, at the bank.

The three groups in front of the wickets in Don Crescenzio's lottery bank melted into one, for ever flowing and ebbing; and the Marquis di Formosa, his hat a little back on his head, showing his fine forehead with some drops of sweat on it, looked on this sight with enchanted eyes, holding his ebony stick between his legs. Sometimes, on recognising a friend or acquaintance before one of the openings, his eyes shone with delight, much flattered that so many distinguished worthy people shared his passion. He opened his eyes wide to see it all, to take in the ever-changing picture, stretching his ears to hear the conversations and soliloquys—for lottery gamblers speak to themselves out loud, even in public—to find out which number among so many mentioned came oftenest into people's mouths, so as to play it that night or next morning. It was warm, and the light was strong in that crowded little shop. But the Marquis di Formosa felt a curious pleasure, a full wide sensation of vitality; he felt young again, and in the pride of health and strength.

In the meanwhile the crowd was not getting smaller; it increased. While in front of white-faced Don Checchino's wicket a lot of students made a row, calling out their own numbers, laughing, and pushing each other, at old Don Baldassare's, in front of the humble crowd were two or three great gamblers, who gave a whole string of numbers, staking tens and hundreds of francs on them. The old clerk wrote slowly, phlegmatically, and read them out before handing the tickets. At Don Crescenzio's, where the work was got through quicker, the scene changed every minute: the clerk came after the soldier-servant sent to stake for his Colonel, a sulky workman gave place to a stupid-looking country nurse, the old lay Sister stuck herself behind the retired magistrate—all were chattering, looking ecstatic, or deeply, sadly engrossed. That was how Don Domenico Mayer looked, the misanthropic Under-Secretary of Finance. He was now standing before Don Crescenzio, his eyes cast down, his cavernous voice dictating ten *terni*, *terni secchi*, on which he boldly played two francs each, to win ten thousand francs, less the tax on personal estate. At the third *terno*, he asked fiercely:

'How much is the tax?'

'Thirteen and twenty per cent,' Don Crescenzio replied playfully, waving his fat white hand in a graceful style.

'Cheat of a Government!' a shrill voice called out behind Don Domenico.

It was Michele the shoeblack, waiting to play his small Friday evening game. He was to play higher stakes next day, when he got the money from Donna Concetta. In the meanwhile he tasted the delight of being there as he waited his turn. At the third *terno secco* Don Domenico explained his game.

'I don't care about taking the *ambo*; fifteen francs are nothing to me.'

'Indeed!' said complacent Don Crescenzio.

He took the twenty francs, folded the coupons neatly, and handed them to him. Getting on tiptoe to reach the wicket, the lame hunchback was already dictating his numbers. He gave the explanation of each.

'This I have played for twenty years ... this is Father Giuseppe d'Avellino's *terno* ... this is the *ambo* of the day ... this is the *terno* of the man killed in Piazza degli Orefici.'

But they were small stakes, seven or eight francs in all, and those waiting behind him got impatient. By a curious attraction, big gamblers went to Don Baldassare, the old man. Ninetto Costa, in evening dress, just showing under his overcoat, his *gibus* hat rather askew on his curly, scented hair, his very white teeth uncovered by smiling red lips, handed his list over to the accountant, while he smoked a Havana calmly, cheerful as usual. He satisfied Don Baldassare's inquiries pleasantly. The sum staked had to be repeated to him as a precaution, not because he wondered at the largeness of it.

'On the first ticket seventy on the *terno*, twenty on the *quaterna*?'

'Yes, that is it;' and he puffed out odorous smoke.

'On the second *terno secco* a hundred and fifty is it?'

'Yes, a hundred and fifty.'

'On the third the whole ticket, two hundred and forty francs. Is that right?'

'Two hundred and forty—that is right.'

The Marquis di Formosa, who had exchanged a smile with Ninetto Costa, strained his ears to hear the ciphers. He quivered, touched with a little envy, regretting he had not so much money to stake. When he heard the whole amount, six hundred and fifty francs, and saw Ninetto Costa pull out this sum lightly to hand to Don Baldassare, he grew pale, thinking how much he could win with so high a risk. He went out, almost choking, to get air at the door. There Ninetto Costa joined him. Both gazed down Toledo, on its crowd and lights, without seeing them.

'You are lucky,' stammered the old nobleman; 'you have money.'

'If you knew all!' said the other, grown grave suddenly. 'I pawned jewels I paid twenty thousand francs for, and I only got five thousand. The pawnshops keep down the loans on Friday and Saturday; they get such a lot of things.'

'What does it matter?—you will win,' said the old man, rolling his eyes, excited by the vision of success.

'On Monday I have a settlement on the Exchange—twenty thousand francs' loss, and not a penny in my pocket. If I don't take something, where will I put my head?'

'You have good numbers?' Formosa asked anxiously.

'I have staked everything. Pasqualino De Feo wanted fifty francs to soothe the spirit. He gave me three *ternos*, two *ambos*, and a *situato*. Then that common girl I pay court to, I gave her a watch. She gave me some numbers, but under a symbol. You understand? Then there are the Cabal numbers we play together, and Marzano's cobbler's ones, and so on. I know if I don't win, Marquis, and a big sum, I must go bankrupt;' and the thoughtless stock-broker's voice trembled tragically. 'I am going to a dance—good-evening,' he said then, lighting his cigar again; and he went off with his nimble step.

Excited by this talk, the Marquis di Formosa went into the lottery-shop again. Now, before the pale, flabby Don Checchino's grill, leaning her elbow on the counter, Carmela, the cigar-girl, using the ten francs Donna Concetta gave her for her earrings, was saying her numbers, faintly, with pauses, playing three or four popular tickets.

'Six and twenty-two—put half a franc on that; eight, thirteen, and eighty-four—two sous for the *ambo* of it, eight sous for the *terno*; then eight and ninety, on the *ambo* another four sous.'

She stopped now and then, as if other sad thoughts distracted her; a flush coloured her delicate cheeks. When Don Checchino made up the account, four francs forty centimes, she took out a roll of copper money and began to count slowly.

'Hurry up! hurry up!' an impatient woman's voice cried out.

She turned round and recognised the woman, an old servant, Donna Rosa, she that served in the house where her unfortunate sister lived. They spoke in a whisper.

'Oh, Donna Rosa, and how is Filomena?'

'She is well; but she is in distress. She sent me to play this number— three girls are playing it, rather, as there has been a wound given, unluckily.'

'Oh, Jesus! God bless her, poor sister! And you—where do you come from?'

'I live in Chianche Road, and I am going home.'

'Greet her for me,' Carmela whispered eagerly.

Pulling her shawl round her, she went away, with her head down, as if overpowered by tiredness. Next to Rosa, the unfortunates' servant, came Baron Annibale Lamarra, fat, pale, panting with his hurried walk from one lottery bank to another. He played many tickets of twenty, fifty, a hundred francs each; but, fearing to be spied on by his miserly wife, whose dower he wasted, in spite of terrible scenes, afraid of being caught by his father, a self-made man, he had got up the fraud of playing a ticket at each place. He ran panting from one lottery to another, trying to believe he would win on Saturday and take back the promissory note from Don Gennaro Parascandolo, the one that had his wife's signature. The thought of it made him shiver with fright. When he got out of Don Crescenzio's lottery-shop he breathed again, and reckoned up mentally. Of the two thousand francs, he had given two hundred to Ambrogio Marzano, the cheerful old lawyer, for arranging with Parascandolo; then he had staked one thousand six hundred francs in different banks. He had two hundred francs left. He would stake them next day, for perhaps he would dream of some good number at night. It was no use risking it all at once. In the meanwhile, from the other door, just as he got out, Don Ambrogio Marzano came in. He stopped to talk with the Marquis di Formosa.

'Have you some good lottery numbers?' Formosa asked anxiously. He clung to the pleasant old man as a bearer of luck.

'I have a forty-nine *secondo* that is a love, my lord!' whispered the enthusiast, so as not to be heard.

'Ah! and what else?'

'Twenty-seven, you know, is the sympathetic number at the end of the month.'

'I have it, too. What do you say of the fourteenth?'

'It is *very good*, my lord; but do you wish really to know the lightning; the dazzling number?'

'Tell me—tell me!'

'I tell you in brotherly love, because when I have a treasure I can't be selfish with it, and keep it to myself. You may have it as a proof of affection— it is thirty-five!'

'Ah!' said the Marquis in a stupor of admiration.

In the meanwhile, still quite serene, Don Ambrogio Marzano went to place his stakes with Don Crescenzio. It is true he had had to give the usual fifteen francs to his Cabalist cobbler. He had given ten to Don Pasqualino, though he did not believe in him much, and a journey to Marano, to take Father Illuminato a tortoise-shell snuff-box, had cost him thirty francs; but he had taken them from a prepayment of law expenses he got from a client, so that the two hundred francs was intact, and he paid it all. Gaetano the glove-cutter, Annarella's husband, whose child was dying, was waiting his turn to stake; but it was a hard week, he had not got the loan of a sou, and had had difficulty in getting an advance of five francs from his master. He staked four of them, keeping back one for the numbers he might think of on Saturday morning.

Now, as night came on, Don Crescenzio and his tired, stupefied clerks had a sort of confused look, like those that have sat too long at musical and dancing entertainments, with dazzled eye and deafened ears; but they went on working. It was the grand weekly harvest, a gathering in of thousands, hundreds, and tens of francs for the Government. Don Crescenzio got a percentage of it, and on good weeks he gave his 'lads' a little extra. Even the people coming in constantly to stake had a queer look. Some were uneasy, some were looking round them suspiciously; others dragged along in a tired way, or their eyes were distracted, as if they were out of their senses. There were those who had just found out numbers, or got money to stake; servants, their day's work over, had run off to the lottery before going to bed; shop-lads, that had just shut up shop, and youths who had run out between two acts at the Fiorentino Theatre, were coming in; and Cabalists from the Diodati Café, or the wine-room of the Testa d'Oro Café, who were all Don Crescenzio's customers, and after long discussion now ended by risking all they had that evening; then a magistrate, weighed down by children and poverty, on his way back from a game of *scopa*, at a sou, ventured the twenty francs that was to feed them for four days; and the pale, sickly painter of saints, having insisted on getting the money for a Santa Candida beforehand, came in just then to stake it, and he was certain to play next morning what Donna Concetta had promised him for the statue of the Immaculate Conception.

Even a very elegant little street carriage stopped, and a hand in pearl-gray gloves, studded with diamonds at the wrist, handed a paper and money to a gallooned footman. The Marquis di Formosa, who had left his seat out of nervousness, and was wandering among the gamblers who came out and in, recognised the profile of a lady of his own set, the Spanish Princess, Ines di Miradois.

'It is true, then, that Francesco Althan takes everything from her,' the old lord thought to himself.

He joined Dr. Trifari and Professor Colaneri as they now came in, still quivering with rage. They quarrelled by the hour about dividing poor Rocco Galasso's seven hundred and sixty francs. Trifari made out he had induced his fellow-villager, Rocco Galasso, to sign, and he wanted five hundred francs. Colaneri made out that Rocco Galasso had signed the promissory note so as to get the examination papers from him beforehand, and by giving them he had gravely compromised himself; he might lose his post through it; therefore the five hundred francs were his. The struggle had been tremendous. They nearly came to blows twice; but Trifari very unwillingly, choking with rage, gave in, because he knew Colaneri had revelations at night—a thing he, a full-blooded heretical blasphemer, did not have. And Colaneri gave in because Trifari brought him many students to do business with for the examinations—a most dangerous thing to do, and he himself was afraid of the risk, but he yielded to temptation to satisfy his vices. In short, they divided the seven hundred and sixty francs. They had met the medium, who asked them in an inspired tone if they wished to do alms of five francs to St. Joseph. They gave it, thinking the question meant numbers, and that they ought to play five for the money and nineteen for St. Joseph's number. All the medium says on Friday evening and Saturday morning means lottery numbers. So that Trifari and Colaneri, after making their game on their favourite numbers, came down at once to play these less probable ones, according to them; then they played the popular numbers, which were three and four, just in case; and at last, leaning on the great wooden counter, they looked in each other's faces with an idiotic grin, still thinking out if they had forgotten anything.

In spite of the late hour, people went on crowding up Don Crescenzio's lottery bank. He would get a large profit this last Friday in March, owing to a flowing back of malignant fever, one of those wild, gathered-up rushes of the slow disease that eats up Naples' fortunes. There were people coming out of theatres who had thought all evening about what ticket to play; they did not wish to put off doing so till Saturday, for fear of forgetting it in the few morning hours left. There were night-cabmen who stopped before the shop, came down from the box, and waited their turn to play, the inseparable whip in hand, with the patient eyes of those accustomed to long waiting; there were those ragged, wretched, wandering night-hawkers, shadowy figures, who shivered with fright in the bright warm gaslight—vendors of newspapers, fritters, pickers-up of cigar-ends, sellers of *pizze*, of beans, of grass for the horses of night-cabs passing from time to time, calling out their wares; and they, too, stopped at the lottery-stand, and went in, not able to resist playing a franc, half a franc, a few sous. The driver and two porters of the omnibus that takes travellers by the last train to the Allegria Hotel came in; whilst the bus-conductors and drivers in Carità Square, as soon as their day's run was over, which must have made them dead-tired, had come to stake on the lottery before going home.

Formosa had not made up his mind to play yet, with that sort of dallying with time all lovers and excitable people go in for. In a corner of the entrance, so as to let people pass, he conversed with Trifari and Colaneri, who did not want to leave either, though they had nothing left to stake.

They stood to enjoy that light, warmth, and crowd, the money flowing in, the lottery-tickets going out, pledges of fortune and riches, and to muse over which of them was the right one. Which? which? Here was the tremendous, delightful doubt, the immense, burning unknown, the mystery that smiled through the veil that cannot be lifted.

After taking a little walk through Toledo, being unable to resist the attraction, Ambrogio Marzano, the lawyer, had come back, too, and joined his little group of Cabalist friends, conversing with them by fits and starts. Quite incapable of not mentioning his number, his crowning stroke, he told them of thirty-five, so that Colaneri and Trifari went in to play it, and he, Marzano, went in to play seventy-three, which Colaneri had given him. No, Formosa was not going to stake yet. But the end of his enjoyment was drawing near; he felt the great moment coming on, and in one of his fervent, mystic bursts he prayed silently to the Lord, the Casa Cavalcanti Madonna, the Ecce Homo he worshipped in his family chapel, to enlighten and inspire him, to do him the one great favour he had asked for years. His friends, after tasting this other drop of pleasure, came out again, and chatted vivaciously about numbers, getting excited with the big shadows that now filled Toledo, broken by that square of light the lottery lamp cast on the pavement. Just then they saw Cesare Fragalà go in. After shutting his shop, the gay confectioner always spent a couple of hours at his club to play dominoes with other tradesmen—grocers, drapers, oilmen, fishmongers— putting down a sou a game. On Friday evening he played these long games, too, but rather distractedly, nervous, in spite of his youthful gaiety, and he made off rather early to go to his dear Don Crescenzio's to make his weekly large stake.

Really, there was a little crabbedness in his gambling ardour, something like a feeling of remorse, of shame at throwing away his money in that way, so he came late to the lottery bank, when there were fewer people about to see and know him. He was put out that evening on Formosa greeting him; it annoyed him to be seen by his neighbour. Then he shrugged his shoulders, and stood by his dearest friend Don Crescenzio, who went on writing, stroking his fine beard, making a lot of fine flourishes with his pen. He began to dictate his numbers to him on and on, showing his white teeth in a smile. Don Crescenzio wrote on quite unmoved. For the six months that Cesare Fragalà played at his bank the stakes had gone on increasing. In that flood of numbers dictated, Don Crescenzio, with his peculiar memory, recognised the medium's numbers—that is to say, his symbols, that everyone had interpreted differently, so that Formosa, Colaneri, Trifari, Marzano, Ninetto Costa, Cesare Fragalà, and all who took their luck on Don Pasqualino's words, played different numbers, and a great many of them, and thus they all managed now and then to make some small hazardous gain—fifteen or twenty crowns over a *situato*, six hundred francs over an *ambo*—very seldom, it is true, but often enough to fan their passion and make them all slaves to Don Pasqualino's cloudy phrases. So with a slight smile, while he was adding up the sum, Don Crescenzio said:

'You, too, are one of Pasqualino De Feo's clients?'

'You know him?' asked Fragalà anxiously.

'Eh, we are friends,' Crescenzio muttered.

'He knows the numbers, does he not?' Fragalà asked, with a quiver in his throat.

'Often he gets them right.'

'How often?'

'When his client is in God's favour,' the agent answered enigmatically. Wishing to end the conversation, he politely handed over the tickets, saying: 'Five hundred and forty francs.'

Fragalà paid stolidly with a tradesman's calm, without changing expression. But when he got out of the lottery-shop, at the door, his smile faded; he remembered he had made his first debt to a money-lender that day, and that he had given security on the shop funds, having also taken out the whole balance to make up the big sum he had staked. It was to get away from these sad thoughts that he joined the group of Cabalists. At one in the morning, standing in front of the gambling place, they neither felt the hours passing, the lateness, nor the penetrating damp; for they burned with that constant inward fire that flamed up from Friday to Saturday. They began the same stories again, at great length, for the thousandth time, interrupting each other, getting heated and excited, staring at each other with wild, humid eyes, as if they were possessed. Cesare Fragalà listened, trying to get the same fever, but not succeeding; for he was only a weak soul, not mad, nor subject to nerves. When they all went over the reasons that made them gamble, such and such material and moral needs, urgent and impelling, that the lottery alone could satisfy, he listened in a melancholy way. At one point he said:

'I—I need sixty thousand francs to open a shop towards San Ferdinando, and make a marriage portion for Agnesina.'

A deep sadness overpowered him. Good, honest, incapable of lying about anything to his wife, he had deceived her for months, like a cheat; he took the ledgers she often stopped to turn over out of her hands, and with hourly caution he tried to hide his vice from her, thus destroying his good temper and ease.

'If it were not for this shop, if it were not for Agnesina——' he muttered, a prey to inconsolable bitterness.

Now, about half-past one, the time came to shut the lottery bank, as the customers became fewer and fewer; and at last the Marquis di Formosa made up his mind to go and stake. Notes in hand, he said the lottery numbers slowly over to Don Crescenzio. There was a slight tremor in his voice, and his eyes stared at the string of figures on the paper, as if he was enjoying himself. The gambling-shop was deserted now. His Cabalist friends, Colaneri, Trifari, Marzano, bringing Fragalà with them, who was in very low spirits, got behind the Marquis di Formosa to listen to his numbers, and either winked approval or shook their heads unbelievingly—in short, they served at Formosa's by no means short gambling operations with the gravity of priests taking part in a Bishop's service. Don Baldassare, the decrepit old man, and pale-faced Don Checchino, stood motionless behind the counter, their eyes half shut, dead-tired with that ten hours' gabbling, thinking of having to go through the same thing next day, from seven till noon, with great heat the last hour. Only Don Crescenzio kept up his calm, placid, Neapolitan felicity, that has its plate of macaroni secure, and serenely watches others' excitement from behind a phantom plate of macaroni, many plates of it in the great imaginative country of Cockayne. The Marquis di Formosa, greatly excited, played high. He put down what Giovanni got from Concetta the money-lender, what the lady's-maid got from Don Gennaro Parascandolo, and seventy francs he got from the pawn-shop for two artistic antique gilt-bronze candle-sticks, found in a lumber-room in his house— two hundred and twenty francs in all. He was still pallid, discontented, and melancholy, suddenly mistrustful of the value of some numbers, sorry not to be able to risk more on others, in despair at the end at not being able to stake on all the others, all that were in his calculations.

So the lover, after a long-wished-for interview with his lady, having got it, sees the moments fly past with frightful rapidity, and is afterwards deeply grieved at not having said to the lady a word of what he felt. This old man, whose ruling passion was not dulled by age, bent his head, crushed suddenly, as if he had lived ten years in a minute. He went out slowly and silently with the others, slow and silent, too, through the dark street leading to his house. They were all cold at that late hour. They shivered, and pulled their great-coats round them, holding their heads down, not speaking to each other. Thus they got as far as Dante Piazza, under the Rossi Palace, where the cabalistic talk began again. They went two or three times up and down the piazza, while the poet's stern white statue seemed to scorn them with its blank eyeballs. They took poor Fragalà with them, eaten up now by overpowering remorse for having thrown away so much money that belonged to his family. But it was no use. He gambled because he was a weak, cheerful creature, pricked on by commercial ambition. He would never be a Cabalist. The others' madness sadly surprised him, and they never could have infected him with it. Still, he stayed with them, feeling that he had not the strength to go home and lie by his wife's side with this remorse on him for having thrown away five hundred francs. He began to look distractedly and fixedly at the shadows, as if he saw some frightful vision. At one point Marzano bowed and went off towards Porta Medina archway, for he lived in Tribunale Road. But the others continued to walk up and down, raving, in the darkness and cold, which they no longer felt. The Marquis di Formosa was the most fervent of all. His eyes sparkled, his figure stood out in the gloom, strong and vigorous, like a man of thirty. Then Colaneri and Trifari took leave. They both lived in a poor house in Cavone Street. Then Formosa went on, with a monologue, speaking to Fragalà, the shadows, or himself. They were going down very slowly towards Toledo once more, when a quiet voice greeted them:

'Good-night, gentlemen!'

'Good-night, Don Crescenzio,' said the Marquis. 'Have you shut up, eh? Was it a good day?'

'Thirty-two thousand five hundred and twenty-seven francs was the sum staked,' said the banker, all in one breath.

Silence followed.

'Do you not play, Don Crescenzio?' Fragalà asked.

'No, never. Good-night.'

'Good night.'

He went off smartly, and they, seeing the lottery bank was shut now, turned back heavily. It was with a sigh that they knocked gently at the palace gate. They were sorry to go home. They parted on the first landing with a hand-shake and a smile.

CHAPTER IX
BIANCA MARIA'S VISION

Both the gamblers went upstairs very quietly, like evil-doers or timid young fellows who have disobeyed their father's orders; each carried a latchkey, and shut the door without any noise. On going into his apartments and his own room, Cesare Fragalà, taking a fit of penitence, shook like a child; only his sleeping wife's placid breathing calmed him a little. He was afraid of awakening her, in case she questioned him, and guessed the truth with that extraordinary alarming intuition women have. He undressed by the slender light of a lamp before St. Agnes, and got into bed with the greatest caution, trembling—yes, trembling—lest he should wake his wife; and in his humble, contrite, desolate heart he swore not to stake another sou. Only this oath and his healthy constitution freed him from sleeplessness, which sits at the bedhead of all gamblers.

Sleeplessness had visited Formosa's pillows. He had vainly tried to read Rutilio Benincasa's mathematical table, to calm his wandering thoughts; the figures danced in a ring before his eyes. He vainly tried to say the rosary, to fix his mind on prayer, to humiliate his heart before the Eternal Will; prayer came coldly and haltingly from his lips. A strong fever of fancy held him, and put his nerves on the rack; it made him start up in his bed, quivering like a violin string: a madness took hold of him, and, from the black darkness and solitude, made itself all-powerful over his thoughts and feelings. He could not stay in bed; in spite of the cold, he got up and dressed, and began to walk about in his freezing room. He did not feel cold; his hands and head were warm; the candle-flame seemed a great blaze to him. All was silent in the house; he never allowed anyone to wait up for him. The two poor old servants—Giovanni and Margherita—whom he had despoiled of their money got on loan, to keep Bianca Maria alive, were sleeping in the closet—tired and sorrowful, perhaps. Bianca Maria was asleep in her cold room many hours ago certainly. But the Marquis di Formosa, devoured by his gambling folly, hoping and despairing of winning from one moment to another, implored God, the Virgin, the saints, the souls of his dead, his guardian angel, Fortune, all the powers of heaven and earth, to help him to win, to get the victory; he forgot his fears as a man and a Christian so far as to ask it from evil spirits, even. Formosa, burning with such madness, could not bear that all in the house should sleep quietly, placidly, while he was torn with anguish and hope. Ah no! he was not afraid of solitude and night, little noises from old furniture, old creaking ceilings, or noisy doors; he was afraid of nothing in that icy house where his wife died of languor and sorrow, where her meek shade still seemed to linger. Fear! He asked, he implored a voice, a revelation, a vision; he would have been pleased, happy, and not frightened, if he had seen something. But his soul was too stained with sin, his heart was unclean from earthly desires; a white soul, a virginal heart, was needed to get this heavenly grace, by which one *saw* what other human eyes were not allowed to see. Bianca Maria was sleeping; she slept, cold creature! though so near to Grace, and still refused to satisfy her father's wishes. He left his room, crossed the passage in front of the drawing-room, and stopped at his daughter's closed door. He listened—no sound. She was sleeping, cold-hearted girl! She had no pity for her father's tortures, and would not pray God and the Virgin for a vision. A dull rage mingled with his Friday madness; he went up and down the passage more than once, trying to go away from his daughter's room; but he could not manage it: his curiosity was so strong to know from her the spirit's revelation that she certainly must have had that night; it could not have failed to come. Don Pasqualino, the medium, after a three days' voluntary fast, after two nights' flagellation on his shoulders and bare, thin breast, had heard from the spirit who helped him that Bianca Maria would get the revelation. The spirit does not lie. Then involuntarily, as if pushed by a force he must obey, he took hold of the door-handle; it creaked, the door opened. But a sharp cry from inside answered to the noise—a girl's cry, whose light, watchful sleep had been disturbed. She rose up in bed, in her white nightgown, her black hair loose on her shoulders, eyes wide open, and hands clutching the coverlet.

'It is I, Bianca—it is I,' the Marquis di Formosa murmured, coming forward.

'Who—who is it?' she asked, shaking with fear, not daring to move.

'I—it is I, Bianca,' he repeated, getting impatient.

She sighed deeply without saying anything, but her breathing was still alarmed. The Marquis had got to his daughter's bed, guided by the faint light of a lamp before a small image of the Virgin.

The girl fell back on the pillows and looked at the ceiling. The Marquis sat down by her bed, and his nervous fingers played with the white fringe of the coverlid.

'Why were you so frightened?' he asked, after a long silence.

'I don't know; it is stronger than I am.'

'When one is in the Lord's grace there is no need for fear,' he remarked sententiously and severely. 'Have you some mortal sin on your conscience?'

'No ... I don't think so, at least,' she said, hesitating.

They kept silence. The Marquis di Formosa looked into the shadows.

'Has the spirit come?' he asked afterwards, in a whispered, mysterious tone.

'Oh, do not speak of that,' she said, sighing again, shutting her eyes, and hiding her face in her hands.

'Has it come?' he insisted; a gambler's cruelty was raging in him now.

'For mercy's sake, if you love me, don't speak of that!' she said, taking his hand and kissing it, so as to move him more.

'Tell me, has it come?' he again repeated implacably.

She, feeling she could not escape that persecution, looked despairingly towards the Virgin, then hid her face in the pillows.

'Tell me, tell me, if it has come!' he cried out, bending over the pillows, as if to breathe his magnetic curiosity into his daughter's face.

'No, it has not,' she said, in a thread of a voice.

'You are lying.'

'I am not.'

'You are lying. The spirit has been here, I feel it.'

'Be good to me; say no more about this,' she said, trembling dreadfully.

'How did you see it? Awake? dozing? sleeping? It was a white figure, was it not, with lowered eyelids, but smiling?... What did it say to you? A very weak voice, wasn't it? Something you alone could have heard?'

'Father, you want to kill me,' she uttered desolately.

These are womanly fears,' said he disdainfully. 'Who ever died through a communication from on high? The meeting of soul and spirit is a spring of life. Bianca Maria, don't be ungrateful, don't be cruel; tell me all.'

'You are trying to kill me,' she repeated, desperately and resignedly.

'You are a fool! Do you wish me, your father, to pray to you? Well, I will; there is nothing else to be done. Children are ungrateful and wicked; they give back cruelty for our love. I pray to you, Bianca, I beg of you, as if you were my patron saint, to tell me all.'

'I will die of this, father,' she murmured, her voice choked in the pillows that helped her to curb her crying and sobs.

'Listen, Bianca,' he went on coldly, keeping in his anger; 'you must believe me. I am a man, I am sane, I am in my senses, I can reason. Well, it is an article of faith with me, as clear as the light, as the sun, that you have had to-night, or will have, a spirit's apparition. It will come to bless our family; it will tell you words of happiness. If it has come, so much the better; your duty as an obedient, loving daughter of the House of Cavalcanti is to tell me all, at once.'

'I know nothing,' she said dryly.

'Do you swear it?'

'I swear that I know nothing.'

'Then this vision will come in the succeeding hours of the night. I am going into the chapel, to pray. I am a sinner, but sinners, too, can ask for grace. I will pray that you may see and feel the spirit.'

'No, don't go away!' she cried out, getting up in her bed and catching hold of his arm with a despairing clutch.

'Why should I not?'

'Don't go away, for the love of God! If you have any affection for me, stay here.'

'I must go and pray, Bianca,' he exclaimed, carried away by excitement, not understanding his daughter's convulsive state.

'No, no—stay; I can't be left alone here, or I'll die of fright.' She spoke restlessly, quite pallid, her trembling hands still clutching her father's arm. She dared not look round. With her head down on her breast, she shut her eyes and bit her lips; while he, in his mad obstinacy, looked fixedly at his daughter, thinking he saw in her that spiritual disorder that must, by a fatality, go with the great miracles that have to do with the soul.

'How do you feel?' he questioned, very deeply and intensely, as if he wished to tear the truth from her soul.

'Stay here, stay here,' said she, her teeth chattering with terror.

'You see something?' he asked suggestively, with an intensity in his voice and will that was bound to influence that fragile feminine frame, broken as it was by the nervous shock.

'I am afraid to see—I am afraid!' she said, very low, leaning her forehead on her father's arm.

'Don't be afraid, dear; don't fear,' he whispered tenderly, paternally caressing her black hair.

'Be silent; keep silence,' said she, with a quick shiver. She continued to lean on his shoulder, hiding her face, shrinking all over. The Marquis put his arm round her waist, to keep up her quivering, feeble body; she hid more, clinging to her father as to a raft of safety. He sometimes felt her quiver all through her nerves.

'What is the matter?' he asked then.

'No, no!' she said, more by gesture than voice.

'Look, look—don't be frightened,' suggested the deluded man.

'Be silent!' she answered, shuddering. He held her up, waiting with a madman's patience that would wait for hours, days, months, years, provided the truth of his delusion were proved.

'Bianca darling,' the Marquis murmured, sometimes encouraging her tenderly. She answered with a sigh, that seemed a lamenting, suffering child's sob. Holding her against his breast, Formosa felt the strong rigidity of that young sickly frame shaken by long shivers. When she trembled all over, he felt the rebound. It seemed to him the implored revelation was imminent. He again said to her, obstinately, pitilessly, 'How do you feel?' She waved her hand, in an alarmed way, as if she wished to chase away a frightful thought or a dreadful vision. What did the agony of that young breast matter to him, the fatal want of balance in the nerves? In that chilly virginal room, a circle of light on the ceiling from the Virgin's lamp alone breaking the shadow, with the quivering form in his arms, the soul trembling before Divine mysteries, he felt it a solemn moment; time and space were not. He, Formosa, was facing at last the great mystery. From his innocent daughter's lips he would know his life's secret, his future: the fatal ciphers that contained his fortune—the spirit would tell Bianca Maria everything, and she would tell him.

'Bianca, Bianca, implore *him* to come and tell you whether we are to live or die. Pray to him, because *he*, the spirit, comes forth from the Divine, to tell you the divine word; pray to him, if he is here near you, or in you, if he is before your eyes or your fancy; pray to him, Bianca, pray to him. Our life is at stake. Save us, Bianca, save us!'...

He went on speaking, incoherently, invoking the spirit's presence, addressing the wildest, saddest prayers to her and to him. The girl, trembling, shivering, her teeth chattering with terror, clung on her father's neck, like a suffering child, fastened like a vice. She said no more, but it was evident the hour, the surroundings, and her father's voice increased her nervousness.

A stifled sob came from her breast, and a very faint, constant lament, like a dying child's, from her lips. He spoke to her all the time, but when he got more urgent, almost wrathful in his sorrow, he felt her arms twitching with despair. Then gradually a change came. To begin with, Bianca's hands and forehead were, as usual, icy cold; she was so bloodless, she had lost her vital heat. Indeed, in that spasm the deluded old man had felt that her whole body was frozen. Suddenly, at intervals, when her teeth stopped chattering and her arms relaxed through debility, he felt a slight heat rising under the skin on her hands and up to her forehead. It seemed a current of heat spreading all through her young body, which filled her impoverished veins with warm blood, and made her forehead and hands burn. He beard her breathing get more distressed; sometimes her breast rose with a long sigh, as if she needed air. Twice he tried to put her head down on the pillow, but she gave a frightened shiver.

'Don't leave me alone, for the love of God!' she stammered, like a baby.

'I won't leave you. Tell me what you see,' he repeated, indomitable and implacable.

'It is dreadful, dreadful!' Bianca stammered, going on trembling, trembling as if she had the body of an old woman of seventy.

'What is dreadful? Speak, Bianca, tell me everything; tell me what you have seen.'

'Oh!' lamented she despondingly.

Now the teeth had given up chattering, her short breathing came from her throat faintly, she burnt all over, and her quick respiration scorched her father's neck where her head leant; besides this, her temples and pulse beat rapidly, but her father, possessed altogether by his madness, in the mysterious half-light of that chilly night, close to the poor drowsy soul in the tortured body, lost all sense of realities. His sick fancy keenly enjoyed the hour's drama, without taking in how cruel it was. He was quivering with joy, indeed, as he believed the great moment of the spirit's revelation had come; the fortunes of the House of Cavalcanti were to be decided that moment. His daughter's uneasiness, terror, spasms, broken words, were easily explained; it was the Favour drawing near. So much time, so long had gone by in unhappiness and wretchedness; now all was to be changed. To-morrow he and his daughter would be rich—have millions! Oppressed and uneasy, Bianca Maria had slid down from her father's breast on to the pillows; her whistling breath was very audible, her eyes shone curiously. Nailed to the spot by his unhealthy curiosity, the Marquis stood by the bed, watching his daughter's every movement by the lamp-light, struck down as she was on that bed of sorrow. Suddenly, as if by an electric shock, her hands clutched the coverlet wildly; a hoarse cry came from her throat.

'What is it?' the Marquis cried out, shaken also.

'It is the spirit—the spirit!' she stammered, her voice changed to a deep cavernous tone.

'Where is it?' the father said in a whisper.

'In the doorway! Look at it; it is there!' she said firmly and forcibly, staring at the door.

'I see nothing—nothing! I am a poor sinner!' Formosa cried out despairingly.

'The spirit is there,' she whispered, as if she heard nothing.

'How is it clad? What is it doing? What does it say? Bianca, Bianca, pray to it!'

'It is clad in white ... it does not move ... it says nothing ...' she murmured in a dreamy way.

'Implore him—implore him to speak to you. You are free from sin, Bianca.'

'It does not speak ... it will not speak!'

'Bianca, pray in God's name, by His strength and power.'

They kept silence. The Marquis di Formosa kept his whole attention on the door where his daughter alone saw the spirit, his whole soul in prayer. She lay still more restless; her burning hands clutched the folds of the sheet between her fingers.

'What does it say?'

'It says nothing.'

'But why will it not speak? Why has it come if it will not speak?'

'It does not answer me,' she replied, still in the same voice that seemed to come from a distance.

'But what is it doing?'

'It looks at me ... looks at me steadily ... the eyes are so sad, so sad. It looks pityingly at me, just as if I were dead. Am I dead, then?'

'Now it will go away without telling you anything!' Formosa shouted out. 'Ask him what numbers come out to-morrow.'

She gave an agonized moan.

'I think it is weeping now, as if I were dead; it looks so to me. Tears fall down its cheeks.'

'Tears, sixty-five,' Formosa said to himself, as if he feared someone would hear him.

'It raises its hand to greet me....'

'Look how many fingers it lifts—look well; make no mistake.'

'Three fingers. It bows to me; it wants to go away....'

'Tell him to come back; pray him to—pray....'

'He signs "yes,"' Bianca Maria went on after a pause. 'It is going away—it has gone; it has disappeared....'

'Let us praise God!' Formosa cried out, kneeling at the foot of the bed. 'The fingers three, the hand five, tears sixty-five; we must find out the number for the dead girl. Let us thank God!'

'Yes, yes,' the girl murmured in a queer tone; 'we must find out the number for the dead girl—we must find out....'

'We will find out,' exclaimed Formosa, laughing like a madman.

He thought no more about his daughter, who was now in a state of high fever with the violence of the *effimere*, that carries off a life in twenty-four hours. She panted, drinking in the air with her open mouth, like a dying bird. The blood beat so wildly in her veins it seemed it would burst them; her whole slender form burned like red hot iron. But the Marquis di Formosa only felt a youthful impatience; he had gone twice to the window to see if day was breaking. No; he had still some hours to wait before he could play the spirit's numbers. It occurred to him he had no more money. How could he play? Not a franc. It was a cruel thing, this continual thirst nothing could satisfy. But he would find the money, if he had to sell the last of his furniture and pawn himself. He would get it, by Gad! now he had got the revelation— now the ministering spirit had deigned to enter his house. His fortune was in his hands; he would put everything on the spirit's numbers.

'Oh, Ecce Homo! Ecce Homo of Cavalcanti House! it was you did us this favour. A new chapel must be added for you, and four lamps of massive silver, always kept lit, in remembrance of what you have done for us.' The Ecce Homo would help him to get the money too. Good and powerful Ecce Homo, the family protector, give money—money to gamble with!

Overmastered by his fervent, passionate thoughts, the Marquis di Formosa spoke aloud, gesticulating with his hands through his hair, wandering about the room like a madman.

Bianca Maria went on raving in a whisper, because her breath was failing, softly, vaguely speaking of Maria degli Angioli, or with deep melancholy of a fresh, laughing, green country place she would like to live in, down there far, far off. But the old man, carried away by his thoughts, no longer listened to her, and as the cold dawn of March burst forth, two deliriums were confused together in that room—father's and daughter's tragically.

In the livid cold light of dawn the Marquis di Formosa wandered in a shaky way, with wild-looking eyes and pallid face, through his flat, searching his empty drawers and sparse furniture for something to sell or pawn. He found nothing. He opened the drawers with trembling hands again, and groped in them, shaking them hard, then he looked around with madness in his gaze, thinking he would like to sell or pawn the bare walls of the house that had once been his. Nothing, nothing! Little by little, eaten up by the lottery, valuable jewels had disappeared, heavy antique and modern silver plate, pictures by great masters, precious books, artistic rarities in bronze, ivory, carved wood—the house was stripped, only the furniture that it would have been disgraceful to part with was left. Alas! nothing could be found to turn into money so as to play the spirit's number. He wrung his hands despairingly; he had left Bianca Maria in a feverish, oppressed stupor, a few confused words still came from her lips, and the servants were still sleeping. He even went into the chapel, wildly; but the lamps burning there were brass. He had bought the altar vases himself when he sold the real silver ones, and had got imitation silver instead. He thought a moment of taking the silver crown from the Virgin's head, and the seven swords in her heart that represent the great agonized Mother's sorrows, but a mysterious dread restrained him.

He went out without being able to say a prayer even, the night's delusion and Saturday morning's feverish haste held him so strongly that dawn. He thought who he could borrow money from, but could not find anyone; he held his beating temples to keep his thoughts together, so as to get what he wanted. All friends of his own rank and his great relations kept away from him after his wife's death; but only after he had laid them all under contribution for his gambling. His present friends? They were all gamblers, all making desperate attempts that morning to go on staking; they would certainly not lend money—each one thought of himself, looked out for himself. New friends? That passion prevented him from finding any, except that morbid set of madmen, damned like himself. A great deal of money was needed, as the spirit had deigned to reveal himself; a fortune must be made that day or never. Suddenly a flash of light struck him: a name came to his mind. He could give him the money; he was a man of honour; he had a lot of money; he would not refuse a Formosa a small loan. While he wrote to Dr. Antonio Amati at his desk, on a leaf torn from a book full of ciphers, he thought he need not feel ashamed to ask a loan from a stranger, for he would give it back that very evening. After he had written, one thought made him tremble: if Amati said 'No'? He was a mere acquaintance, a stranger; money hardens all hearts.

'Take this letter to Dr. Amati, and bring the answer back,' he said to Giovanni, who came in, hardly awake, on being rung for.

'He will be asleep....'

'Take it!' Formosa ordered. He bit his lips, certain now that Amati would refuse; he felt a blush of shame come to his cheek. But he must have money—he must, at whatever cost! He flung himself in the easy-chair, looking at the ciphers on bits of paper scattered on the desk without seeing them; he felt overcome by that irrepressible rage of his ruling passion, at war with realities.

'When he awakes he will give the answer,' said Giovanni, coming in, silently waiting his master's orders.

'Giovanni, give me the rest of the money you have,' said Formosa sullenly.

'I haven't got any, sir,' the other answered, shaking all over.

'Don't tell lies; you have other fifty francs. Give me them at once....'

'My lord, I took the loan of it from a money-lender. I must give it back at so much a week; don't take it from me....'

'That does not matter to me,' Formosa said haughtily.

'Don't take it from me, my lord. If you knew what it was needed for....'

'It does not matter to me' the Marquis said fiercely. 'Give me the fifty francs....'

'They are for getting food for her ladyship....'

'That does not matter to me!' Formosa yelled.

'As that is so, I obey,' said the old servant despairingly, and he took out the other fifty-franc note. The Marquis snatched at it like a thief, and put it quickly in his pocket.

'Your wife has money, too; get it from her,' Formosa went on again coldly.

'Where could my wife get it?'

'She has some. Make her give it to you, and bring it here. Spare me a scene. If your wife denies it, you can leave the house at once, both of you.'

'No, my lord—no; I am going at once,' said the servant humbly.

But a scene followed in there; there was long, agitated talk between the husband and wife. The woman did not wish to let her money be carried off; she cried, wept, and sobbed. Silence at last, and then a moaning.

Giovanni came in again, with his old face distorted, and bent more, as if struck by paralysis. As he put another fifty francs down on the desk, silently, his eyes red with the rare, burning tears of old age, the Marquis was so struck by his appearance that he suddenly relented, and said good-naturedly:

'It is three hundred francs, between yesterday evening and to-day. This evening you will get it all.'

'How am I to get to-day's dinner?'

'I will see about it—at *four o'clock*,' the Marquis said vaguely.

'Her ladyship is ill; she will want a little soup this evening,' the servant muttered.

Then, searching his pockets, with a miserly grimace, the Marquis di Formosa gave three francs to the man, following them with a greedy look.

There was a knock. Formosa started. It was Dr. Amati's answer. It did not matter now if he said 'No.' But as he got the envelope in his hands, he knew by touch that the money he wanted was there, and, red with delight, he put the envelope in his pocket without opening it. He went out now, at eight in the morning, as if carried by an irresistible breath of wind; he went without turning back to look at his sick child, his bare house, his weeping servants, who had given him everything, the neighbour whose visits he had not paid for, and yet dared to ask a loan of money from—he went off, taking three hundred and fifty francs with him, to put it all on the spirit's numbers, while he had left his poor old servants fasting, and had haggled over a little soup for Bianca Maria. No one in the house saw him again till mid-day. His daughter lay in bed, in a burning fever, breathing with difficulty, often asking for something to drink—nothing else. Margherita sat down by the bed, saying the Rosary over to herself to pass the time. She often put her hand on the invalid's forehead, alarmed at its being so hot. The sick girl said nothing; she was sleeping, breathing uneasily. Suddenly, opening her eyes, she said distinctly to Margherita:

'Call the doctor to me.'

'He won't be at home now.'

'When he comes back, then.' And she shut her eyes again.

The doctor only came at half-past four. He stood at the door of the little room, scenting the feverish air.

'You might have called me before,' he said to Margherita roughly.

'Oh, sir, if I could tell you——'

He told her to hold her tongue. The invalid was looking at him, her lovely, gentle eyes wide open, her hand held out to him. The strong man, with the massive head, the good-natured, ugly face, got a look of great tenderness before the fragile creature Affection welled up from his heart. He felt at once that the fever would soon be over: it was falling already, with the suddenness of malaria; but the thorn of that miserable existence, trembling between life and death, victim of a disease he could not find out the meaning of, would stay in his heart.

'Now I am going to order a medicine for you,' he said gently to the sick girl, holding her hand in his.

'No, do not,' she said softly.

'Don't you want any?'

'Listen, listen!' she said, pulling him to her to let him hear better—'take me away!' She trembled as she said this, and Antonio, paling suddenly, struck by an indescribable emotion, could not even answer. 'Take me away!' she added humbly, as if imploring him.

'Yes, dear—dear,' he stammered; 'wherever you like—at once.'

'To the country—far off,' the poor thing whispered, 'where one sees no ghosts in fever, where there are no shadows nor frightful spectres.'

'What do you say?' said he, surprised.

'Nothing; take me away to the country, to greenness and peace with your mother ... before God.'

'Oh dear, dear!' He could say nothing else, this great man, in the supreme emotion, the sweetness of the idyll.

'Far away take me,' she still whispered, looking at him with great, good eyes.

Alone, very sweetly and modestly, they spoke of love without using words.

CHAPTER X
MAY AND SAN GENNARO'S MIRACLE

Gentle April opened all the flowers in the gardens, terraces, and balconies in Naples; wherever there was a little earth warmed by the sun, bedewed with rime, a flower sprang up. Common, uncultivated, popular flowers, quite a humble flora without refinements, having no exquisite colouring or scents, but bright, warm, bursting from the earth with profuse vegetation and plump, full petals. April made the big, sweet-smelling, blood-red roses blossom, and the pinks, beloved of the people—white, pink, variegated—*written on* as they poetically call them, as if these stripes were mystic words; then single and double stocks—white, yellow, red—that the town girls love; they grow them on the damp north balconies of Foria Street; and the mallow with green, perfumed leaves and little pink flowers; but above all, everywhere, roses and pinks—magnificent, velvety, almost arrogant roses, and rich, close pinks bursting their green envelope.

In the damp, dark squares of the low-lying quarters, from Santa Maria la Nova to Porto Piazzetta, from San Giovanni Maggiore to Santi Apostoli, in all these half-popular and cloistral, middle-class and archæological quarters, rose-sellers wandered about; some queer-looking hawkers with big baskets full of cut roses or slips, the root wrapped in a cabbage-leaf, giving such pathetic drawn-out cries that they reached the hearts of sentimental girls. The rose-girl comes into one of these little squares that are always soaking, dripping with dirty, black water, puts the basket on the ground, and sings on in a melancholy, drawn-out voice: 'Roses, lovely roses!' Then women's heads stick out of shops, balconies and gateways, attracted by the long, sad chant, full of melancholy, almost painful, voluptuousness.

Whoever has a few sous, or only one, buys these roses, the slips for the balconies, or cut ones to put before the Virgin, and to scatter, when faded, in the linen drawers. The girl, having sold part of her merchandise, lifts the basket on her head, and goes off, taking up her melancholy cry in the distance, dwelling on the roses' beauty.

That warm May-day all the seamstresses going errands, who found their lovers by chance at the street corners, carried a rose in their hands; all the common folk walking about in the narrow streets round Forcella wore pinks on their white muslin camisoles; the children out from school playing in the streets had flowers; even the servants had flowers on their market-baskets, laid on the provisions wrapped in a white towel.

Really, poetic sentiment was not the only reason that scattered flowers everywhere—at the street corners, in women and children's hands, on washing baskets, flour-sacks, fruit and tomatoes, in the big frying shops at Purgatorio ad Arco, and the old-clothes shops at Anticaglia; it was the quantity one could get for a penny: for a smile, a word, and flowers are so precious to humble folk, who love colour and are intoxicated with the slightest perfume. May-day! In that noon-day sun many dull, gloomy houses of Trinità Maggiore, Forcella, Tribunali, San Sebastiano, San Pietro a Maiella Streets, besides the flowers in the balconies, had put bright-coloured flags, old red damasks, yellow, bright, buttercup curtains, blue silk hangings edged with gold and silver, and many coloured stuffs, kept up in boxes for years, outside the railings for drapery.

The people that live in these tall, black, melancholy palaces, that only get the sun on the terraces, are patricians of old clerical families, very devout and pious, under the influence of all the great old churches around: the Gesù Nuovo, Santa Chiara, San Domenico Maggiore, San Giovanni Maggiore, Pietra Santa, the Sacramentiste, the Girolomini, San Severo, Donna Regina; and finally the influence of the old minster, the grand cathedral, so old, they say, it was a temple of the Sun in Naples' pagan times—or, rather, its early pagan times. There are rich, stern old middle-class families also in the high, dark houses who keep up the customs of their citizen forefathers, and have rigid monastic tendencies. These people, that bright May-day, had taken out of camphored chests silk draperies they had bought at the great factory Ferdinand of Bourbon set up at Terra di Lavoro, or from San Leucio, with its bright, gay factories, for weddings and baptisms held in their private chapels and oratories. A pious folk, that inherits faith in its blood, they are born, live, and die without doubting for a moment. They put all the repressed strength of fancy into that grand mystic dream that rises from the terrors of Hell to the supreme ecstasies of Paradise, having a horror of Purgatory, as if the flesh felt its warm flames; and, dreaming and dreaming on, they come to the last moment with eyes shut in invincible hope.

Besides the May roses and the hedge of pinks blooming on the balconies, in spite of want of sun, these pious folk had put out for rejoicings this May-day their brocades, damasks, and watered silks. May-day! The darkness of old Naples' streets was brightened up by that general wealth of sweet-smelling flowers, with petals scattered on the gray Vesuvian lava stones; and there being so many flowers everywhere, it seemed the sun must be there too. Its presence was felt up there, where the two narrow lines of tall palaces ended in a clear streak of soft blue sky—spring's thin azure. It seemed as if a white sun was down in these narrow openings, Tribunali and Forcella Streets, because so many coloured stuffs, such vivid draperies, waved from the balconies, windows, and terraces. In San Domenico Maggiore Square, especially, the ancient De Sangro and Carigliano Palaces had magnificent brocades; even San Severo Palace, that hides in a dark lane its gloomy vestibule, was dazzling with ancient stuffs. The fresh flowers in the shops, in the tiny balconies of poor houses that come by turns in old Naples with magnates' palaces, on the flat roofs and terraces, out in the air, between earth and heaven; the flowers carried by women, children, humble working people, artisans, beggars even—fresh flowers—formed the people's festival in honour of Naples' protector. That was the explanation, too, of the silk draperies, the gold and silver damasks, the tapestries; it was all the tribute of the old Naples' nobility and burghers to Naples' great patron.

May-day is lovely in Naples, from the air's caressing breath, from the vivid streak of blue sky that manages to make the darkest, most villainous streets gay. May-day is lovely, from the roses that bloom on all sides, seeming to grow from women and children's hands even, as well as all the common garden and field flowers. It is miracle-working San Gennaro's day. It is on May-day his relics are carried from the cathedral crypts—called *Succorpo*, or San Gennaro's Treasury—to Santa Chiara Church, so that the saint may deign, on the prayers of the people, to do the miracle of liquefying his blood. The Bishop of Pozzuoli's head, which was cut off by the executioner's axe, is set in an old gold mask. It bears the Bishop's mitre, enriched with precious stones, and sparkles with a thousand fires. The other relic is the coagulated blood, kept in a very fine crystal phial: through the cold dark clot of blood a straw is visible, going across it and immovable. It was gathered by pious folk present at the Bishop's martyrdom, and religiously preserved. This is the day, the fourth of the flowery, sweet-smelling May calends, that these relics go, borne in triumphant procession, from the cathedral to Santa Chiara Church.

Now, that year 188- it seemed as if the flower of faith grew more vigorously in the people's heart—that devotion to the city's patron burst forth more brightly; for since two in the afternoon the crowd had been rushing along to old Naples, obstructing the narrow streets, lanes and blind alleys. San Gennaro is profoundly popular in Naples, much—a hundred thousand times—more than the real first Bishop of Naples, Sant' Aspreno. But who remembers *him*? He is one of the forgotten ones of the martyrology, which has its shipwrecks in the sea of oblivion, such as happen in other seas.

Sant' Aspreno's little church stands in a lane in the Porto quarter, and is underground; one goes down thirty steps, below the level of the soil; it is merely an oratory, rude, dark, damp, and alarming, where Sant' Aspreno's stick is adored, the pastoral staff of Naples' first pastor. But who goes to Sant' Aspreno's? A few devout people and some lovers of archæological things. San Gennaro, before all the other saints—before Sant' Anna, the powerful old woman, or San Giuseppe, the patron of a good death, next in order to the Immaculate Virgin and the Eternal Father, who are worshipped in Santa Chiara. San Gennaro has the devotion of all lowly Neapolitan hearts to himself. Above all, he was a Neapolitan, born in that black, evil-smelling quarter, Molo Piccolo, where it seems his descendants still live, and take great pride in such an ancestor. He came of Naples common folk, and his family consists of some old working-women, who spend their time between work and prayer, carrying out the *spiritual life*—trying, at least, to reach their great ancestor's perfection in piety. Glorious San Gennaro, the Bishop who suffered martyrdom! His head was cut off by infidels at Pozzuoli, on a great marble stone, which is still preserved: it has a large scar, and three streaks of blood running down; the severed head, being cast into the sea, swam from Pozzuoli to Naples, the face keeping a deathly pallor from loss of blood.

Nor from that day that the saint's head was picked up and preserved, and the coagulated blood put into a phial, to this, has the saint ever ceased to protect Naples. In the maritime suburb, on the Maddalena Bridge, where the little stream Sebeto has to go under a stone arch, the patron saint's statue in marble looks at Vesuvius close at hand, and stands with two fingers raised in a commanding attitude. By that gesture the saint has prevented lava from coming into Naples during Vesuvius' tremendous eruptions; never will the lava dare to pass that limit. San Gennaro, with uplifted finger, says: '*Thou shalt go no further!*' From the most ancient times, twice a year— in soft September, when his name-day occurs, and in flowery May—San Gennaro does the miracle of liquefying his blood before the people. Whilst here at Naples the blood in the phial boils up, making the straw fixed in the cold, dry clot move about, in Pozzuoli the blood on the marble block gets fresh and bright; and whoso standing on the shore has the eyes of faith sees the saint's livid, cut-off head floating in. The miracle is repeated twice every year. When it is later than the usual hour, it is a bad sign; it means a bad year: if he were not to do the miracle ... but the patron saint could not forsake his faithful city. In eruptions, epidemics, earthquakes, his hand is always raised to mitigate and overcome the scourge. All the common people have their own legends about him, besides the great legend of the miracles. The great saint was a Naples man, poor, of the people; there has not been a king, a prince or great lord who has visited San Gennaro's chapel without adding a splendid gift to the patron's wealth. Naples' common folk, to cry up their saint, go about saying proudly and tenderly, 'Even Vittorio! Even Vittorio!' which means that the great King Victor Emmanuel also brought his gift to the patron saint. In former days there were knights of San Gennaro, and his treasury was guarded with hierarchal pomp; the keys were under a solemn trust. There are no longer any knights; indeed, the order is abolished, and the old patrician pomp is rather diminished. But what of that? The saint is stronger than ever, powerful, miracle-working, safe in the people's heart as in an inviolable tabernacle.

That year the people's love for San Gennaro came out stronger than ever, as if a new rush of faith had fortified their souls. At a certain hour the traffic through Forcella and Tribunali was stopped; all who were leaving Naples or arriving had to make a long round to the station by Marina or Foria Road. The cabman told any annoyed fare who asked the reason of the endless journey, 'It was San Gennaro'; and touched his hat with his whip in compliment to the saint. He tried to hurry his horse, not for the sake of being obliging to his fare, but that he himself, after putting up his cab or by taking his stand with it at a street corner, might see San Gennaro's precious blood pass. If all the little streets were crowded with people, all the sumptuous balconies of the patricians' houses and the small, mean balconies alongside were swarming, and in the wide street by the cathedral the crowd was stupendous. That great road that goes down rather too steeply from the hill to the sea from Foria Road to Marina, which was the first surgical cut through old Naples (an energetic cut, but not well carried out; rather ferocious and ridiculous as regards architecture, but certainly sanitary—the Duomo Road, which is the Toledo of old Naples), had then all the majesty of its great days, when the popular flood alarms even those who count over its numbers proudly. People stretched up to Gerolomini and Pendino, above and below, in the two porticos to the right and left of the cathedral; they stood on the broad flight of steps, climbed on the gas-lamps, and even on the scaffolding that has been up so many years for repairs to the west front; there were people there close together, crushed in, choking in the open air, hanging on to iron girders or a beam, and balancing themselves in an extraordinary way on an insecure board. Sometimes a mother in the crowd held up her child to let it get air, and it waved its legs and arms rejoicingly for that throw into the gentle May air. The cathedral police vainly tried to make way for the procession, which was already formed in the church; but when they pushed back the crowd, it surged back again so strongly it went up against the façade of the church.

Suddenly from under the black arch of the great wide-open door, where some torches were burning in the background, solemn psalmody was heard, and the head of the procession appeared amidst silence and stillness in the crowd. Very, very slowly, with an almost imperceptible motion, the Naples religious orders came forward in advance. White and black monks, brown, shoeless, or in sandals, with cape or shaven head, singing holy San Gennaro's lauds, with wandering eyes, and holding bent torches, whose slender flame was hardly visible, being swallowed up by the sunlight. A little boy followed to pick up the great wax drops that fell from the torches. Dominicans, Benedictines, Franciscans, Verginisti, missionaries, Jesuits, monks, and priests in double file were flowing along, carried by the crowd, not looking at it, gazing at a far-off point on the horizon or on the ground. All mouths were open to sing the Latin psalms—severe, stem mouths, like the psalms that came from them, which rose in waves over the crowd's head; and involuntarily, as the religious orders moved along imperceptibly down towards Foria, the devout who knew the Divo Gennaro's Latin prayers joined in the solemn song, while many of the crowd, excited by the air and light and others singing, intoned a wordless psalmody, seized by a mystical fervour. From the bottom of the Duomo Road the crowd, advancing with the procession, went with open mouths; thousands of voices were solemnly singing, the wide sky swallowing up the sound. But those that went on towards Forcella did not leave the Duomo Road open: others took their place, and pushed them on; then, a string of parish priests and the canons of San Giovanni Maggiore having passed, there was a lively tumult among the people, showing evident interest and pleasure. It was caused by the slow filing-out of saints that go with Saint Gennaro, to do him honour in his chapel—there are forty-six of them, either whole statues or busts, in silver. These saints stand on litters, carried on four men's shoulders. These porters disappear among the crowd, so that the saint seems to go along miraculously by himself, all sparkling, over the people's heads. Very, very slowly, as I said, for the crowd was so dense, so congested, the statues sometimes stood motionless, while the people gazed on them with suffused eyes lingeringly, for Naples' devotion loves to feed at length on the sight of their special protectors, who are shut up in the treasury all the year, and only come out that day to bless the poor folk.

As every saint appeared under the dark vane of the great door and went through the people on the way to Santa Chiara by Forcella, there were shouts of joy. The first was Naples' other patron, one who comes next to San Gennaro as a protector, Sant' Antonio. He carries a staff with a tinkling bell on the top, and at his side is the head of the animal he loved. The bell swayed as the saint moved, and rang out cheerfully above the crowd, making them gay, so that they cried out: 'Sant' Antonio! Sant' Antonio!'

Excited, almost sobbing, Carmela, the cigar-girl, asked the saint's protection. He, too, loved an ugly beast, as she loved that ungrateful, hard-hearted Raffaele, called Farfariello. She had been pushed right into the telegraph-office in Duomo Road, and her strained face following his figure showed her hard life and privations plainer than ever. She gazed on the saint's shining face, he who had resisted so many temptations, imploring him to take that love out of her heart, and free her from love's temptations, for it made her gnawing poverty twice as hard.

'Sant' Antonio, Sant' Antonio!' the crowd shouted to the saint as he went off.

'Sant' Antonio, deliver me!' Carmela sobbed out, not knowing she had cried out, and that her neighbours were listening.

But one prays aloud in Naples, whether in the church or the street. Now the Archangel Michael, the triumphant warrior, appeared, tall and agile, in a splendid victorious pose, his dazzling corslet close to his young figure, a helmet on the fair, triumphant head, lance in hand to kill the dragon his foot presses down; Michael, mystic and war-like, saint and hero. Seeing him appear so handsome and breathing out triumph, with the devil wriggling vainly under his feet, the devout had an artistic feeling in their enthusiasm: San Michele was called on by thousands of voices.

Leaning against a column of the portico, to the right of the cathedral, was the Marquis di Formosa. He took off his hat in humble greeting of the brilliant Archangel, for whom he had great devotion; that combination of cherubim and warrior pleased his violent disposition and love of fighting so much. As the splendid, handsome saint came forward, for ever victorious, trampling on the dragon, the old Marquis prayed passionately and fervently that he might be enabled to overcome the dragon of poverty, shame and death that came against him every day; he implored great Michael, overthrower of the devil, to lend him his holy lance to kill the monster that threatened to devour him. San Michele went down the road to the sea also; he was so handsome, flaming with glory in the noon-day light, that the three syllables of his name were repeated over and over again, up and down, as fire runs along a powder-train: 'Michele! Michele! Michele!'

But San Rocco made a diversion, the saviour of the plague-stricken, the people's protector in all epidemics; he is dressed as a pilgrim, with mantle, hood, and staff; he raises the tunic to show the bare knee, with a sore carved on it, a sign of the plague. A faithful little dog follows him—so faithful that people say: 'San Rocco and his dog,' referring to inseparables. This strong friendship, the saint's rather queer figure, in a short cloak, and the dog following—this well-known story, excites affectionate hilarity among the crowd. They look on San Rocco as a dear, indulgent friend they can joke with, as he never gets in a rage.

'Is your knee cold, Santo Rocco?'

'Hi, hi, baldhead!'

'Lend me your great-coat, Santo Rocco!'

But the really devout were scandalized, and insisted on silence. The lovely saint who was a sinner now appeared, the penitent Maddalena, quivering over her bearers' heads, her fine hair falling down her back, her eyes bedewed with petrified tears; behind her, curiously enough, came another saintly sinner, Maria Egiziaca, consumed and wasted by a not less ardent remorse than the Magdalene's. A sort of dull shiver went through all those who saw the statues pass in their midst—it was a quiet excitement that had no outburst. On the widest low step of the flight, under the façade scaffolding, stood Filomena, Carmela's unhappy sister, in blue skirt, gray silk bodice, a pink ribbon round her neck, hair combed to the top of the head, cheeks covered with rouge. She did not hear the insolent hints of those around her. Pulling up her embroidered shawl, she prayed earnestly to the two saints—sinners like herself, but still saints—in blessed San Gennaro's name, to do her the grace of freeing her from her disgraceful life, and she would offer up a solid silver heart.

Then there was a great flutter among the women in the balconies and street. After San Giuseppe and Sant' Andrea Avellino, both patrons of a *good death*, and therefore very dear to imaginative Neapolitans, who have the greatest fear of death; after San Alfonso di Liguori, who is called 'wry-neck,' with loving familiarity, because his head leans to one shoulder; after San Vincenzio Ferrari, who bears the flame of the Holy Ghost on his head, and an open book of the law in his hands—when all these popular saints passed amid shouts, smiles, and affectionate greetings, a fine shining saint, as if newly out of the engraver's hands, with a round, good-natured face and open lowered hands to rain down blessings, came out of the cathedral. It was San Pasquale Baylon, the girls' patron saint—he they make a *novena* to to get a husband; he sends husbands, being an accommodating, joyous saint: all the lassies know the figure, they recognise him at once. From a balcony with a dressmaker's signboard, 'Madama Juliana,' Antonietta the blonde, with her friend Nannina, let fall a rose, that whirled slowly down on to San Pasquale's arm. All felt the devotion, the longing, in that act; quantities of roses were thrown from the balconies and street at San Pasquale. 'Like you, just the same, oh, blessed San Pasquale,' prayed the girls, referring to the husband they wanted.

Now the procession hurried a little; the saints passed quicker, for the impatience of the crowd in front of the cathedral and Duomo Road got tremendous. Great shudders went through the people; all this splendour of silver aureoles and faces, that singular walking over people's heads, and going off towards Forcella, the continuous new silvery apparitions in the great black vane of the cathedral door, gave a nervous feeling even to quiet onlookers.

Cesare Fragalà and De Feo the medium were standing in a little coffee-house doorway to see the procession, but the mild little confectioner, who fled from his shop every day he could, to follow the mysterious lanky medium, had lost the old youthful joyousness and certainty about life—his face had a sickly, care-lined look now. The medium, though he pumped out money every week from the whole cabalistic group, and from others too, still wore his dirty torn clothes, unstarched, frayed linen, and cravat curled up like a wick; his complexion was still yellow with dull-red, scirrhus-like streaks, as if he had barely recovered from a severe fever. The medium always brought Cesare Fragalà along with him now; he insisted on keeping up with De Feo's fantastic ideas, though his simple commercial mind did not understand them; but he was furious, enraged at himself for his want of comprehension. He accused his own disposition, as being too lively, healthy, and stupid to be able to take in the spirituality and refinements of him who had the luck to be visited by the spirits.

Now, Don Pasqualino had told all his devotees plainly enough that a great fortune would come to them that May Saturday, sacred to San Gennaro's precious blood. The gamblers listened greedily; for many weeks, for ever so long, they had not won a half-penny. Except Ninetto Costa, the stock-broker, who made a big profit off some numbers he got from a wine merchant's lad who brought him an account to settle, and Marzano, who got an *ambo* of fifty francs from his friend the cobbler's advice, no one else had got anything, in spite of the inspired friar, or the medium, good spirits or bad, in spite of all their prayers and magic.

Now, Don Pasqualino, who had sucked up hundreds of francs that winter and spring, said that San Gennaro would certainly grant a favour that first Saturday in May, and all the Cabalists believed him, and were scattered here and there among the crowd in Duomo Road, having agreed to meet at Vespers in Santa Chiara. But Cesare Fragalà clung the harder to the medium, the deeper he plunged in the gambling gulf; he had staked a lot that Saturday, and was determined to keep an eye on him. Whenever a saint appeared, the medium turned up his eyes, and prayed in a whisper in the midst of the crowd; Fragalà, alongside of him, crossed himself distractedly. He stretched his ears to hear all the medium said when each saint came out. Now Santa Candida Brancaccio passed, one of the first Naples Christian martyrs, a young woman looking up to heaven, and in her right hand she held a long arrow, that of divine love. A voice called out from the crowd, supposing the arrow to be a pen:

'Write a letter for me to the eternal Father, Santa Candida!'

'The saint is writing for you,' the medium at once chimed in, turning to Fragalà.

'So we hope—that is my hope,' he humbly replied.

A great noise greeted San Biagio, another Bishop of Naples; he is shown blessing the town. For two or three years diphtheria and quinsy had kept the hearts of Naples' mothers in terror, especially among the lower classes. San Biagio is just the saint for throat complaints. When the silver saint came out, amidst clamour, fathers and mothers held out their children to the holy Bishop to get his blessing, that they might escape the dreadful scourge that killed so many innocents.

'San Biase! San Biase!' screamed out the excited, sobbing mothers, holding up their children.

Annarella too, Carmela's and unhappy Filomena's sister, held up her two remaining sons, for the smallest was dead, after having languished a long time. Ah! he would never again be waiting for her on the cellar doorstep, patiently munching a bit of bread till she came back from work. Poor little Peppinello—he was dead! He died of wretchedness in a damp, smelly cellar, from bad, coarse food, with only his little garments to cover him when asleep, always clinging to his mother for warmth. Mother's little flower was dead, starved by the *bonafficciata*, by that terrible lottery that ruined Gaetano, that drove him to steal his children's bread. Annarella would never be consoled for that death. The two left to her were well-behaved and strong, but they were not her blonde, delicate flower. They had dragged her there to see San Gennaro, and when the wretched woman saw so many little ones held up she lifted hers too, weeping and sobbing, thinking her dear flower had not been saved either by San Biase, San Gennaro, or all the saints in Paradise. But as the day went on, the people's emotion increased; everyone was given up to strong emotions that grew stronger every moment from the influence of those around them. In the excited eyes of girls, mothers, the poor, the unhappy, the guilty, all who needed help, whether moral or material, that show of saints got to be like a dream; they saw a shining vision pass, with silvery, dazzling reflections; the names got lost, but the whole procession of the blessed images was impressed on them.

The crowd, now confused and deafened, shaken by religious fervour, did not recognise a group of saints of Naples' earliest ages—Sant' Aspreno, San Severo, Sant' Eusebio, Sant' Agrippino, and Sant' Attanasio, most antique saints, rather obscure and forgotten. A roar like thunder greeted the five Franciscans who keep watch round San Gennaro in the *succorpo*: San Francesco d'Assisi, Di Paolo, Di Ceronimo, Caracciolo, and Borgia. Another shout when Sant' Anna, the Virgin's mother, came out, to whom, say the people, no grace is ever refused. No one troubled themselves much about San Domenico, who invented the Rosary, as no one in the confusion of that noontide hour recognised the proud Spanish monk, except the gloomy Finance Secretary, Don Domenico Mayer. Being pushed by the crowd against a wall, he kept his tall hat well over his eyes, and his arms were crossed in a proud, gloomy way, his lips set in a sad, sceptical smile. The saints went on and on, out of the cathedral's great dark portal, towards Forcella, rather quicker now; the crowd swayed from right to left, as if to free itself from the constraint of that close attention.

The saints' procession was just about finishing, having lasted nearly an hour, from the slowness of the going, and it ended with San Gaetano Thiene, the angelic San Filippo Neri, with the holy doctors Tommaso and Agostino, Santa Irene, Sant' Maria Maddalena di Pazzi, the great Santa Teresa in ecstasy, all ardour and passion, that magnificent saint of Avila, who died of divine love. When the long file of saints finished, and the first of the cathedral canons came out, there was a great movement among the waiting people. All stretched their heads to see better, not to lose a tittle of the religious show; but the noise was unrestrained in spite of this close attention. At last the canons ended also, and finally, under the great embroidered, gold-fringed canopy, appeared the chief pastor of the Neapolitan Church, pallid, his face radiant with a deeply compassionate expression, his lips moving in prayer. Eight gentlemen held up the poles of the canopy, eight choir-boys swung censers of smoking incense around him. The Archbishop, a Cardinal Prince of the Church, walked slowly, alone, under the canopy, his eyes fixed on his own clasped hands; and the whole crowd of women stretching out their arms, men praying, children lisping San Gennaro's name, gazed not at the canopy, gold vestments, or jewelled mitre, but affectionately, enthusiastically at the Archbishop's waxen, clasped hands, weeping, crying, asking favours and pity, gazing fixedly at what he pressed in his hands, now trembling with sacred respect. To it were directed all glances, all sighs, all prayers. The Cardinal Archbishop of Naples held the phial of the precious blood.

In Santa Chiara's fine church, all white with stucco and loaded with gilding like a very spacious royal hall, the crowd was waiting for San Gennaro's miracle. It was not yet night, but thousands of wax tapers, on the high altar and in the side chapels, especially on those dedicated to the Virgin and Eternal Father, lighted up the vast, lovely, graceful church. On the high altar, San Gennaro's head, in a gemmed mitre, the face ornamented with gold, was placed on a white napkin in a gold dish. The two phials of the precious blood stood more in the middle, for the adoration of the faithful. All around the high altar and behind the antique carved wood balustrade that cuts off a large space with the altar from the rest of the church, stood the forty-six silver statues that form a guard of honour to San Gennaro's relics. The Cardinal Archbishop and the canons were doing service at the high altar to Naples' holy patron, that he might perform the miracle; behind the balustrade, to the side of the high altar, stood a solitary, favoured, happy group of old men and women, all in black, with white neckerchiefs and cravats, the men uncovered, the women with a black veil over their hair, a group watched, commented on, and envied by all the other devotees. They were San Gennaro's relations; they alone had the right to go up to the high altar to see the miracle at half a yard's distance.

Then came an immense crowd—in the great single nave of Santa Chiara, in the side chapels, and even outside the two great doors, on the steps and cloisters, where the latest arrivals stood on tiptoe, dazzled by the thousands of tapers, trying to see something, struggling vainly to push a step forward, for there was no more room for anyone. All were agitated and disquieted, from the Cardinal Archbishop kneeling in prayer before the altar to the humblest little woman of the lower class; all were waiting till the heavenly Gennaro carried out the miracle. Most fervently, with head bent over the seat in front, with the trusting piety of a young heart, Bianca Maria Cavalcanti was praying, as the miraculous moment drew near. She prayed to San Gennaro, in the name of his precious blood, to give peace to her father's heart, to give Amati faith; and sincerely, in the great, wise, deep goodness of her heart, she asked nothing for herself. It was enough for her that her father's sick, troubled, tortured heart should have peace; that Antonio Amati's strong, hard heart, besides its human love, should share the highest tenderness of the Divine. Here in a short time one of the greatest miracles of religion would be accomplished. Could not San Gennaro work a miracle in their hearts, if she worshipped with her whole strength? She prayed on, her cheeks flushed with an unwonted fire, a faint blush over them, with a restrained force of mystic enthusiasm, a new passion that had come into her frozen life and brightened it.

At the high altar, his face turned to heaven, breathing intense faith, his voice trembling with overpowering emotion, the Cardinal Archbishop was saying the Latin prayers in honour of Naples' high protector. The whole crowd responded with a long thundering 'Amen!' 'Amen!' came from Santa Chiara's patrician nuns, hidden behind the choir grating.

After the *Oremus*, a moment's silence followed; the fore-running breath of great things seemed to pass over the praying people. San Gennaro's relations at the high altar intoned the *Credo* in Italian impetuously, and the whole church took it up; that ended, there were two minutes of uneasy waiting, to see if the miracle was beginning. But a second, a third *Credo* was soon taken up with vigour, as if the whole people declared its belief, swore it on their conscience, gave themselves over to faith in spirit and truth, impetuously. The Cardinal Archbishop, kneeling, his hands covering his face, prayed on in silence. The *Credo* went on behind him, intoned at short intervals by San Gennaro's relations, and carried on by the whole people. A solemn note stood out here and there amid the general rumble from a desolate heart, a sharp note struck off tortured nerves.... 'I believe!' shouted the people, with a break in the voice which seemed to denote a thousand prayers, vows, and hopes.

Ah! Luisella Fragalà, too, seated in a corner beside the melancholy Signora Parascandolo, was a profound believer. Tears, caused by her excited religious feelings, ran down her cheeks silently. She had a dark presentiment of coming misfortune; she felt it, without seeing or making out what it was, but sure that it was on its way inexorably. She asked San Gennaro for strength, such as he had in his frightful martyrdom, to bear the mysterious catastrophe that was coming on her. Signora Parascandolo was saying the Creed too with the people in a feeble voice; but in the almost frightened pauses, while waiting for the imminent miracle, she, bereaved of her children, begged San Gennaro to grant her a grace, to take her from this land of exile, whence all her children were gone, leaving her alone, groping in the cold and darkness. Rosy Agnesina's happy mother, just like the unhappy mother who was wounded in the past, as she was to be in the future, asked for strength to conquer or to die.

But at the fifteenth *Credo* uneasiness began among the multitude; the words of faith sounded shrilly, like a challenge flung to unbelievers, but they had a quiver of secret dread; the pauses between each *Credo* got longer as the depression of waiting wore out their nerves, then it was taken up again enthusiastically, as if the renewed rush of feeling was terrible, as is the way with crowds.

The wildest in mystic enthusiasm were the old people at the high altar; from behind them a flame ran from one heart to another, carrying the devouring fire into soft indolent temperaments, even to the hearts of sceptics, who trembled as if a rude revolution had struck them and was clearing their eyes. At the twenty-first *Credo* there was anguish in the expectation. All eyes went from the saint's head on the gold dish to the clear crystal phial with its clot of dark blood. The head, in its gemmed mitre and yellow gold mask, sparkled with metallic, rather livid reflections; the blood was still congealed, a stone that prayers could not break. At the twenty-second *Credo*, intoned with a burst of rage, some shouts were heard, calling out desperately:

'San Gennaro! San Gennaro! San Gennaro!'

The feverish prayers recited by the multitude in Santa Chiara, which humbly, forcibly, tremblingly implored a miracle from Naples' holy patron, were fervently said by two women kneeling in the crowd, their elbows on straw seats, and faces hidden, absorbed soul and body in the grace they implored. Donna Caterina, the clandestine lottery keeper, and Donna Concetta, the money-lender, had taken a vow together to San Gennaro for a bishop's heavy gold ring with a large topaz, if he would do them the grace to end their sufferings: either change their lovers, Ciccillo and Alfonso Jannacone's, hearts, make them tolerant of the sisters' enterprises, or change their own hearts, and free them from love of money. A ring, a magnificent ring, to the miracle-working saint if he did that miracle for them; so they both prayed in a whisper, saying their offer over again, monotonously raising their imploring, tearful eyes to the high altar, where the great mystery was imminent. But the people were in a panic already from that delay; they felt a great terror that just that year, after two centuries and a half, the saint, angry, perhaps, with the sins of the people, should refuse to do the miracle that is the proof of his benevolence. The Creed, taken up again after a longer, deeper, and therefore more emotional pause of silence, had an alarmed, almost angry, tone, and burst out with a despairing rush; above all, the old women's voices at the high altar got angry and frightened, trembling with sorrow and terror. In a silent pause, suddenly one of them said, in a voice shaken by devout familiarity, meek jocularity, and uncontrollable impatience:

'Old cross-patch, you want to keep us waiting, eh?'

'San Gennaro! San Gennaro! San Gennaro!' yelled the populace, curiously excited.

Down there, at the bottom of the church, near the wall, where that sweet, faded Madonna, said to be Giotti's, calms the eye with its subdued colouring, Don Pasqualino stood in an attitude that was all prayer; he was standing, but his head and shoulders were bent forward obsequiously, and now and then, when he raised his head from tiredness or inspiration to look at the gilded, painted sky in the church, the whites of his eyes looked enormous, out of proportion, and all colour had left his cheeks; his livid pallor went on increasing. By a magnetic attraction, all those who believed in him and his visions had gathered round him, all disturbed-looking, full of repressed despair, that showed itself in some faces as if they were deep down in sorrow's abyss, for that Saturday, too, had brought them a great disappointment, two hours before, when the lottery figures came out; all were bent by a gnawing remorse, for they felt guilty towards others and themselves. The Marquis di Formosa was bowed, his fine figure looked almost decrepit, for he felt the shame of his disreputable life; he was losing everything, even his daughter, in a slow agony of bad health and wretchedness. Cesare Fragalà's commercial standing was always getting more compromised; he felt his trading correspondents' coldness, his wife's evident low spirits and secret dread, hoping always, but in vain, to set it all right with a big haul. Ninetto Costa was pallid, but smiling, his eyes hollow from sitting up at night and anxiety; he often thought of the catastrophe, choosing in his mind between dishonourable flight and the revolver shot that does not clear scores, but softens people. Baron Lamarra was there, big, fat and flabby, cursing his ambitious beggar-on-horseback dreams, shuddering at the idea of that promissory note signed by himself and his wife. Marzano's gentle smile had got rather idiotic, for he increased his frugality every week so as to be able to gamble; he had given up snuff, smoking and wine, had pawned his pension papers, and was now getting compromised in queer affairs. Colaneri and Trifari were getting no more pupils; the first especially felt himself suspected, discredited, fearing every morning, as he entered the school, to be turned out by order of a superior, or knocked down by the students. All, all, were attacked by that Saturday-evening desolation, the black, terrible hour when conscience alone speaks, loudly, sternly, inflexibly. Still, they were in church, and the most indifferent and unbelieving murmured some words of prayer; they still surrounded the medium, eagerly looking at him as he prayed. One could see from that fascination that he still had power over them, and judge from their eager glances that once the momentary discouragement was past the passion would grow again. Ah! but that hour in the midst of the crowd, breathing out all its unhappiness in prayer, was as frightful for them, who were guilty, as the fatal night of Gethsemane was for the great sinless One.

Despairingly, all fixed their eyes on the high altar, where the burning candles cast reflections on the saint's face.

'San Gennaro! San Gennaro!' the people shouted out as every *Credo* ended.

A wind of terror that the miracle would not come blew over them and burst out in their voices. San Gennaro's relatives were torn with sorrow and rage; they had got to the thirty-fifth *Credo,* and the time was going by with threatening slowness; they, feeling at once offence at their holy ancestor's delay and despair at his anger, called out to him things like this:

'San Gennaro, face of gold, don't keep us waiting any longer!'

'You are in a rage, eh? What have we done to you?'

'Old cross-patch, do the miracle for your people!'

The feeling of rage, tenderness, devotion, and agitation that breathed in these reproaches and pious invocations cannot be expressed. The legend says San Gennaro likes to be pressed, and does not get offended at the remarks his relatives and the populace make to him, and the people's emotion was such that at the thirty-eighth *Credo* each sentence of the prayer was said desperately, as if every word was dragged out by overpowering agony; cries burst out far back:

'Green face!'

'Ugly yellow face!'

'Not much of a saint!'

'Do this miracle—do it!'

The thirty-eighth *Credo* was clamorous; everyone said it from one end of the church to the other: the Cardinal, the priests, men, women, and children, everyone was seized by a mystical rage. All of a sudden, in the great silent pause that followed the prayer, the Archbishop turned to the people; his face, irradiated by an almost divine light, seemed transfigured; his uplifted hands displayed the phial. The precious blood in its thin crystal covering was bubbling up. What a shout! The old church's foundations seemed shaken by it; the echoes were so loud and long that passers-by in neighbouring streets were alarmed; the sonorous bells in the tower seemed to quiver of themselves; the weeping—the sob of a whole kneeling people, cast down on the ground, kissing the cold marble, holding out their arms, quivering with the vision of the blood—was endless.

At the high altar the old relatives lay as if they were dead; one single powerful force bent the whole crowd; there was one lament, sob, prayer; in that long moment everyone mentioned with warm tears and shaking voice his own sorrow and need. At the high altar the Archbishop and clergy now stood up, and sang the anthem in full tones above the organ notes.

CHAPTER XI
AN IDYLL AND MADNESS

Dr. Antonio Amati was deeply in love with Bianca Maria Cavalcanti. That rugged heart that had got like iron in its conflict with science, men and things, that had had to drink up all its tears again, and look on calmly at all kinds of wretchedness—that iron heart which had a great deal of coldness in its simplicity, which, as regards sentiment, was virginal, childishly pure, had opened out slowly, almost timidly, to love. At first.... How had it been at first? The habit of seeing the white, melancholy figure at the balcony windows every day, noticing that gentle, slender apparition among the shadows of the court in these melancholy surroundings. At first it had been nothing but habit, which is often the beginning of love; it creates, strengthens, and makes it invincible. Then came pity, a lively source of tenderness—a source that often hides underground, disappears, seems lost; but, later on, further on, it burst forth gaily, flowing inexhaustibly.

While Bianca Maria's fainting-fit was going on, from the Sacramentiste parlour to her bare room in the Rossi Palace, her transparent face, shut eyelids with their violet shadows, lips as pale as the tender pink of a rose, made him fear more than once she was dead. He often saw that youthful figure again in his mind in a death-like torpor; he saw her as if dead. Pity twined itself round his heart on recalling the sorrowful expression that often crossed the girl's face, as if a terrible secret, a physical and moral torture, went through her soul and nerves; pity led him to wish to save her from her suffering. The day the idea flashed into the great doctor's mind to snatch the pure creature from death, sickness, and unhappiness, whenever his life-saving instinct warned him the struggle was beginning, when he felt the appeal to his intuitive perception of life, to his energy and courage, when his whole strength was summoned up to save Bianca Maria, he knew the word was said that not only the scientist, the man, wished the girl health and happiness, but that the lover was shaking at the idea of losing her. The slight touch of the thin hand, now frozen as if it had no life, then burning with fever, sent flames of passion to his brain. The word was spoken with a lad's simple tenderness and a man's strong resolution, swaying from the purest idyll to violent dramatic possibilities. He was in love. Why not? For one day, one single moment, he had tried to conquer himself, from the natural egotism of a man who has fought and triumphed alone; but accustomed to accept all his responsibilities in life to the utmost, he bowed to love. Why not? He never had loved, for passing attractions towards women, short caprices, leave no trace in the heart. Being children of the imagination, born of a hard, impetuous life, they come back sometimes like a dream, but as indefinite and undecided as dreams; the heart is not concerned.

Dr. Amati, a lonely man, of strong brain and heart, had gained his fortune and reputation at a bound, and up to thirty-eight he wished to know no other joy but helping men, no ease but satisfied ambition. Now he was so completely in love that everything seemed to lose its colour and taste if Bianca Maria was not present, if he did not hear her feeble, sensitive voice.

In love. Why not? In the humblest, meanest, most obscure lives, that warm, bright hour comes—an hour of such vast capacity that it includes all time and space. So, in lives outwardly successful, when the pomp of earthly things opens out, the warm, deep hour comes, inward and intense; all is gathered up in the heart, the soul trembles with passionate strength. Being intensely in love, with all the greater force and violence from any expression of feeling having been rare in past years, a heart like Antonio Amati's gathers up all the friendships missed or neglected: affection for relatives and congenial people; poetic admiration for women that was kept down, never shown, conquered sometimes at the very beginning, and almost always quickly forgotten; all the thousand attachments, petty and great, the human heart fritters itself away on. He was in love knowingly, willingly, tasting all the sweetness of this late fruit of his soul. He found in his retarded passion the thousand and one characteristics and feelings of the love affairs and attachments he had never had. He was done with the great renunciation; he was in love knowingly.

Bianca Maria was in love without knowing it. She was simple and right-minded; she had lived a solitary life, with no conflicts, thinking and praying a great deal; her soul was refined by solitary musing, not by the rough, sore pounding down of a struggling life. From her mother, who had led a sad life, she got a keen, but silent, sensitiveness; from her father she had taken a headstrong loyalty, pride without haughtiness, and uncalculating generosity that delights in giving without interested motives. Over it all was a deep, inbred faith that seemed to be rooted in her, the food of her spiritual life, just as the lamps lighted before the saints are fed on the purest oil, and draw the prayers of the faithful from a distance by their constant, feeble light. She loved unconsciously. Who could have told her anything about it? Her mother had passed away seven or eight years before from a lingering, fatal illness, suffering no pain or sharp spasms; but her heart was pierced with agony for her almost mad husband, who was hacking down the poor feeble stem of the House of Cavalcanti and throwing its branches into an abyss—agony for the poor daughter she left behind to her mad father's guidance, who was going forward to wretchedness, perhaps dishonour.

Bianca Maria remembered; she recalled her mother's face when she was dying, the colour of clay from agonizing thoughts, inconsolable at having to die so soon. These ineffaceable recollections left her grave, made her youth austere, and took away from her all the longings, ambitions, and coquettishness of her age. What did she know of love? Nothing. She lived in a dull way, with no enjoyments, beside a father she respected; but alarmed by his fatal passion, she felt threatened by something obscure, but imminent, and already pinched by poverty, she took to heart the necessary doleful shifts to keep up appearances. She felt an unknown danger in herself like the seeds of death; and now, a wise, strong, good man—an ark of safety in danger, formed to overcome obstacles, to give help; a giver out of consolation, whose presence and voice brought security and hope, strong to lean against; a name never associated with anything foolish; a vanquisher of sickness, pure of any stain—this man held out his hand to save her. Well, she took his hand; it was natural; she could not think of doing anything else but take it and love him.

Unconsciously she loved him, because she must. From her age, temperament, and surroundings, her whole existence, she felt that innocent sort of love that weak natures, beaten down by tempests, have for strong ones.

When Bianca Maria was alone in the dreary suite of rooms where the sparse furniture had got to have a still older, more wretched look, with these old servants always in low spirits, busied in hiding their poverty, in giving it an air of respectable ease, she felt chilled to the heart; she seemed to be old, poor, and neglected like the house and furniture, doomed to languish on in want of everything. And when her father came in, uneasy always, led by his violent passions, his one idea, credulous over vain dreams, giving in to mystic alarms, calling around him a terrifying world of phantoms, she lost her tranquillity at once; her brain whirled, and she saw curious ghostly things with fatal effects. She could not get rid of the nightmare; she felt so weak, so unfit to defend herself from the assaults of that cabalistic madness; she shook all over from the jar to her nerves, from the fever going up to the brain and making it reel.

She always felt very wretched when she was alone or with her father; helpless, without a guide, knocked about by a rushing wind, drawn in by a whirlpool. But if Antonio Amati showed his manly face, his genial strength;

if she heard his firm, rather rough voice, that was smooth for her; if his hand just touched hers, so that she felt a magnetic influence, warmth, youthful vivacity, go through her nerves, she knew she was guided, protected, started on the way of life and happiness. The black clouds moved off with one breath; she saw the blue sky; the fever grew milder, went off altogether, and the sombre ghosts, the fears that blanched her lips, went off at the same time; she quieted down as if a heavenly benediction enfolded her in its sphere of help. She felt like a child again when he was there: Amati was the firmest, safest, strongest.

So she loved him, innocently, unconsciously. This kind of love allows of great humility, great tenderness; it was pure and fervent, it refreshed her. With their different ground-work, the two sorts of love understood each other, melted into and completed one another. That spiritual harmony that is the soul's finest, but also rarest and shortest, experience began the first day she from her dull balcony, he from his stern study, that saw so much agony, beheld each other. Wherever the two minds, feelings, personalities met, the harmony got greater. When she raised her great thoughtful eyes to his, asking in all simplicity for help and affection, he felt his heart bound with a longing for sacrifice. They understood each other perfectly without speaking.

He came from the land, from a small, out-of-the-way provincial town that had little communication with Naples; he had made his name and fortune by struggling with life and death, with men's indifference and hatred, thus getting a formidable idea of his own powers, and only believing in himself. He had plebeian blood and a powerful mind; none of the refinement that comes from breeding and surroundings, the triumph of ideals.

How different from her! She was the daughter of a noble house, refined by instinct, breeding, and surroundings; used to live in meditation and prayer, without a particle of self-reliance to stand out against the ruin of her family, or withstand her father's ruling passion, to save her name or herself. She lived amid privations and discomforts; she had set out too early on the sorrowful stages of the Via Crucis; an unhappy future was before her. How different and far off these two were!

Still, they understood each other, as the secret, mysterious law of love decrees. It mingles everything—feelings, tradition, origin; puts force next to weakness, and binds two persons together irrevocably by their very differences. She did not consider she lowered herself by loving the obscure Southern peasant become a great doctor; he did not consider he stooped to this decaying family, impoverished in blood, means, and courage. The two souls that had to love one another had set out far apart, had had to run through infinite spiritual space to meet, know, join together. It is Plato's grand love theory, that only fools and heartless folk dare to laugh at; the grand theory of falling in love, once more, after a million instances, was to be realized. Did it not seem arranged purposely, that this unknown, common man should reach to fame and riches by his own efforts, getting to know science and life so that he could console the high-born girl's cold, faded, sorrowful youth, languishing in solitude and secret poverty?

When the serving Sister in the Sacramentiste convent ran from the chilly parlour, where Bianca Maria fell in a faint, to the hospital for a doctor, and obstinately insisted Antonio Amati should come to help the invalid, that was the hour of the decisive meeting. The icy, bloodless hands were at last enfolded in the doctor's strong, healthy ones; once more the wonderful attraction by which loving souls overcome time, space, a thousand obstacles, this attraction—unlucky he who has not felt its power—brought together those who were bound to be united. How could it be these two were not to understand each other, if only Antonio Amati could, by his knowledge, save Bianca Maria from the disease sapping her vital forces, if only he could give her health, riches, and happiness? How not come to an understanding if that innocent gentleness, that mild poesy, that source of every affection, if all that was wanting in Antonio Amati's laborious, stern life, could only reach him through Bianca Maria's slight, modest personality?

He was strength, with a serene, just conscience; she was goodness, all unconscious tenderness and mercy. That strength and that goodness called to each other to unite. They were obeying destiny's order to join, so that love should create once more a fine miracle of harmony. When she *had* to will something, she lifted her eyes to her lover's face and drank in will power. When he looked at her he felt the stretched cords of his energy slacken and the great flower of benignity blossom in his heart.

But it was destined that all Amati's experiences in life were to be conflicts, that every reward men of talent and energy get in this life should only be gained by him after a fierce struggle. With love it was the same. A serious obstacle arose between him and Bianca Maria Cavalcanti. It was her father, the Marquis. The first time Amati saw the proud, deluded, violent man, he felt a painful suspicion rise in his mind. He divined dull hostility in Formosa. Perhaps birth, past and present conditions, divided them, the opposite ideas they had of life and its responsibilities. Perhaps the one that came from the earth, bringing forth good like her, scorned this falling away in health, fortune, and respectability. Perhaps he who lived by the arrogant rules of a life given up to luxury, pleasure, and generosity, despised the obstinate, unpolished worker, sparing in pleasures, unfavourable to them, too hard on himself and on others. Perhaps the one guessed the other's scorn, and felt miles apart, with such different ideas that they could never meet. Perhaps the reason of the mutual antipathy, of Amati's coldness and Formosa's hostility, was more inward, deeper, more mysterious. It may be neither dared confess it to himself. In short, it was suspicion, distrust, an unconscious hostility. Indeed, Amati saw in Carlo Cavalcanti the unknown danger that might wreck Bianca Maria's reason and life. It was vaguely, but obstinately, without well knowing why or wherefore; but he felt the danger was there. And Carlo Cavalcanti felt Antonio Amati was his judge— his enemy, I would almost say. Twice, when the doctor was present at Bianca Maria's fainting-fit and at the attack of fever, that made her delirious a day and a night, he said harsh things to the Marquis di Formosa about his daughter's health. The old man listened, quivering with rage, fretting inwardly. He submitted to this deliverer from a dark hour, but he looked haughtily at him, and shrugged his shoulders when he threatened that the girl would die. By what blindness did he always refuse to take Bianca Maria away from that cold, mean house, where all her youthful strength was languishing? At any rate, he obstinately refused, quivering with emotion every time the doctor touched on the subject. It seemed to be from affection, pride, and nervousness, as if he knew what the right remedy was, and could not, would not, make use of it. Full of doubt, the doctor got always nearer to something shady, but he checked himself, fearing to wound certain susceptibilities. The Marquis was poor: how could he change houses? It was natural for him to redden with fright and melancholy when he was told his daughter was fading away to a fatal ending, to frown with offended pride when offers of service were made. Still, his pride had had to give way that Saturday morning he asked Amati for a loan, saying he would give it back during the day. His pride had had to go altogether several other times, always on Saturday, with an urgent note in a large, shaky hand asking for money—more money out of Amati's purse, always promising to give it back the same day, always failing to do so.

He blushed a little as he wrote, his old head bent to weep over his lost dignity as an old man and a gentleman; but his passion was so strong he would have made money out of anything. When the doctor sent him the money in an envelope, and then another sheet of paper, so that the servant should not notice what it was, the Marquis felt mortified, and opened the envelope roughly with a sharp tear, and the blood went to his head. Amati never wrote a reply, but he never refused. In the evening, when father and daughter were in the drawing-room, she working at her fine lace, he going up and down the room to quiet his excited nerves, the doctor would come in. The Marquis could hardly restrain his annoyance, but went forward to meet his visitor with sham heartiness, his face pale. They greeted one another in an embarrassed way, while Bianca Maria's face sparkled. In spite of service rendered, no cordiality grew up between them. They were cold, and took stock of each other, feeling they were enemies. When the doctor, from his native audacity, and that which love gave him, went to sit opposite Bianca Maria and asked her about her health, when they gazed in each other's eyes, the Marquis was troubled, an angry quiver came into his voice. He was the obstacle. It was in vain every time his ruling passion obliged him to ask Amati for money that Amati gave it without hesitation, more delicately each time. It was lowering all the same. This queer intimacy could not rid them of suspicion, want of confidence, antipathy. Perhaps these loans, asked with a lying excuse, lying promises, only dug that gulf of sorrow, shame, and humiliation that is between him who asks and him who gives. Formosa's great dream now was to get money—a lot of money, so as to lead a grand life, after throwing the doctor's sous in his face and turning him out. He ended by hating him for these benefits it was so hard to ask for, that his wretched passion drove him to take.

Antonio Amati understood; he knew Formosa stood in the way. Naturally, he knew what was the greedy mouth that swallowed up all the old man's money, and some that was not his; he knew the fever that destroyed his gentlemanly feeling, that the wretchedness was the result of sin; he knew an irresistible force obliged him to ask for these loans. His only wish was that Bianca Maria should not suffer, that she should get out of these sad, poverty-stricken, mad surroundings, ever since the time she had, in a low state of health, bodily and mentally, induced by fever, told him she loved him and begged him to take her away. He renewed the offer of his country house, where his mother was, more than once. She shook her head, smiled sadly, and said nothing. One evening when she was suffering very much, choking with heat in that flat, airless in summer, icy in winter, he made the offer to Formosa, bringing it out naturally, trying to be cordial. Formosa thought it over a moment. His daughter looked anxiously at him, awaiting his answer.

'It is impossible,' said the Marquis di Formosa concisely.

'Why so?' the doctor asked boldly.

'Just because I choose,' the old man retorted obstinately.

'And you, my lady; what do you say?'

The doctor looked earnestly at her, to give her the strength to rebel. The poor girl's eyelids fluttered once or twice. She looked at her father, then said:

'As my father says, it is impossible.'

He would have liked to remind her then of the sweet words she said to him one day, to take her out of that pit, to carry her far off to the sunny, green country; but he noticed a sudden coldness in her cast down eyes and stern mouth; he felt her soul was escaping from him. He understood he had come into conflict with filial obedience of that deep, unshakable, almost hierarchical kind one meets with in the upper classes, where paternal authority is blindly respected and family reigns absolute. Rage rose in the doctor's heart. He fretted against the obstacle, seeing the power of love crumble in a moment before a simpler but older feeling or instinct, an affection which, besides the ties of blood, had tradition and life in common for it also. He did not say a word, nor cast a reproving glance, as he saw it was a superior power rising against him that for twenty years had held the girl's heart. Love seemed suddenly to have lost its power, as at a word from her father she had been able to give up the idyll she had dreamt over so long in her empty room.

After a little the doctor went away, cold, frozen, like the father and daughter, who looked like ghosts in that great deserted house. He went off with his first love disappointment, which is the bitterest, quivering with rage and grief. When he was alone in his handsome, solitary house, he vainly tried to amuse himself by reading a scientific review. He was wounded in his love and in his self-love.

Like a love-lorn youth, to cheat that bitterness and give a vent to his excitement, he sat down to write a long, incoherent letter full of love and rage. But when he finished it he calmed down. It seemed unjust to accuse Bianca Maria of indifference and cruelty. On reading it over, he thought it ridiculous. He was a man, not a boy; he had white hairs; he ought not to give himself over to boyish outbursts.

'I will tear up the letter,' he said. But he afterwards felt discouraged. The first, purest flower of his poetic love was cut off; the idyll had vanished; the whole future could only be a tragedy.

Yes, the combat between Antonio Amati and Carlo Cavalcanti was secret but obstinate, subtle but very acute. The old man had great power over his daughter; one might say he bent her will to his with an imperious, fascinating glance. He did not wish anyone else should get power over her; he feared to lose his influence. From paternal self-love, that exaggerated jealousy that hates from the beginning those who love their children, or some other mysterious reason, he set himself between his daughter and Antonio Amati when he saw the latter's sway might increase. When they were alone they never mentioned him—on her part out of obedience, for she always waited for her father to speak first, and he never named the doctor.

The maiden was sensitive about this reserve, and got more and more self-contained, already seeing the first sad symptoms of the struggle.

Amati had written her just one letter; she treasured it and read it over and over, because it breathed of honesty, peace, strength, which were altogether wanting in her wretched, disturbed life, with its saddening past, hurrying on to a dark future. She bent her head, even now feeling that love could not save her, for she seemed tied by a sad fatality, by a charm cast over her life. When Antonio Amati came back in the evening, determined not to yield to this extraordinary tyranny of the father's, she looked up timidly at them; the false cordiality and vivacity with which the men greeted each other encouraged her. A pink colour came to her pale cheeks; but if her father frowned or the doctor's voice got hard she became pale and alarmed again. Her father had carefully hidden that he got pecuniary help from the doctor; he was ashamed to confess this loss of dignity his ruling passion had dragged him into. The good, pale maiden took courage when she saw the healthy, hearty hand held out to her to pull her out of her unhealthy surroundings; but when her father abruptly, roughly put away that hand, she trembled; she did not ask why. Her mother had pined away too resignedly for her to dare to rebel. Only she just lived from day to day without going into the disagreements between her father and Amati, letting herself go to the sweetness of the new feeling, trying to escape from her bitter presentiments. But he, a man of science and much given to observation, finding her father's conduct incomprehensible, tried to curb himself so as to tear the secret out of Formosa's heart. He knew the gambling fever devoured him. Sometimes, when he was with Bianca Maria in the drawing-room, two or three of the Cabalist group would come in to ask for the Marquis. He got rather embarrassed. Once he shut himself up in his study with them; voices reached them from there, deadened and indistinct. Twice he went out with them, the doctor's presence making him impatient and nervous.

'Who are those people?' the doctor asked.

'They are friends,' she said, turning away her head.

'Are they yours?'

'No; my father's.'

She let him see she did not wish to speak about them, so he held his tongue. Another time, one Friday evening, Don Pasqualino De Feo came in, with his sickly look and torn, dirty clothes. At once the doctor remembered he had seen him. Yes, at the hospital, where he arrived black and blue, knocked about as if he had got a severe licking; and he remembered his fantastic talk. While the medium was whispering with the Marquis in a window recess, the doctor asked Bianca quietly:

'Is he a friend, too?' But he noticed she got so pale, her eyes so frightened, crushed by fear of something he knew nothing about, that he said no more. He remembered that, on recovering from her long faint, she had tried to send the medium out of the house. 'You dislike him, don't you?'

'No, no,' said she. 'I am foolish.'

She was afraid Amati would interrupt her father's conversation; but finding their talk prevented, they got up to go away. The medium went past with his eyes down, but Amati called out to him:

'You have got over that licking, De Feo?'

He started, rubbed his forehead, and answered, without looking at the doctor:

'I have had favour from him who sent me the misfortune.'

'From whom?' asked the doctor, with a mocking laugh.

The medium said nothing. Formosa got flushed. His eyes sparkled as he answered, in a shaky voice:

'From the spirit.'

'What spirit?' said the doctor jokingly.

'Caracò, the spirit that helps Don Pasqualino,' the Marquis said emphatically.

'Do you believe that, my lord?' Amati retorted, casting on him a scrutinizing glance.

'It is as clear as light,' answered the noble, raising his eyes to heaven ecstatically.

'And you, my lady, do you believe it?' the doctor asked Bianca, examining her face.

She was just going to answer she did not believe, that she was afraid to believe, when a wild look from her father froze the words on her lips. One saw the effort she made to send back a sorrowful cry. Vaguely she waved her hand, and said:

'I know nothing about it.'

The medium cast an oblique glance at the doctor. For the first time an enraged look came over his face and mingled with his mysterious humility. He twisted his neck, as if a hard bone was choking him. He pulled the Marquis's sleeve in an underhand way to get him to go away; but by Amati's words and grin had he found out his utter incredulity, and, like all deluded folk, he felt his faith in the aiding spirit increased doubly, together with a great desire to convince Amati.

'You don't believe in the spirit, doctor?'

'No,' said the latter dryly.

'Neither in good nor bad spirits?'

'In neither.'

'Why?'

'Because there are no such things.'

'Who told you so?'

'Science and facts are enough, it seems to me,' the doctor said plainly.

'Science is sacrilege,' shouted the Marquis, getting in a rage. 'It has been proved spirits do exist; I can prove it to you.'

'It is no use; I would not believe you'—with a slight smile.

'There are spirits; the so-called incredulous deny their existence in bad faith—yes, because they don't know the facts, and then say they are false; because they see nothing, their eyes being blinded by scepticism, they say there is nothing—insincerely altogether.'

The doctor smiled at his excitement, but, glancing at Bianca Maria, he saw she was in torment; he guessed that behind this discussion was the secret of the hostility. Being accustomed to sick and excited people's outbursts, he examined the Marquis with a doctor's eye, following the violent stages of his excitement.

'Quite insincere—quite!' the Marquis screamed out, going up and down the room, speaking to himself. 'Hundreds of honest men, scientists, gentlemen, ladies, have seen, touched, spoken with the spirits, held important interviews with them; there are printed books, thick volumes, about the very thing you deny totally. What do you think this help from the spirits is?'

He stopped in front of Amati to ask him the question. Although the doctor did not want to make him angrier by contradiction, the demand was too direct not to answer it. He glanced at the Lady Bianca, and saw in her face such secret anxiety to know the truth, and such agitation, he brought it out straight:

'I believe it is an imposture.'

The medium cast up his eyes, swimming in tears. Bianca Maria's face got serene, but Formosa's voice hissed with rage:

'Then, you think me a fool?'

'No; but your soul is too loyal and generous not to be easily cheated.'

'Nonsense!' the Marquis called out, quivering—'nonsense! You can't get out of it; Don Pasqualino is a cheat, and I am a donkey.'

'I deny the second part,' said the doctor dryly.

'But you agree to the first?'

'Yes, I do,' said the doctor boldly.

'How do you prove it?'

'There is no need to prove it; I answer because you question me. Besides, now I remember, Don Pasqualino was beaten by two gamblers, enraged because they did not get the right lottery numbers. He told you it was the spirit Caracò.'

'It was all a pretence, the gamblers beating him, so as to keep the spirit's secret.'

'But the two that assaulted him were arrested and confronted with him at the hospital; they had to spend a month in prison.'

'Is that true, Don Pasqualino?' the Marquis asked severely.

The medium looked distressed, as if it were impossible for him to defend himself against an unjust accusation. But the doctor was offended at that request for confirmation.

'My lord,' he said solemnly, 'I am too serious a man and take too little interest to care to go into the business with that fellow. If you have any esteem for me, I beg you to spare me further discussion.'

'All right—very good,' the Marquis said at once, his proud spirit being open to any appeal to good feeling. 'Let us have no more of it; discussions between sceptics and believers can only be unpleasant. Let us go away, Don Pasqualino; perhaps the doctor will do you justice some day. Let us go; I see Bianca Maria is pained also. You must convince the doctor, my dear,' the father added rather maliciously.

'In what way is she to do that?' asked he, astonished.

'She will tell you,' Formosa replied, grinning; and on getting a dismayed look from his daughter, he added: 'Tell him—tell him what you know; I allow you, Bianca. Perhaps he will believe you. You are harmless; you have no interest in cheating; you are not a sham apostle. Tell him all about it; perhaps you will convince him.'

Resolutely he put on his hat and took the medium's arm, as if to give him a proof of affectionate confidence after the way the doctor had abused him. The old noble, Guido Cavalcanti's descendant, with a lineage of six centuries, put his arm into that mean cheat's, who had been shown up as a liar a few minutes before. But who noticed that act that showed Formosa had again shipwrecked his dignity? The two were out of the house already. Bianca Maria and the doctor stood silently; the whole drama of their love seemed to ripen in that silence. With unscrupulous cunning, telling his daughter to speak, let the doctor know all, leaving them alone with that secret between them, the Marquis took his revenge for Amati's scepticism and his daughter's passiveness. He gaily and cruelly lighted the match of a mine, and then went off just as it was catching fire, so that all love's edifice should come down.

'Well, what have you to tell me?' said the doctor at last, keen to know the truth.

'What is it?' she said faintly, coming out of her sad musing.

'Have you not something to tell me? Did your father not advise—almost order you to do so?'

She started. Amati spoke sharply; she had never heard him speak so. She was offended, and became reserved.

'I know nothing,' she said very low. 'I have nothing to tell you.'

He bit his lip angrily. What evil influence had induced him to come between father and daughter in these queer, mad surroundings, all sickness, wretchedness, and vice? What was he doing, with his rough honesty, his vulgar integrity, in that half insane, poverty-struck life? What bonds, what perplexities, was he not making for his own heart, that up to then had kept pure and unmoved? The decisive hour had come. He must break it off sharply if he wanted to escape the fetters that smothered all his old instincts. He was going to make an end of these romantic complications—that subtle, annoying tragedy; his life was a plain one. He got up determinedly, saying:

'Good-bye!'

She rose too. She understood that her father first, then she, had exhausted the lion's patience. Feebly she asked:

'You will come to-morrow?'

'No, I will not.'

'Some other day, then?'

'No.'

'Some other day when you are not busy?'

'No.'

The three 'No's' were said very decidedly. Bianca Maria gave a shiver. He was going away; he would never come back. He was right. He was a strong, serious man, devoted to his work—a work of love and saving others. He was getting involved in a falling away from reason and dignity in the society of people he was helping and being friendly to, and as a return he had been slighted and insulted; and now a charlatan, a cheat, was preferred to him. He was right to go away, never to come back. But she felt lost, a prey to insanity, if she let him go. Looking beseechingly at him, she implored him:

'Don't go away—stay.'

'What is there for me to do here? Ought I to wait for your father to turn me out to-morrow? Because I stood that scene a little ago, must I stand another?'

'I did not do anything to you,' said she, wringing her hands to keep down her sorrow.

'Good-bye!' he said, and nothing else.

'Don't go away—don't go away!'

Two big tears she could not keep back rolled down her cheeks. He had refused to give in to her voice, beseeching pallor, and excitement, but he gave in to her tears. He was a hard man in his success, but a child's, a woman's tears made him forget everything. When she saw him come back and sit down, his good nature making him yield, she did not restrain her choking tears. She sank into her chair again, her face hid in her handkerchief, sobbing.

'Don't cry,' he muttered, feeling that it did her good, but that he could not bear it.

A good deal of time was needed before she could calm herself. She had kept in her feelings too much for the outburst to be otherwise than long and noisy. The June evening was very warm; the scirocco's breath depressed sickly nerves. The only sound was a skilfully played wailing mandoline in the distance up Pontecorvo Hill.

'Listen,' the doctor began, not harshly, but coldly, when he saw she had got quieter. 'I hope you will listen to me quietly. I am an intruder in your family. Don't interrupt me; I know what you would say. I cured you twice; but that is my work; you have no need to feel obliged to me. Don't protest; I know the limits of human feeling. I am an intruder, then. There is nothing in common between you and me; we are different kinds. It does not matter. I, who am not dreamy, seeing you are fading away, that you need the wide, healthy country and solitude, tried to get you away from here. If my dream has not come true, whose fault is it—yours or mine?'

'It is mine,' she said humbly.

'One day,' the doctor went on rather slowly, as if he was thinking over what had happened—'one day you yourself told me to take you away. Do you remember?...'

'I remember....'

'... I thought ... it is no use saying what I thought. I must have been mistaken; but any man in my place would have been. Well, when our dream might have come true, Bianca, tell me, who was it let it fade away?'

'I myself. It was I.'

'You see, then, that I, a man of realities and action, dreamt too much. To your father and you I am a sort of intruder, meddling in your affairs without having any right to, and ineffectually. On the other hand, Bianca, believe me, my whole life has been disturbed through wishing to see you healthy and happy, and from the useless struggle my efforts lead to, for you oppose me yourself. Would I not do well, then, to go away and never come back?'

'You are right,' she said, with a despairing gesture.

'... Still,' Amati went on, striving to hide his agitation, 'I believe—rather, I know—leaving you would cause me great pain. It may be, you too would suffer?' questioning her face.

'I should die of it,' she brought out, sincerely moved.

'Don't say that. But if I am to stay near you, Bianca, to try, against your will and your own weakness, to save your health and fortune, I must be your friend—your greatest, only friend; do you understand? I must have your whole confidence and faith; after God, you must believe in me. I can see that here, in this house, there is a sad secret which your father and you vainly try to hide; but the Marquis di Formosa's feverishness lets it out darkly every minute. Besides this fever, that is at the same time a disease, an overmastering passion and vice, there is something that escapes me, something crueller that tortures you, and you, out of filial piety, respect to your father—fear, perhaps—hide it from me. Bianca, if I am not to know everything, I must go away for ever, and let your life and mine be ruined irretrievably.'

'I love you so,' she said, abandoning her soul to him.

'Darling!' he whispered, patting her brown hair as her head leant for a moment on his strong, faithful heart.

'Promise me one thing ...' she asked in a babyish way.

'Say what it is....'

'Promise me you won't think ill of my father—promise! He is the best of fathers; any girl would be proud to have him. Nothing could shake my respect and love for him. I want you not to blame him for anything—promise me! His fatal tendency is only part of his kindness. He is so unhappy at heart!'

'I promise you, Bianca, to be as indulgent as you could be.'

'That is enough. He is an unhappy man. For years and years our house has been going down. Since when or why I don't remember. I was very little. I don't even know whose fault it is. I don't wish to. I only remember that my mother was pale and sickly; her hands were always cold....'

'Like yours, poor dear!'

'Like mine?' she answered with a pale smile.

'What did your mother die of?'

'Bloodlessness and languor. She faded away ... at the last, she was not in her senses all the time.'

'Did she rave?'

'Yes, slightly,' she answered, blushing to her forehead.

'Don't think of that,' he said, guessing the reason of her blush.

'My father felt mother's sufferings so much! For years a dream had taken hold of him: it was to build up the Cavalcanti fortune, to let mother and me live in style, keep open house, and in one day pour out in charity what now serves to keep us for a year,' she added, with a lump in her throat.

'Keep calm, dear-don't get excited.'

'No, no, let me speak; if I don't I'll choke. A great dream, as large as his heart, noble and generous as his soul, so much so that my mother and I felt gratitude that will not end with life, but must go on beyond the tomb, where one still hears, loves, and prays. But, with his excited fancy, he longed for quick, ample methods of realizing this fortune: methods suited to the case, for a Cavalcanti neither works nor speculates ...'

'It was the lottery,' Amati finished up for her.

'Yes, the lottery; how do you know?'

'I do know.'

'Our misfortune is known to everyone who comes near us,' she went on, quivering with grief. 'Such a misfortune, to crown the others! Mother died of it, from physical and moral weakness. Our whole means are sacrificed to it; it has taken my father's heart from me; when it has destroyed all that is dearest, it will hand me over to wretchedness and death.'

'Don't be afraid, don't fear; everything has a remedy,' he said vaguely, trying to cut short that despairing outflow.

'It can't be cured,' she said earnestly. 'My dying mother, in a lucid interval, said as she kissed me: "Don't judge your father—never be hard on him; obey, be obedient. The passion that eats him up, and is killing me, can only increase with years. This fever will get higher: I have not cured it, neither will you. Leave him to this dream—don't annoy him; if you are unhappy, ask God's help; but respect his years. He only desires our happiness—he is killing me for it; he will make you suffer frightfully, though he is noble and generous. Be merciful to him. It is only so that I can die, as I do, with a quiet conscience." Mother was right. With years he has got unhappier, more eccentric; he is incurable now; he forgets everything, everything—you know what I mean. Some day or other I fear my noble old father, whose gray hairs I ought to honour—that I want everyone to respect—may forget the laws of honour in some dark gambling combination.'

'May God keep him from it!' said Amati, starting.

'May God hear you!' she cried out; 'but I pray so much, and the evil gets worse. If you knew! We are in want of everything: it is the first time I have told anyone. I am quivering with shame, but I can't hide anything from you. He has sold everything: first works of art, then furniture, down to a few jewels mother kept for me—and he adored her!—even the Cavalcanti portraits—though he is proud of his race!—even the silver lamps in the chapel—and he is religious! I live with these two old servants, so faithful neither sin nor poverty has taken them from us! They are not paid: they serve us of the House of Cavalcanti without pay. Do you know, it is by their clever contrivances that the house goes on, that we have enough to eat, and that there is oil in the lamps! I am raising for you the veil of sacred family decency—don't betray us!' He bent and kissed the hand Bianca held out to him, to seal his promise. 'All that money, and more that he gets somewhere—I know not where and have no wish to know—goes in gambling. Friday and Saturday he is wild. Other wretches, like that medium, come for him: his very name makes me shiver with fright and shame; they have queer alarming consultations; they get excited, shout, and quarrel; they use a queer jargon. These are his friends; men of his own rank, his relations, have left him. It may be he asked money from them, got it, and did not give it back, perhaps; it may be the whisper, even, of wickedness makes them avoid us. These Cabalists, men who *see'* —she shivered and looked round—'take his money from him and incite him to play. The day is at hand when he will have nothing left, and he won't be able to gamble. God, God open his eyes, if we are not to perish altogether, the name and the family!'

'Bianca, Bianca, I implore you to be calm,' he said, alarmed at her excitement, following its phases with a doctor's mind and a man's heart.

'I can't,' she cried. 'I have not told you all. Listen: I am a poor, weak creature; the blood runs poor and slow in my veins, you know—you told me so. I have lived either in this sad house or my aunt's convent—that is to say, with my father, always full of his fancies, or with my aunt, whose faith gives her almost prophetic visions. Mother died here; as the gambling passion filled my father's mind, the delusion began to filter into mine against my will. Father speaks to me of ghosts, phantoms, spirits, at all hours, especially in the evening and at night, and I believe in them; you see how frightful that is. The sunlight, seeing people, chases fears away; but evening comes, the house gets full of shadows, my blood freezes; when father speaks of the spirit my heart stops or goes at a gallop; I feel as if I was dying of fear. I get queer singings in my ears. I hear light steps, smothered voices. I see in my mind's eye white-robed figures—they look at me and weep; shadowy hands smooth my hair. I seem to feel icy breaths on my cheek; my nights now are one long watch, or light sleep broken by dreams.'

'There are no such spirits, Bianca,' said he, in a gentle, firm voice.

'I am so weak, so unfit to get rid of delusions. When I have got calmer, father, from his own fancies or the medium's infamous suggestions, comes to torment me. He wishes me to *see* without caring about my feebleness, my fears, not knowing how he tortures me. He speaks of the spirit, wants me to call it up, for I am young and innocent. I try to go against him; vainly I struggle and ask him to spare me, not to make me drink this bitter cup. But it is no use: he is obstinate and blinded; he wants me to see the spirit, and ask what numbers to play. Father has such influence over me, he makes me share his madness to a frightful extent. I shall end by being like him, a poor deluded thing, worn out by night watches and daily delusions.'

She hid her face in her hands, quivering. The doctor looked at her astounded, not daring to say anything.

'And you don't know all yet,' she went on excitedly. 'One day you wrote me a kind, comforting letter, suggesting I should go off to your mother's. What comfort it was! I would have got out of this house at last, where every black doorway frightens me in the evening, and the furniture looks ghostly. I would have gone where there was light, sun, heat, and joy. Well, that night father took an extra mad fit: he came to my room. Wakened from sleep at so late an hour, in the flickering lamp-light, his words put me into a panic; he wouldn't listen to my entreaties, he didn't know he was torturing me, and for two hours he spoke about the spirit that was to appear, that I must evoke; he would teach me the sacred word. He held on to my hands, breathed in my face, filling me with his enthusiasm and faith, and so he gained his end.'

'In what way?'

'I saw the spirit, dear.'

'How? You saw it?'

'As I see you.'

'It was fever; there is no such thing, Bianca,' he said harshly, to bring back her wandering mind to peace.

'You say so; I believe you. But when you are gone, when I have finished my prayers and reading, when I am alone in my room with the shadows the lamps throw, I shall see again that night's vision: my head will swim, my brain whirl, my teeth chatter. Father is in despair now because that night's numbers did not come right; he says I don't know how to interpret; he wants me to call up the spirit again. He thinks now I am a medium, and he gives me no peace. I am not his daughter now; he only looks on me as a mediator between him and Fortune. He watches every word I say, looks enviously at me or haughtily, and goes about thinking of some queer discipline, some privations or other to enable me to see the spirit again, to make my soul pure like my body, and my sight clear. He leaves me alone at the beginning of the week, but on Thursday night he comes and begs me—fancy, he implores me—to call the spirit; that aged man, whose hand I kiss respectfully, kneels before me, as at the altar, to soften me. On Friday he gets wild; he never notices how frightened I get; he thinks it is the coming of the spirits that excites me. The other night, to get away from the torture I find unbearable, I locked my door: I was so bold as to deny father access to my room. Well, he came, knocked, softly at first, then loudly; he spoke to me entreatingly, he ordered me to see the spirit—in a rage first, and then abjectly. I stopped my ears not to hear him, put my head down in the pillows; I bit the sheet to choke my sobs. Twenty times I wanted to open the door, but terror nailed me to my bed. Father wept. Mother, mother, I disobeyed you! You could die for father, but I could not do that for him.'

'Poor darling!' he murmured, trying to calm her down with gentle, compassionate words, petting her hands, as if he wanted to set her to sleep or magnetize her.

'Yes, yes, pity me, for I am so wretched, so unhappy, I envy any beggar on the street. Pity me, because the one person who should love me, take care of my health and happiness, dreams instead about getting money for me, a great lot, and makes me suffer in body, in mind, for it; pity me, for I am an unhappy woman, doomed to a dark ending. In all the wide world, I only have you to care for me!'

They said no more. Bianca Maria's pallid cheeks had got some colour, her eyes shone; her whole heart had been poured out as she spoke, now she kept silence. She had said everything. The bitter secret that implacably tortured her whole existence, on being evoked by love, had come out and had given a shudder of alarmed astonishment to the strong man listening. He said nothing, trying to keep down his own amazement, to arrange his confused ideas. He was accustomed, certainly, to hear lugubrious stories of all kinds of misery, both of body and mind, from his patients; he had lifted the veil from all kinds of shame and corruption; the sorrowful and contrite came to him as to a confessor, and hearts that hid the most horrifying secrets of humanity opened to him. But Bianca's sorrow was so profound, the very source of life being attacked, that it frightened him to see such unutterable wretchedness. Also this girl, wasted by an obscure, unnatural malady, tortured by her own father, that lovely, dear creature, was the woman he loved, that he could not live without, whose happiness was dearer to him than his own. Disturbed, not knowing yet how to set to work before that complicated problem of sickness and delusion, that made the Marquis di Formosa the family destroyer, he found nothing to say to comfort Bianca.

She was worn out now; she felt a vague remorse at having accused her father. But was not Amati to deliver her? Did she not feel quite safe, strong, when he was there? Rousing herself from her exhaustion, she raised her eyes to his timidly, humbly, saying:

'You don't think me bad and ungrateful, do you?'

'No, dear, I do not.'

'Do not judge badly of him.'

'I will cure him,' he said thoughtfully.

CHAPTER XII
THE THREE SISTERS—
CHIARASTELLA THE WITCH

The summer of that year was a bad one for the Neapolitans, morally and materially. Above all, from the end of June the summer scirocco had gone on dissolving into rain; storms covered the bay with black clouds, lightning played behind Posillipo, thunder rumbled from Capodimonte, sudden heavy summer showers raised a pungent smell of dust, and went rushing down the city roads from the hill to the sea like little waterspouts, making the passers-by start aside and run. The poor cabmen, with no umbrellas, ragged, with shabby hats crushed down on their heads, could do nothing but stick their hands in the pockets of their worn-out jackets and keep their heads down. It was a devilish summer, a real correction from God; that was why San Gennaro had been so long in working the miracle that year. He makes no mistakes.

The rushing scirocco lashed up the waves in the bay furiously; they got livid with rage, and foamed under the chill curtain of clouds, and all the bathing-places from Marinella to Posillipo had to take up the boards of their wooden huts to let the raging sea pass through, or they would have been broken to pieces. There lay the great irrecoverable loss, for the long files of provincial people that come from Calabria, Basilicata, Abruzzi, and Molise, to take sea-baths, and fill up the inns and second-class eating-houses, who sit four in a carriage that barely holds two—these country people, who are Naples' summer source of revenue, being afraid of the bad weather, always went on intending to start for Naples the next week, and ended by never leaving their villages at all. Those who had arrived the first week in July, intending to stay till the end of August, on finding they could only have a bathe on one day out of five, and then have to face a stormy sea, got frightened and discouraged, and ended by going back to Campobasso, to Avellino, Benevento, and Potenza, to the great sorrow of the girls and young fellows. It was a lost season.

At the *Fiori* Inn, in Fiorentini Square, the *Campidoglio*, in Municipio Square, and the *Centrale*, at Fontana Medina, there was a void; as for the

Allegria, in Carità Square, one of the greatest resorts of country people, it was a desert.

Very warm days came at times between the stormy ones, which were very exhausting. It was a real African climate, and the bathing-places—De Crescenzio, Cannavacciuolo, Sciattone, Manetta and Pappalordo—had five days' emptiness to one day of too large a crowd of people. The owners shook their heads despondingly, whilst the bronzed, thin, black-toothed, hoarse-voiced bathing-women, shoeless, in shift, petticoat and straw hats, ran after sheets of doubtful whiteness on the dirty brown sands, where the wind caught them and threatened to cast them into the sea. What rain! what rain! The eating-houses in the centre of Naples had poor business, but those who put tables out in the open air on Santa Lucia causeway, the eating-houses that go from Mergellina to Posillipo, the *Bersaglio,* the *Schiava,* the *Figlio di Pietro,* all those whose slender existence depends on fine weather, summer and winter, these suffered most; no one had anything to do, from the cook yawning in the kitchen to the few waiters left, who sat sleepily in the steamy atmosphere that even the storms did not freshen up. Only crawling flies buzzed on the uselessly prepared tables. There was a general idleness; a chorus of oaths and lamentations arose at every new outburst of showers. Even the evenings at the Villa, round the bandstand, where the municipal band plays its old polkas and variations on 'Forza del Destino' of ancient date, where a penny for a seat is all that is needed to be able to enjoy the pleasant sight of a middle-class crowd, seated or wandering round the band, just a penny to sit in the open air and hear the modest concert— even these simple, economical, popular evenings were spoilt. Among the tradesmen's daughters, for whom the Villa means an occasion to show their humble white frocks, sewn and starched at home, to see their lovers, even at a distance, under the flickering gas-lamps, to go a step further on the road, often a long one, that leads to marriage—among these girls there was secret weeping. The chair-hirer wandered through the deserted, damp avenues, full of snails, to see if no one would come to brave the bad weather, or, driven desperate, he settled himself in a corner of Vacca Café to talk over his woes with one of the waiters. What a season!

Don Domenico Mayer's son and daughter, who in other years went every evening to the Villa, walking there and back, so as to spend only fourpence, this year nearly expired with heat and boredom in their Rossi Palazzo flat. Their father was so stern. Their mother was even more sickly and doleful than usual. It was a bad season for the three sisters scattered in different parts of Naples—Carmela, the cigar-maker; Annarella, the servant; and Filomena, the young girl who lived in sin. Above all, their mother was dead in the cellar where she had lived with Carmela, and in spite of having got a pauper's coffin for her from the Pendino district authorities, and her being thrown into the common pit on the great heap of the wretched at Poggio Reale, Carmela still had had to pay seventy or eighty francs for burial expenses, without even having the consolation of knowing that her mother had had a separate grave. For some time Carmela had paid a small weekly sum to a pious *Congregazione* so as to have at her own death, or any of her family's, a separate carriage following and a grave; but debts and wretchedness, gambling resorted to in desperation, had prevented her from going on paying the fees, and she had lost her claim. She was left alone, with no mother, in that damp, dark cellar, in debt up to the eyes, not having twelve francs even to get a black dress or any mourning; she wore a light-coloured cotton with a black kerchief at her neck, and her neighbours criticised her for her heartlessness. Her everlasting lover, Raffaele, had now risen to the highest grades of the Camorrist hierarchy from having taken part in two duels, or *dichiaramenti*, and from having a mark against him with the police; he had got still more haughty to her, especially after her mother's death; he fled from Carmela, and when she went after him at inn doors and suburban taverns, he treated her brutally, all the more that she had got into a wretched condition; she could not give him five francs ever now, or even the two francs he haughtily asked for and she humbly gave.

A subtle suspicion was growing in the girl's mind, and from her mother's death, her excessive poverty, and Raffaele's suspected false-dealing, she lost her head. She often failed to go to the tobacco factory, and lost her day's work, or worked so absent-mindedly, so badly, she was fined and got very little on Saturday. Often during the week she broke her fast with a penny-worth of dry bread dipped in macaroni-water, that a neighbour, not so poor as herself, treated her to. It was too hard, too hard, for one who only wished for others' happiness, to see her mother die of privation, and then thrown into a common paupers' ditch, to mingle her bones with theirs; to see her lover going down gradually the whole ladder of vice, even to prison, perhaps to capital crime; and also to see her sisters fading away for want of moral and physical comfort. Now, with her mother gone to her eternal rest—how Carmela envied her sometimes!—and with Raffaele always going farther off from her, she, feeling her heart as cold as her stomach, went oftener to see her sisters. She thought of going to live with Annarella, for economy's sake, and not to live in such a lonely way; but Annarella lived in a cellar in Rosariella di Porta Medina—she, her husband, and two children, already getting of a good size—in a cellar with a beaten earth floor and walls not white-washed for years. The husband and wife slept on a bed made of two iron trestles, with three squeaking boards laid over them lengthwise, and a big mattress stuffed with maize leaves—the *paglione*, which has an opening in the middle to put in the hand when the bed is made. The girl slept by the mother in the big conjugal bed, and they made up a little bed for the boy every evening upon two broken chairs.

Frightful, utter misery had gradually fallen on the glove-cutter's family. He not only staked his whole week's pay on the lottery, but on Friday evening and Saturday morning he beat his wife, enraged if she had only one or two francs to give him. Now the children were beginning to earn something. The girl worked at a dressmaker's, the boy as a stable-hand; and when he could not get anything from his wife, Gaetano went to the dressmaker's where his little girl worked by the week, called her down, and, by dint of lies, wheedling, or blows, one after the other, he managed always to draw some pence from the child, who got the dressmaker to advance them on her week's pay. With his son, now a boy of twelve, Gaetano behaved still worse. The stable-boy often refused him money, taunting him with his vice and the wretchedness he had reduced his mother to. The father rained down blows on him. The boy, choking with tears, shouted, swore, and struggled. People came up to hear a son call his father a scoundrel, an assassin. Once, when his father gave him a blow on the nose, making the blood flow, he got enraged and bit his hand. On Saturday evening, when they came back to their home, the children carried the marks of their father's blows. The mother, who had forgotten the blows she got herself, found the marks, and wept over her poor children, asking them:

'How much has he taken away from you?'

'Fourteen sous,' Teresina answered sadly.

'He took half a franc from me,' said Carmine, raging.

'Merciful God!' the mother cried out, weeping.

But what she could not get out of her mind was her two-and-a-half-year-old baby, which died from bad milk, bad nourishment, from languishing in that black cellar, which dripped from damp summer and winter. If Peppino was named by chance, she grew pale, and nothing could get it out of her head that her husband's vice had killed her little son. She had religiously kept the big swinging basket that poor Naples children are cradled in (the *sportone*); but she first sold the pillow, then the little maize mattress, and one day of great hunger, not knowing where to get a half-penny, she sold the cradle. Parting from it was so agonizing that the mother sat on the doorstep, not caring who passed, and wept for an hour, with her head in her apron. 'You know, Peppino—you know!' she whispered, as if she was asking pardon of the tiny dead for having sold his cradle.

Now that summer had come in so unsettled and stormy, it had made the family position worse than ever. Of the two half-days' service she did, she had lost one, which meant ten francs. It was the lodging-house keeper: as she had empty rooms, she dismissed her servant. The girl Teresina had had her weekly pay reduced, as the dressmaker had no work; but, not wishing to dismiss the girl straight off, she let her do the house-work out of charity. The coachman that Carmine was stable-boy to went off with his master's family to the country for four months, and would have taken the boy with him; but Gaetano, the lad's father, knowing he could always get some pence out of the boy if he stayed in Naples, by threats, arguments, or blows, prevented him from going to the country. He ordered him to look out for another service in Naples. Carmine shrieked, wept, cursed, threatening to go away secretly.

'I am going away, mother; I am going off secretly, and father won't see a farthing of my money, you know. I will send it to you in a letter; father is not to have any of it.'

'What can I say, darling? You are right to go,' his mother lamented. And that going away of her son tore her heart also.

But the debts they had with Donna Concetta, the usurer, were Carmela's greatest agony, also Annarella's and Gaetano's. Even she had suffered from the bad season, as the debtors almost all failed to pay, and had not even money to pay the interest with by the week. She did not lend a farthing more to anyone; she was embittered and fierce, for even she was feeling the pinch of other people's wretchedness. She shut herself up in the house at night behind iron bars, for she had pension papers and savings-bank books in the house; and that put her in a state of constant fury. She wandered about all day from one street to another, from cellar to attic, from shop to factory, running after her own money, till she was out of breath; for she always went on foot. Devoured with rage from the constant refusals, she began by asking for her interest at least, coldly insistent, and ended up by making a scene, yelling, demanding her 'blood,' as she passionately called her money. But those who most enraged her were Gaetano, Annarella and Carmela. Between them they had got about two hundred francs from her, and she could not get even a centime of the weekly ten francs' interest. Oh, these three! these three! She went to the Bossi factory at Foria, where Gaetano cut out gloves, and had the workman called down sometimes; but, warned by a companion, he got them to say he was not at the factory that day. But she persisted, being suspicious and unbelieving; she walked about in front of the door, and he ended by going down to her, a black cigar ever in his mouth.

The scene began in a whisper, short, energetic, violent: sometimes Gaetano, grinning—for the lottery made him lose all sense of shame— repeated to her the motto of Naples' bad payers: 'If I had it and could, I would pay; but not having it, I can't and won't pay.' But she set to yelling, said she would go to Carlo Bossi to complain, or to the judge; and Gaetano, in a rage, but controlling himself, made answer. What would she gain by getting him turned out of the factory? She would not get another farthing then. The judge? What could he do? The prison for debtors no longer exists in Naples; the Concordia prison has been abolished by gentlemen who could not pay their big debts. Then she got in a rage like a witch; the whole neighbourhood came out to the doors and balconies. He listened, very pale, biting at his black cigar-stump. One day he threatened in a whisper to cut her in pieces. Muttering vague, threatening words, pulling her shawl round her angrily, Donna Concetta went off with the swinging step of rich, lazy women of the lower class, her head a little to one side, her face still discomposed after the scene.

Since she happened to be at Foria, and the cigar-makers' work ended at four o'clock, she went to stand at the door of the factory in Santi Apostoli Square, waiting till Carmela came out, to ask her for her money. She was not the only one that was waiting; other women were at the door who had lent money or clothes to the workers at high interest; and they knew and recognised each other, feeling they had a strong, mutual interest in the laws of usury; they made a long lament together over the tardiness in paying and inexactness of their clients. They all said they were ruined by the bad season and the ill-will of their debtors; the words *'my blood, our blood'* came up always like a wail, as they spoke of the money lost. It was not allowable to send up for any workgirl, but the money-lenders waited, like the cake and fruit sellers, till the workpeople came out. The poor women who were coming from the factory, with sickly faces from the bad tobacco fumes, their hands stained up to the wrist, stopped to buy something to carry home to feed their families on, after their day's work. The money-lenders mingled with pot-herb-sellers, and vendors of parsnips in vinegar and pancakes, and waited patiently, pulling their shawls up on their shoulders—that common trick. At last the women, after being searched, one by one, by an overseer to find out if they had stolen any tobacco, came out. Some slipped away, others stopped to buy broccoli, radishes, potatoes, or some pancake; but the palest certainly were those who were caught outside by their creditors. The palest of all, and not from tobacco fumes, but shame, was Carmela. She tried to lead off Donna Concetta towards Vertecœli Street or Santi Apostoli steps, so as not to let her friends hear what was said; but Donna Concetta went slowly and raised her voice. She wanted her money, her blood; it was a shame not to give it to her; she would have the interest, at any rate. If Carmela had any shame, she must at least give her the interest. The cigar-girl's eyes filled with tears at that abuse, and, having a few pence in her purse, it was impossible to hold out. She handed them to Donna Concetta; but it was so little always that, although she sacrificed her day's meal, it only got her the more abuse. She listened, with her head bent, to Donna Concetta's taunts up Arcivescovato Street and Gerolomini Road; after a time Donna Concetta recognised that the girl had no more money, and that it was useless to worry her.

But Carmela, even when Donna Concetta had gone off, felt the shiver of shame that bitter voice had sent through her, saying such offensive words; and tired, crushed, without a farthing in her pocket after working a whole day, she again felt envy of her dead mother. Of course, she, too, had that vice of gambling, but it was for good ends—to give money to everyone, to make all her friends happy, if she won, to let Raffaele, or Farfariello, as he was called, draw money from her; but to be so severely punished for this venial sin cut her to the heart. Ah! on some days how willingly she would have thrown herself into the well of the building where the factory was, so as not to hear or feel anything more! But Donna Concetta's thirst was not at all quenched by that drop of water, Carmela's pence, and on her way home every evening, before going in at her door, she hurried to the Rosariella Street cellar where Annarella lived. She was generally seated near the bed, and often in the dark, for she had nothing to buy oil with, saying the Rosary with her daughter. Donna Concetta crossed herself and waited till the Rosary was ended, to ask for her loan back, uselessly as it happened every day. Annarella could do nothing now but answer with a sigh or lament, and when Donna Concetta burst into eloquence she began to cry. Then Teresina broke in, speaking to both women.

'Don't cry, mother, to please me.' And to the money-lender: 'Do you not see, Donna Concetta, that mother has not got any money?'

'Dear girl, my darling!' sobbed her mother, choked by all the sorrows of her life.

The money-lender would not be appeased; she was so accustomed to the sham tears of those who wished to cheat her of her money that she no longer believed in any sorrow; it was only when she had exhausted her whole vocabulary of abuse that she decided to go away, slowly, with that sleek walk of hers, muttering that she would do justice with her own hands, against robbers of her blood. The mother and daughter were left alone in the damp, dark cellar's unhealthy heat, and the poor charwoman, responding to an inward thought, exclaimed:

'Soul of Peppinello, do me this grace!'

When Carmela and Annarella afterwards met in the street or the Rosariella cellar, there was a long outpouring of sorrows and interchange of news, when the physical and moral bitterness of their sad existences burst out.

'That lottery! what bad luck, what infamous luck, it was, for it never to give a farthing's winnings, and to take their all—even the bit of bread that just kept them alive!' Sometimes, through speaking about their wretchedness and solitariness, Filomena, the third unfortunate sister, was referred to. 'What was she doing? How could she bear that life of sin?'

Carmela had twice gone to seek her in the alley behind Santa Barbara Steps: once she was out; the other time she found her so cold, so changed, as if struck by remorse, that Carmela, filled with emotion, ran away at once. Another time Annarella had met Filomena in the street, in blue and yellow, with the usual red ribbon at her neck; she asked her why she wore no mourning for her mother.

'I am not worthy,' Filomena had answered, casting down her eyes, and going off with that sliding step on high-heeled, shiny shoes. All through this Carmela felt, besides her open griefs, besides the sequence of wretchedness and humiliation, something she could not take hold of, as if a new misfortune was coming on her head, a crowning fatality was hemming her in, with no way of escape. What was it? She could not say what it was. Perhaps it was Raffaele's increasing coldness, and the brutal way he treated her when they met; it may have been her brother-in-law Gaetano's fierce expression, or that queer look that Filomena gave her: she dared not go to ask for her now.

For some time Annarella and she had been making up a plan to put an end to their difficulties. Among all Naples common folk there are women famed as witches—*fattucchiare*, as they call them—whose witchcraft, philtres and charms cannot be resisted. Some, indeed, have a large practice, much larger than a doctor's would be in the same neighbourhood; almost every quarter boasts of its witch, who can do the most extraordinary miracles, always, however, by God's help and the Virgin's. Well, Chiarastella, the great sorceress, who lived up there at Centograde Lane, near the Corso Vittorio Emanuele, had a tremendous reputation: there was not a shop, cellar, road, square, or street corner where Chiarastella's marvellous deeds were not known and spoken of. It was said everywhere that, to get Chiarastella's spells, you must ask for things that were not against God's will; but no one who attended to this rule had come home disappointed from her little place in Centograde Lane. No one among the mass of Naples common folk dared to throw a doubt on Chiarastella's magic powers. If in the provision stores and macaroni shops, where young and old women love to gossip, or in front of herb-sellers' baskets and barrows, where small folk haggle for three-quarters of an hour over a bundle of borage, and at basement doors, where such long, animated talk goes on; any ignorant woman, on hearing of the Centograde witch's miracles, raised her eyebrows in surprise and unbelief, twenty anxious, excited voices told her of all the deeds done by Chiarastella. In one place a traitor husband had been brought back to his young wife; then a young fellow dying of consumption was cured when the doctors had given him up. Another case was a dressmaker who had lost her customers, and had got them all back gradually by the witch's influence; then there was a heartless girl who drove her lover to an evil life and crime by her coldness, and Chiarastella had set things right. Above all there was the tying of the tongue: that—that was Chiarastella's grand feat. Everyone who had a lawsuit coming off, or a trial in which they might be overcome by their adversary or by justice, where money, honour, liberty or life would be at stake, rushed in desperation for Chiarastella's magic. After hearing about the case, if she considered it moral and in accordance with God's will, she promised to tie the tongue of the adversary's lawyer. The spell consisted of a magic cord with three knots in it to represent the number of persons in the Trinity. Means must be found to put it on the advocate's person, either in his pocket or in the lining of his clothes, on the decisive morning of the trial, and by the help of prayer the rival's advocate would not be able to say over any of his arguments, even if he had them in his mind—his tongue was tied, the suit was lost to him, the spell had secured its object. Examples were quoted where the innocent and oppressed, suffering from man's injustice, had been thus saved by Chiarastella. Carmela and Annarella had thought of applying to Chiarastella for some time, Carmela to try and awaken in Raffaele's heart renewed love for her, she never having had his love, and now it was less hers than ever. Annarella required a spell to get her husband Gaetano to give up gambling at the lottery.

Carmela had been up already at Centograde Lane to make inquiries about getting the magic; she found five francs were necessary; and, besides, there were some small ingredients that had to be bought. Afterwards, if it was successful, just as God willed it, the two sisters would make the witch a good present. Chiarastella certainly never promised anything; she spoke mysteriously, in a doubtful way, and kept deep silence at certain questions. It seemed as if she did not care about money; she contented herself with a small fee for her support, counting on people's gratitude to get a better gift if it was God's will that the thing turned out well later on. Meanwhile, ten francs at least were needed; without them nothing whatever could be done.

Whatever privations the sisters might endure that bad summer, they never would have been able to put aside ten francs between them.

But days went by, and moral wretchedness was as urgent of care as their bodily wants required looking to: it was the only remedy left, so, though much against the grain, Carmela made up her mind to sell her old marble-topped chest of drawers, the chief bit of furniture in her room, that had been bought by her mother as a bride. She barely got twelve francs for it—everyone was selling furniture that hateful summer; there was not a dog left that would buy a farthing's worth of things. She put her few pieces of linen in a covered basket under her bed, and hung her poor clothes on a bit of string from two nails in the wall, where they got damp, but she had her twelve francs.

It was one Sunday at the end of August, after hearing Mass in Sette Dolori Church, that the sisters went towards Centograde Lane. Carmela had shut up her home and carried the key in her pocket. Annarella left her daughter Teresina at home mending a torn dress, after working till midday at the dressmaker's. For eight days now Carmela had not succeeded in finding Raffaele, though she wandered through Naples in her free hours. Gaetano, Annarella's husband, had not come home on Saturday night, nor that morning. In Sette Dolori Church, kneeling at a dark wooden form that the poor must use, as they cannot pay for seats, they prayed earnestly during Mass. Now they were laboriously going up the steps of the steep incline that leads from Sette Dolori Street to Vittorio Emanuele Corso, not speaking, wrapt up in vague hopes and fears. Chiarastella, the witch, lived appropriately in a dark alley. It was quiet, but well enough lighted, and stood to the right of the steep steps that lead from the principal street up the hill to the little outlets Pignasecca, Carità, and Monte Santo. There was a great quietness in that blind alley, but the damp summer scirocco had covered the flint pavement with a thin coating of mud, so they had to walk carefully not to fall, and they made no noise.

'Does she expect us?' Annarella asked, hardly moving her lips. She was panting after going up the steps.

'Yes, she does,' said Carmela in a whisper, as she went in at the door.

They went up to the first-floor, on to the narrow landing. There were two doors facing each other; one was shut fast; indeed, it was fastened by a chain and a heavy iron padlock. It looked as if the dwellers there had gone off after a misfortune, shutting up their dull abode for ever. The door on the left was half open; but the sisters, on hearing a muffled sob, dared not go in without knocking. It was startling for Carmela to pull a brown monkey's paw joined to a big-ringed iron chain the bell inside was hung to. The black, mummified paw gave one a shudder; it was hairy above and pink underneath. It seemed like finding a bit of a swarthy murdered child. The bell tinkled long and shrilly, as if it would never give over. A very old, decrepit, bent servant, with a pointed nose that seemed to wish to go into her toothless mouth, appeared. She signed to the two women to come into the bare, narrow lobby, which was rather damp underfoot. The choked sobbing went on behind another closed door. Soon after the door opened, and a girl of the people, a seamstress (Antonietta the blonde it was), crossed the lobby, her shawl off her shoulders, weeping, her handkerchief at her eyes. Nannina, her short friend, kept one arm round her waist, as if she wanted to hold her up, and went on repeating, to console her:

'It does not matter; never mind about it.'

But on the sobbing getting louder the old woman opened the outer door and sent the girls off, almost pushing them out; then she disappeared without saying a word to Annarella or Carmela. They, already moved by the feelings that induced them to invoke the witch's power, were very sympathetic with the two girls, one so inconsolable, the other so vainly trying to soothe. Leaning at the lobby window, they waited, their eyes cast down and hands crossed over their aprons, tightly holding the ends of their shawls, not saying a word to each other. A great silence was around, in the damp summer sultriness of that long summer noon. Annarella, being gentler, more saddened, and at the same time less infatuated than Carmela, bent her shoulders to her fatal destiny, feeling an increasing want of confidence in any means of salvation, being almost sure that Gaetano would never be brought back to reason by any prayer nor charm. She felt nothing but a growing fear all through her low spirits. Carmela, instead, having an ardent, loving soul that nothing could subdue, felt the flame of passion light up within her. She was not afraid; no, she would have dared any sight or danger to get Raffaele's heart again. But the decrepit servant, bent into a bow, as if she wanted to reach the earth again, appeared in the lobby and made a sign to Carmela to come in. Without making a sound, the sisters disappeared into the other room, and the door shut behind them.

'Here is my sister that I told you of,' whispered Carmela, standing aside to present Annarella, who stood just behind her.

Chiarastella nodded as a salutation. The witch was of middle height, or a little below it, very thin, with long lean hands, the skin of them shiny from sticking to the bones; her body moved automatically, as if she could stiffen every muscle at will. She had a small head, and short face covered with deep red blotches, the jaw very prominent; her complexion was of a warm vivid pallor, and the nose a short one. But her eyes were the interesting thing in the witch's neurotic face; they had a very mobile glance, and the colour varied from gray to green, with always a luminous point, a sparkle, in them; the glance was sometimes shy, then frightened-looking, then seemingly carried away in a spiritual ecstasy; her whole vitality was summed up in them. Chiarastella looked as if she were more than forty, but her hair remained very black, and her forehead was marked by a single deep wrinkle; but when her eyes lighted up, an irradiation of youthfulness spread over her face and person. She wore a black woollen dress, simply made, the usual cut among the common people, only it was ornamented with white silk buttons, and a white silk ribbon hung at her waist, in a knot with two long ends, at the side. White and black are the colours worn by the votaries of Our Lady of Sorrows. A thick crooked red coral horn hung from her neck on a thin black silk cord; in making some careless gesture, the witch often touched this horn. She was seated at a big walnut table that had a closed iron box on it, of deep-cut, artistic workmanship, an antique, evidently. A big black cat slept beside her, its paws gathered up under it. Set round the small room were a little sofa of faded chintz and five or six chairs; that was all that was in it. On the wall was a black wooden crucifix; the figure of Christ, carved in ivory, was a work of art also. She kept silence, with her eyes down. The sisters felt that a great mystery was coming near, and would envelop them.

'We have brought the ten francs,' Carmela said timidly, taking them out of the corner of her handkerchief and putting them on a table by Chiarastella's hand.

The witch did not move an eyelash; only the black cat raised its head, showing fine yellow eyes like amber.

'Have you heard Mass this morning?' Chiarastella asked, without turning her head.

'Yes, we have,' the sisters muttered shyly.

She had a low, hoarse voice—one of those women's voices that seem always charged with intense feeling—and it caused deep emotion in the heart and brain of the hearers.

'Say three *Aves*, three *Pater Nosters*, three *Glorias*, out loud,' commanded the witch.

Standing in front of her, the sisters said the words of prayer; she said them too, in her vibrating voice, her hands clasped in her lap on her black apron. The cat rose on its long black legs, holding down its head. Then, altogether, the three women, after bowing three times at the *Gloria Patri*, said the *Salve Regina*. The prayers were ended. The witch opened the wrought-iron casket, holding the lid so as to hide what was in it, and groped with her fingers a long time. Then, taking out some little things, still hiding them in her hands, she got mortally pale, her eyes became wild, as if she saw a terrible sight.

'Holy Virgin, help us!' Annarella uttered in a low tone, shaking with fear.

Now Chiarastella, with a yellow lighted taper, burnt two queer scented pastilles, which were pungent and heavy at the same time; she gazed intently at the flying smoke-rings; her eyes dilated, showing the whites streaked with blue, as if she was trying to read a mysterious word. When the smoke had disappeared, only a heavy smell was left; the sisters felt stupefied already, from that smell, perhaps. Monotonously, not looking at them, Chiarastella asked:

'Have you made up your mind to work a spell on your husband?'

'Yes, provided that he does not suffer in health from it,' Annarella replied feebly.

'You want to tie his hands, two or three times, so that he never at any time can stake at the lottery, do you not?'

'Yes, that is it,' the other answered eagerly.

'Are you in God's grace?'

'I hope I am.'

'Ask the Virgin's help, but under your breath.'

Whilst Annarella raised her eyes as if to find heaven, the witch took out of the iron casket a thin new cord, looked at it, muttered some queer irregular verses in the Naples dialect, invoking the powers of heaven, its saints, and some good spirits with queer names. The chant went on; the witch, still holding the cord tight in her hand, looked at it as if filling it with her spirit; she breathed on it and kissed it devoutly three times. Whilst she was carrying out this deed of magic, her thin brown hands shook, and the cat went up and down the big table excitedly, spreading its whiskers.

Annarella now repented more than ever of having come, of trying to cast a spell on her husband. It would have been better, much better, to resign herself to her fate, rather than call out all these spirits, and put all that mystery into her humble life. She deeply repented; her breathing was oppressed, her face saddened. She wanted to fly at once far off to her dark cellar; she preferred to endure cold and wretchedness there. It was her sister who had led her into such an extreme measure; she had done it more out of pity for her, seeing her so melancholy, desolate, and worn out by sorrow from Raffaele's desertion. It was not right—no, it could not be—to try and find out God's will by witchcraft and magic in any case. No witchcraft, however powerful, would conquer her husband's passion. She had read one Saturday in his eyes, grown suddenly ferocious, how unconquerable the passion was. She had seen him ill-treat his children with that repressed rage that is capable of even greater cruelty. That witchcraft, you see, with its alarming prelude and continuation, seemed to her another big step on the way to a dark, fatal end.

Now Chiarastella, with sharpened features, her skin more shiny and eyes burning, made three fatal knots in the twine, stopping at each to say something in a whisper. At the end she threw herself all at once from the chair to kneel on the ground, her head down on her breast. The black cat jumped down too, as if possessed, and went round and round the witch in the convulsive style of cats when going to die.

'Mother of God, do not forsake me!' Annarella called out, shaking with fear; but the witch, after crossing herself wildly several times, got up and said in solemn tones to the gambler's wife:

'Take—take this miraculous cord. It will tie your husband's hands and mind when Beelzebub tells him to gamble. Believe in God; have faith; hope in Him.'

Trembling, feeling hot all over from excessive emotion, Annarella took the witch's cord. She was to put it on her husband without his noticing it. She would have liked to go away now, to fly, for she felt the sultriness of the room, and the perfume was turning her brain; but Carmela, pale, disturbed from what she had seen and the commotion in her own mind, turned an appealing look on her to get her to wait.

Chiarastella had already begun the charm to make Raffaele love Carmela again. She called Cleofa, her decrepit servant, and said something in her ear. The woman went out, and came back carrying with great care a deep white porcelain dish full of clear water, looking at it as if hypnotized, not to spill a drop; then she disappeared. Chiarastella, with her face close to the dish, muttered some of her mysterious words over the water. She put in one finger, and let three drops fall on Carmela's forehead, who at a sign had leant forward to her. Then the witch lit a big wax candle Carmela had brought, and went on muttering Latin and Italian words. The candle-wick spluttered as if water had been thrown on the flame.

'Did you bring the lock of hair cut from your forehead on Friday evening when the moon was rising?' Chiarastella's hoarse voice demanded in the middle of the prayer.

'Yes, I have it,' said Carmela, with a deep sigh, handing a tress of her black hair to the witch.

From the iron casket Chiarastella had taken a platinum dish with some hieroglyphics on it, as shiny as a mirror. On this she put the hair, and raised it up three times, as if making a sacrifice to heaven. Then she held the black tress a little above the crackling flame, which stretched up to devour it; a second after there was a disagreeable smell of burnt hair, and nothing was seen on the dish but a morsel of stinking ashes. The incantation went on, Chiarastella singing under her voice her great love-charm, which was a queer mixture of sacred and profane names—from Belphegor's to Ariel's, from San Raffaele's, the girl's protector, to San Pasquale's, patron saint of women—partly in Naples dialect, partly in bad Italian. She afterwards took a small phial from the wrought-iron box, which held all the ingredients for her charms, and put three drops from it into the plate of water, which at once became a fine opal colour, with bluish reflections. The witch looked again to try and decipher that whitish cloud which whirled round in spirals and volutes, and dropped the ashes of the hair in. Gradually under her gaze the water got clear and limpid again in the dish; then she told Carmela to hand her a new crystal bottle, bought on Saturday morning after making her Communion, and she filled it slowly with water from the dish. The love-philtre was ready.

'Take it,' the witch said in her solemn tones, ending the incantation—'take and keep it jealously. Make Raffaele drink some drops of it in wine or coffee. It will inflame his blood and burn in his brain; it will make his heart melt for love of thee. Believe in God, have faith, and hope in Him.'

'It is not poison, is it?' Carmela ventured to ask.

'It will do him good, and not harm. Have faith in God.'

'And what if he goes on despising me?'

'Then, that means that he is in love with someone else, and this charm is not enough. You must find out who the woman is that he has left you for, and bring me here a bit of her chemise, petticoat, or dress, be it wool, linen, or cotton. I will make a charm against her. We will drive in a bit of her chemise or dress with a nail and some pins into a fresh lemon; then you must throw this bewitched lemon into the well of the house where the woman lives. Every one of these pins is a misfortune; the nail is a sorrow at the heart of which she will never be cured. Do you see?'

'Very well, I will try and find out,' said Carmela, in despair at the very idea of Raffaele being unfaithful.

'Let us go away,' said Annarella, who could bear no more.

'Thank you for your kindness, ma'am,' said Carmela.

'Thank you so much,' added Annarella.

'Thank God! thank Him!' the witch cried out piously.

She cast herself down again, kneeling, fervently praying, while the big black cat gently mewed, rubbing its pink nose on the table. The two women went out, thoughtful and preoccupied.

'That witchcraft is not good,' said Annarella, in a melancholy way to her sister.

'Then, what should be done—what can be done?' the other asked, wringing her hands, her eyes filled with tears.

'Nothing can be done,' said Annarella, in a solemn voice.

They went down slowly, tired, worn out by that long scene of witchcraft, which was above their intellectual capacity, and depressed by the tension on their nerves. A man went up the steps of Centograde Lane quickly, turning towards the witch's house. It was Don Pasqualino De Feo. The sisters did not see him; they went on, feeling the weight of their unhappy life heavier, fearing to have gone beyond the limits allowable to pious folk, and that they had drawn God's mysterious vengeance on the heads of those they loved.

CHAPTER XIII
THE CONFECTIONER'S SHOP BANKRUPT

Cesare and Luisella Fragalà had shut the shop that rainy summer evening at nine o'clock, half an hour earlier than usual, because with that bad weather, that boisterous, warm scirocco wind, which made the hot rain whirl round, few people were in the streets, and no one would come out to buy coffee, a bottle of brandy, or a fancy chocolate-box, at that hour in the storm. Only some purchaser of a penny-worth of cough-lozenges came in occasionally, bringing in a puff of wind into the hot shop, dirtying the marble floor with his wet shoes. The evening had been unsuccessful, like the rest of the summer.

Luisella, who was suffering from low spirits, had not had the courage even to go to Santo Jorio for country quarters; it is one of the villages round Naples favoured by the towns-folk. She saw too many clouds coming down on her family peace, just as in the Naples skies, to dare to go from home and leave the shop. The humble pride of a rich tradesman's wife who stays at home with her children and does not think about the shop was all over. She left Rossi Palazzo, that had been the joy of her middle-class ambition, early, only to come back at the dinner-hour, go out again at once, and just come back in the evening to sleep. It was quite another affair from staying with the children.

Little Agnesina, who was three years old now, was a florid, quiet, well-behaved little creature, and often came to see her mother in the shop. She did not ask for sweets or tarts, but, hidden behind the tall counter, she cut out silently those slips of paper that are put like cotton-wool between one sweet and another in the boxes sent to country places. Agnesina made herself useful without making any noise or giving trouble, so that she should not be sent away nor be left at home with the cook and housemaid, who were always bickering. The mother, when she weaned her, would have liked to indulge in a nurse, a Tuscan by preference, so that she should not learn the Naples dialect; but just as she was going to get one, on thinking it over, she felt the subtle bitterness of a presentiment, and gave up the idea. The little girl would have grown up with no training; so, not to be separated so long nor see her unhappy, Luisella allowed her to be brought to the shop now and then.

When Agnesina saw her mother go away in the morning, she ran after her, not crying nor yelling, not saying anything, just looking up in a questioning way. The compassionate mother understood, and to console her, seeing her so quiet and obedient, she made her a promise she might come to the shop later on. That made the tiny arms let go, quite satisfied, as if she had made up her mind to wait. When she opened the big glass door, coming in in her plain cotton frock and big straw hat, she smiled at her mother as if she was a big child already. She silently went to put down her hat in the back-shop without any outburst of greed, very happy to stay beside her mother behind the high counter. Only her mother, after the moment of the little one's arrival was over, got sad. She had never thought of this, of coming to the shop every day for twelve hours to sell caramels and chocolate, to fill paper bags and wooden boxes, always to have to be ready to serve the public, whilst her little one cut paper strips, not saying a word, as neatly as a big girl. She had never dreamt her baby would be a shop-girl, too.

Luisella certainly did not despise a tradesman's life; but she would have liked to be a house, and not a shop, keeper, a housewife, and not a sweetmeat-seller. She had not dreamt of this. She would have liked to sew white work, make her baby's clothes, teach her something—carols at Easter and Christmas, the way to knit stockings, sewing, embroidery, all that is the humble but glorious inheritance of happy wives. But instead she spent her life in public with a stereotyped smile on her lips, not able to say a word privately to her husband and daughter, nor collect her thoughts a single moment. She had taken up that duty of selling in the shop from feeling the financial embarrassments her husband was in. It seemed to her that the shop-lads robbed him, or that they had bad ways with the customers—that, in short, there was need of a woman. For this she gradually sacrificed her whole day. Now no source of commercial aggrandisement was beyond her; while she was a zealous counter-up of pence, she kept house on a still more economical footing always. That was not enough, evidently, because her husband's low spirits began to be still more frequent. It must have to do with large transactions, buying sugar, flour, coffee, liqueurs—matters she could not go into. Cesare kept them out of her reach purposely. Still, she knew the price of goods, and it made her wonder the more at the discomfort they were in. When Cesare, not able to hide the straits he was in, ended by owning that he could not pay a bill, that he had not the weekly money to pay the workmen in the bakeries, she raised her eyebrows in sad surprise, saying:

'I cannot make it out. I do not see why we are so short of money.'

Cesare tried to humbug her, talking some nonsense about Customs and colonial tariffs. He spoke vaguely about losses by some speculations he was not responsible for, saying the whole trade was going to the bad. So she, getting thoughtful, ended by saying:

'Then it would be better to shut up shop.'

'No, for goodness' sake, don't say that!' he cried out.

Ah! she had found out what her misfortune was in the end. Three or four times, without intending it, she had discovered that Cesare was not so honest as he used to be, that he told lies. This made her start with fright, dreading worse evils. When they made up accounts together, he said he had paid so much, at such a price, and it was not true, or he had paid a part of it only. He had got to be a bad payer. The two landlords of the flat and the shop complained several times; they had their burdens, too; they could not wait so long for their money. She had discovered this with a sharp, secret anguish. When she questioned her husband severely, he got pale and red, stammered, letting out his hidden sin by his whole attitude. For a moment Luisella thought she was deserted for another woman, and the flames of jealousy scorched her blood; but Cesare was always so tender and loving, so sincerely and thoroughly in love with his wife, that she was reassured. No, it was not that. She could hardly make out at first what subtle, dissolving element melted away the money in the house. She discovered that the increasing debts were always getting fatally larger, from her husband's growing absent-mindedness, in spite of the sad lies he told her. She could not make out by what tiny wound the blood of the Fragalà house was going drop by drop. It was in vain that the shop was successful, that she did wonders in economy: the money disappeared all the same. She felt a hollowness under the seeming solidity of their commerce; she felt the incurable languor of a body losing all its blood. But she saw no reason for it. It was not a woman, in so far; then who and what was it? Only by dint of searching minutely and lovingly into her husband's daily life had she ended by understanding what it was. First of all, Cesare Fragalà had fallen into the habits of all keen Cabalists; instead of tearing up the lottery tickets he played each week, he was so foolish as to keep them, to compare and study them. One day, in a jacket-pocket, Luisa found a whole sheaf, a week's collection of lottery tickets, four or five hundred francs thrown thus to the greedy Government, given to an impersonal, hateful being, to try for an elusive fortune. Perhaps, in spite of the fright she got then, amid the blaze of light that blinded her, she thought it was the aberration of one week only. But Cesare was too simple about deceiving, for her to go on thinking so.

Luisa's clever eyes now saw that Friday was a day of the greatest excitement with him. She saw his nervousness in the early hours of Saturday, and the evening depression. Now, Luisa's heart was divided by two sharp sorrows that opposed each other: first, seeing their prosperity always flying away, then finding Cesare to be a victim to an incurable moral fever. That fatal period began with her when one may suffer from seeing a loved one given over to a tragic passion, and yet dare not even oppose his self-indulgence, or show one is aware of it. She was still patient, for she disliked the idea of having a grand explanation with her husband, of confronting him with his vice; she still hoped it would be a fleeting fancy.

But, to dash her hopes, day after day she saw Don Pasqualino De Feo, the medium, in the distance, circling round her husband continually, trying not to let her see him; but she guessed he was there, as a woman guesses her rival's presence. She felt the ill-omened, mean beggar was in the back-lane, at the street corner, or under the gateway waiting for Cesare, so as to draw more money out of him, and incite him to gamble again by saying silly fantastic things for Cesare to draw lottery numbers from, figures that would never come out of the urn. Now and then, in spite of Don Pasqualino's prudence that also seemed to be fear, Luisella found him at the doorway, or at the street corner, and looked so coldly and disdainfully at him that he cast down his eyes and went off in his awkward way like a man who does not know what to do with his body. Once Cesare Fragalà named Don Pasqualino De Feo before his wife, watching to see if her face changed; her sweet, affable look went off: she got to have a cold expression, and frowned. He dared not name the medium again. Indeed, he had had to warn him of his wife's ill-will, so Don Pasqualino got still more cautious; if he wanted to call Fragalà when he was at business, he sent a newsboy from the Bianchi corner. But Luisella found out whence these mysterious calls came also; she shook her head as she saw her husband go out of the shop with an affectation of carelessness.

The more the medium circled around, always dressed like a pauper, still torn and dirty, always a sucker-up of money, of everything, the more she felt her husband's rage for the lottery was not a temporary caprice, but incurable vice. Now, on Friday nights, he came in very late; she, pretending to sleep, heard quite well that he was awake, uneasy, turning in his bed, knocking his head on the pillows. Besides, while Cesare's fever did not go down, the shop's prosperity did visibly. The wholesale dealers, seeing that Fragalà was always asking for renewals of bills, or that he barely paid a part of them, got suspicious; they put off sending the goods, they even got to sending them on consignment, which is a grave proof of want of confidence commercially, a thing that ruins a trader; for he has to keep the goods in the Custom-house, not having money to take them out. He goes on paying storage, knowing all the time that the things are deteriorating.

The warning that Fragalà was not quite solvent must have run from Napoli Square to other parts, for he began to find all doors shut if he did not come money in hand; his having signed money-lenders' bills spoilt his credit altogether. Still, his reputation and means stood it so much the more that it was the reputation of all the Fragalàs together. But that could not last. One final blow, and his commercial standing would go also.

Now the bad summer season had come, with a scarcity of country visitors, which caused a languor of all Naples' forces, a crisis that went on increasing among all classes; for everyone lives off strangers in that town of no commerce. It was no use for Luisella Fragalà to give up her change to the country that year for the first time; nothing had come of it. Goods were short in the storehouses from the suspiciousness of dealers, and customers were still scarcer from the bad weather.

Luisella could not manage to keep down her depression now; the pretty young face had got to have a grave expression, her head was often down on her breast. She thought and thought, as if her soul was absorbed in a most difficult problem; for one thing, she saw that her husband's mental malady was always getting worse. He was so sorrowful at some moments, it wrung one's heart to look at him. Besides, the bad weather affected her, too; all suffered from it, rich, well to do, and poor, for in this great country everything radiates, joy as well as grief, good fortune as well as bad. Now she had decided to speak, to question her husband's heart, for the situation was getting gradually worse, it was desperate; in a short time he would be ruined.

Being quite decided now in her loving, strong, womanly heart, having made up her mind to act, she kissed her dear little one, who was so quiet and prettily behaved, saying to herself she would speak, she would bring out everything. Her life was already grievous from her responsibilities as wife and mother; the gay, idyllic time was past for ever, the long sad hour was come when she needed all her courage to influence and convince Cesare. It was really a battle she intended to hold that evening in the steamy shop, whilst the summer rain rattled sadly outside.

It was Friday; still, for a wonder, Cesare Fragalà had not left the shop that evening, as he had got into the habit of doing every week at dusk, not to return till three in the morning, the time the last lottery-shop shut. He went backwards and forwards nervously; twice the usual newspaper boy had come to call him for Don Pasqualino: he answered that the person must wait, because he was busy. Pale and trembling, feeling she had got to an important crisis, his wife followed, with a side-glance, her husband's wanderings. Outside, the rain beat sadly on the windows, the gas-flame looked sickly.

'Shall we shut up shop now?' Fragalà said impatiently.

'It would be best, no doubt,' she said, with a slight sigh, 'especially as no one will be coming in.'

The two shopmen, helped by the porter and message-boy, made haste to put up the iron gates, put out the outside gas, and give a general cleaning up before going away by the little back-shop door in Bianchi Lane. Quickly they said good-night and set off, one by one. The white shop, its shelves brilliant with colour from the chocolate-boxes, was now lit by one gas-jet only. Luisella was seated behind the counter, as usual, and little Agnesina had gone to sleep in her chair, her knees covered with shreds of paper. Cesare often disappeared into the back-shop, as if he could get no peace. Neither of them could make up their mind to speak, feeling that it was a grave crisis that they had come to. She, above all, felt herself choking. It was he who spoke first.

'Look here, Luisella,' he said, in a low voice: 'you know what a bad season we have had.'

'Yes, a wretched one,' she muttered.

'It is a real disaster, I assure you, my dear—enough to make one give up keeping shop. You carry out economies, I work hard ... and it goes from bad to worse.'

'I know that,' she muttered again, as if tired of those grumbles.

'You cannot know the full extent of it ... you would have to deal directly with the wholesale houses to know what ruin — —'

'Come to the point,' she said, rather bitterly.

'Are you angry with me?' Cesare asked humbly.

'No, it is not that,' she replied, in a curious tone.

'Well, I want you to do me a favour—a great favour, so great I am ashamed to ask it, even.'

'Say what it is,' she just uttered, keeping down the pained feeling her husband's words caused her.

'I have a payment to make to-morrow morning....'

'To-morrow, in the morning, do you say?'

'Yes; it is a bill that falls due. I had forgotten it. It is a big bill.'

'Still, you had forgotten it?'

'You know I have got rather confused lately ... in short, I must pay, and I am not ready. I asked in vain for a renewal or if I might pay part only. Everyone wants his money just now. I cannot pay, and there is no money to be had.'

'Then, what is it that you want of me?' she said, looking coldly at him.

'You could help me; you could get me out of this momentary embarrassment. I will give you back the money at once.'

'I have no money.'

'You have some valuables. Those diamond earrings I gave you: they are worth a great deal. One could get a lot for them.'

'Would you like to sell them?' said she, shutting her eyes as if she saw something horrible.

'I would pledge them—just take them to the pawn-shop, only for a few days. They will be redeemed at once.'

'Do you intend to pawn the diamond earrings?'

'And the star—the star Don Gennaro Parascandolo gave you,' he said hurriedly, in an anxious tone.

She said nothing, just kept her head down and looked at the baby quietly sleeping. Then, in a whisper, with an irrepressible shudder, she said to her husband:

'You want to pawn my jewels so as to stake on the lottery.'

'That is not true!' he cried out.

'Do not tell lies. Can you say before me and your daughter that you won't use the money for the lottery?'

'Do not speak to me like that, Luisella!' he stammered out, with tears in his eyes.

'You want them to stake on the lottery with. Have the courage of your vices; don't load your conscience with lies,' his wife answered with the cruelty of desperation.

'It is not a vice, Luisa; it is for good ends I gambled, for good motives, for your sake and Agnesina's.'

'A father of a family does not gamble.'

'It was to open the new shop in San Ferdinando Square. Seventy thousand francs were needed for it, and I had not got it. You know all our money is in use.'

'A family man ought not to play.'

'It was for the happiness of us all, Luisella. I swear to you, believe me, it was because of my love for Agnesina.'

'You don't love her. If you cared for her, you would not gamble.'

'Luisella, don't humiliate me—don't make me out mean. Be kind. You know how much I loved you—how I do love you!'

'It is not true. If you loved me, you would not gamble.'

He threw himself on an iron seat, leant his arms and head on a marble table, and hid his face, not able to bear his wife's anger and his own remorse. He felt great grief and sorrow, only surmounted by that sharp, piercing need of money. With that agony he raised his head again, and said:

'Luisella, if my honour is dear to you, don't force me to make a poor figure to-morrow. Give me your jewels; I will give them back on Monday.'

'Take the jewels; they belong to you,' she said slowly, with her eyes down; 'but do not say you will give them back on Monday, because it is not true. All gamblers lie like that, but pledged goods never come back to the house. Take all the jewellery. What can I say against your taking it? I was a poor girl with no dowry, and you, a rich merchant, condescended to marry me, and gave me a higher position. Should I not thank you for that all my life? Take everything; be master of the house, of me and my daughter. To-day you will take the jewels and stake them; next time you will take the best furniture, the kitchen coppers, the house linen; it always goes on like that. The Marquis di Formosa, too, who lives above us—has he not done that? His daughter has not a bit of bread to put in her mouth now: and if Dr. Amati did not help them secretly, both would die of hunger. Who will help us when, in a year or six months, we are like them? Who knows? Perhaps I will go mad, too, as the poor young lady up there threatens to do. Her father makes her see spirits. It is a scandal amongst all those who know her. But what are we women to do? Fathers, husbands, are the masters. Take the diamonds, pawn them, sell them, throw them into the gulf where your money has fallen and is lost; I do not care for them now. They were my pride as a happy wife. When I put them in my ears and hair, when I opened the casket to look at them, I blessed your name, because, among other pleasures, you had given me this. It is ended; it is all over. We are done with pleasures now; we are at the last gasp.'

'Luisella, have some charity!' he screamed out, feeling his flesh and soul burn from these red-hot words.

'Charity! we will soon be asking for it. The diamonds go to-day, the other valuables next; then all, everything we possess, will disappear. It will all be a flying dream,' she replied, looking in front of her as if she already saw the frightful vision of their ruin.

'Still, I need them; it is necessary for me to take them!' he cried out with the doleful persistence of a desperate man who only feels his evil tendencies pushing him on.

'Who is denying you anything? Even Agnesina has pearl earrings. Put them in; it will make a larger sum. Her cradle has antique lace on it; Signora Parascandolo presented it to her. It is valuable. Take it; it will bring up the sum.'

'Look here, Luisa,' her husband began saying pantingly, emotion choking his utterance, 'I swear to you the money is not intended for gambling; I would not have dared to ask it from you, a good woman, if it was. You have such good reasons to despise me already. But it is a debt for former stakes I made—a terrible debt to a money-lender. He threatens to protest it to-morrow—to seize my goods. This cannot be allowed to happen; a merchant whose bills are protested ought to die.'

'That is true,' she said, hanging her head.

'It may be,' he added after a short hesitation. 'Perhaps I would have taken some of it to gamble with—just a little, only to try and recoup myself—only for that, Luisella.'

'In short, you cannot keep from gambling!' his wife cried out in a rage.

He trembled like a guilty boy, and did not answer.

'Can you not keep from it?' she asked again, attacked by a most terrible fear.

'Look here, this is how it is: it is a perfidious passion. You do not know what it is; you must have felt it to know; you must have panted and dreamt, or you cannot think what it is like. One starts gambling for a joke, out of curiosity, as a little challenge to fortune. One goes on, pricked to the quick by delusions, excited by vague desires that grow. Woe to you if you win anything—an *ambo*, a small *terno*! It is all up with you, for your chance of winning seems certain. Do you see? You feel certain of winning a large sum, as you have managed to get a small amount, and you put back not only all you have gained, but you double, treble the stake in the weeks that follow your success. It is the devil's money going back to hell. What a passion it is, Luisella! It is bad for one to win, and bad not to win. Then the dream, that for seven days keeps you alive, on the eighth day gives you a bitter disappointment; it ends by setting your blood on fire, and to increase your chances of winning at any cost, your stakes increase frightfully; the desire of winning gets to be a madness. The soul gets sick; it neither sees nor hears anything. No family ties, position, nor fortune, can stand against this passion.'

'My God!' she said softly, just as if she were going to fall into a chasm.

'You are right, Luisella, to ill-use me, to strike at me with your scorn; you have a right to do it. I am a bad husband, a worse father; I have beggared my family. You are quite right,' Cesare said again convulsively. 'I was a cheerful, industrious young fellow; all wished me well; my business was going splendidly; you were a joy, and Agnesina a pleasure to me. What fascination has overcome me? That cursed idea I had of winning seventy thousand francs at the lottery to open a shop at San Ferdinando with—a cursed idea that has put the fire of hell into my blood. I wanted to enrich you by gambling, whereas grandfather and father taught me by example that only by being content with a little, by putting sou upon sou, one gets rich. What folly was it seized me? What was the infection? Where did I catch it? What a horrible passion gambling is!'

The poor woman listened to that anguished confession, pale, her lips shaking from the effort she made to restrain her sobs, leaning against the elbows of the chair, feeling crushed by a nameless agony.

'How much have I staked?' Cesare went on. He seemed to be speaking to himself now, without seeing his wife or hearing his sleeping child's breathing. 'I do not know, I do not remember now. The lottery is à great melter-down of money; it is like a crucible the metal runs out of. At first I played moderately; I tried to be moderate and wise about it, as if the lottery was not the most laughable trick that fortune plays on man. At that time I wrote down the money I staked in a pocket-book where I note my ordinary expenses; but afterwards the fever seized me, and has grown so, I remember no more. I do not remember how many thousands of francs I threw away so madly in an ugly dream, a delirium that came back again every Friday. Luisella, you do not know it, but we are ruined.'

'I do know it,' she said very softly, looking at the little one's pink face sleeping in childish serenity.

'You do not know, you cannot know, everything. I have given bills for the money put aside for yearly payments; I have staked the thousand francs we put in the savings bank for Agnesina; I have robbed her of the money I gave her—her own money; I have failed to carry out my bargains commercially. Our correspondents have no confidence in my soundness; they will have no more to do with me; they send me no goods. You see the shop is getting empty; I have no ready money to fill it again. I have not even paid the insurance money; if the shop was burnt down to-morrow, I would not get a farthing. I am a bad payer. You do not know—you can't. I have tried for money everywhere in desperation; put myself in a money-lender's hands, mostly in Don Gennaro Parascandolo's, and they have eaten me up to the bone.'

'Did you borrow money from Agnesina's godfather?' Luisella exclaimed sadly, hiding her face in her hands.

'In money matters no relationship counts; money hardens all hearts. These debts are my shame and torment. A tradesman who takes money at eight per cent. a month is thought to be ruined, and they are right. Money-lending is dishonest both in the borrower and lender. What shall I do? The season is a very bad one for poor and rich; but even if it was a splendid one, the gains would not be enough even to pay the interest on my debts. Just think; it is a miracle that Cesare Fragalà, the head of the Fragalà house, has not yet been declared bankrupt, and a discreditable bankrupt; for a merchant cannot take creditors' money to stake on the lottery. It is theft, you understand, theft, and thieves go to the gallows. After reducing my family to wretchedness, I will take their honour from them by this hellish madness.'

Not able to bear his unhappiness any longer, he burst into sobs, choking and crying like a child. She, shaking with emotion, feeling in her heart a great pity for her husband and a great fear for the future, raised her head resolutely.

'There is no remedy, then?' she said, in her firm voice, like a good, loving woman.

'There is none,' he answered, opening his arms in a despairing way.

'We are on a precipice. I understand—I see it. But there must be some way of mending matters,' she reiterated obstinately, not willing to give in without a struggle.

'Pray to the Virgin for help—pray!' he whispered, like a child—more lost than a child.

'Let us try and find some cure,' she still answered softly.

'You try; I can do no more. I have no will or strength left. You must search for it. I am lost, and nothing will save me.'

The despairing words seemed to echo in the gay, white shop, shining with satin and porcelain. There was a deep silence between the couple. She, wrapped in thought, with the firm, introspective glance of a strong woman, counted over the extent of her misfortune. She did not feel angry now. All rage had fallen at the young fellow's agonized voice. He had been so easy and merry, and now he stammered out piteously his irreparable mistake. What she had heard, the anguish bursting forth from her husband's inward heart, what she had guessed at, and that grievous, impressive spectacle, had done a work of cleansing. All personal resentment had gone from her generous mind. She only felt a strong desire for self-sacrifice, for saving her husband and his home. The littleness that sometimes limited her womanly mind had gone. Her soul rose to unselfish heights of sacrifice. He kept to earth, tied down by his engrossing passion. He did not show even the Marquis di Formosa's greatness under it. His grief, his lamentation, were as monotonous and rhythmical as a child's. She, on the other hand, on meeting misfortune became spiritualized, and let the noblest part of her character rule her. After that wild confession she felt more like a helpful sister, a compassionate mother, than a young wife; more like a high magnanimous protector. She forgot all her natural pretences and affectations as a woman and wife.

He was weeping, with his head down on his arm against the table, like a wretched creature whose unhappiness is really infinite and not to be cured, while she, deep in thought, pondered over means of setting things right. But all at once, with a hush, she told him to say no more. Agnesina had wakened, very gently, as usual, without weeping or crying. Seated queerly on her tiny chair, she was looking at her mother with wide-open, mildly-sparkling eyes. Luisella lifted her out of the chair she was fastened into and bent over to kiss her little one, as if she got strength from that kiss and her requited love.

The tiny one looked at her father without speaking, seeing his head down on the table; then she said, 'Is father asleep?'

'No, no, he is not sleeping,' said her mother under her breath, as she went into the back-shop to take her mantle and hat. 'Go and give him a kiss. Go and say this to him, "Father, it is nothing—it is nothing."'

The obedient infant went to her father, leant her tiny head against his knee, and, in her pretty, singing voice said:

'Father, give me a kiss; it is nothing, nothing.'

Then the poor young fellow's swollen heart burst. The most scalding tears rained on his little one's head.

While tying her bonnet-strings, Luisella, as she heard these desperate sobs, shivered to keep back her tears. But she did not interfere. She let the desolate heart find a vent and take comfort in kissing the little one. She, full of wonder, went on saying under the tears and kisses, 'Father, father, it is nothing.'

'Let us go home,' said Luisella, coming into the shop again, biting her lips, trying to harden her heart.

Still moved, Cesare Fragalà took his little girl in his arms, as he did every evening when she went to sleep in the shop, and put on her woollen hood, tying it under the chin. Luisella went on tidying up the shop a little, taking the key out of the strong box, feeling if all the drawers of the counter were properly shut, with that instinct for working with their hands all healthy, good young women have. They put out the gas, and Luisella lit a taper. Then they went away through the back-shop and the small door that led into Bianchi Lane. It was still raining. The warm scirocco wind beat the tepid summer rain in their faces; but they were not far from home. Cesare put up his umbrella, his wife took his arm to shelter from the rain, the child was perched on his other arm and put her head on his shoulder. All three went along, bowed under the summer storm, not speaking, clinging one to the other as if only love could save them from life's tempest that threatened to overwhelm them. At night, under the rage of heaven, it seemed as if they were going on and on to a sorrowful destiny. But the two innocent ones pressed close to the unhappy, guilty man, seeming to pray for him. They would bring him into safety. They said nothing till they got home, where the servant was waiting for them at the open door. She held out her arms to take Agnesina and carry her to her room to undress her and put her to bed. But the little one, as if she had understood the importance of the time, asked her father and mother to kiss her again, saying, in her gentle, baby tongue, 'Bless me, mother; bless me, father.'

At last they were alone again in their bedroom, where the silver lamp burned before the Mother of Jesus, the holy grieving Mother. Cesare was depressed. But Luisella opened the glass door of the wardrobe at once, where she kept her most valuable things, and stood for a little searching in that half-light. Then she pulled two or three dark leather jewel-cases out.

'Here they are,' she said, offering the jewels to her husband.

'Oh, Luisella! Luisella!' he cried out, agonized.

'I give them to you willingly, for the sake of your honour. I would not dare to keep these stones when we are in danger of failing in honesty. Take them. But by all that has been sweet in our past, by all that may be frightful in our future, by the love you bore me, that I bear you, for our dear child's sake, whose head you wept over this evening, I implore you with my whole heart, as one prays to Christ at the altar, give me a promise.'

'Luisella, you want to kill me!' he cried out, putting his hands through his hair.

'Do you promise to leave all your trade affairs in my hands—debts and dues, buying and selling?'

'I do promise.'

'Will you promise to give me all the money you have or may get, and not try to get money without my knowledge?'

'I will give it to you—all, Luisa.'

'Promise to believe me, only to listen to my advice and what I say.'

'I promise that.'

'Promise that no one will have more influence than me; promise to obey me as you did your mother when you were a child.'

'I will obey you as I did her.'

'Swear to all that.'

'I swear it to the Madonna, who is listening to us.'

'Let us pray now.'

Both piously knelt before the holy images. They said the Lord's Prayer in a whisper, louder at the end. She raised her eyes, and said, 'Lead us not into temptation,' and he rejoined, very humbly and disconsolately, 'Lead us not into temptation.'

CHAPTER XIV
THE MEDIUM'S IMPRISONMENT

The summer rain beat sadly on the pavement; two broad yellow gutters went down the sides of Nardones Road; the sickening sulphurous smell of August storms was in the air. In San Ferdinando Square the cabs had their hoods up, and were shiny all over with rain, dripping on all sides. The long thin horses stood with their heads down, drenched to the bones, and running down with water. The drivers sat huddled up, their shapeless hats over their eyes, keeping their heads down and hands spasmodically fixed in the pockets of their torn capes, as they patiently bore the deluge from the sky. All around was dreary-looking—the royal palace, the porch of San Francesco di Paolo Church, the Prefecture, barracks, and large coffee-houses—all were dreary, in spite of the grandeur of the buildings and the numbers of lights behind the plate-glass windows. There was the majestic edifice of San Carlo Theatre also; but the whole night landscape was wrapped up in the noisy tempest that never rested, and seemed to draw new force from its weariness to beat on houses, streets, and men. There were few passers-by, and these looked like unhappy folks' ghosts walking under dripping umbrellas, or, having no umbrella, they scraped along the wall with coat-collar raised and soft hat soaked with rain. Some few wanderers turned the corner from Toledo Street into Nardones Road, which is a broad enough street in the best quarter of the town; but it has an equivocal appearance, all the same, as if it was uninhabited and unsafe. It had no shady corners, but shutter-closed windows, ill-lit balconies, and half-open doors, where the gaze was checked by a dark passage, had a suspicious appearance. Some great door now and then broke through this doubtful impression, from the brightness of the gas and width of its courtyard, but a shop with far from clean windows, obscured by reddish stuff curtains carefully drawn, a feeble light coming through and small or large shadows showing behind, gave a new feeling of suspicion and uneasiness to the minds of people going home that way who might be bending under the weight of cares and long fatigue.

At one point a woman with a black shawl barely covering her yellow dress and white bodice turned the corner from Toledo Street and went up Nardones Road slowly, holding the corners of the handkerchief on her head tightly between her teeth, sheltering from the rain under a very small umbrella. She went along very cautiously, lifting her feet so as to wet her bright leather shoes as little as possible, lifting her skirt to let red cotton stockings be seen. When she passed under a lamp-post's reddish light she raised her head and showed the face, now sad and tired, for all its commonplace beauty, of Filomena, Annarella and Carmela's unfortunate sister. She got as far as the suspicious-looking shop with the red curtains, and stopped before the plate-glass door as if she was trying to see someone or find out what was going on, and did not dare to open the door. She could make out nothing but some dark shadows with hats on moving about. After hesitating a little, she decided to put her hand on the knob of a small window and open it. She put in her head timidly, and called:

'Raffaele! Raffaele!'

I am coming immediately,' the young Camorrist's voice answered from inside in rather an impatient tone.

She quickly shut the window again and set herself to wait in the rain. A man passed, and cast a queer look at her, his curiosity aroused by meeting anyone in that strange stormy weather at so late an hour. But she cast down her eyes as if she was ashamed, and watched the end of Nardones Road to see who came round the corner, evidently being much afraid of being recognised. Suddenly she gave a start. Two working men were coming along, going up Nardones Road, not speaking to each other, getting all the rain on their shoulders. The one man, old, hump-backed, dragging his leg, turned out to be Michele, the shoeblack, not carrying his block for once; the other, tall and thin, with burning eyes in hollow sockets, was Gaetano, the glover. On recognising her sister Annarella's husband, Filomena gave a frightened shiver and got closer to the wall, as if she wanted to get to the other side of it. She lowered her umbrella, and prayed silently, with lips that could hardly stammer out the words, that Gaetano should not recognise her. She shivered and trembled, fearing the shop door would open and that Gaetano would see the man who was coming out. But Gaetano, as he was getting the full force of the rain on his head, took no notice of the people on the road, luckily for Filomena, nor did the shop door open as he passed. Instead of that, the working men disappeared, one after the other, into a gateway, forty paces off, where some other men had gone in before them. But Filomena felt her cheeks icy under the rouge, from the fright she had got, and she opened the door again to beg and beseech in a whisper:

'Raffaele, do come!'

'I am coming—I am coming,' the young fellow answered in a bored tone, not even noticing that the poor woman was waiting all this time in the rain, at night, in a wind-swept road.

She sighed deeply. Her eyes had no need now of bistre, for a deep line of fatigue went under them, and they were filled with tears. The rain now had soaked through her green cotton umbrella and come down on her head. It soaked her shiny black hair and ran down her face and neck, a warm water, like tears. But she did not even feel the rain trickling, for she felt nothing. She did not see three or four other men come out of Toledo Street, go on to the top of Nardones Road, and disappear into the gateway where Michele and Gaetano had rushed in.

Inside the shop the shadows moved about, and a noise of voices in discussion arose. She got up closer and strained her ears anxiously as she heard Raffaele cursing and threatening. She could not stand the noise of angry voices. Again she opened the door, crying out beseechingly:

'Raffaele, Raffaele, do come!'

Still angrier words burst out on all sides from those drinking and gambling in that wretched coffee-house; then Raffaele came out of the shop, putting on his hat with a bang, as if he was being pushed from inside. On finding himself confronted by Filomena's humble figure, soaking, the rouge running down her cheeks, her face distorted by fear, he cursed impiously, and gave her an ugly shove.

'Come on home—do come!' said she, taking no notice of the push and the curses.

The Camorrist furiously told her to go and kill herself. But it was raining, and he had no umbrella; his short jacket did not shelter him well, so he got under her umbrella, still cursing.

'Be patient with me, be kind,' she said, lengthening her steps on the pavement to keep alongside of him, and lowering the umbrella to his side, so that he should not get soaked.

'But you know you should not come to the billiard-saloon,' said the young fellow, with suppressed rage. 'It bores me to look like a schoolboy being fetched home—it bores me.'

'Be patient with me. I could not help it,' she whispered, drinking in the tears that ran down her cheeks, not being able to wipe them.

'I will leave you—as true as death, I'll leave you! You have your sister's fault. She was so ragged she disgusted me. She came everywhere to look for me, and made my friends laugh at me. I left her for that. Do you understand?'

'Poor sister!' she moaned out.

'You are not ragged, but you get me laughed at just the same. Do you hear?'

'Yes, I know.'

'If you don't give over, I will leave you, as I did Carmela. I am a young fellow of honour, you know.'

'Yes, I know that.'

'Don't come here again.'

'Very well, I never will.'

They still went on with this talk, for he felt enraged at losing his game and at being laughed at by his friends, also at not having any money. She was penitent, feeling that ill-treatment was her just punishment for playing her sister false; so, while he bit at his spent cigar in a corner of his mouth and went on abusing her, taunting her with her unhappy life, calling her every bad name, she went alongside, silent and pale, for all the rouge had run down with the rain. Her wet chemise stuck to her shoulders, and her hair was glued to her forehead with damp. She went on, keeping down the umbrella to his side, bearing his insults; for she was carried away by sorrow and repentance, and said mechanically over and over again: 'It is little to what I deserve.'

Up there all those who went in at the gateway on the right side of Nardones Road had gone up a stair of one flight, opposite the chief staircase, which was a little broader. They went into an apartment of two rooms that was let for an office—so called by the owner because it had no kitchen. But the two rooms were so low in the ceiling, so badly lighted by two small windows, the red brick floors were so cold, the wall-paper so dirty, and the paint of the doors and windows so greasy, that no small notary, poor advocate, doctor without practice, or dealer in doubtful business, stayed there more than a month. The cobbler who served as a porter and the inmates who went down the big stair were accustomed, therefore, to see new faces for ever going up and down the small stair—young and old men, ushers and commission agents, a string of white-faced people, often very queer-looking. Who troubled themselves about the people living there? No one—not even the porter. He got no pay from the occupiers of the flat, and did not care therefore if the tenants were changed. On the big stair busy people lived: house-agents, writing-masters, a third-rate dentist, a midwife, and others of queer professions. They went up and down, taken up about their own interests and business, their decent poverty or unsuccessful ill-doing. They were people who took little notice of their neighbours, so that one might call the office, that always was having new tenants or being left vacant, rather isolated. The ticket 'To Let' stood there on the door the whole year round; every month it was the same. When the apartment was let, then the tenant carried off the key at dusk; when it was vacant, the cobbler kept it on his counter, or, if he was away, he handed it over to the charcoal-dealer opposite. The stair of the apartment was broken in places, slippery and dangerous for those who had not good legs and sharp eyes.

Now, that August the little place had been occupied for a couple of months by a neatly-dressed young gentleman, affecting the style of a provincial trying to be fashionable. He was fat and thick, with a bull-like neck, and his red hair, joined to a florid complexion, gave him an apoplectic look. So the office was opened several times a week for a few hours, and two or three men, or sometimes more, came in. They disappeared up the staircase, and nothing more was heard, nothing showed behind the dirty window-panes; only after an hour or so these men appeared again, one by one, some red in the face, as if they had shouted for a long time, others pallid, as if gulping down repressed rage. They vanished each one by his own road, without even the porter seeing them sometimes.

But one evening of the week, always the same one, seven or eight men met in the office, and then a dirty petroleum lamp, covered by a shade that might cost threepence, lighted up the dirty room. Its only furniture was a rough table and eight or ten chairs, of odd patterns. On that evening the confabulation lasted till past midnight; often some gesticulating shadow showed queerly against the panes; sometimes the men leant out of the window, and looked stolidly into the dull black court, as if they saw the ghosts of their own excited minds. The cobbler, tired with his hard day's work, casting an indifferent glance at the windows of the office, saw it was still lighted up, and, shrugging his shoulders, went off to sleep in his den, a hole under the staircase. The courtyard was not lighted up; the street door was left half open; some people still went out and came in cautiously from the so-called great staircase. Some mysterious night-patient of the dentist, some hurried client to call the midwife, who opened the door mysteriously to go out.

It was after midnight when Dr. Trifari's guests went away from the meeting, all together, silently, hurrying down one after the other to get away as quickly as possible. The last one pulled the office door behind him, and it gave the creaking noise of old rotten wood. The two small rooms that formed the office returned to their solitude, and, with hearts beating high in the excitement of their dream, the party melted away through the town. But this dreary evening the poor cobbler had gone to bed at dusk, wrapping himself up in his ragged bed-covering and torn cape he had worn all day, feeling the chill of the tertian fever and the damp of the stormy weather in his bones. So, in the confusion of the fever that had come on like a block of ice on his chest, he heard the clatter of those going up and down the big stair. Two or three times he seemed to hear voices raised in the office, where there was a window open, and the scirocco wind carried the rain rushing in, and made the oil-lamp flicker. The rain went on falling in the badly-paved court, covering any other noise; then the window was shut, and no more could be heard. Later on the shutters were fastened too, and everything sank again into deep shadow. Still, there was a meeting going on there. Trifari, the master of the house, had been the first to arrive; he lighted the lamp, and went through to the second room to arrange some things, going and coming from it, with his hat a little on the back of his head. In spite of the scirocco wind, it was the first time the colour had gone out of his red face, and some drops of sweat came out on his forehead. Sometimes he stood still, as if he repented of what he was going to do or thought of doing; but he quickly recovered from that momentary depression. When the shrill bell rang the first time, Dr. Trifari gave a start and stood still uncertainly, as if he dared not open it. Still, he went, but he only half opened the folding-door, with great caution, to let Colaneri pass through. The ex-priest's face was rather gloomy, and his shoulders were dripping wet; for his small umbrella, a very shabby one, only protected his head. They said good-evening to each other in a whisper; Colaneri, with cautious glances from behind his spectacles, dried his wet hands with a doubtfully white handkerchief—the fat, flabby, whitish hands that are peculiar to priests. They said nothing to each other. The same complicated anguish bore down on them, so that their Southerners' loquacity was subdued; all the past excitement, beaten down by disappointments following each other, had ended by sapping their strength.

Suddenly, raising his head, Colaneri asked: 'Is he to come?'

'Yes, he is coming,' Trifari breathed between his lips.

'Has he no suspicion of what we are going to do?'

'None at all.'

A gust of wind came into the room and nearly put out the light. It was then Trifari went to shut the window.

'We are only doing what is an absolute necessity,' Professor Colaneri replied, repeating aloud the excuse with which he had been soothing his conscience for some days.

'It is impossible to go on any longer like this,' the doctor remarked in a dull voice; then he lighted a cigar to try and look at his ease, but he did not manage it: he let the match go out.

'The report made against me to the governors is frightful,' said Colaneri in a whisper, with his eyes down. 'I have a lot of enemies—lads I ploughed in the examinations, you know. They reported me to the President of the University as having sold the exercises to some students. They put down the names, too....'

'How could they know all that?' the doctor asked slowly.

'Who can tell? I have so many enemies. The President made a dreadful report; I am threatened....'

'With being turned out?'

'Not only that; there is to be a lawsuit....'

'You don't say so?'

'I have so many enemies, Trifari. It is a serious threat. How will I be able to prove my innocence?'

'You have sold these exercises, then?' the doctor muttered cynically, throwing away his cigar.

'The pay is so wretched, Trifari, and the examinations are all a fraud, too.'

'If they take you to law it will be bad for you.'

'I am ruined if they do. I must have money in hand at any cost this time, do you understand; if not, I am ruined. There is nothing left but to shoot myself, if they take me to law. We must win, Trifari.'

'We will win,' the other affirmed sternly. 'I have a lot of trouble, here and at my home. My father has sold everything; my brother, instead of coming home after his service as a soldier, out of poverty has enlisted in the military police; my sister is not to be married, she has not a farthing of dowry now; she is reduced to making dresses for rich peasants. We had very little, and I have eaten all there was, and there are a number of debts, of calls.... The father of the student whom we forced to sign a promissory note at Don Gennaro Parascandolo's wants to denounce me as a cheat.... We must win, Colaneri; we cannot live another week without winning.... I am more ruined than you are.'

Here the bell rang very gently.

'Perhaps it is him, do you think?' Colaneri asked with a little shake in his voice.

'No, no,' Trifari answered; 'he is to come later, when we are all here....'

'Who took the message to him?'

'Formosa took it.'

'He has no suspicion, then?'

'No, none.'

'Then, the spirit has not told him anything?'

'It looks as if the spirit could not go against Fate, for it tells him nothing about this.'

'It is Fate, I suppose?'

Another ring came. Trifari went to open the door. It was Marzano, the lawyer, the sprightly, good-natured, smiling old man. But sudden decrepitude seemed to have come over him; his pallor had got yellowish, his pepper-and-salt moustache was quite white, and had got thin over his mouth. His smile had gone for ever; evidently, as death drew near, his good opinion of life had gone. He came in sighing. He was soaking, his overcoat shone with drops of water all over, and his lean hands trembled. He sat down saying nothing, and kept his hat well down over his ears, only his mouth kept up the old habit of moving, always chewing ciphers. Now he leant his pointed chin, where a neglected beard was growing, on his stick, being so wrapt in thought he did not even hear what Trifari and Colaneri were saying to each other. Suddenly he, too, having the same engrossing thought, asked: 'Will he come, do you think?'

'Of course he will,' the other two answered together.

'Has he not guessed?'

'He knows nothing about it.'

'These mediums either see a lot or they see nothing.'

'Better so,' the other two muttered.

Dr. Trifari, on hearing knocking at the door, went first into the second room to fetch three or four other chairs, and arranged them round the shabby table. Ninetto Costa and Don Crescenzio, the lottery banker at Nunzio Lane, came in. The stock-broker had lost all his smartness. He was dressed anyhow—in a morning coat; his too light overcoat had big splashes of wet on it; not even a pebble breast-pin shone on his black silk necktie. His fine lucky man's bright smile that showed his teeth had gone too with the smartness. The stock-broker was going on with difficulty from one settling-day to another, taking no more risks, not daring to gamble; he had lost all his audacity; he only managed to keep his creditors at bay: they still had faith in him; because his name was known on the Exchange, because his father had been a model of honesty and he himself had been so lucky, all still believed in his fortune. But the unhappy man knew that the hour of the crisis had come, that he would not even be able to pay the interest on his debts soon, that Ninetto Costa's name would be on the bankrupt list. He had put down everything—his handsome house, carriages, luxurious appliances, journeys, dinners, and English clothes from Poole. But this sacrifice was not enough, for the cancer that gnawed his breast, that ate into everything, was not rooted out. He still desperately played at the lottery, being taken by it now soul and body, shutting his eyes to the storm so as not to see the waves coming that would drown him. Alongside of him Don Crescenzio, with his handsome, serene face and well-combed chestnut beard, had the traces also of beginning to fall off in prosperity. By dint of being in contact with feverish people, just as if he had been touching too hot hands, something of the gambling fever had been affecting him, and through the desperate insistence of the gamblers he had got to giving them credit. How could he resist the imploring demands of Ninetto Costa, Trifari and Colaneri's pretexts, that had a vague threat under them, the Marquis di Formosa's grand promises?—all used different forms of supplication. To begin with, he let them have credit from Friday till Tuesday, the day he got ready the State profits; they, doing a renewed miracle every week, managed to give him what they owed, so that he might be ready on Wednesday; but at last, their resources being exhausted, some of them began to pay a part only, or not to pay anything, and he began to put his own money into it, so that his caution money should not be seized by the State. The gamblers dared not show again till they had got money; then they paid off part of the debt and staked what they had over. One client had disappeared altogether— Baron Lamarra, son of the mason who had got to be a contractor and a rich man. He owed Don Crescenzio more than two thousand francs, and when Don Crescenzio had waited for him two or three weeks, he went to look for him at his house. He found the wife in a furious state. Baron Lamarra had forged her signature on a number of bills, and she had to pay unless she wanted to be a forger's wife; but she was already trying for a separation. Baron Lamarra had fled to Isernia, and from there gave not a sign of life. Don Crescenzio was rudely turned away from the door—that was two thousand francs and more lost! He swore not to give more credit to anyone; but, in spite of the debtors paying him a little now and then, seven or eight thousand francs were still risked, with little hope of getting them back. Eight thousand francs was the exact sum of his savings for several years. Besides, he could not press his debtors much—they had nothing now but a few desperate resources that only came to light from a wicked, burning love of gambling. He now took a lively interest in their gambling, and was anxious for them to win, so as to get his savings back, to recover the money left so imprudently in the hands of these vicious fellows. He watched the gamblers so that they should not go to play elsewhere, now uneasy and sick himself from coming in contact with so many infected people. It was for this reason that the evening's mysterious design was made known to him; they all owed him money, and could hide nothing from him. And in spite of a secret friendship, we would almost say complicity, between Don Pasqualino, the medium, and him, he told him nothing about the mysterious plan; by his silence he seemed to approve of it.

There were five of them already in the small room, seated round the table in different thoughtful or rather absent-minded attitudes. They were not speaking: some held their heads down, and scribbled with their nails on the dusty table; others looked at the smoky ceiling, where the petroleum lamp threw a small ring of light.

'Seven hundred thousand francs have been paid out in Rome,' said Don Crescenzio to break that weighty silence.

'Lucky they! lucky they!' two or three cried out, with a stirring of envy against the lucky Roman winners.

'If what we are doing is successful,' Colaneri muttered darkly, and his spectacles gave a sad twinkle, 'the Government will pay Naples three or four millions of francs.'

'We must succeed,' Ninetto Costa retorted.

'The urn will be under command this time,' said Marzano mysteriously.

Now came renewed knocking, very gently, as if timidity had enfeebled the hand at the door. Trifari disappeared to open it, after asking through the door who it was; he had suddenly grown suspicious. The answer was 'Friends!' and he recognised the voice. The two common folk, Gaetano the glover and Michele the shoeblack, came in; they took off their caps, saying 'Good-evening!' and stood at the entrance of the room, not daring to sit down in such good company.

Outside the wind and rain grew furious, a gutter full of water emptied into the court with a loud swish. Now, under the window-frames, a stream of water came in at the cracks, wetting the window-sills and trickling to the ground, the closed but broken-ribbed umbrellas leaning against the walls in the corners of the room dripped moisture on the dusty floor, and the wet shoes made mud-pies. The men sitting down never moved: they kept up a solemn stiffness and lugubrious silence, as if they were watching a dead person and were overwhelmed with fatigue and the oppression of their funereal thoughts. The two working men standing, one lean, colourless, with a cutter-out's round shoulders, the hair thinned already on the forehead and temples, the other man crooked and hunchbacked, twisted like a corkscrew and old, though his rugged, sharp face was lively still, kept silence too, waiting. Only Ninetto Costa, to give himself a careless look, had taken out an old pocket-book, the remnant of his old smartness, and was writing ciphers in it with a small pencil, wetting the point in his mouth. But they were fancy figures, and his hand trembled a little. His friends said it was from his fast life that it shook. Thus they spent about fifteen long slow minutes that lay heavily on the souls of all those waiting there to carry out their mysterious plan.

'What bad weather we are having,' said Ninetto Costa, passing his hand over his forehead.

'The sky has opened,' Don Crescenzio remarked, yawning nervously.

'What o'clock is it, doctor,' asked old Marzano in a trembling, decrepit little voice.

'It is five minutes to ten,' said the doctor, taking out an ugly nickel watch, the sort that cannot be pawned, attached to a sordid black cord.

'What hour is the appointment for?' asked Colaneri, trying to look as if he was indifferent.

'It was to have been ten o'clock, but who knows whether he will come?' the doctor replied, lowering his voice, putting all his uncertainty and doubt into what he said.

'Who can tell?' said Ninetto Costa profoundly. A long sigh relieved his breast, as if he could not bear the weight that bore him down.

'Are you feeling ill?' Colaneri asked him.

'I wish I was dead,' muttered the stock-broker desolately. Someone shook his head, sighing; another one had the same feeling, evidently, from the expression of his face, and the sad words spread through the damp dirty room under the smoky lamp. Then for a little the summer storm calmed down, fewer drops rattled on the window, and again there came a great silence. Through the wall, no one knew from where, like a slow warning voice, a solemn clock gave ten melancholy strokes. There was a pause between each stroke, and it cast a breath of fear among the men gathered there to plot some cruel device or other.

'That will be the Spirit,' said Don Crescenzio, trying to joke.

'Don't let us jest,' Trifari said, in a severely reproving tone; 'we are occupied about serious matters here.'

'No one wants to make jokes!' Ninetto Costa said chidingly. 'We all know what we are doing.'

'There is no Judas here, is there?' said the doctor, looking round at everyone.

There was a protesting murmur, but it was feeble. No, none of them was Judas, nor was there a Christ among them; but all felt vaguely at the bottom of their hearts that they were going to carry out a betrayal.

'No one is Judas—no one,' cried out the doctor impetuously. 'Swear before God that if there is he must make a bad end.'

'Don't swear, don't swear,' said old Marzano, quite frightened.

Again the bell rang; they all caught each other's eye suddenly, pale and shivering; their fault rose before them. No one moved to open the door, just as if there was a serious peril behind it.

'It will be him,' Colaneri dared to say, not raising his eyes.

'Perhaps it is,' Costa muttered, twisting his pocket-book absently in his hand.

At once all of them regretted that the medium was outside the door. The same shadow of furious disappointment disfigured their faces, hardening them, from the cruelty of a wicked man who sees his prey escaping. The furious instinct that sleeps at the bottom of all human hearts, urged by long unsatisfied passion, burst forth in that delirious form that vice produces in young and old, gentleman and working man. The faces were reserved and hard, strong in their ferocity. Dr. Trifari went forward in an energetic way to open the door. To let the company know for certain that the medium was there, he greeted him and the Marquis di Formosa at once, aloud.

'Good-evening, good evening, Don Pasqualino; we are all expecting you.'

He stood aside to let them go in; the men in the room took a long breath with fierce joy; there was no danger now that the medium would escape them. And he that spoke every night with spirits, who had especial communication by favour with wandering souls, he that ought to have known all the truth, went quietly into the little room where the meeting was, without suspecting anything. He cast, as usual, an oblique glance all round, but the Cabalists' faces said nothing new to him. They had the pallor, contortions, and feverish excitement usual on Friday evening, but he saw nothing else. Only the Marquis di Formosa, who was coming in with him, shivered two or three times; it almost looked as if he wanted to turn back. But the Marquis had been very excitable for some time past. He stammered in speaking, his noble countenance was now degraded by traces of his ignoble passion, he was badly dressed and untidy, had dirty shoes and a frayed collar, and his ill-shaved beard was disgusting and pitiable. He had got so excitable since he no longer had any money, since his daughter's engagement to Dr. Amati. The medium could get no more money out of him, so avoided him, and only saw him at the Friday evening meetings in Nardones Road. But that evening the intimacy had begun again, the Marquis had looked everywhere for the medium, and during the day had given him fifty francs, making an appointment for the evening at ten o'clock; indeed, he had anxiously insisted on this appointment, and the medium had put it down to a disappointed gambler's eagerness to get lottery numbers.

The Marquis's manner on the way to the office had been peculiar, still, Don Pasqualino was accustomed to gamblers' eccentricities, and took no notice of it. He went to sit at his usual place every week near the table, putting one hand over his eyes to shelter them from the glare of the lamp. Around the deep silence still held, broken by a sigh now and then, and on looking at all their pallid, dumb, excited faces the medium felt his first suspicion. He tried to do his usual fantastic humbugging work.

'It rains, but the sun will come out at midnight.'

'That is idle chatter,' shouted Trifari, bursting into an ironical laugh.

The others around muttered sneeringly. Now there was no longer any belief in Don Pasqualino's mysterious words. This want of faith stood out so plainly that the medium drew back as if he wanted to parry an attack. But he tried again, thinking he could profit as usual from the feverish imaginations of the Cabalists by striking a sympathetic chord.

'It rains, the sun will come out at midnight, but he who wears the Virgin's scapulary does not get wet.'

'Don Pasqualino, you are joking,' the glove-cutter said ironically. The medium darted a look of rage at him. 'You need not look at me as if you wanted to eat me, Don Pasqualino. Asking the gentlemen's pardon, you are trying to make fools of us, and we are not the people to allow it.'

'My lord, make that ass hold his tongue,' muttered the medium, making a scornful gesture.

'He is not such an ass after all, Don Pasqualino,' said Formosa, keeping down his excitement with difficulty.

'What do you mean, my lord?' asked Don Pasqualino sharply, getting up to go away; but Trifari, who had never left the medium's neighbourhood, put a hand on his shoulder without speaking, and obliged him to sit down again. The medium sank his head on his breast a minute to think it over, and gazed sideways at the door.

'Sit still, Don Pasqualino,' said Formosa slowly, 'we have a lot to talk about here.'

A slightly agonized expression went over the caller-up of spirits' face. Once more looking round the company, he only saw hard, anxious faces, determined on success. He understood now confusedly.

'Gaetano the glover is not an ass for saying you are making fools of us. What you have been doing for three years past looks like a trick. For three years, you see, you have gone on saying the most disjointed things with the excuse that the spirits said these things to you. For three years you have made us stake the very bones of our necks upon this nonsense of yours; every one of us has not only gained nothing, but thrown his whole means away, from following your rubbish, and we are full of woes, some of them incurable. What sort of a conscience have you? We are ruined!'

'Yes, we are ruined — ruined!' shouted a chorus of agonized voices.

The speaker with spirits had often heard these lamentations, especially lately; but faith had come again into the souls of his followers. Now, he understood they no longer believed in him. Still, hiding his fear, he tried to brazen it out.

'It is not my fault, it is your want of faith.'

'Rubbish!' the old lord shouted in a rage, whilst the others stormed against the medium for repeating to them his invariable reason to account for disappointment. 'Rubbish! how can we have failed in faith when we have believed in you as in Jesus Christ? How can you say faith is wanting when, to reward your overflow of chatter, we have paid through the nose? You have pocketed thousands of francs in these three years. Don't deny it. Have we no faith? We, who have had Masses, prayers, and rosaries said; we, who have knelt and beat our breasts, asking the Lord's favour — have we no faith? Why, we must have had it! How can you account otherwise for the squandering of money, for the way we wasted our own means and our families', thus causing such unhappiness that it would have been nothing but a crime if we had not believed in you? You say we have no faith; you have been our God for three years, you have deceived us, and we never said anything, but went on believing in you after you had taken every penny from us.'

'Everything — you have taken everything!' shouted the company.

'You insult me, that is enough,' said the medium, getting up resolutely. 'I am going away. Good-evening.'

'You do not leave this till we get satisfaction!' the Marquis di Formosa cried out. 'Is it not the case that he will not get out of this till he does?' he asked the assembled Cabalists.

'No, no, no!' the company of these cruel madmen shouted ferociously.

The medium understood, a deadly hue spread over his pallid cheeks, his frightened glance wandered round in a desperate attempt to fly; but the fierce gamblers had got up and made a circle round him. Some of them were very pale, as if they were keeping down strong emotion, the others were red with rage. In all their eyes the medium read the same implacable cruelty.

'I wish to go away,' he said in a whisper, with that hoarse tone that gave such a mysterious attraction to his voice.

'None of us would wish to detain you,' said the Marquis di Formosa with ironical deference, 'if we had not need of you. If you do not give us lottery numbers, you don't leave this!' he ended up by shouting in a fit of fury.

'Lottery numbers, lottery numbers!' hissed Colaneri's thin voice.

'If not, you don't get out of this!' shrieked Ninetto Costa.

'Either give numbers, or you stay here!' thundered Dr. Trifari.

'An end to your fooling; give us the real tip for the lottery,' said Gaetano, grinding his teeth.

'Don Pasqualino, make up your mind that those gentlemen won't let you go away till you have given them lottery numbers—make up your mind to it,' Don Crescenzio remarked wisely. He wished to pretend he was not interested in the question.

'Next week. I promise them to you then; now I have not got them, I swear it upon the Virgin!' stammered the medium, turning his eyes to heaven despairingly.

'What good is next week?' all yelled out. 'It must be to-night, for to-morrow—quick!'

'I have not got them, I have not got them,' he stammered again, shaking his head.

'You must give them. We will make you give them,' the Marquis roared. 'We can do no more. Either we win this week, or we are ruined. Don Pasqualino, we have waited long enough; we have believed too much; you have treated us unfairly. The spirit tells you the real figures, you know them, you always have known them; but you went on mocking at us, telling us silly things. We can't wait till next week; before that we may die, or see someone else die, or go to the galleys. This evening or to-morrow we must have the true numbers. You understand?'

'The true—the true ones!' hissed Colaneri.

'Do not go on talking nonsense; it is past the time for that now,' shouted Ninetto Costa, with the greatest indignation.

Still, in spite of feeling conquered and taken hostage to the unreasonable fury that he had set on fire himself, the medium tried to fight on.

'The spirit does not give numbers by force,' he slowly announced. 'You have offended him. He will not speak to me again.'

'Lies—you are telling lies! A hundred—a thousand times you have told us that the spirit obeys you, that you do what you like with him,' retorted the Marquis. 'A hundred thousand times you have told us that the urn is under orders. Tell the truth; it will be best for you, I assure you. You are at a bad pass, Don Pasqualino; the spirit ought to help you. Our patience is exhausted, so is our money, and other people's, too. The spirit must give you the right numbers.'

Then the medium stood silent for a little, as if he was collecting himself, his eyes turned up showing the whites. Everyone looked at him, but coldly, being accustomed to these antics of his.

'In a little the camellias will flower,' he said suddenly, trembling all over.

But not one of the company troubled himself about this mystic giving out of lottery numbers. Dr. Trifari, who always carried a book of dreams in his pocket, did not even take out the torn book to see what figures corresponded to the camellias.

'In a little the camellias will flower by the sea, on the mountain,' repeated the medium, still trembling.

No one stirred.

'In a little the camellias will flower by the sea, on the mountain,' he repeated the third time, trembling with anxiety, looking his persecutors in the face.

An incredulous snigger answered him.

'But what do you want from me?' he cried out, with a gasp of fear.

'The *real* numbers,' said Formosa coldly. 'We don't believe these that you are telling us can be the right ones; that is to say, just on the chance we will play the numbers corresponding to the mountain, the sea-coast, and flowering camellias. But the *real* figures must be different. While waiting for them, we will play these three, but we will keep you shut up here in the meanwhile.'

'Until when?' he asked hurriedly.

'Until your numbers come out,' retorted the Marquis harshly.

'Oh, God!' said the medium softly under his breath.

'You understand, Don Pasqualino, these gentlemen wish to have a guarantee, and they intend to keep you as a pawn,' the lottery-banker explained, trying to make out that shutting him up was lawful. 'What does it signify to you? What trouble is it to tell the truth? If you have kept them in error up till now, it is time to speak seriously, Don Pasqualino. These gentlemen have a right to be enraged, and I know it. Speak, Don Pasqualino, send us off satisfied. You will stay here till to-morrow at five. When the lottery drawing is over, we will come and take you in a carriage for an airing. Come, come; do what you ought to do.'

'I can't do it,' said the medium, opening out his arms.

'Don't tell lies. You can, but you won't. The spirits obey you,' said Colaneri, letting himself go in a passion of rage.

'Tell them this evening; it will be better for you,' Gaetano the glover muttered in an ill-natured tone.

'Get rid of this obstinacy,' Ninetto Costa advised in a brotherly way.

'Give us the truth—the truth,' stammered the old lawyer, Marzano.

'I can't tell you,' the medium still said, looking at the doors and windows.

Then the Cabalists, on a sign from the Marquis di Formosa, gathered in the window recess. Only Trifari stayed beside the medium. With a threatening, cruel face he put his fat, hairy hand on his shoulder. They spoke to each other a long time, and disputed in a ring, all heads close together; then, having decided, they turned round.

'These gentlemen say they are firmly resolved—as they have a right to be—to get the real lottery numbers, after having made so many sacrifices,' the Marquis di Formosa said coldly, 'and that therefore Don Pasqualino will remain shut up here until he makes up his mind to satisfy our just demands. He cannot go away from here; besides, Dr. Trifari, who is afraid of nothing, will stay with Don Pasqualino. To make a noise would be useless, as the neighbours would not hear; and if by chance Don Pasqualino wished to right himself by going to law, we have an action ready for him as a cheat, with witnesses and documents enough to send twenty mediums to prison. It is better, therefore, to bow your head this time, and try to get off by giving the right numbers. We are quite decided. Until Don Pasqualino allows us to win, he will not get out; Dr. Trifari will sacrifice himself to keep him company. In that other room there is sleeping accommodation for two and food for several days. Between to-night and to-morrow one of us by turns will come every four hours to see if he has made up his mind. We hope he will do so soon.'

'You are trying to kill me,' said the medium with angelic resignation.

'You can free yourself when you choose. We wish you good-night,' the Marquis ended up with, implacably.

And the seven wicked Cabalists passed in front of the medium, wishing him good-night ironically. The medium stood there near the table, his hand lightly placed on the wooden surface, with a tired, suffering expression on his face. He looked now at one, then at another of the Cabalists, as if he were questioning their faces to see if any of them were more civil, and would say a word of release to him. But sad delusions had hardened these men's hearts; the excitement prevented them from understanding they were committing a crime. They went in front of the medium, greeting him, saying a cold phrase or word of condolence without heeding his suffering expression, his entreating eyes.

'Good-night, Don Pasqualino. God enlighten you!' said old Marzano, shaking his head.

'We ask too much of God,' the medium answered in a very melancholy voice.

'Good-night; quiet sleep,' the glover ironically wished him. His words, countenance, and voice had all become cutting.

'So I wish you,' the medium answered darkly, lowering his eyelids to deaden the cruel flash of revenge that shone in his eyes.

'Good-night, good-night, Don Pasqualino,' Ninetto Costa muttered rather regretfully; his frivolous nature was so opposed to tragedy. 'We will soon meet each other again.'

'Of course,' the man of the spirits muttered with a slight grin.

'Good-night,' Michele the shoeblack ventured to remark. He was a keen accomplice in that gentlemanly plot, and thought it made a gentleman of him to be mixed up in it. 'Good-night; keep in good health.'

The medium did not answer him even. He scorned to cast a glance at the deformity, who belonged to the common folk he came from himself, out of whom he could never get any money.

'Pasqualino, do you intend to give these *true* numbers?' asked Colaneri, passing in front of him, still wild with rage.

'I cannot give them like this, being bullied into it.'

'You are joking. We are all your friends here,' squeaked the Professor. 'Do as you like. Good-night.'

'Good-night; the Madonna go with you,' the medium muttered piously, intensifying the mysticism of his voice.

'Dear Don Pasqualino, come, be good-natured before we go,' said the Marquis di Formosa with sudden affability. 'Give us real numbers, and your prison will last only till to-morrow evening at five o'clock.'

'I know nothing,' said the medium, darting a look of hatred at the Marquis, since it was the noble lord who had brought him to this bad pass.

They joined each other at the door to go out, leaving him alone with Dr. Trifari, who went backwards and forwards quietly and coldly from the room alongside, with that icy determination born villains have in carrying out a misdeed. Up till then the medium, except for a shadow crossing his face, leaving its traces of boredom and sorrow, but for a humble, beseeching glance, had given tokens of sufficient courage; but when he saw the others were going away, when he felt he was to be left alone with Dr. Trifari for long hours, days, and weeks, perhaps, all his courage fell, the cowardice of an imprisoned man rose up, and, stretching out his arms, he called out:

'Don't go away! don't go away!'

At that agonized cry the accomplices in that imprisonment stood still; their faces, set like stern judges till then, got suddenly pale. That was the only moment of the whole gloomy evening they realized they were condemning a human creature, a fellow-Christian, a man like themselves, to a frightful punishment. It was the only moment they saw the whole extent of what they were doing in its legal and moral bearings. But the demon of gain had taken possession of them, soul and body, completely. Every one of them, turning back, surrounded the medium, still asking him for lottery numbers, certain real numbers, that he knew, and up till then would not give them. Then, choking with emotion, understanding they were turning the weapons against him that he had wounded them with, the man who had gradually brought the waves of a slow shipwreck over them, who had taken their money and their souls, when confronted with that persistent, malignant cruelty that nothing could soften, that demon his own voice had called up, that real evil spirit he had truly got in communication with, the cowardly medium felt a tremendous fear, and began to sob like a child. The others, alarmed and disturbed, gazed at him; but the demon was stronger than all their wills together. The supreme hour of their life had come for old and young, gentlemen and working men—the tragic hour when nothing can prevent a tragedy, when everything pushes men forward to a tragedy.

Hearing the medium weep like a child, drying his tears with a flaming, torn pocket-handkerchief, none of them felt pity. All felt the warmer, keener desire for lottery numbers to save them from the ruin that threatened them. They left him, to weep meanly, like a frightened fool; one by one, making no noise, they went slowly from that house that had become a prison. He, still going on sobbing, stretched his ears, and heard the door shut dolefully, with that sort of noise that gives echoes in the soul. Trifari, standing behind the door, went putting up chains and bolts, shutting himself up with the new prisoner, with no fear either of the man or of the spirits he might evoke. The hairy red face, when it showed in the shining circle of the lamp, had something animal in it; it showed cruelty and obstinacy in cruelty. On coming in again, the doctor breathed in a relieved way. He looked around, as if the departure of the Cabalists, his friends who had deputed him to be gaoler, pleased him. Now he still went and came from the next room, carrying backwards and forwards all sorts of things. Then he came back from the bedroom, having changed his clothes; he had put on an old jacket instead of his frock-coat. The medium followed all his gaoler's movements closely, for, like all prisoners, he studied his only companion with profound observation. At one point they exchanged a cold, hard glare as from prisoner to turnkey.

'Do you want to smoke?' the doctor asked from a corner of the room.

'I don't smoke,' the medium answered sulkily.

'Won't you sit down?' Trifari asked the medium in a whisper.

'Thank you, I will,' he replied, letting himself down on a chair.

'Do you wish to sleep?'

'No, thank you.'

The doctor sat down, too, then, beside the table, putting one hand over his eyes as if to shield them from the light. There was deep, nocturnal silence. Outside the rain had ended; inside the long, gloomy vigil began.

CHAPTER XV
SACRILEGE—LOVE'S DREAM FLED

Bianca Maria Cavalcanti and Antonio Amati's love for each other had got stronger and sadder. Indeed, the secret sorrow gave some attractive flavour of tears to their passion; what had been an idyll between the innocent pious girl of twenty and the man of forty had acquired dramatic force and depth. Innocently, with the trustingness of hearts that love for the first time, they had dreamt of living, spending their life together, holding each other by the hand as they went on the long road; but Formosa's hostile face rose continually between them. In that troubled summer which had unhinged the Marquis di Formosa's mind more, the position of the lovers had gone on getting worse, together with the old lord's increasing moroseness. People cannot live with impunity alongside of physical or moral infirmities, even if they are heroic or indifferent; and neither Bianca Maria nor Antonio Amati was selfish or indifferent. They did not manage to shut themselves from moral contact with Carlo Cavalcanti, nor to give themselves up entirely to their deep love. Moral as well as physical fevers fill the air with miasma; there is an infectious warmth that sets the atmospheric elements out of balance and poisons the air subtly and heavily, so that the healthiest have to bend their heads, feeling oppressed and suffocated. They were good, honest, and pitiful, their souls were purely filled with love, so that no acid, however powerful, could corrode the noble metal; but the air around was poisoned by Carlo Cavalcanti's moral disease, and they could hardly exist now in that atmosphere.

It was an unhealthy summer. Whatever means of persuasion Dr. Amati used, he could not get Carlo Cavalcanti to send his sickly daughter to the country. Stronger than any argument or anger was the obstinacy of the hardened gambler; he looked on his daughter as a spiritual source of lottery numbers, and put her to torture, so that she might fall into visions again, and he with his disturbed brain, like an old fool, tried to force her to *see*. When the doctor, in despair and anger, insisted she must go to the country, the Marquis, who felt no shame now in asking money from him, promising always to give it back, took up a tone of offended pride, and the doctor, intimidated at bottom by the old lord's grand airs, gave up insisting, and put off the attack till another time. Once he very nearly got Carlo Cavalcanti to go away too, with his daughter, by describing to him the healthy freshness of this out-of-the-way country place, and the old noble almost got ready to start. But he must have made inquiries, and found out that in that small village there was no lottery shop; it was necessary to write or telegraph to Campobasso. Even the telegraph-office was in another village; there were endless difficulties in playing a ticket, and he must have felt at that time more than ever chained to Naples, to the company of gamblers, and to Don Crescenzio's lottery shop. He bluntly refused to go, without giving any reason. The girl bent her head before his decision; she had always obeyed him, and she could not rebel. Amati trembled with rage, angry with her as well; but at once a great pity subdued him. The poor, innocent, suffering girl was wasting away; she could not bear that her lover should refuse to submit. She gazed at him so earnestly with astonished sad eyes that he forgave her for her filial submission.

It was an unhealthy summer. Each year the doctor had kept up the attentive habit of spending a month with his mother, the good old peasant woman in the country, doing the simplest kinds of work—resting, not reading, neither calling nor seeing visitors, keeping always with his mother, speaking the peasant's dialect again, building up his physical and moral health by rustic habits. Well, that year, tied by love's chain, he put off his start from day to day to Molise, feeling all the loss of putting it off, growing pale every time a letter came from his mother, dictated by her to the estate agent—letters that were full of melancholy summonses to come to her. The doctor stayed on in Naples, displeased with himself and others, worshipping Bianca Maria, hating the Marquis. The poor thing's dreams were always disturbed by her father's delusions; she fell off daily in health, and the doctor could do nothing to cure her. All he could manage was that, by offering his carriage, Bianca Maria should take long drives by the sea on the gentle slopes that lovingly enclose Naples. Old Margherita went with her, and sometimes the doctor also dared to go out with the young girl. When he heard of such a thing, the Marquis di Formosa frowned, the old family blood boiled; he felt inclined to punish the bold plebeian, who behaved as if he was affianced to the high-born maiden. But he held his tongue; he had had so many money transactions with Amati, and went on having them every day, keeping up still more pride, decorum, and honour with it. Besides, everyone said, with a compassionate smile, that Dr. Amati would soon marry the Marchesina Cavalcanti, as if the doctor would be doing a kindly act to marry her.

Up there, in green Capodimonte woods, with its hundred-year-old trees, its fields carpeted with flowers, down there along the charming

Posillipo Road, that goes down to the vapoury Flegrei fields, the lovers' idyll began again before Nature, ever lovely in Naples, with its gentle lines and colouring. The maiden's delicate, bloodless cheeks, with the sun and the open air going round her head, got coloured by a thin pink flush, as if her impoverished blood was moving quicker. She smiled sometimes, and threw back her head to drink in the pure air; she managed to laugh, showing white teeth and pinky gums that anæmia had made colourless. Then the doctor, become a boy again, chattered and laughed with her, looking into her eyes, taking her by the hand, sometimes loading her with field flowers. They forgot old Margherita, who forgot them, as she sat on the grass stupefied by the free summer air, as old people are apt to be; but they were so loving and modest with it, that the forgetfulness was no sin. The maiden went back to the house intoxicated with light, sun, and love, her hands full of flowers, her pink nostrils dilated fully to breathe in the pure air still; but as the carriage got into the city streets her youthful smile died away, and when they went under the Rossi Palace entrance she bent her diminished head.

'What is the matter with you?' the doctor asked her anxiously.

'It is nothing,' she replied, the great answer of timid, distracted women who hide their fears.

She went up to her bare, sad room very slowly, but still had a smile for Antonio Amati on the threshold. She went into the house with a resolute look, as if she were keeping down alarm or distaste. Often Carlo Cavalcanti came to meet her, coldly angry, his face distorted by his bad hours of passion. She shivered, while his very look made the blood fly from her face, and chased away the whole idyll of love, took away all the sweetness from the sun and from love. When she got into the drawing-room, she put her big bundle of flowers down on a corner of the table. The old lord questioned her anxiously and greedily about what road she had gone and what she had seen. Bianca answered feebly in short phrases, turning her head away; but he persisted—he wanted to know all she had seen. Nowadays, everything his daughter saw filled him with uncertainties, curiosity, and sorrow; he tried continually to find out in whatever she saw a mystic source of the cipher of lottery numbers. He now considered she was a medium, a much better one than Don Pasqualino, because she was a woman, an innocent maiden, and unconscious of her powers. She did not know it, but she was a medium. Had she not seen the spirit that fatal night weeping and hailing her? He went on wildly with his close questioning, obliging his daughter to follow him in his freaks.

'What have you seen? what have you seen?' the gambler, who forgot he was a father, asked in anguish.

How love's young dream flew away, with its light and happiness! how all the oppressive ghosts of the bare old house gathered round her from that old man raving alarmingly, and obliging her to go through the same terror. Also, every time she mentioned the name of Antonio Amati, her preserver, friend, and lover, the Marquis di Formosa reddened with rage. She saw that her father had ended by hating Amati thoroughly for the very services he had done him, for the very gratitude he owed him. Formosa's face grew so hard and fierce that Bianca Maria was frightened. Her heart was torn between her unwavering daughterly respect and her love for Antonio Amati. Once Margherita hinted before Formosa at rumours of a marriage between her ladyship and the doctor. The Marquis got into a fury and said 'No!' with such a yell that Margherita put her hands to her ears in a fright.

'Still, her ladyship must marry some day,' she remarked timidly and maternally, 'and the doctor might be better than another.'

'I said no,' the Marquis retorted darkly.

From that time forward he spoke in a still more wild and eccentric way. Sometimes in the middle of the many mysterious ghostly incoherencies his mind wandered amongst he came back in speaking to his daughter to a ruling thought—to love looked on as a stain, a sin, an ingrained want of purity in soul and body. The girl often blushed in her simplicity on hearing the abuse heaped on love, and then he praised the chastity that keeps the heart in a state of grace—that allows human eyes to see supernatural visions, and go through life in a sweet, dreamy state. He would get excited, and curse love as the source of all defilement, all evils and sorrow. Bianca Maria hid her face in her hands, as if all her father's strictures fell on her head.

'My mother was a saintly woman, and she loved you,' she remarked one day, repenting at once of her audacity.

'She died from that love,' he answered darkly, as if he was speaking to himself.

'I would like to die like her,' the maiden whispered.

'You will die accursed—cursed by me, remember that!' he shouted, like a demon. 'Woe to the daughter of Casa Cavalcanti who stifles her heart in the shame of an earthly love! Woe to the maiden who prefers the vulgar horrors of earthly passion to the purest heights of spiritual life!'

She bent her head without answering, feeling that iron hand ever weighing more on her life to bend and break it. She dare not tell her lover of such scenes; only sometimes, breaking momentarily the bonds of respect her father held her in, she repeated to Amati her despairing cry:

'Take me away—take me away!'

He, too, now had lost all his calm. He himself was taken by this plan of carrying her off, of taking the maiden away as his comrade, his adored companion—of freeing her from the dark nightmare of a life that was a daily agony to her. Yes, he would carry off the poor victim from the unconscious executioner; he would tear her from that atmosphere of vice, mystery, and sadness; bring her into his house, his heart; defend her against all this folly, these tempests. The Marquis di Formosa would be left to struggle with his passion alone. He would no longer drag to the abyss of desolation he was plunging into this poor meek, innocent girl. Every day this longing to save her grew in his heart, until it became all-powerful. He longed to speak so that his grand dream should become a reality. Gravely and solemnly he had promised Bianca Maria that sad evening she had confided her sad family secret to him that he would save her, and an honest man must keep his promise, even if it induce in him the wildest ecstasies or bring on a sorrowful depression at certain times. He longed to do it. In the meanwhile the days ran on. Some uncertainty still withheld him, even when he was most strongly resolved to ask Formosa for his daughter's hand. He vaguely felt that the answer would be decisive—that after it was said his life would be settled for him. But an important incident all of a sudden made him come to a decision. The Marquis di Formosa, amidst the fluctuations of his mind, kept up his mystical piety, and every Friday he spent hours in prayer in the chapel before Our Lady of Sorrows and the life-sized pierced Ecce Homo crowned with thorns. With that faith of Southerners which has bursts of enthusiasm, but is also bound in by a close net of the commonplace keeping it down to the earth, he constantly mingled heavenly things with all the worldly complications of his ruling passion, and sometimes in his despair he made the responsibility of his ruin rest on his Creator.

'You allowed this to happen; it is all Your fault, Jesus Christ!' the Marquis called out in his prayer. But on terrible days his faith became still more accusing and sacrilegious, unjust. 'It is all Your fault; You allowed it to happen!' he cursed on, tears burning his eyes, his voice choked. Indeed, one evening when Bianca Maria thought her father had gone out, on passing the chapel door she heard angry, sorrowful words coming from it. She put in her head, and saw her father kneeling with his arms thrown round the Ecce Homo. First he deplored his misfortunes; then he set to calling out blasphemies, cursing all the names of the Godhead impiously; then he repented quickly, asking pardon for his untrue and sacrilegious words, until a new outburst of rage came on, and he unclasped the holy image with scorn and threatening words. In his raving he threatened Jesus Christ his Saviour, bound to the column, to punish Him—yes, punish Him—if by next week He did not allow him to win a large sum at the lottery. Bianca Maria, horrified, seeing no end now to his sacrilegious madness, fled, hiding her face in her hand; and, shut up in her own room, she prayed the Lord all night that her father's ignorant heresy should not be punished. Now she always shut herself up at night, to shield her slumbers from her father's influence, because he always wanted her to call up the spirit, and spoke to her of those ghosts as of living persons—in short, keeping her constantly under that frightful nightmare. But she slept very little, in spite of the solitude and silence of her room; for her strained nerves shook at the slightest noise, because she was always afraid that her father would knock at her door, and try to open it with another key, to get her to ask the ministering spirit for lottery numbers. While she was slumbering in a light sleep from which the slightest noise wakened her, she started as if excited voices were calling her, and gazed into the shadow with wide-open eyes, as if she saw a spectre rising up by her bed. How often she got up, half dressed, and ran bare-footed over the floor, because she thought a light hand scratched on the pillow, touched her forehead, or patted her hair! One night, a Saturday, she heard her father going up and down, as she lay awake, all through the house, passing before her door several times, in the wild cogitations of his storm-tossed soul. In a whisper she called down on him Heaven's peace—the peace that seemed to have deserted his mind altogether. But just as she was going to sleep again, a queer, dull noise wakened her, quivering; it was as if a very heavy body was being pulled along, making the doors and windows shake with that dull rumble. Sometimes the mysterious noise quieted down and was silent; after about a minute's pause it began again, stronger, and at the same time more deadened. She remained raised on her pillows, fastened there by an unknown iron hand: what was happening there? She would have liked to cry out, ring the bell, get hold of people, but that rumble deprived her of voice; she kept silence in a cold sweat, the whole nerves of her body strained to hear only. The noise, like an earthquake, was getting nearer and nearer to her door; she clasped her hands in the dark, and shut her eyes hard not to see, praying she might not see. Together with that dragging of a heavy, unsteady object, she heard laboured breathing, as if someone was attempting a task above his strength; then a hard knock, as if her door had been hit by a catapult. She thought her door had violently burst open, and fell back on her pillows, not hearing or seeing anything else, losing her feeble senses. Later on, a good time after, she recovered consciousness, frozen, motionless; she stretched her ears, but she heard nothing else for a long time. In the confusion there now was between her dreams and realities, she believed that all she had heard was only a doleful nightmare that had oppressed her with its terrors. Had she dreamt it, therefore—that queer earthquake, that laboured breathing, that strong blow on her door?

In the morning, having rested a little, she got up easier, and, after saying her prayers, went to her father's room, as she had to do every day, to wish him good-morning. But she did not find him; the bed was unused. Several times lately the Marquis di Formosa had not come home at night. The first time it had caused Bianca Maria and the servants great alarm, but when his lordship came in, he scolded them for having sent to look for him, saying he would not stand being spied upon, he would do what he liked. Still, every time Bianca Maria knew that he had spent the night out of the house she got uneasy; he was so old and eccentric; his madness led him into dangerous company, and made him weak and credulous. She always feared some danger would befall him one of these nights on the road, or in some secret Cabalist meeting. She trembled that morning, too, and went on into the other rooms, thinking over what had happened at night, again asking herself if all that did not point to a dreadful mystery. She found Giovanni sweeping carefully.

'Did his lordship not come home last night?' she asked with pretended carelessness.

'He did come in, but he went out very soon again,' answered the servant.

'He did not go to bed, I think,' she said in a low voice, casting down her eyes.

'No, my lady, he did not,' said old Giovanni.

Margherita came up just then; she said something hurriedly to her husband, who agreed to it, and vanished into the kitchen.

'I asked Giovanni to draw the bucket of water from the well this morning,' the old waiting-woman said. 'I am not strong enough to-day.'

'Poor thing! it tires you too much,' Bianca Maria remarked compassionately, her eyes full of tears.

'I am rather old, but I could do anything for you,' said the faithful one in a motherly voice. 'But I don't know what has come to the bucket this morning; it is so heavy I can't pull it up. I begged Giovanni, who is stronger than I am, to take my place.'

Both went away from there, because Margherita held to the honour of combing out Bianca Maria's thick black tresses. But Giovanni came and interrupted the combing. He called his wife out, not daring to come in, and they chattered together some time, while Bianca Maria waited, her black hair loose over her white wrapper. Margherita came back in disorder; the comb shook in her hand.

'What is the matter?' asked Bianca Maria.

'Nothing, nothing,' the woman uttered hastily.

'Tell me what it is,' the other persisted, looking at the old woman.

'It is that Giovanni, even, cannot pull up the bucket.'

'Well, but why are you alarmed?'

'Giovanni says there is something in the way.'

'Something in the way? What do you mean?'

'He has called Francesco, the porter. They will pull together. Perhaps they will get over the difficulty.'

'What can it be?' the girl stammered, growing deadly pale.

'I don't know, my lady—I don't know,' said the old woman, trying to begin her combing again.

'No,' said the other firmly, waving off the hand with the comb, and gathering up her hair with a pin—'no; we had better go and see.'

'My lady, my lady, what can we do? Giovanni and Francesco are there. We had best stay here.'

'I am going there,' the girl insisted, going towards the kitchen.

Old Giovanni and Francesco in their shirt-sleeves were pulling at the rope with all their strength, and it hardly moved, creaking as if it was going to break. Both Giovanni's and Francesco's faces showed, besides the great fatigue they were enduring, that they were in a great fright.

Occasionally, with heaving sides and cramped arms, they gave up pulling, and cast a frightened look at each other. From the kitchen doorway, in a white wrapper, with her hair down, Bianca Maria looked on, while Margherita, standing behind her, begged her in a whisper to go away for the love of the Virgin! to go away, in God's name!

'But, in any case, what can it be?' asked Bianca Maria steadily, turning to the two men, whose growing fears deprived them of strength.

'Who can tell, my lady?' Giovanni stammered. 'This weight is not a good thing.'

But while all kept their eyes fixed on the well, waiting on in anguish, all feeling a shudder from the delay and fear of the unknown, the *thing* the two men were pulling up hit twice against the sides of the well, noisily from right to left. The dull, heavy noise echoed in Bianca Maria's heart, for it was the same she had heard at night. A little frightened cry came from her mouth; she pressed her nails right into her flesh, wringing her hands to keep down her alarm before the servants. But once more, with a stronger, nearer sound, the *thing* beat against the side of the well.

'It is coming,' said the message-boy affrightedly.

'It is coming,' Giovanni repeated in consternation.

Margherita, standing behind Bianca Maria, could not command her strained nerves; she prayed in a trembling whisper, 'Madonna, help us! Madonna, deliver us!' But what came up to the well-brink, bounding, quivering, with the bucket-rope wound three times round its neck, the chain hanging on the breast, made her yell with fright. It was a man's trunk, water and blood dripping from the forehead over the sorrowful cheeks and bared breasts, water and blood flowing from the wounded side; blood and tears were in his eyes, and over the face and breast, which all had death's livid hue.

Yelling from fright, Francesco and Giovanni ran off, calling for 'Help! help!' The women, mistress and maid, rushed to the drawing-room and fell in each other's arms, the one hiding her face on the other's breast, not daring to raise it, haunted by the frightful sight of the murdered body. It was quite livid, bloody in the face, breast, and enfolded arms, with a despairing look in the eyes and half-open mouth, which seemed to be sobbing. It stood against the parapet dripping blood and water, bound by the cord and chain. The message-boy and the butler had flung downstairs, calling out there was a dead man, a murdered man. At once, on the stairs, the gateway, the whole neighbourhood, the news spread that a murdered man's body had been found in the Rossi Palace well.

Everyone opened doors and rushed to windows; but Francesco and Giovanni's confused, breathless story caused such fright no one dared go in at the Marquis di Formosa's open door, or to the kitchen where the corpse lay. The women were still clinging to each other in the drawing-room; though Margherita tried to command herself for her mistress' sake, she felt the girl's body grow flabby from want of vital force—sometimes it stiffened as in a nervous convulsion. But the great whispering in the palace had got even into the doctor's flat, and his heart was always quivering, expecting a catastrophe. He put his head out of the window and saw people everywhere; the sound of voices came up even to him, saying that a murdered man had been found in the Rossi Palace well, and that the body was in the Cavalcantis' kitchen. Just then Giovanni, on thinking it over that the two women had been left alone, felt sorry that he had made such a fuss, for he knew the scandal would be reflected on the Cavalcanti family, and he was going upstairs again.

'Is there really a dead man?' Amati asked him, not managing to conceal how disturbed he was, in spite of his strength of mind.

'Yes, sir, there really is,' said the butler, with desperation in his eyes and voice.

'Who saw it?'

'Everyone saw it.'

'What! everyone? Did your mistress see it, too?'

'Yes, sir, she did.'

The doctor cast a furious look at him and went into the fatal house, where a tragic breath had always blown from the first moment he put his foot in it, where any queer, doleful tragedy was possible to happen. He wandered about the rooms like a madman in search of Bianca Maria, and found her sitting on a large drawing-room chair, so pale, so terrified, so silent, that Margherita was kneeling before her in alarm, holding her hands, begging her to say a word—only a word.

Bianca Maria glanced at Amati, but seemed not to know him; she kept cold and inert and stiff in her frightened attitude.

'Bianca,' said the doctor gently. She still kept silence. 'Bianca,' he said louder, and he took her hand. At the light touch she quivered, gave a cry, and came back to consciousness. 'My love, my love! speak to me—weep,' he suggested, looking at her magnetically, trying to put his strong will and courage into her. All of a sudden, as if that will and strength had unsealed her lips, she began to cry out:

'The dead man! take him away—take away the dead man!'

'Now, now, don't be frightened; we are taking him away; keep calm,' the doctor said to her.

'The dead man—the dead man!' she cried out, covering her face with her hands wildly. 'For goodness' sake take the dead man away, or he will carry me off. Do not let him take me away, I entreat you, darling, if you love me.'

The doctor gave Margherita a look bidding her take care of Bianca, and went into the kitchen, followed by Giovanni. In the lobby were some people who were already speaking of calling the magistrate; there were the porter, his wife, the Fragalà and the Parascandolos' servants, and Francesco the errand boy, but not one of them dared enter the kitchen, even after the doctor went in. They let him go alone, waiting on silently in the pantry, still wild with fear. The doctor, though accustomed to see dead bodies, being shaken by that catastrophe that affected him so particularly, broken-spirited with the thought of the consequences, went into the kitchen a victim to the deepest melancholy, and the sight of the bleeding forehead, weeping eyes, the tied, wounded hands, the livid trunk, wounded, bleeding, and bound, increased the feeling. But the coolness of a man of science, accustomed to see death, took the upper hand; going right up to it, he saw the head had a crown of thorns, and with perfect stupefaction he understood it all.

It was the Ecce Homo. The wooden, life-sized half-figure of the Redeemer tied to the column, powerfully carved and painted, had all the disagreeable appearance of a bleeding corpse; the well water it had fallen into had discoloured the flesh and the vermilion blood, making it run, with the double magical effect of murder and drowning. Still, Dr. Amati felt his heart tighten on finding out this doleful farce—that mixture of cruelty and grotesqueness. Amazement was his predominant feeling; the strong man only thought of Bianca Maria's great suffering, of her sickness and sorrow, now mortally wounded, perhaps, by this gloomy, mystical, childish madness that the Marquis di Formosa was proud of. All that was urgent now was to save her.

'It is the Ecce Homo,' he said shortly, as he went out to the people assembled in the pantry.

'What do you say, sir?' Giovanni cried out, feeling the same astonishment, increased by horror, of the sacrilege.

'It is the Ecce Homo,' he repeated, looking coldly at them all with that imperious look of his that permitted of no reply. 'Go into the kitchen, dry it, and take it back to the chapel.'

They looked at each other, asking opinions; having got over the horror of a dead man, the outrage on the Divinity shocked them.

'You may send for the priest afterwards,' he said, 'to give a blessing;' for he knew the heart of the Naples folk.

The girl was still lying on the armchair, her eyes covered with her hands, always muttering to herself:

'The dead man—the dead man, dear love! Take him away. Get the dead man carried away.'

'There is no dead man, dear,' he said, with the gentleness that came from his great pity.

'Yes, yes there was,' she whispered, shaking her head in a melancholy way, as if nothing would convince her to the contrary.

'There was no dead man,' he answered gravely, feeling it was necessary to bring her back to reason.

He tried to take her hands from her eyes, but they stiffened, and an agonized expression came over the girl's face.

'Look at me for a moment,' he whispered in an insinuating tone.

'I can't—I can't!' she said in a sad, mysterious voice.

'Why not?'

'Because I would see the dead man, love—my love!' she said, still with that deep sadness that brought tears to the doctor's eyes.

'Dear, I swear to you that there is no dead man,' he replied again gently, as persistent as with a sick child.

In the meanwhile he tried to feel her pulse, and the temperature of her skin. Strange to say, while she seemed almost delirious, her hand was icy and the pulse was slow and feeble. It gave him a pang at the heart, for that want of life and strength showed him a continuous incurable wasting away. He would have liked to find out about that curious disease which made the blood so feeble and the nerves so irritable, but his heart loved Bianca Maria too well for his science to keep its clear-sightedness. He could not find out the secret of the impoverished blood or the disordered nerves; he only understood thus, darkly, that her constitution was wasting away from weakness and sensitiveness. He did not think of medicine or rare remedies; he just thought, in a confused way, he must save her—that was all. Ah, yes, he must snatch her at once from that madman's claws—this poor innocent girl that was subjected daily to being startled by this hopeless folly; he must take her away from that growing wretchedness of soul and body, from that fatal going downhill to sin and death—his poor darling who only knew how to suffer without rebellion or complaint. He must act at once; he was a man and a Christian. He must save this unhappy girl, as he so often had saved people from hydrophobia, or as, on one occasion, he had saved a wretched man who had got tetanus. At once—at once—he must save her, or he would not be in time. Where was the Marquis, then? Where was the cruel madman that staked his name, his honour, his daughter?

'Sir, it is done,' said Giovanni, putting in his head at the door. The old servant was very pale. After being relieved from the terrifying impression of what he thought was a murdered corpse, the serious insult his master had done to the Godhead came to disturb his humble religious conscience. That figure of the Redeemer, with the cord round His neck, hung down in the well, as if it was the mangled remains of a murdered man—to see that representation of the meek Jesus so scorned made him think that his master's reason had given way; such sacrilege must bring a curse on the house. He called out Margherita, to tell her what had happened, while the neighbours round about—on the stair, at the entrance, and in the shops—were going about saying that the Ecce Homo of Cavalcanti House had done a miracle, resuscitating a man that had been murdered, by putting Himself in his place. Everywhere, in different ways, they got lottery numbers out of the extraordinary event.

'The dead man, poor fellow!' the girl went on, half unconscious, the voice like a faint breath from her lips.

'Do not say that again, Bianca Maria. Believe what I say,' the doctor replied with gentle firmness. 'There was no dead man; it was the Ecce Homo statue.'

'Who was it?' she cried out, getting up and looking wildly at him.

He gave a start. He thought it was the crisis, her mind having wandered so long, so he repeated, trying to influence her by his steady gaze:

'It was the Ecce Homo figure. Your father flung it in the well, with a rope round its neck.'

'My God!' she shrieked in a loud voice, raising her arms to heaven. 'God forgive us!'

She fell on her knees and bent forward, touching the ground with her lips. Weeping, praying, sobbing, she went on imploring the Lord to forgive her and her father. Nothing served to quiet her, to get her up from the ground, where she often burst out in long crying-fits. The doctor vainly tried gentleness, kindness, force, violence; he did not succeed in quieting her. Bianca Maria's excitement increased, though there were some stupefied intervals, after which it burst out louder again. Sometimes, while she seemed to be keeping calm, a quick thought crossed her brain, and she threw herself on the ground, crying out: 'Ecce Homo! Ecce Homo, forgive us!'

The doctor looked on, shuddering, his head down on his breast, feeling his will powerless, his science useless. What was to be done? He called in Giovanni and wrote two lines on a card—an order for morphia, which he sent for to the druggist's. But he was afraid to use it: Bianca Maria was not strong enough to bear it. She despairingly, with strong, queer vitality, beat her breast, muttering the Latin words of the *Miserere*, weeping always, as if she had an inexhaustible fountain of tears.

This had gone on for an hour, when quietly the Marquis came into the room. He looked older, wearied, and broken with the weight of life.

'What is the matter with Bianca Maria?' he asked timidly. 'What have you done to her?'

'It is you that are killing her,' the doctor said freezingly.

'You are right—quite right. Darling, I am an assassin!' shrieked the old man.

That man of sixty cast himself at his daughter's feet, trembling with shame and humiliation, shaken by dry sobs. Under the doctor's eyes the scene went on, with filial and paternal positions reversed. That bald, gray-haired father, with his tall, failing form, full of dread and sorrow, shedding old folks' rare burning tears, feeling the whole horror of his fault, bent before his young daughter, begging her to forgive him, with a childish stammer in his voice, just like a boy relieving his childish repentance by crying. The daughter was still trembling from the great wound his inconsiderate cruelty had given her soul; it was quivering with the gall his cruelty still poured into it, while her father's humiliation made her groan still more dolefully. To the strong man, whose life had always been an honest, noble struggle, directed always towards the highest ideals, both of them seemed so weak, so wretched, so utterly unhappy—the one as torturer, the other as victim— that he once more regretted the time when the tragic Cavalcanti family had not got hold of his heart, to grind it to powder. But it was too late; that misery, unhappiness, and weakness struck him so directly now that Amati, strong man as he was, suffered in all these spasms, and could not control his instinct to give help, the feeling that was the secret of his noble soul.

'Forgive me, dear—forgive your old father; trample on me, I deserve it—but forgive me,' the Marquis di Formosa went on saying, seized with a wild, grovelling humility.

'Do not say that—do not say it. I am a wretched sinner; ask forgiveness of Ecce Homo, whom you have insulted, or our house is accursed, and we will all die and be damned. For the sake of our eternal salvation ask Ecce Homo to forgive you.'

'Whatever you wish, whatever you order me, I will do,' he answered, still grovelling, holding out his hands beseechingly; 'but Ecce Homo deserted me, Bianca Maria—he betrayed me again, you see,' he ended by saying, again seized with the rage that had led him to do the sacrilegious, wicked, grotesque act.

'You frighten me,' she cried out, stepping back and putting out her arms to prevent him touching her: 'you—a man—wanted to punish the Divine Jesus. Ask for forgiveness if you do not want us all to die damned.'

'You are right,' he muttered, frightened, humbled again. 'Do what you like with me. I will do penance. I will obey you as if you were my mother. I am a murderer, a scoundrel.'

The Marquis threw himself into a chair, broken down, his breast upheaving, his head bent, and keeping a glassy stare on the ground. His daughter was standing in a white dressing-gown that modestly covered her from head to foot, her black hair loose on her shoulders, and she had the dreamy, sorrowful look of one walking in her sleep, wakened from wandering, pleasant dreams. The doctor broke in:

'Bianca Maria,' he said.

'What is it you want?' she replied, feebly looking at her father, who was still plunged in deep dejection.

'Your father is much distressed; you are in pain—you must both forget this sad scene. Will you listen to kindly good advice from me?'

'You are goodness and kindness itself,' she whispered, raising her eyes to heaven. 'Speak—I will obey you.'

'This has been a very sad time, Bianca Maria, but it may bring good fruit. Your father and you have wept together—tears cleanse. By your common sufferings, by the love you bear him, you ought to ask your father not to humiliate himself so far as to ask your pardon, but to promise you, in the name of all you have suffered, to do what you will request him later on, when you are calmer; tell him so, Bianca Maria.'

The girl's mobile face, which had been drawn and quivering, at the doctor's commanding, quiet, amiable words, at that voice that had the magic power of giving her ease and faith in life, was getting tranquillized. Her soul, broken and tired, was resting.

'So be it,' she whispered, as if she was finishing an inward prayer aloud. Going up to the big chair, where her father lay looking quite broken down, she bent towards him, and in a very gentle voice said:

'Father, you love me, do you not?'

'Yes, dear,' said he.

'Will you do me a favour?'

'I will do everything—all, Bianca Maria.'

'I only want one favour for my good, for my future health and happiness; promise to do it.'

'Whatever you like, dear; I am your servant.'

'It is a great favour. I will tell you later on, when we are in God's grace again, when we are both quieter, what it is. I have your word, father, your word—you have never failed.'

'You have my word,' he said, panting as if he were not fit to go on talking.

She understood; she bent with her usual filial submission and touched his hand with her lips; he lightly touched her forehead as a blessing. She went to Amati, held out her hand, and looked at him with such loving intensity that he grew pale, and, to hide his emotion, bowed down to kiss her hand. Slowly dragging her slender person, from failing strength, she went out of the room, leaving the two alone. The old man seemed wrapped in deep and rather sad reflections, for he raised his face to heaven and cast it down in an anguished way, shaking his head as if discouraged. The doctor saw that the right moment had come.

'Can you listen to me?' he asked very coldly.

'I would prefer ... I would like to wait for some other day, rather,' the Marquis answered in a feeble voice.

'It will be better to have the talk out to-day,' Amati said, with the same commanding coldness.

'I am much disturbed ... very.'

'It may be that from what I tell you you will find something to soothe you. You know that I am devoted to you.'

'Yes, yes,' the other said vaguely.

'I cannot say much to prove my devotion; I try when I can to act in that spirit. I am sincerely attached to both of you.'

'We know it; our debt of gratitude is great.'

'Do not speak of that. For some time past I have wished to tell you of a hope of mine, and I dared not. You know me better than to suppose that any material interest would influence me. You see, my lord, I do not want to recall the past to your memory, it is so sorrowful, but it is necessary to do it. You and your daughter have been in poor circumstances for some years, and it is certainly not your daughter's fault. Your intentions are loving and holy; they have a high motive all honest men must approve of—the setting up of your house and fortune, to get happiness for your daughter; it is a good intention, I do not deny it. I myself admire this noble wish of yours.'

The Marquis held up his head now and then, glanced at the doctor with a flutter of his eyelids, showing approval of what he was saying, with such care and delicacy not to offend, not to cast an old man down more, for he suffered so much from his humiliation.

'But the means,' the doctor went on to say—'the means were risky, hazardous, very dangerous. Your passionate desire for fortune made you go beyond bounds, made you forget all the sufferings you were unconsciously spreading around you. Do you not see, my lord? You have sickness, wretchedness, around you, and in you. Passion has carried you away, and the loveliest, dearest of women, your daughter, must fall into the abyss with you.'

'Poor darling! poor darling!' the Marquis muttered pityingly.

'You love your daughter, do you not?' Dr. Amati asked, wishing to touch all the chords of feeling.

'I love no one but her; I love her above everything,' Formosa said quickly, with tears in his eyes again.

'Well, there is a way of protecting that innocent young life from all the physical and moral anguish that daily eats it up; there is a means of taking her out of these unhealthy surroundings of decent but stern poverty that she suffers from in every nerve; there is a means of securing her a healthy, comfortable future, with the peace and quietness her pure soul deserves; there is a way for her to recover, and it is in your hands.'

'I tried it, you know,' the Marquis di Formosa said despairingly; 'but I did not succeed.'

'You do not take my meaning,' the doctor went on, barely keeping in his impatience, as he saw that the Marquis was still blinded. 'I am not speaking of the lottery, which has been so disastrous to your family, a torment to your daughter, the despair of all who love you and wish you well. How can you suppose I was referring to the lottery?'

'Still, it is the only way to make money—a lot of money. Only with that can I save Bianca Maria.'

'You are making a mistake,' the doctor answered still more coldly. 'I am speaking of something else; ease and fortune can be found elsewhere.'

'It is not possible. There is no limit to what one can win at the lottery....'

'My lord, I am speaking seriously. This madness of your Cabalist friends does not influence me; indeed, it infuriates me when I think of the sorrow it causes. I can recognise the good intentions, but they stand for an unpardonable frenzy. Never refer to it with me again—never!'

Formosa looked up; his face, which till then was undecided and disturbed, got icy and hard. That 'never,' said so firmly by Antonio Amati, made him frown rather.

'What methods are you referring to, then?' he asked in a queer voice, in which Amati noted hostility again.

'Perhaps to-day we are too excited; let us put off talking about it till another occasion,' muttered Amati, who saw he was about to lose an important advantage. 'To-morrow will do.'

'There is no use in delaying,' the Marquis di Formosa insisted coldly and politely. 'As it has to do with Bianca Maria's welfare, I am ready.'

'Give me your daughter for my wife,' said Dr. Amati quickly and energetically.

The Marquis di Formosa shut his eyes for a moment as if a bright light dazzled them, as if he wanted to hide his flashing glance, and did not answer.

'I think I am offering your daughter a position worthy of the name she bears,' the doctor went on again at once, determined to go to the bottom of it, 'for my work has brought me money and credit; it is no use being modest. I will work still harder, so that she may be rich, very rich, happy, and in an assured position, protected by my love and strength.'

'You love Bianca Maria, do you?' Formosa said, without looking Amati in the face.

'I worship her,' he said simply.

'Does she love you?'

'Yes, she loves me.'

'You are a liar, sir!' the Marquis di Formosa answered, in a deep voice.

'Why insult me?' asked the doctor, determined to stand everything. 'An insult is no answer.'

'I tell you that you are lying, and that you have no ground for saying you are loved.'

'Your daughter told me that she loves me.'

'That is all lies.'

'She wrote it to me.'

'Lies. Where are the letters?'

'I will bring them.'

'They are not genuine. All lies.'

'Ask her.'

'I will not ask her. My daughter cannot love without having told her father.'

'Ask her about it.'

'No, she confides in me. You lie.'

'Question her on the subject.'

'She would have spoken to me before; my daughter is obedient; she tells me everything.'

'It does not look as if she did.'

'I am her father, by Gad!'

'You have often forgotten that you are; she may have forgotten it this time.'

'Dr. Amati, don't go on speaking on this subject,' the Marquis said, with cold, ironical politeness.

'I insist on it, it is my right; I have not lied. Besides, I spoke distinctly; I offer myself to your daughter, who is sick, poor and sad, as husband, friend, protector, to care for her, body and soul, to love and serve her as she deserves. Will you give me your daughter? You ought to answer this.'

'I will not give her to you.'

'Why will you not?'

'There is no need for me to give my reasons.'

'As the refusal is insulting, I have a right to ask them. Perhaps it is because it is I am not of noble birth?'

'It is not for that.'

'Do you not think me young enough?'

'It is not that, either.'

'Have you a particular dislike to me?'

'No, I have not.'

'Why is it, then?'

'I repeat that I do not choose to tell you the reason; I can only answer "No."'

'You will not agree even if I wait?'

'No.'

'You give me no hope for the future?'

'None.'

'Not in any circumstances?'

'Never,' the Marquis said decisively.

They said no more. Both were vexed in a different way.

'Do you want your daughter to die?' said the doctor, after thinking a minute.

'Never fear, she won't die; there is something keeps her up.'

'To-morrow she, a Cavalcanti, will be a beggar.'

'I will make her a millionaire, sir; I alone have the right to enrich her.'

'I told you that I love her.'

'Nothing can equal my affection.'

'But woman's destiny is love in marriage, and to have children.'

'Of common, vulgar women, but not of Bianca Maria Cavalcanti. She has a very high mission, if she will carry it out.'

'My lord, you will ruin her.'

'I am saving her. I assure her immortal fame and immortal life.'

'My lord, I beg, you see how I implore, I who have never prayed to anyone. Don't say "No" so obstinately without even consulting Bianca Maria. You are preparing a new, heavy sorrow for her. You give me no chance of living for her, and insult me, an honest man, like this for no reason. I beg you think over it; don't make up your mind at once.'

'To-morrow or any other time would be the same. It is "No"—always "No"; nothing else but "No." You will not get Donna Bianca Maria Cavalcanti,' he said, grinning devilishly.

'Think it over, my lord. If you still say "No" to me, I must go away for ever. Do not sever our ties so roughly.'

'You are free to go as far as you like. We will not see each other again. Perhaps it would have been better had we never met.'

'That is true. I am going.'

'Go, certainly. Good-bye, sir.'

'Before going away, however, I want to question your daughter here, before you. We are not in the Middle Ages; a girl's will goes for something, too.'

'It does not.'

'You are mistaken. I will ask her. I will go away when she tells me to go. Call her, if you are loyal and a gentleman.'

The old lord, challenged in the name of honour, got up, rang the bell, telling Giovanni to send in his daughter. The two enemies stood in silence until she came in. She had got back all her calm with the facility of all very nervous temperaments, but a glance at the two she loved disturbed her mind at once.

'I leave the word to you,' said the doctor politely, bowing to the Marquis.

'Bianca Maria,' the other began, in a solemn voice, 'Dr. Amati says he loves you. Did you know that?'

'Yes, father.'

'Did he tell you?'

'Yes, he did.'

'Did you allow him to tell you?'

'Yes; I listened to him.'

'You have committed a great fault, Bianca Maria.'

'We are all apt to do that,' she said in a low tone, looking at Amati to gain courage.

'But there is something much worse. He says that you love him. I told him that he lied—that you could not love him.'

'Why did you call him a liar?'

'Can you possibly ask me, Bianca Maria? Is it possible that you are so lost to all sense of shame and modesty as to love him and tell him so?'

'My mother loved you also, and told you so: she was a modest woman.'

'Keep to the point—do not call witnesses. Answer me, your father. Do you love this doctor?'

'Yes, I love him,' she said, opening out her arms.

'I will never forgive you for saying so, Bianca Maria!'

'May God be more merciful than you, father!'

'God punishes disobedient children. Dr. Antonio Amati asked me for your hand. I said "No": "No" now, to-morrow—for ever "No"!'

'You do not wish me to marry Dr. Amati, then?'

'No, I do not. In reality you do not wish it, either.'

She did not answer; two big tears rolled down her cheeks.

'Answer, my lady,' said Amati, in so anguished a tone that the poor girl shivered with grief.

'I have nothing to say.'

'But did you not say that you loved me?'

'Yes, I said so; I repeat it—I will always love you.'

'Still, you refuse me?'

'I do not refuse you. It is my father who rejects you.'

'But you are free; you are not a slave. Girls have a right to choose. I am an honest man.'

'You are the best, truest man I have ever known,' said she, clasping her fragile hands, as if in prayer. 'But my father will not allow me: I must obey.'

'You know you are causing me the greatest sorrow of my life?'

'I know, but I must obey.'

'Do you know you are breaking my life?'

'I know, but ... I cannot do otherwise. Mother would curse me from heaven, father would curse me on earth. I know it all: I must obey.'

'Will you give up health, happiness, and love?'

'I give it up out of obedience.'

'So be it,' he cried out, with a quick gesture, as if he were throwing off all his weakness. 'We will only say one word more. Good-bye.'

'Will you never come back? Are you going away?' said she, shaking like a tree under a tempest.

'I must go. Good-bye!'

'Are you going?'

'Yes; good-bye.'

'Will you never return?'

'Never.'

She looked at her father. He made no sign. But she felt so desperate for herself and for Antonio Amati that she made another trial.

'A little while ago, father, you promised me, in a time of terror and repentance, to do whatever I wanted. I ask you to do this one thing. It is this: let me marry Antonio Amati. A gentleman's word, a Cavalcanti's, is sacred. Will you break it?'

'I have my reasons—God sees them,' the Marquis said mysteriously.

'Do you refuse?'

'For ever.'

'Would nothing influence you—neither our prayers, nor your love for me, nor my mother's name—would nothing induce you to consent?'

'Nothing.'

'He says "No," love,' she whispered, turning, looking around her with a wandering eye. But Antonio Amati was too mortally wounded to feel compassion for another's suffering. Now one single wish possessed him, that of all strong minds, to lock up the great catastrophe of his life, scorning barren sympathy, and fly to solitude. He needed darkness, silence, a place to hide, to weep in, to cry out in his sorrow. The girl before him was the image of desolation, but he saw nothing, felt nothing: compassion had gone out of his heart; he felt all the unforgiving selfishness of great suffering. 'My love, love!' she still repeated, trying to give expression to the anguish of her passion.

Do not say that, Bianca Maria,' he said, with the bitter grin of the disappointed man; 'it is no use—I do not ask you for it. We have spoken too much. I must go.'

'Stay another minute,' she said, as if it meant putting off death for a little while.

'No, no—at once. Good-bye, Bianca Maria.' He bowed low to the Marquis.

The cruel, impassible old man, whom nothing would move, for his eyes saw nothing but his mad vision, returned his bow. When the doctor passed in front of the girl to leave the room she held out her hand humbly, but he did not take it. She made a resigned gesture, and looked at him with as much passion as an exile for ever banished from his country can express. It was no time for words or greeting; divided by violence, they were leaving each other for ever; words and greetings were of no use now. He went away, followed by Bianca Maria's magnetic gaze, without turning back, going away alone to his bitter destiny. She listened longingly for the last sound of the beloved foot-step, that she would never hear again. She heard the entrance door shut quietly, like a secret prison door. All was ended, then! Her father sat down in a big chair, thoughtful but easy, leaning his forehead on his hand. Quietly she came to kneel by him, and, bending her head, said:

'Bless me.'

'God bless you—bless you, Bianca Maria!' said the Marquis de Formosa piously.

'Your daughter is dead,' she whispered; and, stretching out her arms, she fell back, livid, cold, motionless.

CHAPTER XVI
PASQUALINO DE FEO'S WILL

Don Gennaro Parascandolo, the money-lender, had for some time past been coming very often to the big gateway in Nardones Road. He went up the big stairs to the second floor, where he enjoyed real love with a poor good girl, a flower of delicacy and innocence he had found on a doorstep one evening. The wretched girl was just going to ruin. He, with his usual money-lender's prudence, had made her believe he was a poor clerk, a widower with no children, who would certainly marry her if she proved good and faithful.

The unlucky Felicetta, whose name was a mockery, lived like a recluse, served by a rough girl, her only companion. She spent her time longing for her lord and master's presence, though she did not even know his real name; and, in spite of a physical distaste, she was full of gratitude to this good Don Gennaro, who had freed her from the danger of a dreadful fall by promising to marry her when, later on, she had ended her probation of virtue and faithfulness. She was a tiny, neat little woman, with rather fine features, and a quantity of fair hair, too great a weight for her small head. Cast out on the world by a curious fate, she would certainly have fallen into an abyss if she had not met at a decisive moment Don Gennaro, who spoke to her kindly, gave her something to eat, took her to an inn, and finally hired a little flat for her in Nardones Road, where she spent her time crocheting and getting her humble marriage outfit ready, expecting Don Gennaro's visits daily, and smiling to him with lips and eyes, like the good girl she was! Besides, the money-lender, who took off his diamond rings and gold studs when he went to see her, was quite paternal with her. Every little gift—for he kept her in decent comfort only—was made so pleasantly that it brought tears to Felicetta's eyes. Though he was her lover, Don Gennaro treated her so respectfully that she went pondering in her innocent, grateful heart how she could show her gratitude and affection.

Don Gennaro, the hard money-lender, who had seen so much weeping and despair without troubling himself, was very tender with her. He often spoke sadly to her of his two handsome sons who had gone to the dark world of spirits. He got sentimental, and brought flowers like a timid young lover, asking her to pray for him; also for his dead little ones, he added, wishing to join these two loves that were so curiously different.

'For them it is no use,' replied Felicetta humbly; 'they are angels.'

Little by little Don Gennaro had gone deeper into this love-affair, more than he would have desired, still using all precautions, so that Felicetta should find out nothing about him, and no one should know about his love-affair with the poor girl. He could not restrain himself. His man's heart of ripe years, familiar with life, flamed with youthful passion. He came every day now to Nardones Road, changing the time, but spending long hours in Felicetta's simple, loving company. At the end of that stormy summer he had given up his usual autumn trip, and was forgetting his precautions, bringing gifts to the girl, who took them rather astonished; but he explained he had just succeeded to a little money.

'Then, we will get married,' the young woman said timidly, for she felt her bad position.

'I am getting my papers sent from my village,' Don Gennaro answered, sighing, regretting to the bottom of his heart he had a wife.

But one holiday, after taking a few turns in Toledo Street, when he had gone down by Sant' Anna di Palazzo to Nardones Road, carrying a bag of sweets in his hand for his lady-love, as he was going up the stairs, he heard a sort of call or whistle behind him, evidently to make him turn his head. He did turn, though he could not quite make out if it was a whistle or a loud signal that had called his attention. It had been a mysterious call, that was all, one of those voices that come from the soul. However much he looked round, above and beneath, going close to the railing, he saw nothing, could find out nothing. Annoyed at being detained on that stair, where he was always afraid of being discovered, he hurried into Felicetta's rooms. Still, all the time of the visit he was put out; he thought, secrecy being the foundation of his happiness, it had crumbled away with that voice calling to him. Indeed, next day, right under the entrance, he met the Marquis di Formosa coming down the small stair, looking as if he were in a dream. Really, they were not on speaking terms now, though they knew each other; but that day, both feeling put out, they stopped in front of each other, watching one another.

'Busy as usual,' the Marquis di Formosa muttered, in a hoarse voice that gave an idea of emotion, for it looked as if rage had made him lose his voice.

'Yes, like yourself,' Don Gennaro replied darkly.

'I have no business to do,' Formosa replied, in a still more undecided and shy manner. 'Is Signora Parascandolo well?'

'She is quite well,' Parascandolo said, at once suspecting something under the question. 'How is Lady Bianca Maria?'

'She is rather in poor health,' the old man said, hanging his head.

'Good-morning, my lord,' Parascandolo answered at once, taking the opportunity to go off.

'Good-morning, sir,' Formosa said, touching his hat, and looking after the usurer mechanically.

He went slowly up the big stair, frightfully bored by that meeting, thinking at once he must change houses and carry Felicetta off to a far-away part; and he slackened his steps to see if the Marquis were asking the porter where Don Gennaro Parascandolo was going to. But Formosa had gone off. When the usurer got to the second landing, again he heard a whiff; a flash passed before his eyes, as if the mystical warning was being repeated persistently because he had taken no notice the first time. Again holding on to the railings, he thought over where that call could come from, and told himself he must be dreaming, as there was nothing about. That love, carefully hidden, made him as superstitious as a woman.

'There must be spirits in this house,' he said to Felicetta during his call, as he could not get over his absent-mindedness. 'Twice in coming upstairs I felt as if someone was calling me, and I could not make out where the voice came from, or if it really was a voice.'

'Do you believe in spirits, then?'

'Well, who can tell?'

'This house has certainly a queer lot of lodgers,' said the girl. 'Day and night a number of suspicious-looking people come and go. The other evening, as I was watering my flowers on my balcony, I thought I heard cries and complaints coming from the first-floor. Then all was silent; I heard no more.'

'They must have been spirits,' said Don Gennaro, laughing unwillingly. 'Would you like to go to another house?'

'Yes, very much—a small house, with more sun.'

'On the Vittorio Emanuele Corso would you like?'

'It would be too grand for me.'

Don Gennaro was still thoughtful when he went away. As he was on the first-floor landing, he thought he saw two people he knew go down the small stair—the advocate Marzano and Ninetto Costa. They, heated in argument, did not see or pretended not to see him, because they owed him a lot of money, and he held a heap of stamped paper against them. But the money-lender was put out; he felt a mystery growing around him, while a burning curiosity took hold of him to know the truth. So that the next day, after wandering about all morning to find a new house for Felicetta, having found her a nook in that open quarter between Vittorio Emanuele Corso and Piedi Grotta, as he was coming back to tell her so, he stood on the stair on purpose, waiting. And the call, the fluttering, the secret voice, was heard like a suppressed summons. He peered about; this time he saw. He saw two windows of the flat that looked on to the great door, one with closed shutters, the other of obscured glass half open. There, just for a second, through the glass, an emaciated, despairing face showed that cast an imploring look at him, then disappeared, and a thin hand and white handkerchief waved to call him. Then the hand went out of sight. The darkened window was slammed violently, and the shutters were closed as on the other window. Don Gennaro turned round to go down at once to the isolated flat, but then he stood still, confused. What did it matter to him what was going on there? Who was it who showed himself imprisoned inside there? He remembered his features vaguely, though he barely had seen them. He did not know him. It had to do with a stranger; but whether he was a stranger or not, Don Gennaro's mature prudence took the alarm. Perhaps it would be best to go and give the alarm at the police court. He thought better of that, too; for many reasons it was best to have nothing to do with the police. But the idea that someone was shut up, calling for help, for days past, who would perish perhaps without his help, put him in a great state. A mysterious crime was going on; his Southerner's curiosity burned within him, and his coolness as a man who had seen many ugly scenes encouraged him to help the unlucky man. At last he went downstairs, and, crossing the small yard, he went up the damp, broken stairs. After thinking a minute, he knocked and rang. The little bell tinkled mournfully, but no sound came from inside. He knocked again; not a sound. Then time about with ringing the bell, he knocked with his ebony stick. The silence was like that of an empty house. Twice he stooped to the keyhole, and said: 'Open, by Gad! or I will go and call the police.' The second time, when he had shouted louder, he thought he heard a whisper, and he waited again. No one came to open at the loud ring he gave. Then he began to go downstairs, determined to call the police authorities. It was on the last step that he again met the Marquis di Formosa. The latter raised his head and grew pale as he recognised Don Gennaro. Still, he had the courage to ask:

'How come you here?'

'There is something wrong going on up there, my lord,' said the money-lender coldly, lighting a cigarette. 'I am going to a magistrate.'

'Why should you call in a magistrate?' the old man stammered, in a nervous way.

'I tell you that up there a disgraceful thing has happened, or will happen, and, as I am an honest man, I cannot allow it. Will you come with me to the magistrate?' and he looked him straight in the eyes.

'Don Gennaro, don't let us exaggerate. Perhaps it is a joke among friends, or a just punishment,' said Formosa, getting excited.

'I do not wish to know anything about it. I only know that a man asked my help. I know I knocked, and they would not open.'

'What exaggerated talk are you going on with?'

'Something bad is going on.'

'We will go upstairs. I will induce them to open,' said the Marquis, making up his mind to have as little of a catastrophe as possible, as it had to be.

Silently they went up together. Formosa gave two long rings, the known signal.

'Who is it?' asked a muffled voice, speaking through the keyhole.

'It is I, doctor; open, please.'

'But you are not alone.'

'It doesn't matter—open.'

'If you are not alone I will not open, as you know,' Trifari said angrily from inside.

'Open the door; it will be better for everyone, doctor,' the Marquis di Formosa negotiated. 'If you do not open the ruin will be greater. Don Gennaro Parascandolo here knows all; he wants to go to a magistrate.'

'At any rate, I am not going away,' Parascandolo said from outside. 'I will only go for the purpose of calling the police.'

'Oh dear! oh dear!' Formosa muttered with a senile quiver.

A step was heard going and coming, then a slow rattle of chain-links, and Trifari's face, with long, red hair growing unevenly on it, showed in a slit of the door.

'Open, open!' said the money-lender, grinning, going on, without seeing the bloodthirsty glance Trifari cast on him.

On going in, a smell of smoky oil caught the nostrils, of cooking done in an airless place, of not very clean people, who have lived shut up for a long time. The front-room and the so-called dining-room were dirtier than ever, with dust, lampblack, bread-crumbs, and fruit-skins. The house was like an animals' lair, when they have been shut up in their dens for days and weeks from fear of the huntsman. On a chair, pale, with hollow cheeks, pinched nostrils, bloodless ears, his blue lips half open, as if he could hardly breathe, the medium lay stretched out, his limbs flaccid, his beard long and dirty, his hair hanging in curls on his neck.

Trifari, to make him stand up, gave him two blows, one on the arm, the other on the shoulder. It brought quite a new sort of doleful expression on the unlucky impostor's face.

'What are you doing? Are you not ashamed?' shouted Don Gennaro, quite scandalized.

'He treats me so at all hours of the day,' the medium muttered in a thread of a voice.

'Keep up your courage; you will come away with me,' said the money-lender, handing him a flask of brandy that he always carried.

'I shall not have the strength, sir,' said the other feebly. 'They have killed me, shut up here, with no air nor light, with this stink that makes me sick. I have generally fasted or got poor food, and been worried all the time to give lottery numbers. I was often beaten by this hyena of a doctor, that the Lord has brought into existence, for my sins. It is agonizing, sir; I am in agony.'

'How could you do that to a man—a fellow-Christian?' Parascandolo asked severely, looking at the other two.

'See who is preaching!' shouted Trifari. His impudence was indomitable.

'You, my lord, a gentleman!' said Parascandolo, making out he would not speak to Trifari.

'What would you have? Passion carried me away,' said the old man, quite humiliated, shivering from other remembrances also.

Just then came in at the door, which had been left open, Colaneri, the viperish professor, and Don Crescenzio the lottery-banker. On seeing a stranger, recognising Don Gennaro, they understood all, and looked at each other dismayed, especially Don Crescenzio, who was a Government official, as he said.

The money-lender went on smoking coolly, whilst the medium, getting weaker, let his head fall back on the chair. The house, which had been a prison for a month now, had an ugly, sordid look, and the artificial light of the lamp in full day wrung the heart like the wax tapers round a bier. Really, Don Pasqualino looked like a corpse.

'Have so many of you set on one man?' the money-lender asked, without directly addressing anyone.

'Why did he not give the lottery numbers at once?' yelled Colaneri, pulling at his collar with a priestly gesture. 'No one would have done anything to him then.'

'You could be sent to the galleys for this, you know,' said the usurer rather icily.

'Don't you speak of the galleys; you ought to have been there long ago!' hissed the ex-priest.

The other shrugged his shoulders, then said:

'Don Pasqualino, have you the strength to get up? I want to take you away.'

The four looked at each other, grown pale suddenly. It was natural that, the thing being discovered, the medium should go away; but the idea that he would be taken away to the open air, free to come and go, and to tell what had happened—this escape from persecution made them very frightened.

'I have no strength to move, sir,' said Don Pasqualino complainingly. 'If they wanted to kill me, they could not have found a better way. God will punish them;' and he sighed deeply.

There were two knocks at the door, and two other couples came in— Ninetto Costa and Marzano, Gaetano the glover and Michele the shoeblack. Not content with coming every day, every two hours, in turn, to ask for lottery numbers, with the monotonous perseverance of the Trappist monk who says to his fellow, 'We must all die,' on Friday there was always a full meeting. Then it was a case of torture in the mass; it was the reckless conduct of those fallen to the bottom of the abyss, who still hope to get up out of it—of those hardened by passion, who see light no longer. Indeed, their cruel obstinacy had increased, because of the evil action they were doing and the persecution they had carried out against Don Pasqualino. Instead of feeling remorse, they were in a frightful rage, because even their violence had had no effect, since not one of the lottery numbers, whether given by symbol or straight out by the medium during his imprisonment, had come from the urn. The first cold douche on their wrongheadedness came when Don Gennaro Parascandolo arrived. It was only then they noticed the wretchedness and dirt of the prison where they had kept the man shut up, the cruelty of Trifari the gaoler's face, and the suffering look on the prisoner's—then only they understood that they might be prosecuted for such a crime, and that they were at Don Pasqualino's and Don Gennaro's mercy. Dumb, frozen, amazed, they did not even ask how the prison had been discovered. They now felt the heavy weight on the heart that is the first moral personal punishment of sin. The Marquis di Formosa was the most humiliated of all; he remembered he had brought the medium there, and he already saw his name dragged from the police-court to prison, then to the assizes. Now the Cabalists turned imploring looks on the two arbiters of their fate. Don Gennaro Parascandolo methodically went on smoking.

'Above all, doctor,' he said, throwing the smoke in the air, 'put out the light and open the window.'

'I won't take orders from you!' Trifari shouted. He was the only one unsubdued; he was wild at his prey escaping.

'Do you really want to go to San Francesco,' Parascandolo asked quietly, meaning the largest prison in Naples.

'They ought to put you there!' yelled the liverish Cabalist, who had got half mad from having to watch Don Pasqualino.

'I will wait till you pay me the lot of money you owe me,' remarked Parascandolo.

'Don't you wish you may get it!' said Trifari impudently.

'Someone will pay—father or mother—to avoid a trial for cheatery,' the money-lender added without putting himself about at all.

All the men looked at each other, shivering. Each of them owed money to the usurer, even Don Crescenzio. The only two who did not—Gaetano and Michele—were worried as much by Donna Concetta. Even Trifari held his tongue; the idea of being shamed in his village before those old peasants, whose secret plague he was, made him groan already like a wounded beast. Stolidly he went to open the windows and put out the smoking lamp that gave out a horrid smell of blackened wick. The bystanders' eyelids fluttered at that strong light of day; all faces were white, and the medium's was like a dying man's. The usurer gave him another sip of brandy, which he drank drop by drop, being hardly able to get it down.

'Now we will call up a cab,' said Don Gennaro.

'What! are you going to take him away?' asked Ninetto Costa in despair.

'Do you want me to leave him here for you to carry off a corpse?'

'What an exaggeration!' muttered the other vaguely. 'Don Pasqualino is accustomed to living shut up.... You are ruining us, Don Gennaro.'

'Think of your other woes,' said the money-lender gravely.

The other, struck by his words, said no more. All of them trembled, seeing the medium was trying to rise; slowly, leaning on the table, and only by a great effort, taking breath every minute, opening his livid mouth with its blackened teeth, did he succeed. The enchantment was broken altogether; now the medium was escaping for good. He would go to the police-court, and accuse them of keeping him in custody—of cruelty and ill-treatment. But at heart they thought this of less consequence than the medium's getting away, for, to revenge himself, he would never give them lottery numbers again. Would they were sent to gaol, if only they got right lottery numbers, for they would be able to corrupt justice and escape. The dream had fled; the source of riches was going, flying off. Nothing, nothing now would induce the medium to give them lottery numbers—certain, infallible ones. Every step he tried to take on his thin, shaky legs gave them a pang.

'If you don't take heart, Don Pasqualino, we shall stay here till evening,' Don Gennaro remarked.

He was in a hurry to be off. Indeed, his position among them was not very safe. All owed him money. If they had been bold enough to carry out one imprisonment, they might well carry out another more useful and profitable. Don Gennaro, indeed, took the command by his coolness and strength, but were not these men desperate? Yet they were feeling that break-up of moral and bodily strength, that weakness, that comes to the most finished scoundrels when they have carried out some wicked deed, having put all their real and fictitious strength into the enterprise and obtained no result. At any rate, it was better to go out.

'Gentlemen, I wish you good-morning,' he said, taking his hat and cane, seeing the medium was scratching at his coat with skinny hands to clean it.

'I would like to say a word to each of these gentlemen,' the medium requested.

There was a whispering. All crowded round him who spoke with the spirits, while Parascandolo was already in the lobby and held the door open as a precaution.

'One at a time,' said the medium. 'It is a kind of will I am making. I want to leave a remembrance to every one.'

He took them aside one by one in the window recess. He looked them in the face and touched their hands with his feeble, cold fingers. The first was Ninetto Costa.

'Look here, Ninetto: don't give up hope; remember, there is always a revolver for a finish up.'

'That is true,' he said, trying to find a number in the words.

The second was Colaneri, the ex-priest.

'There is the gospel for you; it opens its arms,' whispered the medium.

'Thank you for reminding me,' said the other, half cheerfully, half sadly, taking the double meaning of the advice.

The third was Gaetano, the glover.

'Why are you a married man? I would have advised you to marry Donna Concetta, who has so much money.'

'Has she a lot?'

'Yes, a great deal.'

'You are right, it is hard luck.'

The fourth was Michele, the shoeblack, the hunchbacked dwarf.

'If you were not so crooked and old, I would advise you to marry Donna Caterina, she that has the small lottery.'

'But I am crooked,' said the shoeblack sadly.

'Well, work hard.'

The fifth was Marzano, the lawyer, his head shaking, but still burning with the frenzy.

'You know, thousands of sheets of stamped paper are sold in Naples: why do you not try for a license?'

He whispered rather than said it, and the old man looked wonderingly, suspiciously at him, and went off hanging his head.

The sixth that came up was Dr. Trifari. He hesitated, for he had ill-treated the medium too much in the prison days. Still, he was treated with great civility.

'To get rid of your worries, why do you not sell all in your village and bring your parents here?'

'I never thought of it. I will consider it.'

The seventh was Don Crescenzio, the lottery-banker at Nunzio Lane, whom Don Pasqualino had had a long intimacy with. They spoke in a whisper. No one could hear what was said.

'How foolish Government is!' said the medium.

'What is that you are saying?' cried out the other, alarmed.

'I say, how stupid Government is.'

'I don't know what you mean.'

'You do perfectly.'

The eighth to come up was the Marquis di Formosa. He was rather timid, too, feeling that he had done most wrong to Don Pasqualino.

'The spirit spoke to me again, my lord.'

'What did he say?'

'He told me that Donna Bianca Maria Cavalcanti was a perfectly lucid soul, but that, as I said, man's touch would defile her; it would make her obtuse and unlucky, unable to have further visions.'

'Donna Bianca shall die a virgin. Tell the spirit so,' the old man said proudly.

'Well, Don Pasqualino, are we to stay here till evening?' said the money-lender, coming in. 'Have you finished with these gentlemen?'

'Yes, I have done,' said the other in a strange voice, as if he had got back his strength in some queer way.

While the medium looked in his pockets to see if he had a torn handkerchief and a dirty pack of cards he always carried with him, and then put on his shabby hat, the Cabalists had gathered in a group, but they were not speaking. What he had said in its true and symbolical sense as a hint, a suggestion, had deeply moved them.

'Gentlemen, may God forgive you!' the medium cried out in a queer way, with a slight smile, as he went off.

They hardly greeted him, but glanced at him remorsefully. None of them dared make an excuse for the ill they had done him; each of them felt the nail riveted that the medium had driven in. The two went down the small stair very slowly, for the medium often threatened to fall. The usurer did not go so far as to offer him his arm; the medium was much too dirty. When he came to the doorway and looked around, drinking in the free air, tears came to his eyes.

'I thought I would never get out alive,' he said as he got to the carriage.

'Where do you wish to go?' asked Parascandolo.

'To the police-court,' said the other in a feeble voice again.

He was spread out in the carriage like a serious invalid. Don Gennaro frowned rather, and, not to make people stare, he had the carriage hood put up. They went on to Concezione Street.

'Do you intend to denounce them?' Parascandolo asked.

'You do not know how they have tortured me,' muttered the other, knocking his head against the carriage hood whenever there was a jostle, as if he could not keep his head straight on his shoulders.

'So you will take them up, will you?'

'For thirty days I, an unhappy man, in bad health, was shut up with no air nor light and a stinking oil-lamp, whilst they who behaved so badly to me took their exercise.'

'Why did you not give them the lottery numbers?'

'Just because— —' said the medium mysteriously.

'Don Pasqualino, you don't know the lottery numbers,' said Don Gennaro, laughing.

'What does it matter to you?'

'Nothing at all; but you must be frank with me.'

'Yes, sir, yes, sir,' said the medium humbly; 'but why did they endanger my life? What harm had I done them?'

'Don Pasqualino, you ate up several thousand francs belonging to these gentlemen, to my knowledge,' Parascandolo went on in the same laughing tone.

'It was all charity, sir—charity.'

'Really, was it all charity?' Don Gennaro sneered wickedly.

'There was some little thing for myself, sir,' Don Pasqualino sighed out, with a flash of malicious amusement in his eyes.

'Then, there is no use in going to the police-court?'

'We had better go there, all the same; you will be satisfied with me.'

They got down at the big gateway in Concezione Street, where the guardians of the public safety were going and coming. It was a tremendous effort to the medium to go up the stairs; he lost his breath at every step.

'Rather an effort, eh?' the usurer said more than once.

'Don't leave me, don't desert me!' the medium sighed out.

At last they got to the first-floor, where Don Gennaro, respectfully saluted by the ushers, asked if there was a magistrate present. There was not. The head-clerk was there; he had them shown in at once, and was most ceremonious.

'Here is Signor Pasqualino De Feo; he wants to make a statement,' said the money-lender, setting to smoking a cigarette, after offering the head-clerk one, looking the medium straight in the eyes.

'I wished to know,' said he feebly, 'if anyone has come to say I had disappeared.'

The inspector took a thick ledger, and turned it over as he smoked.

'Yes, sir,' he said. 'Chiarastella De Feo, living in Centograde Lane, wife of Pasqualino De Feo, stated that her husband was unaccountably absent. She feared imprisonment or misfortune.'

'What misfortune, what imprisonment, could there be?' the medium called out, smiling ironically. 'Women always talk nonsense.'

'She said it had happened to you before, though she could not state under what circumstances.'

'Why should they have shut me up?'

'To drag lottery numbers from you.'

'Did my wife say that I knew lottery numbers?' said the medium with a little laugh.

'Do not believe it, inspector; it is nonsense,' Parascandolo added laughingly.

'I wish to state, to avoid mistakes, that, being at Palma Campania, at Don Gennaro Parascandolo's villa there, I was so ill I had to stay there a month without being able to write to my wife. Then I thought every day I would soon be able to return.'

'You witness that this is true, do you, sir?' said the inspector carelessly, not giving it any importance.

'Yes, I do, sir.'

'Then it is all right. He would have given you lottery numbers during this month's illness of his, I suppose?' asked the police official, still grinning.

'Of course he did,' said Parascandolo, in high good-humour.

'But what use are they to you? With a poor employé like me it would be different.'

'Don Pasqualino, if you are strong enough, give the inspector lottery numbers.'

'You are making a fool of me,' muttered the medium.

They said good-bye, and the inspector advised De Feo to go to his wife's house at once, as she would be anxious.

'Did you not see that I did as you wished, sir? I forgave those who had offended me,' said Don Pasqualino as they went downstairs.

'You are too good,' the other answered, rather ironically.

'I do not intend to make a merit of it, for there is none. I would never have accused these gentlemen.'

'Ah!' said the other, standing still for a moment. 'Why is that?'

'It would not suit me to do it.'

'I see. But why did we come here, then?'

'It was necessary to make a statement, for the police were looking for me.'

'Is your wife such a simpleton?'

'What! my wife? She is very fond of me; she is nervous for me, and says we must retire from the profession.'

'What profession is it?'

'Don't you know? She is the famous witch of Centograde, Chiarastella.'

'Ah, I remember. Her witchcraft is like your knowing lottery numbers, is it?'

'Her magic is true,' said Don Pasqualino thoughtfully and sincerely.

'And does she believe in your being a medium?'

'Yes, she does,' said the other, hanging his head. 'My wife is in love with me.'

'In love with you?'

'Yes, with me.'

'You are a queer lot,' said the money-lender philosophically. 'And, meanwhile, you have saved the eight scoundrels.'

'How have I saved them? Did you understand the advice I gave them all?'

'No, I did not,' Don Gennaro answered, surprised at the malicious tone of his voice.

'I left them each a remembrance,' the medium replied, in a shrill voice.

'Will they obey you, do you think?'

'As sure as death,' said the medium dolefully.

He bowed to Don Gennaro, and, with renewed strength, went off quickly towards Municipio Square. Parascandolo looked at him as he went off, and felt for the first time a shudder at cold malignity.

CHAPTER XVII
BARBASSONE'S INN—THE DUEL

In the little Barbassone inn, on the road that goes down from Moiariella di Capodimonte to Ponte Rossi, there were no customers that clear winter morning. It was really an outhouse on pillars, roughly built, and on the ground-floor there was a big, smoky kitchen with a wide, grimy fireplace and a large hall, where rustic tables were set out for eating and drinking. On the upper floor, which was reached by a queer outside staircase, the host and his wife slept in the room over the kitchen. The other bare room, used as a storeroom, was full of black sausages and stinking cheese, strings of garlic hung on the walls, and bunches of onions and winter marrows strung on osier withes. Below, in front of the inn, were two or three arbours, that must have been covered thick with leaves in spring and summer, but now they were bare, showing the wooden framework. Under the arbours were dusty, broken tables covered with dry, rustling leaves; and at the side of the inn was a bowling-green, surrounded by a low myrtle hedge. The host had had a wooden stair made inside, leading from the ground-floor to the upper rooms; and a door at the back opened on to the fields. From the first-floor windows could be seen the suburbs of Naples, Reclusorio Road, the railway-station, the swamps outside the town, and the Campo Santo Hill. Two roads went up to the inn; one came from Moiariella, the other from Ponte Rossi. There was the way from the fields also, but it did not count.

However, if the neighbourhood of the country inn was deserted, some company were certainly expected, for the servant in the kitchen that fine quiet morning was giving hard blows to some pork chops on a big table. On the stove a kettle was boiling for a macaroni. Before the inn door the host, a sagacious-looking peasant, was washing fennel and salad in a bowl on the ground, throwing away the bad leaves to the thin fowls that were clucking about. The hostess of the Barbassone was away; her husband often sent her out when it suited him, to buy fresh fish, tripe, or whatever could not be got at Capodimonte market. He stayed at home with the old servant, who was busy in the kitchen helping him; and there was a son of his, about twelve years old, who waited on the customers. This boy was now employed in the kitchen grating down some white nipping Cotrone cheese, that looks like chalk and burns the throat, but Naples throats do not object to it.

It was a soft, quiet time near noon. The host often looked to see if anyone was coming from the low road of Ponte Rossi, or if anyone was coming down Moiariella road, but Barbassone's keen face was as serene as the December morning. He bent down again to soak the lettuce-leaves in the already earthy water of the basin, when, without his having seen her, a black figure of a woman rose before him. She was a girl a little over twenty, but so worn with fatigue, want and sorrow she looked years older, and her great black eyes burned in her lean face. She was Carmela, the cigar-girl, Annarella and Filomena's unhappy sister, Raffaele or Farfariello's despised love. She had come on foot, so naturally made no noise. A thinly-veiled excitement was mingled in her face with the weariness after her long walk. She was dressed like a vagrant in a cotton frock quite washed out, with a rag of a red shawl round her neck and a rumpled cotton apron at her waist.

'Good-day, gossip,' she said, greeting the host with Naples common folk's favourite title.

'Good-morning, lass,' he answered, looking at her suspiciously.

'Can I have a glass of wine?' she asked, keeping down a tremble in her voice.

'Are you alone?'

'What about it? Am I not able to pay for a glass?'

'You may drink the whole cellar,' the host said in a tone of affected carelessness, and he stood aside to let her into the room, following her to a table.

She sat down on a rough chair, after glancing round quickly. There were no customers.

'Is it Gragnano wine you want?'

'Yes, sir.'

'Half a pint of Gragnano wine!' shouted the host towards the kitchen, cleaning the table with his apron.

'Do you wish anything to eat?' he then added, still staring at the girl.

'I am not hungry; I am thirsty,' said Carmela, casting down her eyes. 'Give me a penny-worth of dry chestnuts.'

The host slowly went to get those white, shrivelled, hard chestnuts that provoke thirst. In the meanwhile the boy brought a caraffe of greenish glass full of dark wine, stoppered by the usual vine-leaf. Carmela began to munch the chestnuts slowly, drinking a mouthful of wine at times.

'Will you do me the pleasure?' she said to the host, who was hovering about rather uneasily.

'Thank you, I will,' he said.

He never refused, and, as there was only one glass, he took a long pull at the bottle, making the wine gurgle, then drying his lips.

'How quiet you are out here!' said the girl, trying to start a conversation. 'Have you customers always?'

'Not always. It is according to the weather.'

'People from Naples come, do they not?'

'Yes, I have them sometimes.'

'Here are two francs. Buy a cap for your boy,' she said, seeing the host was suspicious.

He took the money unhesitatingly and pocketed it, then stood to be questioned.

'A set of young fellows are to come here at mid-day, are they not?'

'Yes, I expect some.'

'One Farfariello is to be with them, I believe?'

'Yes, I heard that.'

She gave a deep sigh.

'Is he your brother?' the inn-keeper asked.

'He is my lover.'

'There are no women with them,' the host remarked carelessly.

'I know that,' she said, shaking her head. 'But not only they are coming. Don't you expect others?'

'Another set of men may be coming.'

'What to do?' she cried out, feeling her fears justified.

'To get dinner, of course.'

'Is there nothing else?'

'Nothing. At Barbassone's it is the only thing to do.'

'On your honour, is that all?'

'I give you my word. While they are in my house nothing can happen.'

'Yes, but what about afterwards?'

'I have nothing to do with that. When they have gone three yards away, I have no more to do with them, do you see.'

She said no more, and got quite thoughtful. A wine-stain was on the table, and she lengthened it with her finger, making a pattern with the wine.

'Gossip, will you do me a kindness?'

'Don't speak like that.'

'A real charity, gossip, that God will give you back on that handsome son of yours. Let me be present at this dinner in some room aloft—any hole where I can see without being seen.'

'My dear, Barbassone never meddles with doubtful affairs.'

'If you love your son, do not say no to me. It is not a plot, I swear it by the Virgin! It is an idea, a fancy of mine. I want to see what my lover is doing.'

'Yes, to make a scene—a quarrel.'

'I will not move, sir; I swear it by my eyes! I just want to look on at this dinner—nothing more.'

'Do you promise not to come out of the room?'

'I swear I will not.'

'Nor try to speak to anyone?'

'No, no, I won't.'

'If you are found out, do not say that I put you there.'

'Of course not.'

'Come with me,' he said sharply.

She started after the host, who left the hall and went up the outside stair to the second-floor. Carmela gave a glance from the parapet up the two roads that lead from Naples to Barbassone's inn, but they were quiet and deserted. Not the slightest noise of a carriage or footsteps came up in that noontide silence. The inn-keeper took Carmela across the room where he and his wife slept, and opened the door of the smaller one alongside where the inn provisions were kept. A whiff of rancid lard and ripe cheese caught Carmela by the throat and made her cough.

'You will be all right here, my dear,' Barbassone said to her, leading her to a window that looked to the front of the inn. 'If these honest fellows come, they will dine down there in the arbour. You will see their every movement. Only you must promise you will stay behind the window-glass.'

'Yes, sir, I will,' Carmela promised.

'You are not to go down, whatever happens. Do you understand? I don't want to get into a scrape with my customers.'

'Yes, sir; I will not go down, never fear,' she said in a low tone, half shutting her eyes, as if she saw a frightful sight before her.

'If not, I will shut you in.'

'There is no need of that. As I love the blessed Virgin, I won't move.'

'Good-bye in the meanwhile,' said he, going away.

'God will reward you,' the girl called out after him.

The long waiting began, and to the love-lorn maiden these minutes had the weight of lead. Still, she stood motionless behind the dull, dirty window, and her warm breath dulled the panes more. There were a couple of bottomless chairs and a wooden stool in the room, but she did not think of sitting down. She was too anxious to mount guard at the window, looking at the two sunny roads that mild winter's day, examining the peaceful landscape, where city noises were silent. Only twice she went backwards and forwards in that room full of black sausages and brown cheese, choked by their bad smell, and she saw there was another window that looked to the back of the inn, over the fields going up to Capodimonte. It was perfectly silent on that side too.

As time passed, a sharp anguish caught her heart. Perhaps the man who had told her of Farfariello's and his friend's trip to Barbassone's inn had cheated her, or she might have misunderstood what he meant. Farfariello, his friends, and the others, perhaps at that time were already in some other place, and all might be happening far off, without her being able to stop it. Perhaps it had happened already. She often turned her eyes to heaven, praying that it should not be so. At one time, not managing to keep down her uneasiness, she pulled her rosary from her pocket and began to say *Ave Marias* and *Pater Nosters* mechanically, thinking of something else. Seeing a dreadful vision, that made her despairing heart go out to the Virgin, for her to save Raffaele from misfortune '*and in the hour of our death*,' she caught herself saying aloud once. It was just then a noise of wheels and a cracking of whips came from Capodimonte Road, and Raffaele and three other youths, almost the same age, appeared in a cab.

'Oh, Our Lady of Sorrows!' sobbed out Carmela from behind the window.

Raffaele paid for the cab, and, contrary to the usual habit in these country trips, that the driver always shares the pleasures of the day, this time the horse turned round and went back the way it came. The young fellows, with trousers tight at the knee and caps hanging by one hair, were now making a great uproar in the lower room, perhaps because dinner was not ready. The boy quickly spread the cloth on one of the tables which ought to have been shaded by the leaves of the arbour, but it was bare. In the meanwhile, quite calmly, these youths set to playing bowls, waiting till the macaroni was ready. Raffaele especially went about quietly, with that low-class ease that charmed Carmela's heart.

'May you be blessed!' she whispered, rather reassured by that calmness.

Now, seated at four sides of the table, pulling macaroni into their plates from a big dish in the middle, Raffaele and his friends ate straight on with youthful appetites, improved by the wintry country air. They drank a lot, and often lifted their glasses of bluish dark wine, and, looking fixedly at each other, said something and drank it off at a gulp, without winking. Carmela, though she heard no voices, understood that they were drinking healths, or to the success of something.

Up till then, everything had gone on like a commonplace joyous winter trip, on a fine sunny day in a quiet country place: the inn, the host in the doorway, the boy serving the table, and the four fellow-guests, looked perfectly easy, in sympathy with the quietness around. But again there was a noise of wheels from Ponte Rossi Road, and an ostentatious whip-cracking. Raffaele and his friends looked up, as if out of mere curiosity, while Carmela, cut to the heart by that sound, felt her legs giving way, and she prayed the Lord silently to give her the strength not to die just then.

It was a party like the first one—of four young fellows with light trousers, tight at the knees, and neat black jackets, wearing their caps over one ear. Carmela recognised the one that led the party—Ferdinando, called the l'Ammartenato Teaser. He said something to the driver on paying him; the man listened, bending down, then went off slowly the road he had come, without turning his head. The two parties looked straight at each other solemnly, and bowed very punctiliously. Raffaele and his friends went on eating quietly; the other four took off their hats and hung them on the bare boughs. Macaroni was much quicker served for them, perhaps because the host had got ready enough for the two parties, so that at one time, as Raffaele's friends were eating slower and Ferdinando's were hurrying their mouthfuls, they got to the same stage, then went on together to the next course, swallowing, in two gulps, pork chops and lettuce salad, and drinking glasses of wine one after another as if they were water. While they were drinking, the two tables glanced at each other now and then quite indifferently. In spite of the quantity of wine swallowed they seemed to keep very cool; some of them lay back in their chairs occasionally in a calm way. Still, all that calm and free-and-easiness was the same at each table, curiously alike, as if the two sets had made a tacit agreement; but it fell short of the gaiety natural to Neapolitans on an outing, when laughter, shouts, and songs rise to heaven. Sometimes the youths round Raffaele, nicknamed Farfariello, bent towards him, and he smiled proudly; it was the only sign of cheerfulness in the company. Ferdinando—Ammartenato as his nickname was—did not smile even; his set tossed glasses of wine down their throats always, not moving a muscle. Carmela looked on from above; her lover's smiles, the wine drunk off by the two sets, and their peaceful free-and-easiness, did not reassure her. Amongst other things, she saw the movement of the lips, but did not hear the words. It seemed to her that a deep silence was between these people, who understood each other by signs; it was a doleful silence, in the midst of country peace. A slow, ever-increasing anguish oppressed her breathing, as if her heart had contracted and only beat at intervals; her whole will was in abeyance. She stood, leaning with her forehead against the dusty window, rigid, her sad eyes fixed on Raffaele's face, as if she wanted to read what was passing through his mind. Now the inn-keeper and his boy brought the fruit—that is to say, dried chestnuts and a bundle of celery with white stalks and long, thin green leaves—and with it more wine. Then, all of a sudden, after his father had whispered something in his ear, the little boy took off his apron, put on his cap, and started off running up the Ponte Rossi Road. As it was getting near the end of the meal, Carmela felt her brain giving way; she had one single desire growing in her mind to go down, take Raffaele by the arm, and carry him off with her, afar, where neither *cammorristi* nor *guappi* could reach. She dared not. For a month before that Raffaele had been cold and hard to her, avoiding her persistently, so that she got to places he had been at always ten minutes after he had left. He had let her know, too, that it was no use; in any case, he would have nothing to do with her.

'He might at least tell me why, and I would go away satisfied,' she cried out, weeping, to those who had repeated Raffaele's words.

But she had not seen him for a month; in fact, if she knew that two sets of Hooligans were going that day to a mysterious appointment at the Barbassone inn at Ponte Rossi, it was from an indiscretion of a chum of Raffaele's. He had said it, looking her straight in the eyes, with a secret meaning she could not help guessing, so that she left him at once, and on foot, from her low-lying quarter, she had dragged herself up there, panting, sorrowful, biting her lips, not to cry out nor weep.

She dared not go down; she felt Raffaele would abuse her and chase her away rudely, as he had always done lately. She shook at his angry voice and contemptuous words. Now the dinner was coming to an end very quietly; the two sets were smoking cigars, gazing into vacancy with the solemn satisfaction of people who have dined well and are getting ready to digest. For a time the peace that rose from the surroundings was such, and the youths were all so quiet, that for a moment Carmela felt her anguish soothed, and she hoped it was a tragic dream. Only for a moment, to fall deeper again into a sorrowful abyss, where the moments passed with dramatic slowness.

Ferdinando's party rose. The four young fellows, with the usual cheap swell gestures, pulled up their trousers, tightening the straps, dragged down their jackets, and set their caps haughtily across their heads. They went away, passing beside Raffaele's table solemnly; then they all touched their hats, and the others answered, saying the same word. Carmela could not bear what; it was 'Greeting.' They went away; she gave a sigh of relief. But instead of returning by Ponte Rossi, whence they came, and where perhaps the carriage was waiting for them, Carmela saw them go round the house, and one by one. She had run to the window that looked on to the inn-keeper's garden and the fields, and saw them disappear behind a green screen of trees. Panting, she ran again to the other window, that looked on to the inn-yard, where Raffaele's party were getting ready to go off also. All was safe if they took the Capodimonte Road, whence they had come. It would only mean that there had been two dinners, with no after-thought nor consequences. The preparations had been somewhat slow, but at a signal from Raffaele all hurried, while he, with a spent cigar in a corner of his mouth, paid the reckoning quietly. He got up, stretching his arm for his cap, which was hanging from a bough; in doing it his waistcoat pulled up, and Carmela saw something shining at his trousers belt. It was a revolver. Yet for a last moment she still hoped. Perhaps they were going away peacefully by the quiet country roads to the noisy town; and, at any rate, Raffaele always carried a revolver, a small-sized one. But in a moment the horrid fact she dreaded looked to her like a certainty. Very quietly Raffaele and the other three youths turned, not by Capodimonte Road, but behind the inn, through the garden, following the same road as the other set, and making up to them—that is to say, walking quietly with their springy step one after the other. She could bear it no longer; she felt something give way within. She ran to the storeroom door; the man had locked her in, evidently, for it would not open. She, wild, blind with grief and rage, began to shake the door, which was old and worm-eaten, so that it offered little resistance. The bolt the host had drawn broke with the rattling, and she very nearly fell on the landing from the shock. She went down the outside stair at a bound, but on the last steps she found the host, his shrivelled peasant's face very pale, for he had heard all the noise. He stood in her way.

'Where are you going?'

'Let me pass—let go!'

'Where are you going? Are you mad?'

'Let me go, I say!'

He caught hold of her wrists and looked her in the eyes.

'Are you the woman they are going to kill each other for?'

'Holy Virgin, help me! Let me go!'

'Do you want to get killed?'

'Yes, yes! Let go of my wrists!'

'Do you want them to kill you?'

'It doesn't matter if they do,' she cried, slipping from his grasp with a powerful wrench.

Running, panting, sobbing, her hair loose, clapping on the nape of her neck, her dress beating against her legs and throwing her down, then getting up again, crying, filling that serene country silence with her despair, she ran after the two sets of men by the same road, turning behind the same hill with green trees. She found herself in a narrow country road, and instinctively followed it, feeling it was the right one. She went on and on very swiftly, bursting with sobs, her ears alert, questioning the silence. But on the right a harsh, sharp sound made her jump; just after it came another shot, then another. She rushed into the field where the two files of low-class duellists were going on firing at each other at a short range. Throwing herself on Raffaele, she shrieked wildly.

'Go away!' he said, trying to free himself.

'No, I will not!' she shrieked.

'Go away!'

'I will not.'

'It is not for you; go away!'

'That doesn't matter.'

All this took place in a minute; the shots went on echoing dolefully in the country air. In an interval she slipped down on the ground, her arms spread out, with a bullet in her temple. Carmela's fall was the signal for flight, especially as, the virginal stillness of the country air having been broken by the many revolver-shots, people from Capodimonte village were heard arriving by Ponte Rossi Road. Hurriedly the two sets went off across the fields by a marked path, and quickly disappeared. On the duelling-ground only Carmela was left lying on the grass, blood flowing from her temple. Beside her, Raffaele, looking pale, tried to stanch the wound with a wet handkerchief. But the blood went on spouting like a fountain, making a red pool round the girl's head. She opened her eyes feebly.

'Tell me who it was for.'

'Don't think about that. Think of your own health,' he said in an agitated way, looking around.

'People are coming now; make your escape,' she said, thinking only of his safety.

'Can I leave you like this?'

'It does not matter; someone will help me. Fly, or you will be arrested.'

'Adieu,' he said, feeling relieved. 'We will see each other again at Pellegrini Hospital; I will come and ask for you.'

'Yes, yes,' she whispered, shutting her eyes and opening them again. 'Fly! Adieu.'

He rushed off, too, very quickly, without looking back; she followed him with her glance, half sitting up, holding the handkerchief to her forehead, while the blood flowed down her neck and shoulders into her lap. She was alone. She was holding her head down in her great weakness, when some peasants, a magistrate from Capodimonte with some police, and a gardener from the Royal Palace grounds came up at the same moment. They had to put her into a chair that the Barbassone inn-keeper had brought out, and carry her. They went slowly, the same road as she had come. She lay with her legs swinging against the chair, her arms limp, her head going hither and thither, and at every shake of the chair spilling big drops of blood on the ground. Before the inn, where the two tables with wine-stained cloths still stood, the chair was put down.

'Would you like anything?' asked the magistrate, a swarthy man.

'Only a little water to drink,' she said, opening her eyes slowly, as if her eyelids were too heavy.

Meanwhile they put a cold-water bandage on the wound till a cab could be got to take her to Pellegrini Hospital.

'How do you feel?' asked the magistrate. He wanted to go on with the inquiry, as he saw that her strength was failing.

'I feel better; it is nothing.'

'Who was it did this to you?'

'Nobody,' she said quietly.

'Who did this to you? Tell me! I will find out, at any rate,' the magistrate insisted.

'No one touched me' Carmela muttered.

'It was a duel, was it not? How many were there?' the magistrate asked loudly, his heart hardened by now.

'I don't know.'

'How many were there?'

'I know nothing about it.'

'Take care, or afterwards I will have you put in prison.'

'It doesn't matter,' she said, shutting her eyes.

'It was for you, was it, that these shots were fired? Was it for your sake?'

'No, no, it was not,' she said, her face suddenly growing sorrowful.

'Who was it for, then?'

'I don't know; I know nothing,' she added decisively, as if she was not going to answer any more.

The magistrate shrugged his shoulders in a rage. But another inquirer was coming along Ponte Rossi Road—a woman dressed in green cloth, embroidered in pink, and a pomegranate bodice, her shiny black hair dressed high, and cheeks covered with rouge. It was Filomena, Carmela's unfortunate sister.

She came up panting, her face discomposed, her hair not kept up by the silver comb, the patent-leather shoes quite dusty, holding a handkerchief at her mouth to keep back her sobs. When she saw the crowd evidently round a wounded person, she rushed into the group; crying out wildly, and pushing people aside, she fell on her knees by her sister, showing the self-forgetfulness of a frightful sorrow, and groaned out:

'Carmela dear, how did this happen?'

The other opened her eyes—her face showed a sorrowful amazement; she tried to caress Filomena's black hair with her weak hands, but her livid fingers trembled.

'How did it happen?' Filomena exclaimed, sobbing noisily, while warm tears ran down her cheeks and washed off the rouge.

'It happened just like that,' said Carmela, and nothing more.

'Carmela, who had the audacity to do this to you? Who was the assassin? Bring him to me,' cried Filomena.

'Try and find out the truth,' the magistrate whispered in the woman's ear. He made a sign to the others to stand aside for a little and leave the sisters alone. Now they had bound the girl's head up roughly, and under the bandages her face seemed tinier, more worn, as if rubbed down smaller by the hand.

'My sweet sister, my sweet sister!' Filomena went on saying, still kneeling before Carmela.

'Don't cry—why do you cry?' said the wounded girl, in a curious, solemn, deep voice.

'Tell me who did it!' Filomena said her. 'It was for Raffaele, was it not? Was there a fight? I knew it—I knew it; but I did not get here in time. Holy Virgin, why did you not let me get here in time? I have to see my sister like this because of not getting here in time.'

A livid look had come over the wounded girl's face on hearing this; her eyes had got wide open. With a violent effort she raised her head a little, and said to Filomena, staring at her:

'Tell me the truth.'

'What do you wish, sweetheart?'

'I want you to tell me—but think of the state I am in, think of that first.... I want you to tell me all.'

Then the other, fallen into deeper affliction, shook all over and held her tongue.

'They have had a duel,' Carmela brought out with difficulty, keeping her eyes on her sister. 'There were eight of them; Raffaele was there, and Ferdinando the Ammartenato—they were fighting for a woman.'

'Holy Virgin!' Filomena said, going on weeping with her face in her hands.

'Who was the woman?' asked the wounded girl, putting her hand on her sister's head, and almost obliging her to raise it. Filomena only looked at her, her eyes filled with tears.

'It was you—it was you,' the wounded girl said in a cavernous voice.

The bad woman threw herself back, raised her arms heavenward, and cried:

'I am a murderer—I am the cause of your death!'

Carmela's face got clay colour; in a whisper, stammering, as if she could not use her tongue, she too said:

'Murderer! murderer!'

'You are right—you are right, Carmela: I am a wretch!' Filomena cried, stretching out her arms. A moment after, the blood soaked the bandage round the wounded girl's head, and blood began to drop from her nose. The magistrate, who had run up, frowned, and signed to the cabman, who had come forward to take the girl to Pellegrini Hospital, to stop.

'Forgive me, dear,' Filomena wept out, cast down at the foot of the chair. But Carmela no longer heard her. Blood flowed from her mouth and trickled down from her nose, falling on her breast; the earthy pallor of the face spread to the neck; her half-open eyes showed the whites only; her hands, lying on her knees, pulled at her wretched, dull dress, as if searching, with that motion that gives a frightful impression of terror and sorrow. All of a sudden she opened her mouth—her breath was failing her.

'Carmela darling!' Filomena cried out, understanding, getting up on her knees, panting. But from her mouth, black already, a loud, long cry came out, as profound as if it came from her tortured vitals, sorrowful as if all the complaints of a life-long agony were in it—a cry so loud and doleful it seemed to shake everything around—men and things—and make the neighbourhood lose colour. Carmela's light hand was still vaguely searching for something, and ended by finding Filomena's head, where it rested, grew cold and stiffened. The dead woman's face was quite cold, but it was tranquil now. Silently bent forward under the forgiving hand, the survivor sat there, and the country around was silent also.

CHAPTER XVIII
TO LET

The fourth of January, 188—, very early in the morning, the porter's wife at Rossi Palazzo, formerly called Cavalcanti, put a step-ladder against the architrave of the entrance door, to the right, and stuck three bits of paper on the pipernina stone, with 'To Let' printed on each piece. The three notices said that three large suites of rooms, so many in each suite, were available, and could be seen at such an hour. Coming down the ladder, the woman sighed dolefully. For years none of the Rossi Palazzo suites had been to let; everyone was very comfortable and stayed on. She had got to know them all well. In the four months houses are looked for in Naples, from the fourth of January to the fourth of May, she had peacocked about at her ease always. She had not to go up and down stairs with house-hunters, as the Rosa Mansion woman next door or the Latilla woman had to do; she did not risk changing tenants that liked her for new ones that might be unpleasant. Instead of which, this very year three large flats were empty at the same time: one on the first floor—the Fragalàs'; two suites on the second floor—Dr. Amati's and the Marquis di Formosa's. It was a real catastrophe for the porter's wife, who never would get any rest for four months, and get no pay for her trouble. Altogether, three large suites to be empty was really a misfortune. 'Just like my luck,' said the porter's wife to those who condoled with her and asked the reason of these changes. She told the reason the tenants were going at once, so that people should not believe Rossi Palazzo was damp, that it threatened to fall, or that the owner had got an idea of raising the rents. Nothing of the sort. It was misfortunes. All are liable to them. It was natural Don Cesare Fragalà and that good soul Donna Luisa should leave the house where they had been married. It was splendid, really—a gorgeous apartment, but they could not pay the high rent any longer. The husband had gambled everything away at the lottery; he was loaded with debts and ruined. Also, his confectioner's shop in Santo Spirito Square had gone out of his possession, for his wife, fearing bankruptcy was at hand, had decided to sell everything: jewels, plate, and furniture were all to be sold, everything luxurious got rid of, and a composition be made with their creditors. They were to go into a small house, and look out for a clerk's place for her husband, to keep the family agoing. The porter's wife and her gossiping friend remembered the two gorgeous parties for Cesare's marriage with Luisella and at little Agnesina's birth—all the great style of these receptions, the sweets, wine, and ices. It was an overthrow.

'Good gracious!' muttered the inquirer, man or woman. 'Did he lose all that at the lottery?'

'He lost all. They are left without a farthing, if they pay their debts; and Donna Luisa insists on paying. She may die from it, but she will pay.'

'What a scoundrel of a husband she has got!'

'We are not masters of ourselves,' the porter's wife prosed solemnly; 'we are all flesh.'

She was sorry, very, that the Fragalàs were going off to who knew where. She would never see them again. Most of all, she was sorry for little Agnesina; she was so good, placid, and obedient. She already went to the infants' school, tiny little body! Her mother went with her and brought her back carefully every day. They were a good sort, and it had to be seen who would come in their place.

The Cavalcantis' going away was a thing that had been foreseen for some time. The Marquis had paid no rent for several months, and Signor Rossi had stood it. He had allowed something to be paid on account now and then, partly because the Marquis di Formosa had been the old owner of the house and sold it to him, and he did not want to turn him out forcibly. How patient he had been! Now he could stand it no longer. In the Cavalcanti household they were often short of five francs for food. The Marquis had carried off the most necessary furniture piece by piece, selling it to a dealer in Baracchi Square. Donna Bianca Maria, poor soul! often dined off a hot dish that her aunt, Sister Maria degli Angioli, sent her from the Sacramentiste convent. The two old servants, Giovanni and Margherita, tried for outside work. The woman darned stockings and silk-knitted goods; the man copied papers for a magistrate's clerk. They were in such wretchedness that but for feeling shame the door-keeper would often carry up a dish of her macaroni or hot vegetable soup; but she dared not. They were gentlefolk, and bore their wretchedness silently. Besides, for want of a dower, Donna Bianca Maria Cavalcanti had been rejected as a sister of charity. By the new laws it was not allowable to go into other monasteries or orders; the new Government would not even let one be a nun.

'Then are they going away in May?' asked the inquirer rather pityingly. 'Where are they going?'

'Who can say? But I can tell you that her ladyship will not see that day. She is so ill; she wastes away like a taper; she says nothing, but when she has the strength to show at the window, she looks like a shadow. She does not go out now; indeed, she has no clothes to go out with, and if she had them she would not have the strength to go a step. Poor lady! to think her father could have got her married if he had chosen.'

'To whom? Why would he not allow it?'

Here began the woman's third sorrowful recital, the departure of the third tenant, Dr. Amati, that she earned such a lot of money by, from his sudden summonses to sick people. Alas! he was going away; indeed, he had gone, putting her on the street, poor woman, for she would never earn another farthing. Just fancy that Dr. Amati, who was so rich now, and earned as much as he liked, just out of charity, he was such a good man, had wanted to marry the Marchesina, she was so sweet and lovely; and she had been in love with the doctor, too, from her soul, because he had helped her in her illness—because she had known no other man—in short, because he only could get her out of that beggary. Well, it was not to be believed, but the Marquis di Formosa had said 'No,' and had persisted in saying 'No,' always making his daughter lose that bit of good luck she would never have again.

'What do you say?' her questioner cried out. 'It seems impossible.'

'Indeed, yes, it looks like a lie, but the Marquis di Formosa said "No." He felt quite honoured and pleased that Dr. Amati had asked for his daughter's hand, but some forbears of his long ago had left a written paper, in which it was said the last woman child of the family was not to marry—she must die a maid; and if this command was not carried out, a great punishment from God would come on her. No one knew what tears the Marchesina had shed, but her father had been firm. So that Dr. Amati—one evening they had had a great dispute—to avoid further occasions for anger, and to get the idea out of his head, had taken a month's leave from the hospital, left all his patients, and gone off to his native village to see his mother. Then he came back to Naples, but he would not even put his foot in Rossi Palazzo; he had gone to live in a furnished house in Chiaia Road. At Rossi Palazzo his flat was closed with all his furniture and books which the doctor no longer read; sometimes the housekeeper came to dust, and went away again. In a short time now the furniture and books would be carried away, too, and in May the flat would be empty. Poor Donna Bianca Maria, how often she had seen her come to the window of the inner court and gaze on Dr. Amati's closely-shut balcony! She made one's heart sore, that poor child of the Virgin, wasting away with sickness, melancholy, and wretchedness. Really it looked as if there was no more oil in the lamp. Margherita, her maid, when she spoke about her, cast down her eyes not to show she was weeping. But the Marquis was not wrong to obey his grandsire's wishes; there is no trifling with God's vengeance.'

'Ah! it was written,' remarked the gossip approvingly, quite thoughtful. 'It was written, my dear. When it is God's will, what is to be done?'

House-hunters began to flock in to inspect the flats to let in Rossi Palazzo, and the door-keeper's hard times began—it was never-ending, from ten in the morning to four in the afternoon, up and down the stairs. Every time a family arrived in front of the office and made the usual inquiries, she shook her head and got up, sighing, to go with them to the first or second floor. She went in front, going up very slowly, turning round to chat with the usual familiarity of small people in Naples, making her keys rattle, as they hung from her waist; asking if they wanted to see the doctor's rooms, for he had given her charge of them. Monotonously wandering through the huge rooms, rather severely furnished, where the stern moral impression of a great science—a great will—was still present, and all the human misery that had come there to ask help, she praised up the house and Dr. Amati, the famous doctor that all Naples admired, or, as she said, the whole world.

'Ah,' said the visitors, much impressed; 'and why did he leave this house, then?'

Very hastily she replied that the doctor was going to marry and needed a larger house, or that his business had gone in another direction, or that he was going to a smaller apartment, having taken a consulting-room at the hospital; in short, any lie that came into her head—such hurried, unlikely lies that the house-hunters, endowed with natural suspiciousness, would not take it in at all, and interrupted her with: 'All right; we will come back.' But they did not come back at all; indeed, the solemn, solitary look of the flat, with too many books, too many surgical appliances, and even the chair-bed of black leather that the sick lay on to be examined, that looked like the first step towards the tomb, left rather a sad impression, so they went away hurriedly, speaking low, still more alarmed by the doctor being away, the feared and respected god of medicine. They fled, never to return, a cloud over their spirits, not at all anxious to come back to be dispirited by these solemn, thought-inspiring surroundings.

The door-keeper, standing in the doorway, saw them go off quickly towards Toledo Street, where there was movement, light, and gaiety, and in spite of their vague promises, hesitatingly made, she knew they would never come back. 'Nothing is arranged, dear,' she often said, with a wearied air, to the neighbouring door-keeper at the Rosa Mansion. Nothing was settled, even for the flats that the Fragalà and Cavalcanti families were leaving. It looked as if the house-hunters noticed the bad luck that came from these two flats, where so many tears had been shed, where so many were still being shed. In the Fragalàs' house, brave, melancholy Luisella had got rid of a great part of the furniture; the fine red drawing-room was now bare of its old brocade couches, and the child slept in its parents' room. Their way of living was of a sudden meaner, smaller, being restricted to the bedroom and dining-room. Sometimes the visitors found the family at dinner at two o'clock. Cesare Fragalà kept his eyes on his plate, eating stolidly. Luisella said nothing, but kept rolling bread-pellets in her fingers. Little Agnesina, well-behaved and good as usual, looked at her father and mother alternately, taking care to make no noise with her spoon and fork, not to disturb them. When the visitors came in, the father of the family got paler and the mother cast down her eyes. Both of them at each visit felt having to leave the house: their wounds smarted and bled afresh. The little one looked at them, and said over in a whisper:

'Mamma, mamma!'

The visitors, led in by the door-keeper, felt they were in the way, and excused themselves, going on into other rooms while the woman spoke volubly to take off their attention. When they saw the drawing-room, parlour, and lobby empty, they gave queer glances at each other, so that the door-keeper shivered with impatience, cursing in her heart all who go away from houses and those who go looking for them, also those who go round to show them—that is to say, herself, who had this hard fate. The visitors asked the stock questions rather suspiciously:

'Why are they going away?'

Then she made up her mind and whispered:

'They have failed in business.'

'Ah, is that it?' exclaimed the visitors, much interested.

On the stair she gave particulars—told the reason of the failure, spoke of their former riches and the want of any comforts now; told about Signora Luisella's courage and her husband's rage for gambling on the lottery, and poor little Agnesina's good behaviour. She seemed to understand having come into the world and grown up at a bad season. The house-hunters listened full of interest, with that skin-deep emotion peculiar to Southerners; but from what they had seen, as well as from what they had heard from the door-keeper, they got a singular impression of evil fate—a doom weighing down an innocent, good family; a hard destiny, destroying all the sources of happiness and energy.

The house-hunters turned their backs on the Fragalà household and Rossi Palazzo slowly; but they still felt sad, and spoke to each other about there being implacable, unforeseen, overpowering disasters, sometimes coming on humanity. Some attributed it to perfidious fate, some to the evil eye; others were philosophical over the passions of humanity, especially for gambling, still repeating the phrase that includes all the indulgence and forgiveness of Naples' folk: 'We are not our own masters.'

It was difficult to get into the Marquis di Formosa's flat. Often Margherita objected to anyone seeing the house, in spite of its being the right hours for visits. The door-keeper talked her over, feeling rather annoyed. She raised her voice and asked, 'How ever would a house be let, if no one could get in to see it?' Sometimes she managed to get in by slipping through the half-open door. All stopped speaking at once, for from the freezing bare lobby to the bare frozen drawing-room there was such cold, such a smell of old dust displaced, that it gave one a shudder. Big dull stains on the walls marked the outline of large pieces of furniture that had once been there, which the Marquis had sold to use what they fetched for staking on the lottery. One saw the big hooks and nails that the pictures had been hung from, and a heap of old yellow paper lay on the ground in a corner of one empty room. Where curtains had been fastened to the doors and balcony windows, there were holes in the plaster, for they seemed to have been violently torn away.

The chapel, too, had not a saint left. Our Lady of Sorrows and the Ecce Homo had been sold, also the vases and ornaments—even the fine napkins with old lace, so that the despoiled altar had a doleful, desecrated look. Sometimes the visitors, on going through the house, met a slight girlish figure in black, her shoulders wrapped in a shabby shawl, the lady's heavy black tresses seeming to make her face still more bloodless. She gazed at the visitors with her sorrowful eyes as if she did not know what was going on; a shade of grief reanimated them for a moment when she remembered it meant they had to leave that roof, their only refuge. The woman said in a whisper, 'It is the Marchesina!' nothing else, and that apparition was like the outline of an irreparable disaster. Sometimes the house-hunters, followed by Margherita and the door-keeper, came to a closed door. The waiting-woman rather hesitated, but on a hint from the door-keeper she made up her mind to knock.

'My lady, may we come in?'

'Yes, yes; come in,' a feeble voice answered.

Then all saw a wretched maidenly room, freezing with cold, where a pale creature in black, wrapped in a worn shawl, was seated by the bedside, or getting up quickly from her kneeling-desk. Then, abashed, they just gave a quick look round, muttered vaguely some excuse, and went off, the maiden following them with her thoughtful, sorrowing eyes. On the stair they dared to speak. They asked the woman, as if speaking of dead people or things:

'*What was their name?*'

'The Cavalcantis; he is a Marquis,' said the door-keeper.

Then the visitors would go off, taking with them a deep impression of people and things that are extinct.

CHAPTER XIX
DON CRESCENZIO'S TRIALS

Coming out of the Finance Department, from the Secretary's room, having got to the lobby, Don Crescenzio staggered and had a singing in his ears.

'Do you feel ill?' asked the usher anxiously, for he knew him.

'No, it is nothing; it is from this first heat of spring,' he stammered. And he brought his hands across his forehead, which was covered with cold drops of sweat. Still, to try to look at ease, he pulled out a cigar and lit it.

'Is business good?' the usher asked the lottery banker, while he was carefully putting out the match.

'Well, just so-so,' said the other, giving a sketchy sort of smile.

'It would be grand to get the right figures,' the usher muttered; 'one would like to spit in this infamous Government's face,' he added in a whisper.

'But no one knows the right figures—no one does,' the other cried out as he went away. But when he was under the portico and got out to the open air, he felt dizzy again; he had a singing in his ears and nearly fell. He had to stand a good minute, leaning on the stone posts of San Giacomo Palazzo door, which opens on to Toledo Street, seeing the usual crowd in that thoroughfare swim before his eyes. It was larger than usual, from its being the first fine spring day, which brought out more people than usual. He only saw a confused crowd without distinct outlines. He heard a great noise without distinguishing either words or voices. Only, while he went on smiling instinctively, he saw sharply marked in his mind the corner of the writing-room where the Finance Secretary had turned his cold, severe glance on him. He heard the exact sound of the Secretary's words ringing out as clear as if they had just struck the drum of his ear. The Secretary had been very stern with him. He could no longer be lenient to the lottery banker, for he had been too lenient already; he did not want to seem an accomplice of his fraud. 'Fraud,' he said and repeated, in spite of the deadly pallor that came over Don Crescenzio's face on hearing the cruel word.

One cannot play tricks with the State; it gives no credit. Every week lately, when Don Crescenzio came to hand over the profits, he was short of money, and had had to ask the Minister of Finance at Rome to make allowances for him and give him time. This had happened every week. But the State is not a bank which can grant delays. It makes others wait, but it will not. Every time he mentioned the State the word filled the Secretary's mouth severely and sonorously, and he frowned a little. Don Crescenzio listened, with his head down, starting when he heard named that mysterious being who gets all and gives nothing; who has no heart or bowels, and holds out open hands to take and carry off everything. Ah! the Secretary had been decisive in his cruelty. By Wednesday he must pay up all in full—stakes and the debt in arrears; if not, the downfall was unavoidable: the State would seize the caution money and prosecute Don Crescenzio for his indebtedness. He had just given one sob at the Secretary's last words.

'You lose the caution money, and you go to prison if you don't pay up,' the worthy official wound up his remarks with.

Don Crescenzio had set to imploring then. He had a wife and children; if he had been so foolish as to give the gamblers credit, was he to be ruined for that? If they would give him time, he would force the men to pay; he would give back the State the uttermost farthing. He was an honest man; in short, he was cheated, slain.

'You gamble too, and on credit,' the Secretary said haughtily.

'I only did it to try and recoup myself.'

'An honest lottery keeper never plays himself. It is immoral in a citizen to play.'

'Then the State is immoral also.'

'The State cannot be immoral, remember that. Think of how you are to pay; I can do no more for you.'

Still, he had begged, sobbing, that they would not cast him into prison; indeed, they could not require a man's death, being men and Christians. But he had made that scene before twice, and had managed to get a month's, a fortnight's grace. This time the Secretary looked so freezingly at him that Don Crescenzio had understood. This was the end, really. He must either pay or go to prison. He took leave, always feeling that word *Wednesday*, *Wednesday*, cut into his brain. It was true he had a young wife and two babies; a small family, that with Neapolitan good-heartedness and good-nature he had accustomed to living freely, going from a fine holiday dinner at home to a grander country excursion, and to celebrate all the feast-days with good eating. They gave each other presents of heavy gold jewellery, and, though contenting themselves with hired carriages, had always a secret wish to keep a carriage of their own; and he bought earrings, rings, and brooches for his wife, and presented her with shiny jet mantles such as our towns-folk love. And all this came while living off the income from the lottery bank; indeed, he speculated a little with Government money, but did not gamble on the lottery ever. This was past, the time of purity and innocence. When had he staked the first time—he, who ought to have kept himself from that contagion, and only lived off the lottery, without letting it fasten on him, live off it as one may drink poison without dying of it, though the same poison laid on an open wound will kill? When had he first staked? He did not remember now; he saw confusedly a great *Wednesday* stand out with such vivid heat that it seemed like a live coal, as if it must burn him. It was all a confusion, in which the mental disorder of the Cabalists who crowded into his shop, touching him with their feverish hands and infecting him, and their money—got God knows how or where—passing from their hands to his, all gave him the impression of a tragedy. That mental malady that burned in their blood, young and old, rich and poor, powerful and insignificant, had passed on to him; from being with them, breathing their atmosphere, it had soaked through everything, and come into his very life. First of all, greed of gain had made him give credit to the Cabalists, keeping back always so much per cent. off their stakes when they played on credit, while he asked for delay from the Government; then, as the deviations became continually larger, as the hole got deeper till there was a precipice down to it, he began to gamble too, unlucky wretch, tempting Fate, having the delusion he was in her favour, and playing on credit, with the huge delusion that he might win a large, an immense sum.

Ah! the unlucky wretch, he knew quite well that hardly anyone ever wins. He was well acquainted with the frightful law of averages, that shows that winning is so rare it is difficult to find cases of it. It is an infinitesimal chance, like one planet meeting another every two or three hundred years by inflexible sidereal laws. He knew well that Government always wins, always; that it takes sixteen million francs from Naples alone every year— from all Italy, sixty million of francs. But what did that signify? He went on giving credit to the Cabalists; he showed at their meetings; he lent a hand to imprison Don Pasqualino, being blinded himself. The vulgar luxury of his house increased; his wife got fat, she was red and shiny from eating too much, and now she was going to have another child. She wore a cream silk dress covered with lace; her fat hands, laden with rings, lay on her already rounded figure with that quietly satisfied air of women easy in their feelings. What a disaster if on Wednesday he did not bring the money to the

Secretary! He, his wife and children, and the one to be born, would be in wretchedness, and he himself in prison.

Now, every time the word 'Wednesday' came to the mind of the handsome lottery banker, with his well-kept chestnut beard and white hands, a little warm blood flowed into his pale cheeks, and he felt them burn like two flames of fire. He had dragged himself away from the San Giacomo doorposts, and was going among the crowd, letting himself be carried along, feeling a slight dizziness that came from his being wrapt up always in the same maddening idea. He must do something, gain money, try and get it from those who owed it to him and had it, so that on Wednesday he and his family would not be ruined. Where was he to go? He must look for money at any cost; he would drag it from his debtors' vitals. He was not going to die for them; he would not go to San Francesco for these four scoundrels, who had drawn him into dishonest courses. Money, money was what he wanted; he thirsted, hungered for it; it was his soul—his body asked for that only. Money, or he would die; that was all.

Now, having made up his mind, he set out on the search for some of those indebted to him. They had gradually all deserted his shop, not being able to stand his constant demands for money. They took to some other lottery bank the few pence they managed to get hold of by some dark miracle, God knows how or where. Out of fear for his just anger, they had even taken away his profits, ungrateful now, as well as dishonest. However, he knew where they all lived; he wished to set on them; he would not let them go till they felt his despair as if it was their own. He would wait at their homes, at their doors, in the streets they went through; he would speak to them, shout at them, and weep. He would give them such a fright that the State money would be got out of them, dragged out by his rush of despair. It was a question of life and death; his wife and children were not to be sent to beggary because he had been too easy, too weak, too much of a boy. He must get the money—he must. The crowd had now carried him to the upper part of Toledo Street, while he was making up a good plan in his head how to carry out best this burning desire to save himself in a way likely to effect his purpose. Let us see: where would he go first that springtide noon? Where would he say his first word? He must make no mistake; he must try and strike a sure blow, or otherwise.... He could not think of non-success; it was a notion he could not bear. Now he had stopped in Carità Square, fixing his eyes, which had a thick cloud before them, on Carlo Poerio's statue. The people passing hustled him on all sides; the shouts of street-sellers and voices of passers-by struck him as a vague, indistinct noise. He thought a minute of going to the Marquis di Formosa's, the person most largely indebted to him; but amongst them all the Marquis was the one he was sorriest for, from his own misfortunes; also he was the one least likely to have money. Now, Don Crescenzio did not want to begin by being unkind to an unhappy man, nor did he want to make a bad start; he was too much afraid of not succeeding—he was too discouraged. He would go last to the Marquis di Formosa—afterwards, as a last resource. The safest of those he had given credit to was Ninetto Costa, the stock-broker—the safest because, in spite of his falling behind with his payments, he always could get money to borrow; some still believed in his star. Ninetto Costa had got into debt several times with him, but had always paid until the last time, when it was for rather a large sum; but for three weeks past he had got so out of pocket he could not give a farthing to Don Crescenzio. What did it matter? Costa was a moneyed man.

The lottery banker went forward towards the Exchange, knowing this was an hour that Ninetto Costa would be there for certain. But among the band of bankers, stockbrokers, merchants, and outside brokers, who were chattering, talking things over, and vociferating, he looked vainly for him for a quarter of an hour. Then he asked two or three men for him, and got a bad reception. Some shrugged their shoulders, others gave an ironical smile, and all set at once to speak of their own business, leaving Don Crescenzio alone. He, who with the extraordinary trustingness of people in desperation had gone in there quite quieted down, already sure of a good result, felt a burning from his mouth to the pit of his stomach. But where was Ninetto Costa, then? He remembered having gone to call on him once at Carolina Road, where the smart stock-broker had a set of rooms furnished with striking youthful luxury; but he had changed his house some time before—it was at the beginning of his downfall. Now Don Crescenzio remembered having gone with him one evening, on leaving the meeting in Nardones Road, up Taverna Penta Road to a very ordinary house there, which Costa was reduced to, just opposite San Giacomo Road. He must find him, at any rate, whether alive or dead. Ninetto Costa would give him the eleven hundred francs he owed him, and at least a part of the debt to Government would be paid; a small part, it is true, but something, at least. He went up again towards Taverna Penta Road, and the sulky door-keeper looked at him, and said:

'Fourth-floor.'

'But is he at home?'

'I don't know,' she grumbled.

Patiently, determined not to be discouraged by anything, he went up the narrow, steep stair, and from the landings and doors came out the sound of children's whining and women's quarrelling voices and noisy sewing-machines. On Ninetto Costa's door was a torn visiting-card fastened up by four pins. He knocked twice. No one came; there was no sound from inside. He knocked louder, the third time—nothing yet. The fourth time he gave the bell a hard pull, and a very light step could be heard; then no sound nor movement, as if the person who had come to the door was listening intently.

'Don Ninetto, it is I. Open—especially as I know that you are in the house, and I won't go away,' the lottery banker said in a loud voice.

There was a few minutes' pause again. Then the door opened softly, and the stock-broker's face appeared, sadly altered. Now all his youthfulness, prolonged by high living and cosmetics, had fled. His hair was sparse on the temples and on the top of his head. Two flabby, yellowish bags underlined his eyes, and thousands of small wrinkles came down in all directions, marking the face indelibly. The jacket that hardly covered him had the collar turned up, as if he were cold or wished to hide his linen.

'Is it you?' he asked, with a sickly smile.

He brought Don Crescenzio into the parlour, a shabby lodging-house sitting-room with red chair-covers and curtains dulled by smoke, and sat down opposite to him, looking at him with dull eyes which had lost all expression.

'It is I. I went to look for you at the Exchange. Have you not been there to-day?' Don Crescenzio asked, feeling a burning at his stomach again.

'No, I did not go to-day.'

'Why not?'

'No matter.'

'Have you not been there for some time?'

'Not for—yes ... for three or four days.'

'What have you been doing?' Don Crescenzio asked anxiously.

'Nothing,' said the other, with a gesture that was too clear.

'Have you gone bankrupt?'

Ninetto Costa shut his eyes, shivering, as if he did not want to see something; then he said:

'Yes, I have.'

'This is ruin, ruin!' shouted Don Crescenzio, throwing up his arms heavenwards.

The other bit his moustache convulsively.

'At least, you have kept something. That eleven hundred francs you owe me—you must have kept it, have you not?'

Ninetta Costa looked at him dreamily.

'If I do not get this eleven hundred francs by Tuesday evening, I must go prison!' the lottery banker shrieked out.

Ninetto Costa hung his head.

'I must go to prison, and my family will have no bread. You must give me the eleven hundred francs, you know!' shrieked Don Crescenzio in a great rage.

'I have not got it.'

'Look for it.'

'I shall not find it. No one will give it to me.'

'You must find it; I cannot go to prison for you. Find it.'

'It is impossible, Don Crescenzio,' said the stock-broker, with tears in his eyes.

'Nothing is impossible when it has to do with a debt like this, when it is a question of saving an honest man from ruin. For pity's sake, Don Ninetto; you know how dear honour is.'

'Yes, I do,' said the other, turning his face away.

'For pity's sake don't forsake me. I have done you a favour; don't be so ungrateful.'

'I have not got a farthing, and I cannot find one.'

'But have you no friends or relations left?'

'None—not one. I have gone bankrupt; that is enough.'

'What will you do?'

'I am going—going to Rome,' the stock-broker brought out, after a slight hesitation.

'What to do?'

'Who knows? Perhaps I shall make my fortune there.'

'But you ought not to forsake me; you, a man, must give me the eleven hundred francs before you leave.'

'I have not got it. I can't get it. Don't torment me, Don Crescenzio; I have not a farthing.'

'Give me your signature to a bill; some banker that you are acquainted with will cash it.'

'All my bills are presented.'

'Pawn your jewellery.'

'I have sold it all.'

'Then give me your watch.'

'It is sold.'

'Then ask your mother or your uncle.'

'My uncle will perhaps do me the kindness to support my mother. The mother of a bankrupt, you understand, is never very well received.'

'For how much have you failed?'

'For two hundred thousand francs.'

'All through the lottery, was it?'

'I lost all there,' Ninetto Costa said, with a decided gesture.

'But how can you leave me to such ruin?' Don Crescenzio rejoined, nearly crying; 'how have you the heart?'

'How have I the heart?' the other said, in a shaky voice. 'I am leaving my mother with nothing to support her, you know. I am going to Rome. If I make any money I will send you some.'

'When do you go?'

'To-morrow.... Yes, to-morrow.'

'Can you send me money by Tuesday?'

'I don't think so, Don Crescenzio—I don't think so,' Ninetto Costa said, with desperate calmness.

'It must be by Wednesday, you know; if not, I am ruined.'

'I was ruined three days ago.'

'Holy Virgin! who has blinded me?' the lottery-keeper said, crying.

'You want to kill me before the time,' Ninetto Costa muttered.

'What are you saying?'

'Nothing. But keep calm. Everything may come right gradually.'

'Wednesday is the last day I have got—Wednesday.'

'Perhaps Government will give you time. Find out some way; write to the Minister, write to the King. I must start off.'

He pointed to a small bag, not half full, with a feeble smile.

'But, really, can you not give me anything?'

'I would do it, Don Crescenzio, but I swear to you that I have not got a farthing. I am off to Rome; then I will see....'

Disappointed and excited, Don Crescenzio got up to go away, half angry and half sorry for Costa. He wanted to rush off in search of his other clients; he wanted to find money, to leave that sad house, the sad company of a man more desperate than himself. He wanted to go away. Ninetto Costa looked at him in a dull way, keeping up that pallid smile on his white lips, the absent-minded smile of a man quite indifferent to earthly affairs. Still, the other once more insisted in a vague way, as if in justice to himself, thinking he had not done enough to get his money. But the stock-broker gave him such a suffering look he said no more.

'Good-bye, Don Crescenzio; for—give me.'

'Good-bye, Don Ninetto; don't forget me at Rome.'

'Have no doubt of it,' said the other, in a weak, queer voice.

They took each other's hands without pressing them—cold, feeble hands, both. As in a dream, Ninetto Costa went to the door with the lottery banker; silently they looked at each other, but did not speak. Then the door shut again with such a queer *decisive* sound that the lottery banker, going slowly downstairs, gave a start. He felt almost inclined to turn back; it came to his mind that Costa had told him he had not a farthing, and, then, that flabby travelling bag with nothing in it. But the thought of his own sorrows distracted him from his pity and from any suspicion of greater misfortune. Now, still on foot, to spare the money for a cab even, he began to run up Toledo Street, as if prodded by a goad, to go to San Sebastiano Road, where Marzano, the old lawyer, lived, another indebted to him. He, too, because of his professional position, even if he had no money to pay up at once, would be able to get a loan; at any rate, he owed eight hundred francs to Don Crescenzio, and he would give them to him; indeed, Don Crescenzio would sit there till he got them, even if he had to wait till night. He knew his house very well, a poor house indeed: for Marzano staked everything— all he earned—and he even supported a cobbler at sixty francs a month, a Cabalist, who wrote lottery numbers with charcoal on dirty pieces of paper.

Don Crescenzio went up the steps four at a time, running, because a voice in his heart told him he would find the money at Signor Marzano's; he felt a good presentiment. Still, when he put his hand to the iron ring that hung from a greasy cord, a sudden alarm took him, the fear of not succeeding, a horrible fear that paralyzed his strength, the nervousness of the unfortunate when life and death are at stake. A dragging step was heard, and a shrill voice asked:

'Who is it?'

'Friends—a friend,' the lottery banker stammered hastily.

The door opened suspiciously, and the cobbler's mean face showed, all marked with pimples. His blear, red, stupid eyes stared at Don Crescenzio.

'Do you want to see the lawyer?' he asked, drying his hands on a dirty apron.

'Yes, sir.'

'He cannot attend to you.'

'Is he busy?'

'He is ill.'

'Ill, is he? Not much the matter, I hope?'

'He has had a stroke. Wishing you better health——'

'Good God!' shouted Don Crescenzio, throwing his hat down on the ground in despair.

'It was the lottery did it.... Indeed, he always starved himself; he did not live well. He ate very little and drank water, you see.'

'Oh, God! God!' Don Crescenzio whispered in lamentation.

'It is God's will,' the cobbler said softly, pulling out a little bit of dirty paper and taking a pinch of yellowish snuff. 'When it is God's will, what can one do?... Don't despair. Till the last there is hope.'

'I know that; it is why I am so despairing!' shrieked Don Crescenzio.

'I have a right to complain,' the silly fellow rejoined. 'I would have got him a fortune. I expected peace in my old days from him, and in the meanwhile, by his own folly, he is at death's door, and leaves me to wretchedness. Do you see?'

'But how was it? how did it happen?'

'Wait a minute. I am just coming.' And he went out of the room.

Don Crescenzio looked round him, stupefied with sorrow. The wretched room had no other furniture but some old lawyer's bookcases, choke-full of dusty papers, a small table, and two soiled straw chairs. There was a glass on the table, with two fingers of bluish wine in it—the thick, heavy Sicilian wine. The floor had not been swept for a long time, the wall was full of spiders' webs, the window-panes were covered with dust, and a smell of dirty staleness and mustiness caught the throat. And this was the lawyer's house—of him that had been one of the best advocates of his day, and had earned thousands of pounds in his profession! Don Crescenzio felt his heart bleed; his hands were like ice. Had he come here, to this abode of poverty, shame, and death, to look for his eight hundred francs to save himself? What madness, what madness his had been! Would it not be better to run away, as he was finding everywhere the same traces of dishonour and wretchedness—everywhere? But the cobbler came back.

'What is he doing?' Don Crescenzio asked in a whisper.

'He is in a stupor.'

'Is he asleep?'

'No; it is from the disease.'

'What has been done for him?'

'He has been bled; then, he has an ice blister on his head, and another on his chest.'

'Does he speak at all?'

'He does not understand what is said.'

'Has he become powerless?'

'Only on his right side.'

'What does the doctor say?'

'What can he say? It is a case of death.'

'Is the doctor coming back?'

'Who can say? There is nothing to pay him with. I found seven francs and a nickel watch that won't pawn. I have spent three francs already on ice. When the seven francs are done, we are at an end of our resources.'

'But how did it happen? how did it happen?' Don Crescenzio asked again desperately.

'Humph! there has been such a lot of things. He has had some unpleasantnesses, you see. A man is always a man.... He needed money ... he tried to get it in all sorts of ways.'

'What did he do?' asked the other, alarmed.

'Evil-minded people say he forged stamped paper—washing, you know, what was written on it already, and putting it to use again. But it can't be true. He leaves me to beggary; he has been ungrateful to me; but it can't be true. I will never believe it. It seems that the ill-natured people got at the President of the Consiglio dell' Ordine, who called him rather ugly things. It seems, in short, there were unpleasantnesses.'

'Poor man! poor man!' Don Crescenzio called out in a low voice.

'This summons to the President was a fatal thing for him. You may think for an honest man to feel himself insulted is unbearable. Signor Marzano wished to go away to some village where there is better breeding.'

'To go away at his age with seven francs in his pocket!'

'I would have gone with him,' the silly cobbler muttered modestly. 'I was getting ready to go with him, out of love to him; and as to the money — that is the real reason of the stroke.'

'How could it be?'

'You know, sir, that my mathematical labours, with God's help, have always brought in some money to the advocate.'

'Yes, some small sum every three or four months,' Don Crescenzio remarked sceptically.

'You are mistaken; one may say that I benefited him, and these wretched sixty francs he gave me every month, for me not to clap on soles any longer, but work at necromancy, were not even the hundredth part of what he won each month. Now he is leaving me, ungrateful fellow! like this ... enough: I may tell you I had given certain numbers to him symbolically, numbers that must necessarily come out; and they did come, you know.'

'Then, he won?'

'No, nothing; he did not understand — he staked on others' figures — his mind is not trustworthy now. When he knew it he got the stroke.... To your health, sir.'

'But had you really told him what were good numbers?'

'I swear it before God; but he did not understand.'

'Why did you not play them?'

'You know quite well that *we* cannot play.'

'Ah, yes, that is true.'

They stopped speaking; the cobbler put the glass to his lips and took a sip of wine.

'I would like to see him,' Don Crescenzio said suddenly.

They went into the small bedroom; it was poor and dirty like the study. Marzano, the advocate, lay on a wretched iron bed, raised on pillows, whose covers were of doubtful whiteness; a lump of ice was on his bald head, another on the bare, skeleton-like breast, and his thin, small body was covered by a brown horse-blanket. On the night table was a tumbler of water with a bit of ice in it; the dying man's right hand was wrapped in the blood-letting bandages. All his right side, from the face to the foot, was struck rigid, numb already, while his left hand went on trembling, trembling, and all the left side of his face often twitched convulsively. A confused stammering came from his lips; all his gentle, good-natured expression was gone, leaving on that old face, half belonging to death already, the marks of a passion that had got to be shameful.

'Signor Marzano! Signor Marzano!' Don Crescenzio called out, leaning over his bed.

The sick man set his eyes, veiled by a curious cloud, on the lottery-keeper's face, but the expression did not change nor the stammering stop.

'He doesn't recognise you,' said the cobbler, taking snuff.

Don Crescenzio left the room at once, feeling the nightmare of it weighing on his mind.

'You are his friend: will you leave him something?' the cobbler asked. 'I have only four francs; he will die like a dog.'

Then all Don Crescenzio's suppressed sorrow burst out.

'He owes me eight hundred francs, and I am ruined if I do not get it by Wednesday. He is dying; but I am left, and I am tortured. He will die; but my children will sleep on church steps in a month. He at least is dying, but we shall all come to desperate straits, you see.'

'Excuse me, I did not know,' the cobbler said, alarmed.

'I have been assassinated,' sobbed out the other.

'Be quiet, he may hear you; what can you expect from him?' And he took the last sip of the bluish wine left in the bottom of the tumbler.

Don Crescenzio fled. Now at intervals he felt his head going, and he needed to say the word 'Wednesday' to gather himself together. Still, instinctively, with that automatic style of moving of unhappy people who go to meet their destiny, he went up by Porto Alba again towards Bagnara Lane, where Professor Colaneri lived. He, too, owed him money, and promised to give it week by week, but had always sent him away with empty hands or put him off with small sums. The ex-priest lived on the fourth-floor of a house in Bagnara Lane, with an unlucky clear-starcher who had given heed to his blandishments and passed for his wife. They had four unhealthy children with big heads and crooked legs, and all lived in two rooms—quarrelling, crying, beating each other, and weeping all day. He had hidden from the clear-starcher that he had been a priest; the unlucky woman, thinking to become a lady, gave in to him, and for six years had lived in a state of servitude, between holding children and doing servant's work of the roughest kind amid indecent wretchedness, among that brood of ugly, howling, for ever hungry children, whom she avenged herself on by slaps for the blows her husband was liberal with towards her. It was a hellish house, where the father was always sulkily thinking over mean, sometimes guilty, methods of getting money for gambling. Twice Don Crescenzio had gone there, but he had been present at such disgusting scenes that he had rushed away, hunted out almost by the laundress's bad words and the four demons' howls. But now what did that matter? Colaneri owed him seven hundred francs and more; of a debt of nine hundred francs he had only paid two hundred in three or four months, or rather less. Colaneri, by Gad! was not ruined like Ninetto Costa, or apoplectic like Marzano—Colaneri must pay.

'Is Professor Colaneri at home?'

'Yes, sir,' an old woman who acted as door-keeper said.

Then he went up quickly; the laundress came to the door to open, unkempt, a greasy kitchen apron over a shabby dress. Her cheeks were fallen in, her breasts emaciated, and a tooth was wanting in front, through which she whistled a little.

'I would like to see Professor Colaneri.'

'He is not here,' she said quickly, leaving the other still outside.

'He is in—I know he is,' said Don Crescenzio in a rage. 'At any rate, it is no use denying it. I will wait for him on the stairs: he must come out some time.'

'Then come in,' she said unwillingly. As the lottery-keeper was coming in, a dirty boy with water on the head got a slap. Whilst he waited in the room that served as a parlour, study and dining-room, from beyond—that is to say, the kitchen, in the bedroom, and even the landing-place—cries burst out from the quarrelsome family. But in a silent interval the Professor came in, putting on an old jacket all spotted with grease, and setting his spectacles on his nose with an ecclesiastical gesture.

'I have come for my money,' Don Crescenzio said brutally.

'I have got none,' the debtor answered sulkily.

'That does not matter to me. You must give it to me.'

'I have no money.'

'Find some. I must have my seven hundred francs, you know.'

'I have not got it.'

'Give a lien on your salary: get a loan that way.'

'I have not got a salary now.'

'What! are you not a professor now?'

'No; I have been dismissed from my post.'

'What! are you dismissed?'

'Yes—turned out by force. I was accused of selling the examination papers to the students.'

'It was not true, of course?'

'Of course not. But the plot to ruin me was well arranged. The Senate advised me to resign.'

'So you are on the pavement?'

'Yes; I am destitute.'

Then only Don Crescenzio noticed that Professor Colaneri's face was pallid and distorted. But this third disappointment enraged him.

'I don't know what to do to you; you must give me the seven hundred francs, at any rate.'

'Have you got five francs to lend me?'

'Don't talk nonsense! I want my money—for to-morrow at latest, mind.'

'Crescenzio, you are putting a man already on the rack to torture.'

'That is fine chatter. I can't go to San Francesco on your account. You are so many murderers. I go to Costa for money, and find that he has failed—that he is going off to Rome, to do he knows not what. If it is true, he is going to Rome ... and I get no money. I go to Marzano, and find him half dead. Here you tell me you are on the pavement and have no money.'

'We are all ruined—all of us,' muttered the ex-priest.

'Well, you all want to kill me, do you? But when you needed credit I gave it to you ... and now you want to kill me and my family! But you have got sons also; you must think about feeding them—to-morrow and every other day; you ought to do something. You will think of me—think of my babies—think that we are Christians, too!'

'Do you know what I must do to-morrow to give my little ones bread?'

'What do I care? I know you will give it to them. I know that my children are not to go fasting while yours get their food.'

'Well, listen: I am not a priest now; I have been excommunicated, I am outside the pale of the Church; therefore I will get no help there. I had a professor's post, a good safe thing, but I have lost it; I needed money too much. Don't ask me for sad confessions. I will not get my post again, nor any other; I am a marked man.'

'But what is the use of telling me about these sorrows? I know about them. I know they will do my affairs no good.'

'Look here, then: I have no outlook; now, as I have put unlucky beings into the world, I feel that it is my duty to give them bread—at least that. I have gambled away on the lottery what they had as a certainty, an unfailing resource; but it is folly to think of that. Therefore I have taken the great decision, once for all.'

'What are you referring to?' asked Don Crescenzio, much astonished.

'To-morrow I am going to accept the offer the Evangelical Society has made me. I will become a Protestant pastor.'

'Oh, God!' said the lottery-keeper, astonished above measure.

'As you say,' said the other, gulping as if he could hardly swallow.

'And you will give up our religion?'

'I am leaving it through hunger.'

'And that other ... do you believe in it?'

'No, I do not.'

'And how will you set about preaching?'

'I will do it; I will get accustomed to it.'

'You will have to abjure, will you?'

'Yes, I have to do that.'

'Will it be a grand ceremony?'

'A very grand one.'

They spoke in a whisper, and Colaneri's cynical face was distorted, as if he could not stand the idea of abjuring. Don Crescenzio, too, in his astonishment, had forgotten his sorrow.

'You have got to apostatize?'

'Yes, I must apostatize.'

'Well, your priest's orders have been taken from you.'

'Still, to deny the faith is a different thing,' said Colaneri darkly.

'Then, it distresses you very much to do it?'

'I hate to do it.'

'How much will you gain by it?'

'Two hundred francs a month in some village they will send me to.'

'It is hardly enough for bread.'

'To each of my boys that turn Protestant they will give a small sum. I will be able to marry their mother.'

'But to have to leave Christ's religion!' exclaimed Don Crescenzio, with that horror of Protestantism that is in all humble Neapolitan consciences.

'What would you have? It is hunger drives me to it,' Colaneri muttered desperately.

He seemed now altogether changed, even in his character; it was clear to him now how fatal his rage for gambling had been; he saw what he had done against himself and his own gifts, and he felt an unconquerable distaste for that apostasy. He had done wicked things; he had descended to crime, even, of a coarse kind, having got corrupted in that unhealthy atmosphere; but now he found the punishment in front of him, he trembled and lost all his bravery; he trembled at having to deny his faith, his God, for a loaf of bread.

Don Crescenzio looked at him and said nothing, amazed. He had always thought Colaneri a scoundrel, and, if he had given him credit, it was only because he thought he could seize his salary. But now, on this decisive day, he saw him cast down, moved to his inmost soul by an awful fear of the Divinity he had already betrayed and insulted, whom he was again outraging by his apostasy. Don Crescenzio, although small-minded, felt the agony of that conscience that was now fighting in its last outpost, having got to the stage where human endurance ends, the hardest, most wearing hours in life. So he dared not say anything more to him about the money. He stammered:

'Your wife—what does she say?'

'She would like to prevent me doing it, except for the children's sake.'

'The poor children, must they lose their souls also?'

'They are innocent. The Lord sees; He will be just. Besides, why has He set me with my back to the wall? For each child that enters the Protestant Church they give me a small sum.'

'When will this come off?' Don Crescenzio asked, after hesitating.

'In a month. A month of instruction is needed for the poor innocents.'

'It will be too late for me,' the other said in a low tone, still thinking of his money.

'I will give you a receipt if you like, then.'

'It is too late. I am ruined.'

'What a punishment—what a punishment!' the apostate said, hiding his face in his hands.

'I am going away,' Don Crescenzio said, prostrate now, in a state of utter depression.

'Be patient.'

'What is the use of patience? it is a punishment! You spoke the truth just now: it is a chastisement! I am going away; good-bye.'

They did not look at each other nor say another word; both of them felt seized and cowed by the frightfulness of the punishment, not feeling any more rage or rancour in that breaking-down of all pride and vanity that the Divine chastisement brings. When he was on the stairs, Don Crescenzio was seized with such faintness that he had to sit down on a step, and stay there confused, neither seeing nor hearing in that moral numbness that comes on after great excitement. How long did he stay there? In the end, it was the step of someone going up and brushing past him that roused him, and with that start all his frightful pain came back unbearably. He rushed downstairs helter-skelter, and ran through the streets like one in a dream, urged on as if someone with a straight, unbending weapon were pushing him with the point. He got to Guantai Street, to the little inn, Villa Borghese, a resort of country people, where for four months past Trifari had lived with his father and mother, who had left their village at his bidding. The two humble peasants had managed, from youth to old age, to put some pence together and buy some bits of land by working eighteen hours a day and eating stale black bread, being content with beet soup cooked in water, with no salt, and sleeping all in one large room, with only a bed and a chest in it, upon a straw pallet; and this they bore for the sake of making their son a doctor, handing on to him all their peasant's vanity, making him have an unbounded longing to be a gentleman, a great man, superior to everyone in the country-side, so giving him, unknowingly, that rage for gambling that, according to him, was to make him grow rich suddenly, very rich, so as to crush everyone with his power and luxury.

But in a few years his whole professional career was ended, for he scorned it and gave it up; he had begun to lead a life of shameless indebtedness, expedients, and dodges. He had begun by deceiving his parents, and had ended by weaving for himself nets of intrigues and embarrassments. His father and mother gloomily, in the silence of their peasant souls that know of no outlet, had sold off everything gradually, going on sacrificing themselves for this son that was their idol, whom they adored because he was made of better clay than themselves. They were at last so reduced, so chastened in their pride, they waited in their old house for their son to send them ten of twenty francs now and then for food. And he did it; bound to his old folk by a fierce love made up of filial instinct and gratitude, he shivered with shame and grief every time they told him, resignedly, that in spite of being well on in years they would have to go back to work in the fields to earn their daily bread, so as not to be a burden upon him. But these helps had got to be less frequent; the rage for gambling blinded him so he could not even take ten francs off his stakes to send to the unlucky peasants. The finishing stroke was when he wrote imperiously, ordering them to sell the last house they had left, the old home with its sparse furniture and kitchen utensils, to bring the money and come and live in Naples with him; they would spend less there, and be more comfortable.

It was a dreadful blow, for these unhappy folk held so to the habit, now become a passion, of living in their own house and village, and the very word Naples frightened them. Still, saying not a word of their sufferings, they kept up their pride, told the villagers they were going to live as gentlefolk with their gentleman son at Naples, and had obeyed. They had haggled for a long time over the price of the old house and those few bits of old furniture they got at the time of their marriage; but at last, hoarding up the few hundred francs they had got for them carefully in a linen bag, and travelling third class, they got to Naples, frightened, not sad, but buried in that dumbness that is the only sign of a peasant's ill-humour.

They had lived four months at that inn, in two dark rooms; for they were on the first-floor with their son, who always came in at a very late hour, sometimes when they were getting up. They had no occupation, and never spoke to each other; staying up in their own room, they looked with melancholy, surprised eyes on all the extraordinary Naples people that moved about in that narrow, populous road, Guantai Nuova. They stayed hours and hours, wrapt up in gazing on a sight that stupefied them; but they were incapable, however, of making any complaint, though they were suspicious of everything, of the spring bed, of the bad, greenish glass of the mirror, of the miserable dinners served in their own rooms. As it was a thing they were not accustomed to, they thought they were living in unheard-of luxury. They disliked the servants, who scoffed at the two peasants, and the washerwoman, who brought back their coarse shifts all in holes, and loaded them with abuse in the true Naples style if they made any remarks.

Sometimes, getting over their instinctive shyness about speaking, they told their son to take them away from the inn and hire a small house, where his mother would cook and do the house-work; but he pointed out to them that would require too much money, and they would do it later, when he had got the fine fortune he was expecting from day to day.

In the meanwhile, their fortune grew smaller, and every time they loosened the linen purse at the end of the week, their hearts gave a twinge. Often, when they pulled out the money, they saw their son's eyes brighten up, as if an irresistible love-longing filled them; but he never asked them for it—one could see he put a check on himself not to ask. But each day he became gloomier, wilder; he no longer ate with his parents, and spent his nights outside, not coming back to the inn, so that even into these peasants' dull minds had come the idea of some danger threatening.

The mother told her beads for hours, that the Lord would have pity on their old age; whilst the father, being sharper, and more experienced, thought that perhaps some bad woman was making his son unhappy. But they said nothing to him; even the luxury they lived in, as they thought, although they paid for it themselves, seemed to them a condescension on their son's part, a favour he did his parents. Like him, without understanding or knowing why, they began to hope for this fortune that was to turn up, some day or another, to make them gentlefolk. The old peasant-woman's purple lips were constantly moving, saying prayers, in the small, mean, dark room of the Guantai Street hotel, whilst the old man went out every day, going always the same road, that is to say, into Municipio Square, and from there to the Molo, to gaze at the blackish sea, the ships in the mercantile port, and the men-of-war in the military one; he was fascinated and struck only with that in all the great town, going nowhere else, knowing nothing of the rest of Naples, being afraid of the noise of carriages, and dreading thieves perhaps. He retraced his steps slowly, looking round him suspiciously.

They never went out with their son—never, as they were just peasants and so dressed. They always refused when he feebly invited them to go out with him, guessing, in spite of their dulness, that it would not please him to show himself with them. He was so handsome, such a gentleman, in his great-coat and tall hat. But one evening he came in more excited than usual. Quickly, in rather a hard voice, such as he had never used to them, Dr. Trifari told his parents that his business, his big affair, his plan for getting rich, in short, required money to be laid out, so they should hand him over these last few hundred francs they were keeping in reserve; do him this last great sacrifice, and he would give it all back a hundredfold. He spoke quickly, with his eyes down, as if he did not wish to intercept the dreadful, chilled, despairing look the two peasants exchanged, feeling struck to the heart, frozen. The father and mother held their tongues, looking on the ground; then he, speaking quicker, in an anxious tone, trying to soften his harsh voice, implored and implored, begging them, if they loved him, to give him the money if they did not want to see his death. They, without making any remark, glanced assent at each other, and with senile, quivering hands the father undid the linen bag and took out the money, counting it slowly and carefully, starting again at each hundred francs, following the money with a troubled eye and a convulsive movement of the lower lip.

There were four hundred and twenty francs, the whole fortune of the three. Pale at first, the doctor got very red, his eyes filled with tears, and before either of them could stop him, he bent down and kissed his father's and mother's old brown, rugged, horny hands that had worked so hard. Not another word had been said between them, and he was gone. He did not come back to the hotel in the evening; but now they did not take any notice of his being absent. Still, the next day he did not come back to dinner; it was the first time it had happened. They waited till evening, but he did not come. The peasant woman told her beads, always beginning again; they ended by dining off a bit of bread and two oranges they had in their room.

Dr. Trifari did not come back the second night either, and it was about noon of the second day that a letter, with a half-penny stamp, by the local post, came, addressed to Signor Giovanni Trifari, Villa Borghese. Ah! they were peasants, with dull intellects and simple hearts; they never imagined things, or even thought much; they were curt, silent people. But when that letter was brought to them, and they recognised their son's well-known and loved writing, they both began to tremble, as if a sudden, overpowering palsy had come on. Twice or thrice, his rough spectacles shaking on his nose, with the slowness of a man not knowing how to read well, and having to keep back his tears, the old peasant read over his son's letter, in which, just before starting for America, he said good-bye to them filially and tenderly; and, feeling the gentle, terrible letter getting well printed on her mind, the old woman kissed her beads and gave a low groan. Twice an inn servant came in, with the sceptical look of one accustomed to all the chances and changes of life. He asked them if they wanted anything to eat; but they, blind, deaf, and forgetful, did not even answer. When, towards six o'clock, Don Crescenzio came in, after knocking fruitlessly, he found them, almost in the dark, seated near the balcony in perfect silence.

'Is the doctor here?'

Neither of the two answered, as if death's stupor had overcome them.

'I wished to know if Dr. Trifari was here.'

'No, sir, he is not,' the old father said.

'Has he gone out?'

'Yes, he is out.'

'How long has he been absent?'

'He has been away a long time,' the old peasant muttered, and a groan from his wife echoed him.

'When is he coming back?' shouted Don Crescenzio, very agitated, taking an angry fit.

'I can't tell you; we don't know,' the old man said, shaking his head.

'You are his father; you must know.'

'He did not tell me.'

'But where is he gone? Where is that scoundrel gone?'

'To America—to Buenos Ayres.'

'Good Lord!' Don Crescenzio just managed to bring out, falling full weight on a chair.

They said no more. The mother devoutly clutched her rosary. But both Trifari's parents seemed so tired that Don Crescenzio felt desperate, finding everywhere different forms of misfortunes, and greater ones than his own. Still, he clutched at a straw; above everything, he wished to know all about it, with that bitter enjoyment a man feels in tasting the full agony of his misfortune. He, too, had fled, then; he, too, had escaped him; that money, too, was lost—lost for ever.

'But who gave him the money to get away?' he cried out in an exasperated tone.

'Are you really friendly to him?'

'Yes, yes, I am.'

'Truly are you?'

'Yes, I tell you.'

'Here is his letter. Take it; you will find out from it.'

Then by the faint light of fading day he read the unhappy man's long letter. Eaten up by debts and his ruling passion, not knowing where to lay his head, he wrote to his parents, taking leave of them on going to make his fortune in America. Of the four hundred francs it had taken about three hundred and fifty to pay for a third-class ticket on a steamer, counting in a few francs for his keep the first two or three days in Buenos Ayres. He owned up to everything. He was the cause of his own ruin and of his family's. He cursed gambling, fate, and himself, swearing at bad luck and his own bad conscience. He sent back a few francs to the two poor old folks, begging them to go back to their village, to get on as well as they could, until he was able to send them something from Buenos Ayres. He told them to go home, and he would not forget them, and the money would just serve for two third-class fares to their village; nothing would be left over to buy food even. He begged them on his knees to forgive him, not to curse him. He had not had the courage to kill himself, for their sakes; still, he begged them to forgive him. Though he was leaving them like this, he implored them not to give him a curse as a parting provision on this wretched journey of his. He was starting with no luggage or money, and would be cast into the ship's common sleeping-place. The letter was full of tenderness and rage: abuse of the rich, of gentlemen and Government, came alternately with prayers for forgiveness and humble excuses.

Don Crescenzio read twice over that agonized letter written by a man enraged at himself and mankind, feeling himself wounded in the only tender feeling of his life. He folded it absent-mindedly, and looked at the two old people. It seemed to him that they were centenarians, falling to pieces from decrepitude and hard work, bent by age and sorrow.

'What are you going to do now?' he asked in a whisper, after a short time.

'We are going to our village,' the old man muttered. 'To-morrow we will go by the first train.'

'Yes, yes, we are going back,' the poor old woman groaned, without looking up.

'What are you to do there?' he rejoined, wishing to find out the full extent of all that misfortune.

'We are to work by the day in the fields,' said the old man simply.

He examined the two, so old, tired, and bent, now making ready to begin life again so as to get bread, to dig the ground with shaking arms, bending their brown faces and sparse white hair, under the summer sun. Struck to the heart by this last blow, feeling the chorus of misfortune growing around him, he did not open his mouth about the money he was to have got from Trifari; indeed, feverishly, he felt such pity for the two old folk that he said to them:

'Can I do anything for you?'

'No, no, thank you,' the two said, with the despairing gestures of those who expect no more help.

'Keep up your courage, then.'

'Yes, yes, thank you,' they muttered again.

He left them without saying more. It was night now when he went down into the street. For a moment, feeling confused and dismayed, he thought, Where was he to go? Anew, set along by quite a mechanical goad, he took courage, and, crossing Toledo Street, went up to the high part by San Michele Church, where the Rossi Palace stood out dark and lofty. In that mansion lived the last of those largely indebted to him, the most desperate of all. So as not to have a bad omen at the beginning of the day, he had kept them to the last. But he had found money nowhere; and now, with the natural rebound of the unhappy who fight against their misfortunes by that strength of hope which never dies, now he began again to believe that Cesare Fragalà and the Marquis di Formosa would give him the money in some way—that it might rain down from heaven.

When he went into Cesare Fragalà's flat, led across an empty dark room by little Agnesina, who came to open the door, carrying a half-burnt candle, he had at once regretted he had come. Husband, wife and daughter were seated at a small table, with a cloth too small for it, taking their supper silently, looking at every little bit of fried liver they put in their mouths for fear of leaving too little for the others. The child especially, having a healthy youthful appetite, measured her mouthfuls of bread so as not to eat too much of it. Cesare Fragalà sat very solemnly, all traces of a smile having gone from his face, and looked at the tablecloth with his brows knit. His wife, the good Luisella, with her big black eyes, on whose brow the happy mother's diamond star had shone, had now a humble, subdued look in a plain stuff gown. Quietly with her calm eyes the child looked serenely, with a martyr's patience, at the visitor, as if she understood and expected the request he was about to make. Before that gentle, thoughtful child's eye Don Crescenzio felt his tongue tied, so it was with an effort he stammered out:

'Cesare, I am come about that business.'

A flame of fire burned in Cesare's cheeks. The wife gave up eating, and the child cast down her eyelids as if the blow were coming on her own head.

'It is difficult for me to do anything for you, Crescenzio; you don't know all our embarrassments,' Cesare said faintly.

'I do know—I know,' said the other, hardly able to keep down his feelings; 'but I am in a worse state than you are.'

'I don't believe you can be,' muttered the merchant, who had gone through the bankruptcy court a few days before, in a dreary tone; 'I don't think you can be.'

'Your honour is safe, Cesare, but I am not to save mine. What can I say? I add nothing more.'

And, not able to bear it any longer, feeling Agnesina's sympathetic eyes on him, he began to weep. A little evening breeze coming from a half-shut balcony made the lamp quiver. It was a fantastically wretched group, the husband, wife, and daughter clinging to each other, all most unhappy, looking at that wretched man sobbing.

'Could we not give him something, Luisella?' Cesare timidly whispered in his wife's ear, while the other mourned vaguely.

'How much do you owe him?' said Luisa thoughtfully.

'Five hundred francs ... it was more. I paid part of it.'

'Was it a gambling debt?' she asked coldly.

'Yes, it was.'

'What was he saying about honour?'

'He gave us credit. If he is not paid, Government will have him put in prison.'

'Has he children?'

'Yes, he has.'

She went out of the room. The two men looked sadly at each other, and the girl gazed at them both with her kindly, encouraging eyes. After a little Luisa came back looking rather pale.

'This is our last hundred-franc note,' she said, in her pleasant voice. 'There is only a little small change left for ourselves; but the Lord will provide.'

'God will provide,' the child repeated, taking the hundred-franc note from her mother's hands and giving it to Don Crescenzio.

Ah! at that moment, before these poor people, who counted their mouthfuls of bread, who stinted themselves of the last remnant of their money to help him; at that moment, in the midst of sad, gentle expressions on the faces of ruined folk, who still kept faith and compassion, he felt his heart break; he shook as if he was going to faint. For a minute he thought of not taking the money; but it seemed to him charmed, made sacred by passing through that good woman's hands and the brave little girl's. He only said quiveringly:

'Forgive me, forgive me for taking it.'

'It is nothing,' Cesare Fragalà said at once, with his easy good-nature.

'You are so kind, so kind,' Crescenzio muttered, as he took leave, looking humbly at the two—the woman and the child—who bore misfortune so bravely.

Cesare went out of the room with him.

'I am sorry it is so little,' he said; 'it won't do you any good.'

'It is worth a hundred thousand, as far as the heart is concerned!' the lottery-keeper exclaimed sadly. 'But I have to give four thousand six hundred francs to Government, and this is all I have got.'

'Have the others given you nothing?'

'Nothing. I found nothing but misfortunes and bad luck everywhere. I am going up to the Marquis di Formosa's now.'

'Don't go there,' said Fragalà, shaking his head; 'it is no use.'

'I will try.'

'Don't try for it. They are worse off than we are. They dread every day they will lose Lady Bianca Maria. Her father has lost his senses.'

'Who knows? I might get it.'

'Listen to me: don't go. You might come in for some ugly scene.'

'Some ugly scene! What do you mean?'

'Yes, the Marchesina gets convulsions; she cries out frightfully in them. Every time we hear her we leave the house. She cries out always, "Mother! Mother!" It is agonizing.'

'Is she mad?'

'No, she is not. She calls for help in her fits. They say that she sees.... Don't go there; it is no use. Do what is right.'

'Very well. Thank you,' said the other.

They embraced, as sad and excited as if they were never to see each other again.

Now, when Don Crescenzio got to the Rossi Palazzo entrance, after hurriedly going downstairs almost as if he feared to hear the Lady Bianca

Maria Cavalcanti's dying cries behind him—when he got out on the street alone, amid the people going and coming from Toledo Street that soft spring evening, he suddenly thought it was all over. The hundred francs his weeping had dragged from the Fragalàs' wretchedness was shut up in his otherwise empty purse in his great-coat pocket. Just there he felt something like an increasing heat, for that money was really destiny's last word. He would get no more; all was said. His desperate resolutions, his growing emotion, his day's struggle, running, panting, speaking, telling his wrongs, weeping, and the great dread of ruin tarrying with him, had done nothing but drag the last mouthful of bread from his most innocent debtor. A hundred francs—a mockery to the sum he had to pay on Wednesday, without fail. A hundred francs, no more; a drop of water in the desert. He felt it, for he had used up a lot of strength and excitement, and had only managed to drag these few francs from the Fragalà family's honesty; so he felt flabby, weak, and exhausted. That was the last word. Then there was no more money for him; he must look on himself as ruined—ruined, with no hope of salvation. A cloud—perhaps it was tears—swam before his eyes. The flow of the crowd took him to the bottom of Toledo Street; he let himself be carried along. He felt that he was the prey of destiny, with no strength to resist; he was like a dry leaf turned over by the whirlwind. He could do nothing more—nothing; all was ended. Some other people still owed him money. Baron Lamarra, Calandra the magistrate, and two or three others owed him small sums. But he did not want to go to them even; it was all useless, all, since, wherever he had gone, wherever he had taken his despair, he had found the marks of a scourge like his own—the gambling scourge— that had sent them all to wretchedness, shame, and death like himself.

He dared not go back to his home now, though it was getting late. He had gone down by Santa Brigida and Molo Road to Marina Street, where he lived in one of those tall, narrow houses one reaches by gloomy alleys from Porto, which look on to rather a dull sea between the Custom-house and the Granili, and from Marina Road, where fishermen's luggers and boats are anchored and tied up. Among the thousands of windows he gazed at the lighted-up one where his wife was putting the babies to bed. But he dared not go in—no. Was it not all ended? His wife would read the sentence, the condemnation, in his face, and he could not bear that. An increasing feebleness took hold of him; he felt as if his arms and legs were broken, and in the darkness and silence—where only the cabs taking travellers to the evening trains, only the trams going to the Vesuvian districts, gave a touch of life to the dark, broad Marina Road—not able to stand, he sat down on one of the seats in the long, narrow Villa del Popolo, the poor folk's garden that goes along the seashore. From there he still saw, though further off in the distance, like a star, the lighted window in his little home. How could he go in to bring tears and despair into that peaceful, happy little atmosphere! That innocent infant and the other about to come into the world, the mother so proud of her husband, of her little boy: must he—*he*—make them quiver with grief and shame that evening? This would be unbearable for him. How tremendous a punishment it was, falling on everyone's head, as if all were accursed, and destroying health, honour, fortune, everything!

In a dream, going on from one thing to another, he knit together all the threads of that chastisement that started from himself and returned to him, going on from his despair to that of others, while he still gazed at the slight beacon where his family were waiting for him. He saw again Ninetto Costa's pale, worn face, setting out for a much longer journey certainly than to Rome, leaving his mother a bankrupt suicide's name; he saw Marzano the advocate struck with apoplexy, his lips bloated, amid the frightful wretchedness that left no money to buy more ice, whilst a dishonouring accusation had been made against him, shaming his gray hairs; then Professor Colaneri, chased away from the school, accused of having sold his conscience as a teacher, and, after having cast off the clerical robe, now obliged to give up the religion he was born in, of which he had been a priest; he saw Dr. Trifari sailing in an emigrant ship, without a farthing, short of everything, while his old parents had to go back to dig the hard earth so as to earn their living; and Cesare Fragalàs resigned surrender, which ended the name of the old firm, and left him to confront a future of wretchedness. Finally, above everything, the illness Lady Bianca Maria Cavalcanti was dying of, while her father had not a bit of bread to put in his mouth. All, all were being punished, great and small, nobles and common folk, innocent and guilty, and he with them—he and his family, struck in all he held dearest—his means, home, happiness, and honour—a band of unfortunates, where the innocent were the ones that had to weep most, where little infants, girls, and women paid for grown men's mistakes, and old people, too—a band of wretched ones—to whom, in his mind, he added others that he knew and remembered. Baron Lamarra, with the accusation of forgery held over him by his wife, had gone back to work as a contractor, in the sun on the streets, among buildings in course of construction; and Don Domenico Mayer, the hypochondriacal official, who one day in despair, not being able to move for debt, had thrown himself from a fourth-floor window, dying at once; and Calandra the magistrate, who had twelve children, was so badly reported on that every six months he ran the chance of being put on the shelf; and Gaetano the glover, who had killed his wife Annarella with a kick on the stomach when she was two months gone with child: but no one knew anything about it except his children, who hated their father, as every Friday he promised to kill them also, if they did not give him money. All—all of them were at death's door, yet living on, amidst the pinching of need and the canker of shame. And he, finally, who had his family there in the little house waiting, while he had not the courage to go back, feeling that the first announcement of their misfortune would burn his lips. It was all one chastisement, one frightful punishment—that is to say, the hand of the Lord bearing heavily on the wicked, the guilty, and striking them to the seventh generation; or, rather, the same sin, the same guilt, that infamous, cursed gambling, had got to be an instrument of chastisement against those who had made an idol of it; for the gambling passion, like all others that are outside of life and real things, had the germ, the seed of bitter repentance, in the vice itself. They were struck where they had sinned, or, rather, by the sin itself. It was just one long burst of weeping from all eyes, even the purest ones, a burst of sobs from the cleanest lips; a crowd of poor, honest, innocent creatures struggling amidst hunger and death, paying for others' mistakes, giving the guilty the remorseful thought that they had cast the people they loved best into this great abyss. Not one safe, not one, of those who had given up their life to gambling, to infamous, wicked gambling, that eater-up of blood and money. Not even he or his family were safe; he, too, was broken; his children were to be reduced to holding out their hands. The punishment was too great; it was unbearable. What had he done to have to go to prison like an evil-doer, that his wife should be ashamed of belonging to him, and his children would never mention his name? What had he done to have to stay there in the street like a beggar, who dare not go back to his den, having got no alms from hard-hearted men? Ah! it was too much, too much! What fault had he committed?

A couple of policemen went through Marina Street, and cast searching glances into the darkness of the footpaths in Villa del Popolo; but the shadows were deep, and the men did not notice Don Crescenzio lying at full length on a seat. But he, by a quick change of scene, saw before him his lottery shop in Nunzio Lane, on glowing Friday evenings and anxious Saturday mornings, when the gamblers crowded to the three wickets in his shop, their eyes lighted up by hope, their hands quivering with emotion. He saw again the placards in blue and red letters that incited gamblers to bring more money to the lottery. He saw again the number of advertisements of Cabalists' newspapers and the mottoes: 'So you will see me'; 'It will be your fortune'; 'The people's treasure'; 'The infallible'; 'The secret unveiled'; 'The wheel of fortune.' He remembered the medium's frequent visits and his fatal intimacy with all the other Cabalists, spiritual brothers, and mathematicians, who excited the gamblers with their strange jargon and impostures. He saw it again at Christmas and Easter weeks, when the gambling became wild, fierce; for people have such a longing to get into the long-dreamt-of Land of Cockayne. And he always saw himself pleased with their illusions that ended in a sad disappointment; pleased that that mirage should blind the weak, the foolish, the sick, the poor, the sanguine—all those who live for the Land of Cockayne; pleased that everyone should get the infection, that no one was safe; quite delighted when, at great festivals, the rage increased and the stakes augmented his percentage. He saw it all clearly: his own figure bending to write the cursed ciphers and the lying promises in the ledger, the gamblers' crimson or pale faces distorted by passion. He bowed his head, crushed, feeling he had deserved the punishment, he himself, his family, on to the seventh generation. The lottery was a disgrace that led to illness, wretchedness, prison—every sort of dishonour and death. And he had kept a shop for the infamous thing!

CHAPTER XX
BIANCA MARIA CAVALCANTI

For three days in the Marquis di Formosa's house a deep silence had reigned. The doors, oiled in their hinges and locks, shut and opened with no noise. The two old servants, Giovanni and Margherita, walked on tiptoe, not saying a word, like shadows gliding over the floor—or, rather, they made no movement. Giovanni, seated on the single straw chair that furnished the lobby, Margherita seated at the sick girl's bedside, gazing at the pale face sunk in heavy stupor in the sickly slumber of high fever, both kept quite still. The doctor, some sort of a medical man, called in from Berriolas', the neighbouring druggists, said that above everything any noise would have a bad effect on the patient's brain, and at once in the house every sound, even sighs, were hushed. Not a word was said above the breath, for those old servants were accustomed to being silent and motionless. It looked already as if they had been overtaken by the long last rest. Then the doctor asked for the family practitioner. When they mentioned Dr. Amati's name, he at once proposed to send for him. He needed him. The Marquis di Formosa's anxious face got icy, and the two servants looked just as sorrowful. Then he suspected something, shook his head, and set to treating the patient himself, covering her burning head with ice, giving her quinine every two hours to try and bring down the high fever, the raging typhoid, giving her strong nourishment, but without making any improvement, never managing to overcome the state of coma she was in, except by raising a queer delirium, mingled with spasmodic nervous convulsions; for the blood-poisoning by typhoid was complicated by serious nervous disorders.

'What do you say about it, doctor—what is your verdict?' asked the Marquis di Formosa on the stair landing.

'If it was only typhoid there might be some hope; but the whole nervous system is overthrown. We run the risk of meningitis. I tell you again, you must call Dr. Amati in; he knows the patient.'

'It is impossible to do so,' the Marquis answered sharply.

'Then I do not answer for the consequences,' said the other, going off.

Going back into his daughter's room, the Marquis di Formosa stiffened his pride against the doctor's request, which tortured his fatherly heart. That man, who had taken his daughter's heart from him, would never enter his house again and bring his evil influence on her. Bianca Maria was young and strong; she would get over the illness. Thus he persisted in his haughtiness, and went back to sit at his sick daughter's bedside. He leant over that face that always got more bloodless, and called to his daughter just above his breath.

She was lying sunk in that torpor of typhoid, with a lump of ice on her motionless head, her hands joined as if in prayer, the usual attitude of typhoid patients. Still, she heard that breath of a voice. She did not answer, she did not open her eyes, but, with a slight contraction of her muscles, she drew her eyebrows together frowningly, as if annoyed; and her hand made a constant motion, always the same, obstinate, discouraging, to keep her father at a distance. He leant down again, hurt and offended, saying in a whisper that it was her father—her own father, who loved her so fondly, who wanted to make her well; he was the only person who really loved her.

But the bored expression got stronger on the poor invalid's face—the patient, as the doctor called her—and the slender, obstinate, uneasy hand went on driving away the Marquis di Formosa. The old man had difficulty in keeping down a rush of anger that rose to his brain, and he went to sit a little distance off, folding his arms across his breast, his head down, submitting, humbling himself. Margherita alone got an answer when she asked Bianca Maria anything—if she would drink any of that strong beverage, marsala, beaten up egg and soup, that is given to typhoid patients, or if she wanted the ice-bag changed. The girl, without opening her eyes, answered either way by a wave of her slight hand. And the Marquis di Formosa was obliged, if he wished to know anything, to watch the old waiting-woman's face. At certain times, in despair at that obstinate ostracism, he went out of Bianca Maria's room and began to walk up and down in the drawing-room; but often his excited footsteps made too much noise, and Margherita's worn face came to the doorway. He stood still. She made him a sign to be quiet; the noise did harm to Bianca Maria.

'Here, too, do I annoy her?' he asked, quivering.

And as Margherita agreed, 'Yes, it was true,' even in the distance he made her suffer, to keep down a feeling of rage, he took his hat and went out of the house. Then the flat fell back again into its great stillness; Giovanni slumbered sadly in the hall, whilst Margherita leant over the invalid's pallid, burning face to breathe out some gentle word to her. Making an effort, the poor girl smiled for a single minute, and the old servant, satisfied, went back to her chair, muttering words of prayer to herself, without taking her eyes off Bianca Maria.

Very, very late, after having wandered through the streets, tiring himself by walking, ill-dressed, unbrushed, having lost all care for his appearance, quite unrecognisable, the Marquis di Formosa came home to find the door open, as if they had heard his footsteps from a distance. Margherita came up to him in the dark with her ghost-like step.

'How is she?' he asked.

'Just the same,' she sighed out.

'What does the doctor say?'

'He orders ice and quinine. He again asked for Dr. Amati to be sent for.'

'I told you never to mention that scoundrel's name!'

'Hush!' she hissed out respectfully, and she went away.

The Marquis was seized by so profound an anguish that, the old faith rising again in his heart, he sought for a place to kneel down and pray the Lord that He would save his daughter, and free him from that agony. Alas! the small room used as a chapel at first, where Bianca Maria and he had prayed together so often, was empty: he, after having abused the saints and the Virgin, after having done the sacrilege of punishing Ecce Homo, had sold the saints, Virgin, and Ecce Homo to stake the money at the lottery. There were no more guardian saints in Cavalcanti House; the Virgin and her Divine Son had withdrawn their saddened eyes from insult. There was nothing left in that house, nothing. During these last days, throughout the poor girl's illness, they had lived on alms; that is to say, off some allowance inexhaustible pity of Gennaro Parascandolo the usurer's wife had granted to Margherita and Giovanni's tears and entreaties.

The Cavalcantis were holding out their hands for alms now! For many weeks he had had no money to stake, and he avoided Don Crescenzio's lottery bank, as he had not the many francs he owed him to give back; but when Friday came, though he knew they were reduced to private begging, knowing that what he did was a domestic crime, he came to Margherita to implore her to give him two francs, or only one, to gamble with. Only on that Friday, confronted by Bianca Maria's illness, he had not dared; he was struck incurably. That girlish body, stretched on what perhaps might be her death-bed; that head crushed down under the heavy bag of ice; that profile, pinched as if it was rubbed down by an inward hand; that eyebrow, that frowned on hearing his voice only; and that hand, that hand above all, that chased him away constantly, obstinately, a victim to a dumb, lively horror—all that had broken down the last energies of his old age.

Illnesses of old people make the old thoughtful and melancholy, but young people's illnesses frighten them as a thing against the order of Nature. Ah! in these moments of anguish, he felt so weak, so old, so worn-out, an organism with no vitality, a lamp with no oil. And shaking, trembling, not even looking towards his daughter's bed, he went to sit in his usual place, letting himself go, as if he had to sit there and wait for death.

Only one thing could give him back a flash of energy—that is to say, a flash of hatred—and it was the name of the loathed doctor, which was repeated from time to time by the new doctor or mentioned by his own servants, who referred to him in spite of his express orders against it. She, Bianca Maria, had never mentioned it. In the doleful convulsions that had come on before that typhoid she had raved at great length, cried out over and over again, calling for her mother, 'Mama, mama!' like a child in danger, like a lost child; nothing else. Vainly in these low ravings, in that confused muttering, that long, disconnected chatter, he had stretched his ears to hear his own name or the scoundrel's who had taken his daughter's heart from him. She had always called for her mother, no one else. And he trembled, shivered, in case of hearing that name coming from her lips, still keeping up in his old age and tiredness, in his growing weakness, that dull rage, that implacable hatred. Sometimes, when the delirium got higher and higher and haunted him, he ran away from the room, stopping his ears, always fearing she would call on that name. Outside he stood thus, waiting, undecided, and very agitated.

'What is she speaking about?' he asked Margherita when she, stupefied and frightened, came out of the room.

'She wants her mother,' the other muttered, crying silently, for it seemed to her a forerunner of death.

And the typhoid went on, finishing its first week, not yielding to the ice or the quinine, keeping always between a hundred and four and a hundred and five degrees, as if the mercury in the thermometer had stuck at that doleful figure, a funereal cylinder that nothing was of any use now to bring down.

'How much is it?' the old father made inquiry with anxious eyes from Margherita, who was looking at the thermometer held against the sick girl's burning skin.

'A hundred and four degrees,' she muttered under her breath with infinite despair.

Implacable figure! To bring down the fire that burned away Bianca Maria's blood and nerves, seeing that quinine taken by the mouth in large doses had no proper effect, quinine was now injected with a tiny, pretty silver syringe into the patient's arm. Not having the strength to open her eyes, she raised herself with difficulty, propped up on pillows, and held up in Margherita's arms, and her head shook, the black hair stuck to her temples, and dripped moisture from the chill of the ice-bag. They had to hold up her head, too, for it went from side to side. Then, baring the poor arms all dotted by the silver needle, a new burning, painful puncture was added to the others. She started, but only slightly, as if no pain was worse than that sleep. Sometimes she opened her eyes, and set them on Margherita's face, and they were so sad in their expression of weariness, so muddy in colour, dry, and indifferent now to all earthly sights, that a glance from them wrung the heart. It looked as if they had emptied out the fountain of tears. When her father and Margherita saw these doleful eyes in front of them, they gave a start.

'My child! my child!' the old man said to her, holding her hands.

Then she, disturbed and tired, lowered her eyelids at once, and sank anew into that stupefied state in which the only two signs of vitality were her laboured breathing and the high temperature. Very seldom did the quinine injections succeed in bringing down the high fever; there was a slight discouraging variation, nothing more.

Only on the morning of the tenth day she seemed, all of a sudden, in a better state. It was sleep instead of torpor, and in the comforting sleep a cold sweat ran over her forehead, which Margherita wiped off carefully. The poor old woman followed tremblingly every minute of that sleep, as if she guessed intuitively Bianca Maria's life was to depend on it; and while she said her prayers over mentally, her whole attention was fixed on the loved face sharpened by illness, that seemed to be getting back renewed brightness. Whilst the sound sleep lasted, Margherita's vigilant ear heard a noise in the flat. She got up on tiptoe and went out. It was the Marquis di Formosa coming in again, and he questioned her with his eyes anxiously.

'She is resting; she is better—she is much better,' muttered the poor old woman, putting a finger to her lips to enjoin silence.

The father's dry eyes filled with tears; it was the first good news in ten days' anguish and fears. He, too, went into his daughter's room, sitting down in his usual place, watching the thin face, where the great nervous tension seemed to have given way to a favourable crisis.

Margherita, so as not to disturb Bianca Maria's sleep, dared not make use of the thermometer to find out her temperature, but her heart told her the fever had certainly gone down. Then, both silent, she praying inwardly and the Marquis di Formosa fishing up some shreds of prayer from the depths of his clouded conscience, they spent two hours watching over the invalid's quiet sleep. It was dusk when she opened her eyes—the large eyes that had been shut for ten days by fever's burning, leaden hand, and at once Margherita leant over her, questioning her:

'How do you feel?'

To her astonishment, the girl, instead of answering with a wave of the hand or a nod, said in a very feeble voice:

'I am better.'

Also the Marquis di Formosa had come up beside the bed, and, quivering with joy, he said over and over again:

'My child! my child!'

'Do you want anything?' the waiting-woman asked, for the sake of hearing the feeble voice which had gone to her heart.

'No, nothing; I feel better,' the invalid whispered, with a sigh of relief from her unburdened breast.

Her father had taken hold of her hand, gazing affectionately at his daughter. And she, who for ten days had driven him away from her bed by her look and the waving of her hand, smiled on him this time. It was a flash of light. He could do nothing but stammer out:

'My child! my child!'

And Margherita went out of the room cheerfully, as if her young mistress were safe—safe for ever from the frightful danger she had gone through for ten days. The Marquis di Formosa had sat down at the head of the sick girl's bed, and, holding her slight hand in his, he felt his darling's fleshless fingers pressing now and then a little harder on his own, as a loving caress. Twice or thrice he leant over and asked, 'Would you like anything?' She had not replied, but that rapid flash of a smile had come back. It was night already, and faces could not be made out any longer, when, on a new question from her father, Bianca Maria replied: 'Yes, I do.'

'What do you want? Tell me at once!'

'I want the doctor at once,' she said.

'Do you feel ill?' the old man asked, misunderstanding her.

'No; I want Dr. Amati.'

Her father put his hand over the girl's on the coverlet, but he said nothing.

'Do you hear? I wish for Dr. Amati,' she repeated in a louder voice, that already had a quiver of annoyance in it.

'No, my dear, it cannot be,' he replied, trying to restrain himself, thinking of her illness, and remembering her danger.

'I want Dr. Amati,' she said in a loud voice, raising her head from the pillow with a peculiar motion. It seemed, indeed, to the old man that she had ground her teeth after having announced for the fourth time her strange demand.

'It is not possible, my dear,' he muttered, trying to hold in his own burning rage.

'Go and call Dr. Amati! Go at once!' she shouted, as if giving him an order.

'You are mad!' he cried out, rising from his seat. 'I will never go.'

'Yes, yes, you will!' she yelled, rising on the pillow, clutching at the sheet with her clenched hands; 'you will go at once, and bring him here directly. I want Amati beside me—always with me. Go at once!'

'No, no, I will not!' he shouted in his turn, not knowing what he was doing. 'He will never put a foot in here while I am alive.'

Margherita had run in, quite upset, in despair a second time, but still more despairing from the new turn the illness had taken. Hardly had Bianca Maria seen her, when she called out to her:

'Margherita, if you love me, go and call Dr. Amati.'

'I forbid you to; do you hear?' the old Marquis shrieked to the woman. He was so exasperated that his hands shook, his eyes gave out sparks.

'For goodness' sake, miss, do not get in such a state; remember you are talking to your father. Please, my lord, remember my lady is ill; she is not in her right mind.'

'I am not mad; I want Dr. Amati,' the girl still cried out, clenching her fists, grinding her teeth, rolling her eyes so convulsively that only the white of the eyeball could be seen.

'Holy Virgin! Holy Virgin!' Margherita went on sobbing out.

'For the love of God, if you are fond of me, go and call Dr. Amati!' the sick girl sobbed out, her head swaying about, sometimes rising from the pillow and falling back upon it.

'She is mad! she is mad!' shouted the old man, raving.

'My lord, go away outside; I beg of you, go away,' Margherita implored, seeing that his daughter fixed her eyes, now full of intense rage, then with keen sorrow, on her father, and that the sight of him made her still more frantic.

'I am going away—I am going away; but she will not see Dr. Amati!' he shouted, going outside, feeling he could bear it no longer.

But from the drawing-room, whither he had borne his anger, he heard a loud shriek, loud and agonizing, as if the patient were driving her nails into her flesh; and after that shriek another, lower, but equally agonizing, such a cry of unbearable sorrow quivered in it, and words spoken now loudly, now in low tones, that came to him confusedly. The girl had fallen into convulsions. Suddenly the sounds quieted down, and then, still trembling from a mixed feeling of rage, pity and fear, he went near the room; but he did not go in, merely calling Margherita to the door.

'How is she?'

'She is worse, much worse,' she said, weeping silently.

'But what is she saying?'

'She wants Dr. Amati.'

'That she will never get.'

These short discussions, however, though the invalid sank at intervals into a state of coma, were heard by her, and twice on coming out of that torpor the loud shrieks had burst out anew, with a quivering of all her muscles, especially with a frightful knotting together of the muscles in the nape of the neck. Throughout the cries that name, the name the poor thing had worshipped so long in secret, that name that had been for her the sign of salvation—that name came up again always obstinately in her delirium, proclaimed by the soul that knew no fetters now; imperiously, gently, despairingly, with such an outflow of love that Margherita and Giovanni, who ran in to keep down the hysterical girl's arms, felt their hearts breaking. From the other room, as the sick girl raised her voice, sometimes shrill, then deep, calling upon Dr. Amati, the Marquis di Formosa started and shuddered, with that obstinate, blind hatred of old people who cannot forgive. Vainly, vainly he tried to think of something else—not to hear, not to feel the despairing sorrow of that appeal. It was no use keeping down his head and stopping his ears, trusting to the farthest-off room in the house; that clamorous complaint still reached him persistently—nothing could be done to check it. It was a nightmare now, and in spite of the distance, in spite of closed doors, he heard clearly and distinctly the words of love and sorrow in which Bianca Maria called on Dr. Amati; the words got printed on his mind, and hammered on his brain like a persecution.

That went on for an hour and a half, and she did not quiet down nor stop speaking, finding new strength, nervous strength, to call, and call as if her voice, as if her calls, were to go through the wall, across the streets, were to get to the man she longed for to save her. Oh, that nightmare, that nightmare! to hear his daughter's ravings! She who had thrust him away from her bed, now was making desperate appeals to another man. Now and then, as if to put an end to that talking, imploring madness, he went close to the room door, and heard Margherita's level voice, as she held her mistress clasped in her arms, trying to calm her, whilst she went on as if she had no ear for other voices, as if she had to call for Dr. Amati until she saw him come into her room. And her old father went off wild and desperate, shaking with rage and anguish, not knowing what to do; now grovelling, now ferocious, still unsubdued; keeping up his hatred, not able to calm down, his blood boiling in his veins, and a shortness of breath oppressing him. But at a certain stage he heard the bell ring, and someone go into the flat, and then into Bianca Maria's room. Formosa stood still, motionless, astounded. Who had come in then?

When Margherita came into the room where he had taken refuge, and called him with a wave of her hand, he followed her meekly. Beside the sick girl's bed, holding her twitching arms and looking into her eyes, was the doctor in charge, Morelli, whom poor Margherita had called in. But Bianca Maria, even under the doctor's strong hands, even under his scrutinizing glance, went on trembling; her head rose convulsively from the pillow, her neck stretched forward, getting rigid, and then her head fell back again, worn out, still with a continued slight movement backwards and forwards, whilst unweariedly she went on saying, sometimes low, then shrilly, 'Amati ... Amati ... Amati ... I want Amati....'

'But what is the matter with her?' asked Formosa, clasping his hands, with tears in his eyes.

'She must have had some strong excitement two or three hours ago: had she not?'

'Yes, I fear so.'

'Was it from some alarm, some noise?'

'I ... I don't ... quite know.'

'Well, she got excited? Did she cry out?'

'Yes ... she did.'

'Why did you let her get excited? Why did you not let her have what she wanted? Do you know the danger your daughter is running?'

'I do not know ... I know nothing. What do you expect me to know?' the old man shouted, holding out his hands, beseeching like a child.

'The danger is of meningitis,' said the doctor through his clenched teeth.

Now the invalid had half opened her eyes. The doctor examined her pupils. Her eye seemed glassy, rigid, as her whole person had got.

'Doctor, what is it? is she dead?' yelled the old man, as if he were mad.

'It is temporary paralysis, from meningitis.'

'What is to be done?'

'Well, we will see. Meanwhile I beg you to have Dr. Amati called in.'

The old man looked at him, disordered.

'What do you say?'

'Send and call Amati. Do you not see she wants him?'

'... She is raving.'

'Yes, sir; but when she asked for him, she must have been conscious; and even in delirium you must obey her, my lord.'

'Am I to obey?'

'Your daughter is in a serious state; it is better to satisfy her.'

'Is she in danger?'

'You may lose her from one hour to another. She has no strength to bear up against meningitis.'

'Doctor, doctor, do not say that!'

'My dear sir, do you want me to tell you the truth, especially as the poor patient cannot hear us? First of all, you would not allow Amati to be called; then you let the young lady get into this state of exasperation.... You will not go on with this refusal? The girl is dying....'

'O holy God!' blasphemed the Marquis.

'I will go to Amati's house,' Morelli said.

'... He will not come.'

'Why should he not? Was he not the doctor in charge? He is an honest man; he is a great doctor.'

'... He will not come,' Formosa repeated.

'Then go yourself, my lord.'

Now, whilst Formosa made a despairing gesture, the sick girl had started up, and again rapidly through her clenched teeth she had begun to say: 'Amati! ... Amati! ... I want Amati!...'

'Do you hear?' said Morelli.

'But I cannot!' shouted Formosa, 'for I turned that man out of my house. I would not let my daughter marry him. I cannot humble myself to him.'

'Very well, but my lady is dying,' said the doctor, holding down the girl's hands, which were clapping together.

'Go and call Amati! For mercy's sake, for the love of God, do not give me up! Call Amati!' groaned the invalid.

'My God! what a punishment! what a punishment!' the old man cried out, tearing his hair. 'But, doctor, give her something; do not let her die!'

'... Amati! ... Amati! ... I want Amati!' she said, raving, rolling her eyes fearfully. Then, falling back again, worn out, on the bed with a fresh stroke of paralysis, the only living thing in her was her voice, asking for Amati; still the only idea of her wandering reason was Amati, Amati, Amati.

'I will write to him,' the old man said desolately, going to another room whilst the doctor was trying to put new ice on Bianca Maria's burning head.

The Marquis di Formosa was writing, but it was unbearable, the shame of having to give in, and the words would not come from his pen. He tore two sheets. At last a short letter came out, in which he asked Dr. Amati to come to his house, as his daughter was ill—nothing more. When he had to write the address he nearly smashed the pen. Then, not looking Giovanni in the face, he told him to run to Dr.—yes, to Dr. Amati's. The poor old thing ran, whilst Morelli gave calomel pills to his delirious patient, who was crying out, for the pain in her head had got unbearable, frightful. Her father, having carried out his first sacrifice, felt he was going mad with these howls, fearing lest he should begin to howl and howl like her, as if he had caught meningitis from her. Now that he had written the letter, carried out an unbearable sacrifice, the Marquis di Formosa began to wish that Dr. Amati would come soon, at least. It was impossible for him to bear these cries, laments, and groans any longer, where one name came up continuously. Now he was counting the minutes for Giovanni to come back, straining his ears if he heard the noise of a door opening. Time was passing, and the sick girl, in spite of ice, in spite of calomel, was raving, with glaring eyes, a prey to the inflammation that seemed to be burning up her brain. Here was a door opening; someone was coming towards the room where the Marquis di Formosa had taken refuge in his desperation. It was Giovanni alone, and he looked so tired, so old, so sad, that the Marquis shivered as he asked him:

'Well?'

'Dr. Amati is not coming.'

'Was he not at home?'

'He was not. I waited for him under the portico; then he came back....'

'Well, then, what happened?'

'He read the letter ... and he said he was too busy; that the young lady was sure to have a good doctor.'

'Did you not ... beg ... him to come.'

'I did, my lord. He got severe then, and went away muttering something that I did not understand.'

'You ought to have gone upstairs and insisted.'

'I had not the courage.'

'But do you not know my lady is dying for want of him? Do you not know that?'

'I do know it, my lord; but the doctor used me ill. I am a poor servant.'

'He is right,' said the old man slowly; 'I insulted him deeply.'

'My lord, my lord, go yourself; he will not refuse you.'

'You are mad.'

'For the young lady's sake.'

'He will refuse. He will insult me.'

'For her sake.'

'No, no; it is too much to expect....'

'But, my lord, you said it yourself: my lady is dying.'

'Go away!' shouted the Marquis brutally, driving his servant away.

He was left alone. His pride rebelled against the idea of humbling himself before the man he had abused. He suffered frightfully; his daughter's voice, now muttering in a low tone, now yelling shrilly, calling out 'Amati,' gave him a feeling of physical pain, of a red-hot iron scorching his flesh. Within him, however, as time passed, as the girl's danger increased, a work of clearing away was going on, in which all the old and the new rebellions of his haughty feelings went on tumbling down, and in place of the pride came a tremendous pity, a great affection, an immense sorrow. The hours flew by whilst he walked up and down, gnawing at the curb of the last chains in which his heart was bending, till at last it sank to the earth; and that eternal delirious voice which could say nothing but the name of Antonio Amati never ceased. He no longer shook with anger; hatred was silent, and when Dr. Morelli, having gone away and come back, asked for Amati, he replied:

'He has not come. I am going myself.'

'Will you bring him?'

'Yes, I will.'

It was very late, however, when he set out on foot to go to Santa Lucia Road, where Dr. Amati was now living. It was nearly midnight, and people had turned out in Toledo in the mildness of the April evening. In spite of being old, the Marquis ran through the streets, urged by a nervous force, and when he got to the big gateway of the palazzo Amati lived in, he went up the stairs rapidly, not giving any answer to the porter, who asked where he was going.

'Tell Dr. Amati that the Marquis di Formosa is here,' he told the housekeeper, who came to open the door to him.

'Really ... he is studying.'

'Tell him, I beg of you. It is very urgent ...' the old man implored; his pride was completely gone. She went off, and came back again at once, making the Marquis a sign to come in. He crossed two sitting-rooms, and came to a study all in shadow, where the lamp-light was concentrated on a large table scattered with papers and books. But Dr. Amati was standing in the middle of the room, waiting. These two men, who had hated each other so much, looked at one another, with the same sorrow they had in common, and pity for the unhappy dying girl cut short all rancour. They looked at each other.

'What is it?' Amati asked in a weak voice.

'She is dying,' said Formosa with a despairing gesture.

'Of what?'

'Of meningitis.'

An earthy pallor spread over the doctor's face, and two lines formed themselves about his lips. And he dared not make the Marquis any reproaches. Had he not himself forsaken the poor girl, though he had promised and sworn to save her? Had he not through pride left the delicate, sickly flower a prey to all moral and physical evils? Both of them were guilty, both.

'Let us start, then,' he said. They went out together, called for a cab, and had the hood put up, as if they wanted to hide their sorrow. They did not speak during the drive. Only whilst he bit at his spent cigar Dr. Amati from time to time asked some medical questions.

'How long has she had meningitis? is this the first day of it?'

'Yes; but she has had typhoid fever for nine days.'

'Had she high fever?'

'It went up to a hundred and four and a hundred and five.'

'Had she bad headaches?'

'Frightful headaches.'

'Did she have convulsions?'

'Yes, at intervals.'

'Does she roll her eyes about?'

'Yes, she rolls her eyes.'

'Do the muscles at the nape of her neck contract?'

'Yes, they do.'

'Was there some reason for it?'

'Yes,' said the father humbly, almost sobbing out his monosyllable.

'Did she get calomel?'

'Yes; Morelli gave that.'

'Did it not soothe her?'

'No, not a bit. Often she is paralyzed, but for a short time.'

'It is just meningitis,' the doctor muttered thoughtfully.

The carriage went on and on, as well as it could with an ordinary night horse. They were not getting there yet, and they had already urged the driver to hurry.

'Is she delirious?' the doctor asked again.

'I do not know—I am not sure if it is delirium; but she is always speaking convulsively.'

'What does she say?'

'She calls out for you.'

'For me?'

'Yes—always for you.'

Ah! the doctor's heart broke on hearing that. The old father heard him say, like a frightened prayer, 'My God!' They said nothing more. They found the door open. Poor old Giovanni had waited for them on the landing, leaning over the railing, looking into the entrance-hall, anxious to see them arrive, but certain that the doctor would come.

'How is she?' asked her father at once; he had a constant need of being reassured.

'Just as she is bound to be,' sighed the old butler, going on in front. 'She is much the same.'

'Is she still delirious?'

'Yes, still delirious.'

They went in very softly to the small room. Dr. Morelli had gone away a little while before, leaving a short note for Dr. Amati. But he went straight to the sick girl's bed. Her voice, tired now, but still impassioned, went on always repeating Amati's name, but her head was sunk in the pillows, and her eyes half shut. He saw everything at once, and the disorder of his mind must have been tremendous, for he could not manage to control his face— he, the strong, invincible man. And he hesitated a minute before replying to the unhappy, raving girl who went on calling to him, fearing to cause too strong an impression on her nerves; but he could not resist the feeble voice that went straight to his heart and made it bleed with tenderness; he said:

'Bianca Maria.'

What a cry the answer was! She got up, her face suddenly flaming; her eyes grew enormous. She threw her arms round his neck, and leant her head on his breast, crying out:

'Oh, my love! my love! how long you have been in coming! Do not leave me again—never forsake me; it is so long since I have been calling for you—do not leave me.'

'Do not fear; I will not leave you ...' he muttered, trying to overcome his emotion, petting her fine, ruffled, tumbled hair.

'Never go away from me again—never!...' she cried out passionately, clinging with her arms round his neck. 'If you forsake me I shall die.'

'Keep quiet, Bianca Maria, be quiet—do not say such things.'

'I will say so!'—she raised her voice, irritated at being contradicted—'if I have not you it is death for me. But you will not let me die? Ah, do not leave me to die!'

'My darling, be quiet—be quiet,' he said, not able to control himself, trying to loosen the chain of her arms round his neck.

'Do not lift me from here! do not make me let go!' she shrieked, making desperate motions with her head. 'If you make me let go, I feel that death will take hold of me....'

'Oh, Bianca, Bianca, be quiet, for my sake! do not kill me!' said the strong man, now become the weakest and wretchedest among men.

'Death will catch hold of me! it is here behind me! I feel it! You alone can save me! Do not let me die—I do not wish to die: you know I do not wish to die!'

'You will not die. Hush, my dear, or you will get worse. I am here: I will not go away ever again—I will not leave you!'

'... I do not wish to die!' she ended up, again getting a little quieter. They remained like that for some time. The father was standing at the foot of the bed, leaning against the bed-rail, with his eyes down, feeling in his broken pride, in his wounded soul, the full weight of the chastisement the Lord was heaping on him, as a punishment for his lengthened sin.

Very softly, seeing that the girl had stopped speaking, that her eyes were closing, Dr. Amati tried to put her head back on the pillow; but she felt the movement, and while he bent down she drew him to her at the same time, and he had to stoop, since her arms would not let go. They remained like that, she dozing, he leaning over in an uncomfortable position, in such anguish at her state and his own powerlessness that the sensation of physical discomfort did not affect him. Grief took such a violent hold of him that he seemed about to suffocate, not being able to weep, cry out, or speak now the unhappy girl was dozing; but sometimes she gave a start, and an expression of painful annoyance came over her fleshless face. An idea seemed to come into her mind: either she heard a voice the others did not, or saw some fanciful sight, for her eyelids fluttered and her lips drew back from her whitish gums. Then she opened her eyes, as if she had found out where that noise, that sight, that disagreeable impression, came from, and with a thread of voice, which only the doctor heard, she called:

'Love!'

'What is it you want?'

'Send him away.'

'Who do you mean?'

'My father.'

The doctor turned pale, and did not answer. He gave a side-glance at the old man, who was still standing at the foot of the bed with his eyes cast down in sorrowful thought.

'I beg of you, send him away,' she began again, speaking into his ear.

'But why do you wish it?'

'Just because—I don't wish to see him. Send him away. He must go away.'

'Bianca Maria, remember he is your father.'

'Look here—listen,' she said, pulling him nearer to her, so that she could speak lower. 'He is my father,' she whispered; then, with a smothered fear and an immense bitterness, 'but he has killed me!'

'Do not speak like that,' he replied, turning his head the other way that she might not see his feelings.

'I tell you I am dying through him. I am not raving, you know; I am in my senses,' she replied, opening her eyes wide with that babyish trick of dying children that drives mothers mad with grief.

He shook his head, as if he could not tell what to do nor what to say.

'Send him away!' she insisted, in a rage, with the fatal outbursting fury of meningitis.

'I cannot do it, Bianca Maria....'

'If you do not send him away yourself, I will get up and shriek out to him to go away, never to come before me again—never, for the future: do you hear?'

'Wait a moment,' he said, as he made up his mind, resigned.

And he left her, loosening himself from her, putting back her thin arms on the coverlet. She followed him with her glance, never taking her eyes off him, as if through them she could know what Dr. Amati was saying to her father in a low tone.

Dr. Amati, with great delicacy and a shudder of grief that made his voice shake uncontrollably, was explaining to him that meningitis is a frightful malady which burns the brain, breaks the nerves, and makes the unlucky patients attacked by it rave for days and days: it incites them to constant anger, and fury, even. Poor Bianca Maria was a victim to this fancy, that she could not bear to have anyone in her room; and that if he loved his daughter, if he did not wish to hear her burst out into wild talk, would he be so kind as to go into another room?...

'Did my daughter tell you that?' the old man asked, deadly pale, with his eyebrows knitted.

'Yes, it was she who said it.'

'Does she wish to have no one in her room?'

'No, no one.'

'Except yourself, is that it?'

'Yes, I may stay.'

'Does my daughter turn me out?' shrieked the old man.

'For goodness' sake, my lord, do not get irritated! Have pity on your daughter, yourself, and me.'

'I will not go away unless she tells me herself, do you hear? Bianca Maria!' the Marquis called out, going up close to the bed.

She looked at her father with the greatest intensity, as if she was answering him.

'Bianca Maria,' shouted the exasperated old man, 'is it true that you do not want to have me in your room? Say yourself if it is true. I do not believe this man. You must say it yourself.'

'It is true,' she said in a very clear voice, looking at her father.

He cast down his eyes, where the last tears of old age were showing, and his head sank on his breast, overcome by the inflexible punishment that came to him from the raving girl—from his dying victim. He went out without turning round. And stooping, as if he were a hundred years old, alone, speechless, he went away to what had been his study, where only an old table and a chair were left. There, lying forward with his face in his hands, with no conception either of time or things, the old sinner sank into the immeasurable bitterness of his punishment. Sometimes Bianca Maria's voice came to him, feeble or loud, ever telling Amati:

'I do not want to die—I will not die! Save me! save me! I am only twenty! I will not die!'

The voice, the despairing words, said in delirium, but which still seemed to be a lament and a curse, had a cruel effect on him. He had not strength left to get up and go out, to leave the house alone, to die like a dog on some church steps, unwept for and unregretted. He did not get up to go beside the dying girl, for his daughter had turned him out, keeping by her the only person she had loved.

'I will not die, love! I will not die!' the delirious girl was saying.

'She is right—she is right,' her father thought, giving a start.

Whilst the hours went by he heard, from where he was, the doctor going backwards and forwards, in his effort to save the girl's life, the hurried orders, Giovanni going out and the assistant doctor coming in. He had no right now to come forward and know what was going on, and, in fact, he was forgotten there, as if he had been dead for years and years, as if no Marquis di Formosa had ever existed. Would it not be better for him if he were dead, since everyone had forsaken him? 'It is what I deserve,' he thought to himself.

He strained his ears sometimes, as if the noises that came to him were to tell him that his daughter was getting better, that the doctor was giving her strong, effective remedies; but, except for the servants, the assistant, and the doctor going about their work, he heard nothing else but the constant agonizing cry: 'I will not die! I will not die! Love, save me!'

He sank into a slumber, with his old head resting on his arms, towards dawn, still hearing in this slight unconsciousness that same cry of anguish. It was Giovanni who wakened him, at full daylight, by bringing him a cup of coffee. The father, turned out of his daughter's room, questioned the servant with his eyes.

'She is still in the same state—just the same.'

'Then, not even Amati can save her—not even him?'

'He is trying to, but he is in despair.'

The Marquis di Formosa spent three days and nights in that room alone, not seeing a bed and hardly touching the little food that was brought in for the three days and nights that Bianca Maria's dying agony lasted. The old man's face, always of a reddish tinge, in spite of his age, was now streaked with purple, his white hair, when Giovanni and Margherita came to him, was tragically disordered. Only, from seeing their crushed state, he asked them no more questions. Did he not hear her still raving, crying out that at her age she did not want to die, she would not die, adding the most heartrending supplications and cries?

The two servants told him nothing; his hearing had got more acute, and not a word of the raving went past unheard. Still, that very vitality of nervous strength, that strong voice, deluded him as being a sort of health, and in the short intervals of silence he almost wished the raving would begin again. But the third day, in the morning, a new painful sensation drew him out of that stupor. The delirious girl, in a choked voice, was calling for her mother, begging *her* not to let her die. Sometimes she stopped speaking; he looked round him, alarmed at these sudden silences, which got longer, starting when again Bianca Maria began to cry out:

'Mother, I will not die! I will not—I will not, mother dear!'

About two hours after midnight, on the third day, still seated by his small table, slumber came upon him, with the raving still echoing in his ears. How long did he sleep? When he wakened, the silence was so profound that it frightened him. He waited to hear the voice crying out not to die yet. There was nothing. He counted the time from the wasting of the candle; two hours must have gone by.

A horrible fear took hold of him; he dared not move. He looked under the doorway arch, and saw Margherita's white face looking at him. He understood. Still, mechanically he asked:

'How is Donna Bianca?'

'She is well,' the old woman said feebly.

'When did it happen?'

'An hour ago.'

'Did she not ... did she not ask for me?'

'No, my lord.'

He tried to get up; he could not. He thought that death would lay hold of him there, on that seat, at once, since young people of twenty die before old men of sixty. Now Dr. Amati had come into the room. He was unrecognisable; a deadly weight had broken down all his moral and physical energies. Great silent, child's tears rolled down his cheeks. They said nothing for a time.

'Did she suffer a great deal?' the father asked.

'Yes, frightfully....'

'Were you not able to do anything to ...'

'No, I was able to do nothing,' the doctor said, beaten, holding out his arms as he owned to the most horrible of his failures.

The old man, his face now rigid in tragic expression, was not crying. Like a child who is not to be comforted, Dr. Amati took him by the hand, lifted him from his chair, and said gently:

'Come and see her.'

They went. The Marchesina di Formosa Bianca Maria Cavalcanti was lying on her small white bed, her head rather sloping on one shoulder, the waxen hands, with discoloured fingers, clasped over a rosary. A soft white robe had been put over her wasted body. The violet-shaded mouth was half open, the clayey eyelids lowered. She seemed very much smaller, like a girl in her teens. On her face there was only the haughty seal of death, that soothes all and forgives all. It was not serenity, but peace.

From the doorway the two men gazed on the small figure, with long, black hair flowing over it. They did not go in; motionless, both kept their eyes on the mortal remains, and Amati repeated gently, as if to himself, like a child whom nothing could comfort:

'There should be flowers—flowers....'

The old man did not hear him. He looked at his dead daughter, saying not a word, giving no sigh; he bent his great frame and knelt down in the doorway, holding out his arms for forgiveness, like old Lear before the sweet corpse of Cordelia.